DARK MAGIC

JAMES SWAIN

A TOM DOHERTY ASSOCIATES BOOK · NEW YORK

This is a work of fiction. All of the characters, organizations, and events portrayed in this novel are either products of the author's imagination or are used fictitiously.

DARK MAGIC

Copyright © 2012 by James Swain

All rights reserved.

A Tor Book
Published by Tom Doherty Associates, LLC
175 Fifth Avenue
New York, NY 10010

www.tor-forge.com

Tor® is a registered trademark of Tom Doherty Associates, LLC.

ISBN 978-0-7653-6791-4

Tor books may be purchased for educational, business, or promotional use. For information on bulk purchases, please contact Macmillan Corporate and Premium Sales Department at 1-800-221-7945 extension 5442 or write specialmarkets@macmillan.com.

First Edition: May 2012
First Mass Market Edition: May 2013

Printed in the United States of America

0 9 8 7 6 5 4 3 2 1

ALSO BY JAMES SWAIN

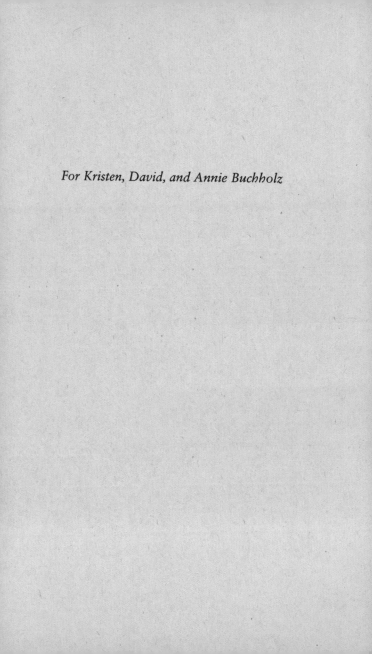

For Kristen, David, and Annie Buchholz

ACKNOWLEDGMENTS

Thanks to Katharine Critchlow, my editor at Tor; Charlie Randall of H&R Magic Books; the incredible Bill Malone; Eric Raab; my agent, Robin Rue; and the best in-house editor a writer could have, my wonderful wife, Laura.

If witches could do any such miraculous things,
as these and other which are imputed to them,
they might do them again and again,
at any time or place, or at any man's desire.

—Reginald Scott
The Discoveries of Withccraft, 1584

PART I

TIMES SQUARE

1

Visiting the spirit world was never easy. The other side was a shifting landscape of light and dark, where time moved forward and backward, and often stood still. It was here that fierce battles between the forces of good and evil were constantly being waged, with the earth's outcome weighing in the balance. A visitor could get hurt, if he was not careful.

Peter Warlock knew the risks. He'd visited the spirit world many times, and always returned unharmed. He was at home there, as much as any person could be.

Striking a match, he lit the three white candles sitting on the dining room table in Milly Adams' apartment. The wicks sparked to life, and he gazed into the faces of the six other psychics sitting around the table. As leader of the Friday night psychics, it was his job to make contact with the spirit world. Clasping the hands of the two women sitting beside him, he shut his eyes, and began to recite the words that allowed him to communicate with the dead.

"In darkness, I see light: in daylight, I see night.
Shadows as bright as sunshine, the blind able to see.
This is the world we wish to enter.
We ask the eternal question, yet no one seems to
*   know.*

Who is the master of Creation?
Who can explain, or from the future tear the mask?
Yet still we dream, and still we ask.
What lies beyond the silent night, we cannot say."

His world changed. He found himself standing on the sidewalk in an unknown city. Swirling images bounced around him like a kaleidoscope, with scenes flashing by at warp speed. Men, women, and children staggered past, all of whom were dying before his very eyes. The images were torturous, and he twisted uncomfortably in his chair.

"What do you see?" Milly asked, squeezing his hand.

Peter tried to focus. He had a job to do, no matter how painful it might be.

"I'm standing on a street corner in a major metropolitan city. Something terrible has just occurred, and scores of people are dying on the sidewalk and in the street."

"How are they dying?" Milly asked.

"They're gasping for breath and going into convulsions. Then they just stop breathing."

"Is it some type of attack?"

"I'm not sure. I don't see any guns or bombs going off or anything like that."

"Which city are you in?"

"I can't tell. There are too many shadows to make out the street names."

"Present day?"

"I think so. I see a movie poster on a building for a remake of *The Untouchables*."

"That comes out next week," Holly Adams whispered, squeezing his other hand.

"Look hard, Peter," Milly said. "You have to find out where this attack is taking place."

Still in his trance, Peter stepped off the curb to search for a familiar landmark. A city bus screamed past, the driver slumped at the wheel. It careened off several parked cars before plowing into a storefront and toppling over. He was just a visitor to this world, and there was nothing he could do to help the driver or the passengers inside.

Peter scanned the street. A large skyscraper with an imposing spire on its roof caught his eye. He'd seen the silver ball drop from that spire on New Year's countless times.

"Oh, no," he whispered. "It's here in New York."

Milly gasped. "Are you sure?"

"Yes. Wait. Everything's coming into focus now. It's nighttime in Times Square. The theaters have let out, and the streets are jammed with people. Something awful is happening to them, and they're grabbing their heads and screaming and dropping to the ground. Cars and buses are crashing into each other as well, their drivers dead. It's total chaos."

The rest of the table exchanged worried looks. To Peter's left sat Milly's niece Holly, an aspiring witch attending Columbia University; to her left, Reggie Brown, who used his psychic powers to pick winning horses at the racetracks and beat the casinos, and who was the largest donor to good works in the city. To Reggie's left sat Lester Rowe, a Scottish-born psychic who lived on the Lower East Side and only traveled uptown to attend Milly's gatherings. To his left, Max Romeo, a world-famous magician, now retired. Beside Max sat Madame Marie, an elderly Gypsy who read Tarot cards out of a dusty storefront in Greenwich Village. Rounding out the circle was Milly, the grande dame of psychics in New York, who could trace her bloodline directly back to the witches of Salem, Massachusetts.

"Ask him, Max," Madame Marie whispered.

Max nodded. He knew Peter the best, having taken the boy under his wing after his parents had died, and turned him into one of the world's foremost magicians.

"When, Peter? When will this happen?" Max asked.

"I can't tell," Peter replied.

"Look around, see if you can spot something that will tell you the day."

"The shadows are back. It's all out of focus."

Max slapped his hand forcefully onto the table. He did not tolerate anything but perfection from his student. "Look harder, Peter. There has to be something there."

"I'm trying."

"Try harder," Max implored.

Peter spun around, seeing nothing that would tell him the day of the week. His ability to look into the future was as much a curse as it was a gift, and he nearly shouted in frustration.

"It's not working."

"Try the news tickers on the office buildings," Holly suggested. "They usually have stories running across them. That should tell you."

"An excellent idea," Max said. "Concentrate on the buildings."

Times Square had become a dead zone, and Peter tried to block out the carnage, and determine the exact day he was seeing in the future. Taking Holly's suggestion, he studied the office buildings, and spotted the digital news ticker that ran across the front of the ABC News building that included an ESPN ticker for sports. The score for a Yankees game against the division rival Rays caught his eye. He was an ardent baseball fan, and knew that the game was to be played on Tuesday afternoon at the stadium in the Bronx.

"It will happen in four days," he announced.

"Are you sure?" Max asked.

"Yes, Max. I'm looking at the score to a baseball game that hasn't been played yet."

"Well, at least we have some time," Milly said, sounding relieved.

Peter began to fade. Entering the spirit world was exhausting, and took all of his strength. He started to pull out of his trance, then stiffened.

"What's wrong?" Holly asked.

In the median of Times Square stood a menacing figure dressed in black. His hair was shorn to within an inch of his scalp, his face chiseled. He was unaffected by the scores of dying people, and looked like the Grim Reaper.

Peter had run out of gas. Pitching forward, his forehead hit the table with a bang.

"Oh my God, Peter!" Holly exclaimed. "Are you all right?"

Peter waited for his mind to clear. Lifting his head, he looked into Holly's sweet face.

"I'll live," he replied.

"You scared me."

"I think we're done," Milly declared. "Good job, Peter."

"Yes, Peter, that was a splendid effort," Lester said.

Everyone rose and patted him on the back. Each week, they gathered in Milly's apartment and conducted a séance to see what evil was coming in the days ahead. In that regard, they had succeeded. Only, as Peter knew, the hard part was now to come.

They retired to the living room, and took their usual spots. Peter abandoned the comfy leather chair he usually sat in, and stood at the window, gazing at the blazing lights of Times Square thirty blocks away. In four days, it would be turned into a living hell, and he wrestled with how to deal with it. It was Milly who broke the silence.

"Tell us what you're thinking," she said.

Peter turned from the window. "We need to act quickly. The usual method of contacting the authorities isn't going to work. We must get their attention right away."

"He's right," Reggie said, chewing on his pipe. "We can't send them a letter, and expect they'll open it in time. Something else has to be done."

"I agree," Milly said. "Any suggestions?"

"We could bombard them with anonymous e-mails," Holly offered.

"Anonymous e-mails can be mistaken as spam, and never seen," Reggie reminded her.

"You're right. Sorry."

"How about a good old-fashioned phone call?" Lester suggested. "We can buy one of those devices that alter a person's voice, in case the call is taped."

"Phone calls can be traced," Milly reminded him.

"Even cell phones?" Lester asked.

"Naturally."

"How about running a banner behind a plane? Those usually get people's attention."

Lester had a knack for finding humor in just about any situation. This time, no one laughed, and the living room fell deathly quiet. Down below, a police cruiser passed the apartment building, its mournful siren punctuating the still night air.

"There's no getting around it," Peter said. "We need to make direct contact with the authorities. Since I'm the one who saw the attack, I should do it."

"You can't go to the authorities," Milly said. "Look at what happened to poor Nemo."

Peter knew perfectly well what had happened to Nemo. Once the government had discovered that Nemo was psychic, they'd stuck him on an estate in Virginia, where his handlers put him through vigorous interrogation sessions in an effort to find out what the government's enemies were plotting. It was a wretched existence, and Peter hoped it never happened to him, but that still didn't change the situation.

"I still have to do it," Peter said.

"But why risk direct contact?" Milly asked. "Isn't there some other way to tell them?"

"How do I pass along information that I don't understand? I saw people dying in Times Square, but there was no blood, or gunfire, or explosions. Did some kind of bomb go off? Or was it something else? The authorities are experts at figuring out puzzles like this. I have to tell them what I saw. It's the only way to prevent a catastrophe from happening."

Milly sprang off the couch and crossed the room to where he stood. She grabbed his forearm and gave it a healthy pinch, just like she had when he was a little boy.

"They will never let you go, Peter. Once you start talking, they'll realize you're not normal, and then it will be over for you. Is that what you want? Never to see any of us again? And what about your career? Are you willing to toss that away as well?"

Peter said nothing. An uneasy silence fell over the group. Madame Marie cleared her throat. Everyone shifted their attention to hear what the old Gypsy had to say.

"I know you like my own son," Madame Marie said. "You are a headstrong young man, and prone to making rash decisions. Think about this before you act. You have four days in which to make a decision. Use them wisely."

"Yes, Peter, do think about it," Max added. "There's a lot at stake here."

"A good night's sleep will do the trick," Lester joined in.

"That and a hot toddy always worked for me," Reggie added.

They were the closest thing to a family that Peter had, and he would weigh their words carefully. Tomorrow was Saturday, and he had a matinee in the afternoon, and another show at night. He bid them goodnight, and Milly walked him to the door.

"Please let me know what you decide to do," she said.

"I will, Milly. Thank you for your advice."

"Like you ever listened to me."

"I've always listened to you."

"But have you ever obeyed?"

Hardly, he thought. He kissed her on the cheek. "Goodnight."

"Be safe, Peter," she said.

"And you as well," he replied.

His limo was idling at the curb, waiting to take him home. He spent a moment trying to clear his head. A little voice was telling him to go to the police, and tell them what he'd seen. It was the right thing to do, only it would lead to questions that he wasn't prepared to answer. His friends were right. He needed to sleep on it, and come up with a better plan of attack.

A chill swept through his body. He looked up and down Central Park West, sensing another presence. Was Nemo trying to contact him? His friend could do that, and without thinking, he stepped off the curb. In the clouds was a translucent face that looked like Nemo's.

"Peter, watch out!"

A city bus was hurtling toward him. He jumped back onto the curb, then gazed into the sky. Nemo was gone. Holly stood behind him, her teeth chattering from the cold. He draped his leather jacket over her shoulders.

"What were you doing?" she asked.

"A little star-gazing. What's the mood upstairs?"

"Not good. They're afraid you'll do something rash."

"Me? Perish the thought."

"You need to be careful. No one wants you to disappear. Especially me."

A single tear ran down her cheek. Growing up, he'd babysat for Holly, and shown her magic tricks to keep her entertained. She was the little sister he'd never had, and one of the few people he ever confided in. He hated to see her so upset.

"I'll be careful," he promised.

"You're not crossing your toes, are you?"

"Toes and fingers are uncrossed."

"I worry about you. Were the things you saw really that bad?"

"I've never seen anything like it."

"Could it have been terrorists?"

"I don't know. That's why I have to contact the authorities."

"You know best." She slipped out of his jacket and kissed his cheek. " 'Night, Peter."

"Goodnight."

He watched her go back inside, and climbed into the limo. Herbie, his African-American driver, put down his newspaper and glanced into his mirror.

"You look wiped out, boss. Ready to call it a night?"

"Yeah, Herbie. Let's beat it."

Peter poured himself a Scotch from the limo bar. He didn't drink often, and when he did, there was a reason. The drink burned going down, and cleared his head.

"Do you have something to write on?"

"Pen or pencil?"

"Pencil, please."

Herbie passed him a yellow pad and a pencil. "Which way home?"

"Through the park. It's usually quiet this time of night."

Herbie entered Central Park through the 72nd Street entrance. The park was empty, save for a die-hard jogger and a man walking his dog. Switching on the reading light, Peter stared at the blank pad. The key to stopping the catastrophe in Times Square would be finding the man he'd seen standing in the median. If he could get a drawing to the police, they could track the man down, and avert the disaster. He wouldn't have to talk to them—just get the drawing in their hands, and call the man a threat. It sounded like a plan, and he began to sketch.

He was a passable artist, and the man's face slowly took shape. Square chin, a scar on his left cheek, another beneath the hairline on his forehead. Flat nose, possibly broken a few times. Soulless eyes. Whoever he was, he'd lived a harsh life.

Peter appraised his work. It was a decent likeness, only something was missing. He added a scowl to the man's face. That did the trick. He'd captured the thing about the man that was so unnerving. He could watch innocent people die without caring.

They'd reached the 72nd Street exit on the east side of the park. Herbie got onto Fifth Avenue, and headed south to 62nd Street, where he hung a left. They pulled up in front of a nondescript brownstone on a street of quiet elegance.

"So what are you drawing?" his driver asked.

Peter passed the sketch through the partition. Limo

drivers saw hundreds of faces every single day. Maybe Herbie could help.

"Ever see him before?" Peter asked.

Herbie had a look. He shook his head, and passed the pad back.

"If I gave you a copy of this sketch tomorrow, could you e-mail it to other drivers you know, and tell them to be on the lookout for this guy?"

"Sure," Herbie said.

"Good. I'll see you in the morning."

Peter climbed out of the limo. The driver's window came down, and Herbie stuck his head out. "If you don't mind my asking, who is that guy, anyway?"

The pad was clutched in Peter's hand, the face staring up at him. The harsh streetlight accentuated the man's utter callousness, and Peter could not help but shudder.

"He's the Devil, Herbie, and we need to find him."

"Got it, boss. See you in the A.M."

Peter climbed the steps to his brownstone. The downstairs lights were burning brightly. Liza had stayed up. A warm drink was waiting, and something good to eat. She was wonderful that way, and made him happy in ways that no one had ever managed to before.

He hurried inside.

2

New York's Meat Packing District was not where people went to see live theater. Located on the West Side, the district's once gritty meat-packing plants were now occupied by nice restaurants, late-night clubs, and fashion boutiques. The neighborhood had found new life, and a soul all its own.

Peter had chosen to stage his full-evening magic show in the district for this very reason. By avoiding bustling Times Square, he did not have to compete with the musicals, revivals, and serious dramas that fueled New York's Theater District. He was the new kid on the block, and his fans ate it up. Each night, they flocked to his shows, desperate to find out what this young miracle-maker would do next in the abandoned meat-packing plant that was his stage.

Peter stood inside his dressing room. It took longer to get ready for a magic show than it did to perform one. He was nearly done with his preparations, and he adjusted the elastic pull that ran up the right sleeve of his jacket. The pull was one of his favorite props, and it let him make small objects disappear in the blink of an eye.

He stood in front of the mirror and tested the pull. Picking up a playing card, he secretly attached the card to the pull using a small clip. By extending his arms, he made the card race up his sleeve. To the mirror, it looked like real magic.

"Hey, Peter, can you talk?"

It was Liza, speaking through the inner-canal earpiece

that he wore during his show. Along with being the love of his life, Liza was his assistant, the best he'd ever had.

"As well as the next guy," he said into the tiny microphone sewn into his shirt collar.

"Very funny. Everyone's in their seats. It's a good crowd."

"Sold out?"

"Yup. The last tickets got bought right before the doors opened."

"That's great. Is Snoop there with you?"

"He's standing next to me. Ready to go over the details?"

"Let 'er rip."

A magician's assistant wore many hats. Liza and Snoop worked as ushers, and chatted with the patrons as they were led to their seats. Any valuable information they gleaned was passed to Peter before the show began. Magicians called this preshow work. It allowed them to know intimate details about the audience before ever stepping foot on stage.

"Here we go," Liza began. "Row A, seats five and six are an older couple from Battle Creek, Michigan, named Wayne and Marilyn Barcomb. Their son, Michael, is about to graduate from NYU Medical School. Michael's sitting in seat seven. He was talking on his cell phone as they got seated. I think there's a young lady in the wings."

"Engaged?" Peter asked.

"It sounds that way. She's going to meet the parents on Sunday."

"Did you get her name?"

"Suzanne."

"Another med student?"

"Yes—how did you know?"

"Just a guess. Great job."

"Thanks, Peter."

Snoop went next. Before joining the show, Snoop had been a computer hacker, and had gotten his nickname because he enjoyed sticking his nose into other people's business.

"You're going to love this," Snoop said. "Row F, seats eight through twelve are five ladies who could be stand-ins for *Sex and the City*, but actually work in the media department of the J. Walter Thompson advertising agency here in New York. One of them is celebrating a birthday, but I couldn't find out which one."

"The birthday girl's sitting in seat number 10," Peter told him.

"Cut it out."

"I'm serious. I'll bet you lunch."

"No thanks. How do you know she's in seat number 10?"

"Simple deduction. Five ladies are out on the town, and one is having a birthday. The birthday girl will sit in the middle so none of her friends will feel left out."

"Wow. I'm impressed," Snoop said.

"Merci. Keep going."

Snoop recited the rest of the things he'd overheard while taking patrons to their seats. One lady had a poodle who'd eaten a box of chocolates, and nearly died. Another woman was worried that a passport for a trip to Paris might not come through in time. And one poor man was a recent victim of identity theft, and had been forced to cut up his credit cards. It was just enough information for Peter to open up the door to a person's psyche, and plumb their thoughts.

"Want to add anything, Zack?" Peter asked.

Zack handled ticket sales and worked the door. He was a muscle head, and cut an imposing figure. Zack had once handled security for a heavy metal band, and had a sixth sense when it came to spotting trouble. "Sure do. A strange guy with a British accent approached me in the lobby, and asked if you still accepted challenges during the show. He had this way about him that bothered me. When I asked him what he had in mind, he told me to piss off."

"Was he drunk?" Peter asked.

"I don't think so."

"Stoned?"

"His breath was clean."

"Off in the head?"

"No, he acted pretty normal."

"Think he's a troublemaker?"

"He sure came across that way. Want me to give him a refund, and ask him to leave?"

Everyone in show business had to deal with hecklers. Throwing the guy out on his ass was an option, only there was always the chance he'd file a lawsuit, and cause bigger headaches.

"Leave him alone," Peter said.

"You sure?" Zack replied.

"Positive. Tell me what he looks like, so I can be on the lookout."

"He's in his mid-thirties, about six-foot tall, real athletic-looking, with a snarl on his face like a junkyard dog," Zack said. "He's got a bad vibe."

Lying on his dressing room table was the sketch Peter had drawn after last night's séance. He picked up the pad and stared at the man he'd nicknamed the Grim Reaper.

"Is he dressed in black?"

"Yeah. He looks like a funeral director. How did you know?"

Because I saw him last night talking to the dead. He continued to stare at the pad. What were the chances of the same evil man buying a ticket to his show? About one in a million. He tossed the sketch onto the table.

"Where's he sitting?"

"Last row, on the aisle," Zack said.

"Keep an eye on him. Any sign of trouble, throw him out."

"You still didn't tell me how you knew what he was wearing."

"I guessed."

"You're going to have to tell me how you do that someday."

A backstage buzzer went off. There were five minutes left before the curtain went up. They had a show to do, and Peter put the strange man out of his mind.

"Good job, everyone," he said. "Now, let's go make some magic."

3

For an audience attending Peter's magic show, it was about the experience.

Entering through blackened front doors, patrons stood in an unheated lobby listening to a haunting piano composition by avant-garde composer Philip Glass. No food or drink was sold, although eco-friendly programs were available, provided a ten-dollar donation was made to a homeless shelter which Peter supported.

Fifteen minutes before the curtain rose, ushers clad in black led ticket-holders down a long, claustrophobic hallway that had not been painted since the days a sausage-processing plant had occupied the building. The stains on the walls were dark and menacing.

The hallway led to a cozy six-hundred-seat theater designed by the magician himself. The stage had no curtains or visible props, just a handful of shadows produced by muted lighting. The seating was tiered, the chairs plush and comfortable. From the ceiling hung silk screen posters of famous magicians past. Houdini, The Amazing Dunninger, Thurston, Blackstone, and Carter the Great all gazed down.

Once in their seats, patrons were handed a sheet which outlined the house rules. Cell phones and cameras were forbidden, as was any electronic recording. During the show, Peter would invite members of the audience to request tricks from his repertoire which were not on the bill. Whenever possible, he would accommodate them.

The format was unique. Peter wanted the audience to be a part of the performance. To accomplish this, he took chances, and could not always predict how each show would come out. It was risky, yet he'd discovered it was why people came to this unlikely area of the city to see him work. They wanted to be part of something unique, and he was not about to disappoint them.

"Good evening, ladies and gentlemen, and welcome to *Anything's Possible,*" Liza's voice boomed over the PA. "Before we begin tonight's performance, please turn off your cell phones. Remember, no electronic recording of any kind is permitted. Thank you, and enjoy the show."

The house lights flickered before going dark. The theater grew hushed. A flash of light hit center stage, followed by a curling puff of smoke. Peter stepped through the cloud wearing a perfectly tailored black Italian suit, his black hair worn short and slicked straight back.

"Good evening, and welcome to my show," he said.

The applause was generous. He was becoming the face of magic to a generation that had grown up social networking on computers, his tricks endlessly discussed on forums, Web sites, and in chat rooms. For many, the scrutiny would have been unbearable; for him, it was simply another opportunity to showcase his art. He stepped to the foot of the stage.

"I was bitten by the magic bug as a boy. I bought my first tricks at the age of eight, and practiced until I could do them right. It took a long time. While I was practicing those tricks, I imagined all the things I would do if magic really was possible. This became the focus of my life: I wanted to turn the things I'd imagined into reality. I suppose you could say that I became a magician well before I was able to perform a single trick. Being a magician started in my imagination, and has never stopped. Please enjoy the show."

He stepped back. A collective gasp filled the theater. The empty stage had been transformed into an enchanted sanctum filled with beautifully decorated props and apparatus. Like the young magician, they'd simply appeared out of thin air.

For the next hour, Peter did everything a wizard could possibly do. Objects appeared, disappeared, were burned and made whole, elongated, autographed, and vanished, without any visible clue to where they'd gone. A long darning needle was thrust through the magician's arm, yet produced no blood or visible wound. Eggs became birds; cats turned into barking dogs; the lovely Liza was transformed into a ghost, her essence flying across the stage where it entered into a bottle like a genie. Before the audience's disbelieving eyes, the bottle grew to giant size, with a giggling Liza curled up inside. A pistol was shown to contain real bullets. It was fired at the young magician, who caught the bullet between his teeth, and spit it on a plate. A member of the audience was asked to write the name of any playing card on a piece of paper. The paper was burned, and the ashes rubbed on the magician's forearm, causing the name of the card to mysteriously appear. A borrowed dollar bill was given a vigorous shake. More bills appeared, the money floating into lucky hands in the audience.

To close the first half, Peter clapped his hands three times in quick succession, and a puff of smoke enveloped him. When it had cleared, he'd disappeared along with every prop on stage.

The audience cheered. It had been a breathtaking joyride of deception, with each trick building purposefully to the next. Now, it was time for everyone to catch their breath.

The intermission was short. Few people left their seats, content to talk among themselves, and compare notes about what they saw, and didn't see, to try and make sense of it all.

The second act soon followed. For many, this was what they'd come for, the test of wills and skills that Peter presented to his audiences each night. It started innocently enough, with the young magician standing downstage.

"You just saw my favorite magic," he began. "Now, it's your turn. If you have a favorite trick, or something you've heard I've done, raise your hand, and I'll try to accommodate you."

Down in the first row, the five ladies from J. Walter Thompson smiled up at him. He leaned toward the lady celebrating her birthday with his eyebrow upraised. The psychological reaction was impossible to resist, and she raised her hand.

"Your name, please," Peter said.

"Katherine," the birthday lady replied.

"Today you're celebrating your birthday, aren't you, Katherine?"

"Why yes, I am."

"And this is your twenty-ninth birthday, correct?"

Katherine was several years older than twenty-nine, and grinned.

"What trick would you like me to do, Katherine?"

"Read my future," she replied.

"Certainly."

Reading the future was Peter's most requested trick. People who believed their future *could* be predicted were perfect subjects, and through body language and facial expressions, often communicated their innermost feelings and desires to him. He began slowly. "You are currently in the middle of a relationship, but are fearful it won't work out. Give it time, and you'll know exactly what course to take. Your job at the advertising agency is going well; there may be a promotion in the works. You own a dog which you adore, and you wish you could spend more time with him. I see many more pets in your future."

"Oh, my God! You're so right!" Katherine exclaimed.

He had batted a thousand with Katherine. It hadn't hurt that her pants were covered in dog hair. Before he could field another request, a voice with a thick British accent rang out.

"Hey! I have a request. Pick me!"

The voice came from the last row. A patron rose from his seat, and the spotlight quickly found him. Peter could not believe his eyes. It was the Grim Reaper, in the flesh.

"Call 911," he whispered into the mike in his collar.

"Why? What's wrong?" Liza whispered into his earpiece.

"Just do it."

"What should I say?"

"Tell them we have a dangerous person here." To the man he said, "Your name, please?"

"If you were psychic, you'd know that," the man shouted back.

A murmur rippled through the crowd. Whoever he was, he was about to ruin the show.

"I'm looking through the ticket log right now," Liza said. "Here we go. The ticket was picked up at will-call. The name used was Wolfe. No first name."

How appropriate, Peter thought. The Grim Reaper is named Wolfe. He brought his hand to his forehead, and pretended to concentrate.

"Your name is Wolfe," he announced.

The man in the last row blinked. *Score one for the good guys,* Peter thought.

"Very good," his heckler said.

"Thank you. I rather like it myself. Now, what is your request?"

"I have an object in my pocket wrapped in tissue paper. Tell me what it is."

"Of course. Please come up on the stage."

"No. Tell me what it is first."

Zack appeared in the back of the theater, ready to hustle Wolfe out the door. Peter had something else in mind. If he could get Wolfe on the stage and stall, the police could come and arrest him.

"Sir, for all I know, you could have a dozen objects in your pocket, and want to trick me," Peter told him. "If you'd like me to tell you what a particular object is, come onto the stage, and I'd be happy to oblige you."

"You win."

Wolfe hustled down the aisle, and climbed the stairs to the stage. He was built like a rugby player, and had one scar on his left cheek, another beneath the hairline on his forehead. The horrific image of dead people in Times Square flashed through Peter's mind. It was *him*.

"Please take the object from your pocket so we all can see," Peter said.

Wolfe removed the mystery object from his jacket pocket. It was wrapped in white tissue, and not very large.

"Tell me what it is," Wolfe said.

The theater had grown deathly still. Peter gazed at the object. He'd been plumbing people's thoughts since childhood, and didn't think Wolfe would pose any problems.

"The object is something you always carry with you, isn't it?" Peter asked.

"Yes, it is."

"And you've had it for a long time."

"Right again."

"Here's what I want you to do. Form a mental picture of the object in your mind. Imagine yourself wrapping the object in tissue paper earlier tonight. Can you do that?"

"I suppose."

"Do so, and I'll read your thoughts, and tell you what the object is."

Wolfe scrunched up his face and Peter read his mind. A picture filled with shadows began to form. The shadows faded away to reveal Wolfe standing in a dingy hotel room by a dresser. On the dresser lay a leather wallet, a handful of change, a Zippo lighter, a passport, and a worn pocketknife. Wolfe wrapped the pocketknife in tissue, and slipped it into his pocket. The picture disappeared. Peter smiled thinly. He was going to end the show on a high note, Wolfe be damned.

"The object in your hand is a pocketknife," the young magician said. "Am I right?"

Wolfe opened his mouth, but nothing came out.

"Please answer me."

"You're bloody good, you are," Wolfe said.

"Thank you. Please show the audience that I'm correct."

Wolfe tore away the tissue paper to reveal a worn pocketknife with a mother-of-pearl handle. The resulting ovation was long and hard.

"The police are coming," Liza said into his earpiece. "Do you want Zack to grab Wolfe when he comes off the stage?"

"Yes," Peter whispered back.

"I'll tell him."

Peter began to escort Wolfe off the stage. Only the Grim Reaper had something else in mind. Flipping open the knife, he pointed the blade at the young magician.

"We're not done," Wolfe said.

The savage look on his face was as easy to read as a newspaper headline.

"You came here to kill me," Peter said.

"I most certainly did. You're the best I've ever seen."

"What's that supposed to mean?"

Wolfe flashed a sick grin and charged him. Someone in the crowd screamed. *Not tonight*, Peter thought. Taking a hand-flasher from a hidden pocket in his jacket, the young magician fired off a load of flash paper that went straight into Wolfe's eyes.

Wolfe staggered backward, the knife slipping from his hand. The sarcastic Brit didn't seem so menacing anymore. Peter slugged his attacker in the mouth.

Zack leapt on the stage, and tackled Wolfe from behind. The two men began to wrestle.

"The police have entered the building," Liza said into his earpiece.

A pair of New York's finest came huffing down the aisle. They did double-time up the steps, and joined Peter on stage.

"Where is he?" one of the cops asked.

Peter looked at the spot where Zack and Wolfe had been standing. Both men had disappeared. He knew what had happened, and motioned to the cops.

"Follow me," the young magician said.

4

Wolfe and Zack had fallen through a spring-loaded secret trapdoor in the stage. By the time Peter and the cops reached the basement, Wolfe had escaped through a back exit, while Zack was knocked out cold.

"Damn it," Peter said.

"We'll take care of your friend," one of the cops said. "Go finish your show."

Peter hurried back to the stage. The audience was still in their seats, waiting for the show to end. He asked a dozen people to stand up, and began to read their minds, calling out dates and anniversaries and anything else he could pull from their thoughts. By the time he was done, he was exhausted, and could barely speak.

The audience rewarded him with a standing ovation.

As the crowd was filing out, more cops arrived. A pair of detectives led him to his dressing room. Their names were Sal Dagastino and Colleen Schoch, and they were straight out of a TV cop show. Short and annoying, Dagastino barked questions like a drill sergeant, while Schoch, who was pretty enough to be a runway model, said little.

"Let me see if I've got this straight," Dagastino said, scribbling in a notepad. "Wolfe tried to stab you. You blew flash paper into his face, and your assistant grabbed him. They started wrestling, and fell through a secret trapdoor. What's that for?"

"I make myself disappear during the show," Peter said.

"I always wondered how that worked. Your assistant hit his head and was knocked out, which let Wolfe escape. That about sum it up?"

"Yes, detective."

"Show me how the flash paper trick works."

"I'm not allowed to reveal my secrets. It's the magician's code."

"Show me anyway."

Peter pulled the hand flasher from his pocket, and pulled the trigger. A blinding flash of white light appeared a few feet above their heads.

"Pretty neat. I need to keep it . . . as evidence," Dagastino said.

Peter handed him the device. One of his gifts was the ability to peer into the future. He saw Dagastino standing with a teenage boy who was his spitting image. Dagastino handed the boy the device, and he fired it off, burning his hand.

"Don't let your kid play with it," Peter said without thinking.

"Who told you I had a kid?" the detective asked, pocketing the device.

"No one. It's what I tell everyone."

"Thanks for the warning. Next question. Your assistant called 911 before Wolfe attacked you. Why did she do that?"

Peter couldn't tell Dagastino the truth without revealing he was a psychic. He hated lying to the detective, but saw no other choice.

"Wolfe made some comments before the show that bothered me," he said. "When Wolfe came on stage, I sensed he was going to cause trouble, so I told Liza to call 911."

"You sensed it?"

"That's right. His vibes were bad."

Dagastino scribbled away. Peter breathed a sigh of relief.

"How did Wolfe pay for his ticket? Credit card or cash?" Dagastino asked.

"Someone came to the theater and paid cash. The ticket was waiting at will-call."

"So there's no paper trail."

Peter shook his head.

"Think you'd recognize Wolfe if you saw him again?" Dagastino asked.

"Absolutely. We were as close as I am to you."

Dagastino produced a photograph from his jacket, which he passed to Peter. The photo showed Wolfe passing through an airport security check, and had the date and time stamped in the corner. It had been taken two days ago.

"This him?" the detective asked.

"Yes. If you don't mind my asking, who is he?"

"I can't tell you that."

"Come on. He tried to kill me."

"I still can't tell you."

Reading minds was hard when the subject wouldn't play ball. Peter realized he was going to have to pull the information out of Dagastino one piece at a time.

"You're searching for Wolfe, aren't you?" Peter asked.

Dagastino flipped his notepad shut, and said nothing.

"Wolfe's a bad guy, isn't he?" Peter went on.

Silence.

"A *real* bad guy."

Dagastino looked confused, and glanced nervously at his partner.

"He slipped into the country a few days ago and shouldn't have, and now every cop in New York is looking high and low for him," Peter said.

"Who the hell told you that?" Dagastino snapped.

"No one."

"Then what are you, a mind reader?"

"Whatever gave you that idea."

"Stop the wisecracks. Now, who gave you that information?"

Peter felt himself starting to lose his temper. If he wasn't careful, he was going to say something really stupid. He'd already taken enough of a risk talking to the detectives, and decided it was time to end the interview. He went to the door and twisted the handle.

"I'm sure you can find your way out," he announced.

"Are you throwing us out?"

"That's right. Have a nice night."

Dagastino left the dressing room in a huff. Instead of following him, Schoch stayed behind. She looked vaguely familiar, and Peter tried to determine where they'd met before.

"Tell me why you did that," Schoch said.

"Your partner is a jerk. He had it coming to him."

"Dag's trying to do his job. Wolfe's dangerous. You need to help us find him."

"How dangerous?"

"I can't tell you that."

This was going nowhere. Wolfe was going to kill scores of people on Tuesday night if he wasn't apprehended. Schoch impressed him as trustworthy, so Peter shut the door.

"I'm going to tell you something about myself that can go no further," he said.

Schoch crossed her arms, and waited.

"I *am* a mind reader. Earlier tonight, I read Wolfe's mind. I know why he's in New York. He's planning an attack in Times Square on Tuesday night, right as the theaters let out."

Schoch uncrossed her arms. "You're a mind reader?"

"That's right."

"Excuse me, but that's impossible."

"No it's not. Think of a number, any number. Got one?"

"Yes . . ."

"Two hundred and seventeen."

"How the hell did you do that?"

"I read your mind. Now, listen to me. Wolfe is some kind of mass murderer. He won't use guns or bombs or anything like that. People will simply fall down on the pavement, and die. Now tell me who Wolfe is. Maybe I can help you find him."

Schoch bit her lip, thinking about it. Trust ran both ways. She finally nodded.

"All right. Here's what we know about the guy who attacked you. Wolfe is a member of a cult called the Order of Astrum that's based out of the United Kingdom.

Their symbol is tattooed on Wolfe's neck. It got spotted in the surveillance photo Dag showed you."

"What kind of cult?"

"They practice dark magic."

"Any idea why he tried to kill me?"

"No. Now tell me how the mind reading works. It sounds very useful."

"It's a gift," he explained. "I have to connect with a person to read their thoughts. Sometimes, all I get are bits and pieces of what they're thinking."

"So Wolfe let you read his thoughts."

"Yes. It was almost like he was testing me."

"If we find Wolfe, would you come down to the station, and read his mind?"

Peter hesitated. This was exactly what had happened to his friend Nemo. Nemo had gone to help the police, and had done such a good job that he'd never been seen again.

"Let me think about it," he said.

P eter escorted Schoch to the back exit of the the- ater. Telling her about his psychic abilities hadn't been as difficult as he'd thought it would be. She was easy to talk to, and inspired trust. He opened the back door. A black Volvo was parked in the alley, Dagastino was at the wheel.

"Tell your partner I'm sorry I pissed him off," Peter said.

"I will." Schoch paused. "You don't remember me, do you?"

He plumbed her face. He *had* met her before. But where?

"I thought you looked familiar," he admitted.

"I was the first officer on the scene when your parents died. I took care of you that night."

Peter felt like he'd been punched in the stomach. The memories came rushing back, and he envisioned Schoch in a dark blue uniform. "You took me to the station house, and fed me ice cream. You were very kind, although I'm afraid I wasn't much help. The doctors said I repressed the memory of what happened."

"You tried very hard. I always appreciated that. I still think about the case."

"It's been closed for a long time," he said quietly.

Opening her purse, Schoch removed a business card, and stuck it into his hand. "Call me if you remember anything else about Wolfe that might be helpful."

"I'll do that. Please don't tell anyone what I told you," he said.

"About the mind reading? Don't worry. Your secret's safe with me."

Not everyone could keep a secret, but the bond that had been cemented between them long ago told him that Schoch could be trusted. She walked outside and got into the waiting car.

"Goodnight," she called to him.

Peter glanced at her card. Schoch worked out of the 19th Precinct on the Upper East Side, not far from where he lived. This area of the city wasn't in her jurisdiction, and he found himself wondering why she and her partner were here.

As the Volvo pulled away, a strange thought occurred to him. Schoch had been there the night his parents had perished, and now she was here, questioning him about Wolfe. It was too much of a coincidence. The two events were somehow connected.

He ran into the alley wanting to ask her, but the car was already gone.

5

Peter went inside. Each night, he followed a ritual. First, he bid goodnight to the menagerie of winged and four-legged assistants that he used in his show. Then, he inspected his props so they'd be ready for tomorrow. Satisfied that everything was just right, he stood in the center of the stage, and soaked up the darkness. Normally, he spent this time being thankful that he got to do the thing he loved for a living. But tonight was different. A man had tried to stab him, and he didn't know why. It would eat at him until he learned the answer.

He left through the theater's front doors. Liza, Snoop, and Zack huddled beneath the canopy, trying to stay dry in the pouring rain. Liza looked upset, and gave him a hug.

"Are you okay?" his girlfriend asked.

"I'm fine," Peter replied.

She gave him a look. The first time he'd laid eyes on Liza, she'd been performing aerial contortions as part of a troupe of Chinese acrobats with Cirque du Soleil. Small-boned and petite, she had an oval face and simmering light brown eyes that could peel back his soul.

"All right, I'm not fine," he confessed.

"You left the hidden microphone in your collar turned on," she said. "We overheard your conversation before the battery died. Detective Dagastino sounded like a flaming jerk."

He started to panic. He'd never confided in Liza about his psychic powers. Nor had he told Snoop or Zack, and he wondered how much of his conversation they'd overhead.

"Did you hear what his partner, Detective Schoch, told me?" Peter asked.

His assistants shook their heads. He was safe for now.

"Let's go. I'll tell you in the car," he said.

His limo was parked at the curb. They piled into the backseat, and made themselves comfortable. The glass partition slid back, and Herbie stuck his shiny bald head through the opening. "You okay, boss? Liza told me what happened."

"Just a little shaken up. It could have been worse," Peter replied.

"I'll say. Where to?"

"Nowhere. Just drive around."

"Nowhere it is."

Herbie headed south. Soon, they were being bathed in the soft yellow street lights of Greenwich Village. The sidewalks were empty, the foot cops and street people nowhere to be seen. There was no lonelier city than New York when it rained.

The back seats of the limo faced each other. Peter held hands with Liza, while staring at Zack and Snoop. Snoop's usual sheepish expression had been replaced by a worried look. Zack pressed an ice-pack on the golf-ball-sized lump on his forehead.

"Here's what the detective told me," Peter said. "The guy who attacked me is named Wolfe. He slipped into the country a few days ago, and the police are hunting for him. Wolfe belongs to a secret cult called the Order of Astrum. They're supposedly into dark magic."

Zack sat up like he'd been hit with a cattle prod. "Wolfe's part of the Order?"

"That's right. You've heard of them?"

Zack slipped back into his seat. He looked disgusted, and stared out his window.

"The heavy metal band I did security for dabbled in dark magic," his head of security explained. "When we were touring England, members of the Order came backstage after a show, and asked the band to join up. When the band refused, they threatened us. A few days later, our bus got firebombed. We ended up cancelling the tour, and coming home."

"Do their members have a special tattoo on their neck?" Peter asked.

Zack nodded. "Every member of the Order gets a shimmering silver tattoo inked on the side of their neck. It supposedly lets the Order keep track of them."

"Like a homing device?"

"I guess."

The limo braked at a traffic light. A loud rapping on the passenger window made everyone jump in their seats. Zack cautiously lowered his window. A panhandler stood in the gutter, hacking violently.

"Spare some loose change?" the panhandler asked.

"Take a hike," Zack said.

"I just need a couple of dollars. I haven't eaten all day."

"You heard me. Beat it."

The panhandler lowered his eyes. Peter leaned forward to get a better look at him, and saw a proud man humbled by a series of tragic events beyond his control. His situation wasn't going to change unless someone helped him, and Peter extracted a handful of hundred-dollar bills from his wallet, and stuck his arm out the window. "Hey, I think you dropped this."

"Oh, my God," the panhandler gasped.

"Go ahead. It's yours."

The panhandler took the money with tears in his eyes. "Thank you, thank you."

"Get some warm clothes, and a place to sleep."

"Yes, I will."

"And go to a clinic for that cough."

"I'll do that, too. You're very kind."

"Goodnight."

The light changed, and the limo drove away. Zack hit the button to raise his window. His eyes shifted to Peter's face. "I know you're into helping people, but you're going to have to cut it out until Wolfe is caught. It's too risky."

"I'm never going to stop helping people," Peter said.

"All right. Then you need to get more security, especially at the theater."

"All right. Double the security."

"For yourself as well."

Peter didn't need a bodyguard. He was tuned in to Wolfe, and would sense the next time the assassin came calling. Only he couldn't tell Zack that, so instead he said, "I've got Herbie watching my back. Right, Herbie?"

The glass partition slid back. "You say something, boss?"

"Zack thinks I need extra security so I don't get killed."

"No one's going to kill you while I'm around, boss. I've got bills to pay."

Everyone laughed. Feeling a gentle tug on his sleeve, Peter looked at Liza.

"Wolfe said something strange before he tried to stab you," his girlfriend said. "Do you remember what was it?"

"Wolfe said, 'You're bloody good, you are.' Then he charged me."

"What's that supposed to mean?"

"I think he was complimenting me."

"But he tried to kill you."

"Maybe he was testing you to see how your magic stacked up," Zack said.

The limo fell silent. It was an angle that Peter hadn't considered.

"Wow, that's heavy," Snoop said.

Snoop was trying to be funny. Only no one laughed.

Snoop and Zack shared a loft on Greene Street in SoHo. Peter dropped them off, and then had Herbie drive to his brownstone on the Upper East Side. It was still raining as they pulled up, and Peter and Liza got out. The driver's window lowered.

"Is this guy Wolfe really trying to kill you?" Herbie asked.

"Afraid so," Peter replied.

"Why? What did you do?"

"I don't know. He's part of some strange cult."

"That's bad stuff. What time do you want me here tomorrow?"

Tomorrow was Herbie's day off. On his off days, Herbie had custody of his teenage daughter, whom he was trying to help raise. Peter didn't want him missing that.

"Don't worry about it, Herbie. If something happens, I'll call you."

"You got it. Sound the alarm, and I'll come running."

"Thanks. I appreciate the concern."

The limo glided down the rain-slick street. Peter unlocked the front door, knowing how lucky he was to have people like Herbie working for him. There was no price tag for loyalty or friendship. It had to be earned every single day.

They entered the brownstone. From the street, the building appeared nondescript, its gray stone walls shoddy compared to many of its affluent neighbors. But like most things in Peter's life, appearances were deceiving. His home had three floors and a sundeck on the roof, three spacious bedrooms with cathedral ceilings, a living room with a working fireplace, a gourmet kitchen, a workshop, a study, a basement big enough for a wine cellar, and a Pilates room with an Allegro Reformer. Upon entering for the first time, visitors could often be heard to exclaim, "Oh, my God!" at the enormous collection of brightly painted magic tricks, theater posters, and stage illusions crammed into almost every room. He had practically grown up inside a magic shop, and it was only fitting that he now lived in one.

They moved through the downstairs without turning on the lights. Liza stopped at the stairwell, and slipped her arms around his waist.

"I'm going upstairs to take a hot bath. Are you sure you're okay?"

"I'm okay," he said.

"You don't sound okay. Stop worrying. The police will find this guy."

"I sure hope so."

In the kitchen, he poured himself a glass of juice, and drank it standing at the window. Shadows danced in the courtyard behind the building like dancers in an otherworldly ballet. Talking to Schoch had brought back painful memories, and it would be a while before he'd be able to fall asleep. He'd been seven when his parents had died, and his memories of them were faint. He'd tried to learn as much about them as he could. It was the only way he could stay close to them.

Their names were Henry Butler Warren and Claire Abigail Higgins, and they hailed from the town of Marble in southern England. Their relationship had been straight out of a storybook. They'd grown up together, attended the same college, gotten married, and moved to London to become professors at a small university. Peter had come later, when his parents were well into their forties.

One day, his parents had packed up their things, and moved to New York City, where they'd taken teaching jobs at Hunter College. The move had been traumatic for their son—a new city, strange customs, his classmates making fun of his accent—and they'd struggled to make it work. They'd argued a lot, and he remembered one exchange in the kitchen where a glass thrown by his mother had shattered against a wall. But in the end, they'd never stopped loving each other. That was what he remembered most.

He felt a sharp stabbing in his chest. People said that time healed all wounds, but that wasn't true when the two people you loved most were taken away from you as a child. That was a pain that he'd never quite gotten over.

He went to his workshop. It was filled with tricks that needed repairs. In the corner sat the Spirit Cabinet. Created by the Davenport Brothers in 1875, the illusion had stood the test of time. The trick was simple. The magician entered the cabinet and sat on the stool. Members of the audience tied ropes around his wrists and ankles, with the ends fitted through holes in the doors to ensure he could not move. When the doors were closed, ghostly manifestations occurred, courtesy of an assistant hidden in a secret crawl space. Or, you could perform the trick the way Peter sometimes did, and let real ghosts do the work.

Peter liked ghosts, and ghosts liked him. They'd been talking to him for as long as he could remember, and would sometimes do favors for him. They were his friends, as much as a ghost could be a friend to someone on the other side. Perhaps by talking to them now, he'd better understand what had happened tonight.

Try it, he thought. *Nothing to lose.*

He entered the cabinet, and shut the door. Inside was a stool with a tambourine lying on it. He picked up the tambourine, and parked himself on the stool. Then, he began to shake the tambourine. The sound had a profound effect upon him, and a shudder passed through his body.

A few minutes passed. The first rule of dealing with ghosts was patience. They had their own timetable, and there was no getting around it.

He heard a faint noise that sounded like a chorus to a song. He strained to make out the words. It *was* a song.

> *"My spirit and my voice in one combined,*
> *The Phantom of the Opera was there inside my*
> *mind."*

He smiled to himself. He hadn't heard those lyrics in a long time.

Then, his world changed.

He was standing inside the lobby of the Majestic Theatre, singing the chorus to the dark musical he'd just had the privilege to see. The lobby was filled with people; mostly adults, but a fair number of children as well. None of them were smiling, except for him.

"Peter, hurry along," his father called out.

His parents stood by the entrance, dressed in warm winter clothes. His father was tall and thin, with unruly gray hair and cheeks the color of tomatoes. His mother was a half-foot shorter than her husband, and might have passed as his daughter had her hair not been snow-white. Peter joined them, and his mother buttoned his coat.

"How did you like the show?" she asked.

"It was scary," he said. "I loved it."

"What did you like the most?"

"The music. It was so spooky. I can't stop singing it."

"I'm glad you liked it. Your father has a surprise for you."

With a smile on his face, his father reached into his pocket, and removed the *Phantom of the Opera*'s soundtrack. His son squealed with delight.

"Can we go home now so I can listen to it?" Peter asked.

"Not yet. We've got another surprise for you," his father said.

Peter looked into his father's eyes, and saw singing waiters and a table covered with giant plates of pasta. They were going to Mamma Leone's, his favorite place to eat.

"Can I have the fried pastry for dessert?" Peter asked.

"We'll see. Now, come along, or we'll miss our reservation."

Outside it was snowing, the flakes the size of silver dollars. Standing on the sidewalk was a beggar playing the theme from *Phantom* on an old violin. The music was as enchanting as a siren's song, and Peter could not help but sing along.

"Don't dawdle," his father said.

Next to the beggar was an open violin case into which Peter tossed a handful of coins.

"You play very well. Perhaps someday, you'll be in the show," the boy said.

"I can only hope," the beggar replied.

"*Peter!*"

"I have to go now. Good luck."

His parents had turned into an alley beside the theater which was used as a shortcut by theatergoers. Peter hurried to catch up to them.

"Wait for me," he called out.

Three men rushed past, knocking Peter to the ground, and ripping his pants. The boy stifled the urge to cry. Lifting his head, he saw the men holding guns to his mother and father's backs. They hustled his parents to a waiting car at the end of the alley.

"*Mother! Father!*"

His parents were being shoved into the back of the car. His father was fighting back, and one of the men struck him on the head with his gun. The gift of prescience could be a terrible thing, and Peter knew at that moment that he was never going to see his parents alive again.

"*No!!*" he shouted.

He jumped to his feet, and ran toward the car. As he came out of the alley, the car pulled away with his parents and their abductors inside. One of the abductors was visible through the side window, and Peter saw a man with crooked teeth and a twisted nose. On the man's neck was a shimmering tattoo whose silver color made it look alive.

"Give me my parents back!" Peter shouted at him.

His world changed again. He was back inside the Spirit Cabinet, banging the tambourine. The chorus from *The Phantom of the Opera* had been replaced by the sound of a man's tortured breathing. After a moment, he realized he was listening to himself, panting for breath.

He was not alone.

The shimmering tattoo he'd seen on the abductor's neck hovered directly in front of him. Staring into its center, he saw his parents' distraught faces as they were whisked away to their doom, and felt himself shudder again.

He had wanted a sign from the other side, and he'd gotten his wish. The Order of Astrum had murdered his parents, and now they'd sent an assassin to kill him.

6

Wolfe traveled light. Toothbrush, shaving kit, fake ID, a few thousand in American money, a Zippo lighter from his army days, a disposable cell phone, a laptop, a single change of clothes, and the pocketknife. From time to time, one of the items would break or need replacing, and he'd go through a short period of adjustment. They were his only possessions, and he was attached to them.

Wolfe was sick about losing the pocketknife. It had been given to him as a small boy by an uncle. He had eaten with it, killed with it, and used the corkscrew to open bottles of wine. It pained him that it was now lying in a police evidence bag. It was not the fate he would have hoped for his knife. Better if it had ended up sticking out of the young magician's chest, like he'd planned.

The cab braked. "Seventy-eight Christopher Street. That will be ten bucks," the driver said.

Wolfe settled the fare. Soon he was standing on one of the West Village's narrow streets. He checked the street for any signs of police. Seeing none, he approached a parlor with a hand-painted sign in the window that was home to a Gypsy fortune-teller named Madame Marie. As he opened the front door, a buzzer went off in his ear. He went in.

The parlor was small and scented with sandalwood, the walls covered in dark burgundy fabric. A round antique table sat in the room's center flanked by two wingback chairs. On the table was a dog-eared deck of Tarot cards, and nothing else.

"Anybody home?" he called out.

"We're closed."

The voice was female, and had come from behind a beaded curtain.

"The sign in the window said you're open until midnight."

"Don't believe everything you read. Come back tomorrow. We open at ten sharp."

"Are you Madame Marie?"

"Yes."

"I need to see you now. I'm leaving tomorrow."

"Leaving?"

"Flying home to England. I was told you were the best fortune-teller in New York."

"You can't come back some other time?"

Wolfe heard a slight hesitation in Madame Marie's voice. When it came to sound, he could hear things that other people could not. It had happened while he was in the army, after nearly being blown up by a roadside bomb. Ever since, his hearing had been phenomenal.

"It's really important. Please. I'm desperate."

She let out a sigh. "Have a seat. I'll be right out."

Wolfe took the chair closest to the door and looked around the room. He could tell from his surroundings that Madame Marie was the real deal. Fake fortune-tellers used a variety of props and cheesy gimmicks to get their clients to tell them what was on their minds. Some had their clients sit at glass tables so they could read their body language, or write questions on trick clipboards which took impressions of their handwriting. Wolfe had visited psychics all across the world, and knew their tricks. None of that subterfuge was in evidence here. Real fortune-tellers didn't need tricks. They simply gazed into their tea leaves or crystal balls, or laid out their Tarot cards, and told you what they saw. Some were better than others at peering into the future, and some, like Madame Marie, had powers that bordered on prescience. That was why she was on Wolfe's hit list of psychics to kill in New York.

The curtain parted, and the lady of the house entered. In her seventies, she dressed like a Gypsy, with long flowing robes, and wore a mystical five-pointed gold medallion around her neck to ward off evil spirits. She greeted him with a dip of the chin, and slipped into the other wingback. Her eyes were puffy with sleep.

"Good evening," she said rather formally. "What is your name?"

"Jeremy," Wolfe replied.

"Good evening, Jeremy. My name is Madame Marie. One hundred dollars, please."

Wolfe paid up. The money disappeared into a hidden fold in Madame Marie's clothing. She picked up the Tarot cards and began to shuffle them.

"Have you been fighting, Jeremy?"

Wolfe hesitated. If he lied to her, she'd know it. Better to tell the truth, and see what happened. "I had a slight altercation earlier. Am I nicked up?"

"Your breathing is accelerated, and the side of your face is pink and swollen. You came to me during a time of stress. This must be very important to you."

"It is."

"Good. I like to help people when I can." The Tarot cards made a soft purring sound as they cascaded between her wrinkled hands. "Do you have a question for me?"

Wolfe nodded. Before he ended his victim's life, he was required to test them. If they passed, they died; if they failed, they were spared, and he went on his merry way.

"Go ahead," she said.

"Will my mission be successful?" he asked.

She smothered a yawn. "Is that why you're here in New York? A mission?"

"That's right."

"Very well. Let us find out."

She cut the deck, then dealt a row of three face-up cards onto the table. Her bony forefinger swept over them, and her eyes narrowed.

"What do you see?" Wolfe asked.

"Your childhood was harsh. You left home at a young age to seek a new life. You had dreams of becoming successful and wealthy. Instead, you joined the army, and became a merchant of death."

"I followed the orders I was given," he said defensively.

The old Gypsy looked up. "I'm only telling you what I see. I'm not passing judgment."

"Right. Sorry."

She resumed studying the row of cards. "The service

changed you. You see the world differently now. Sometimes, late at night, you lay awake and wonder what your life would have been like had you chosen another path."

"Would it have been different?"

"Yes, much different."

"How so?"

She pointed at the card of the juggler. "You would have become an entertainer."

A shudder passed through his body. His boyhood dream had been to play drums in a rock 'n' roll band, and tour the world. He didn't want to hear any more.

"Tell me about my mission."

Madame Marie dealt another row of face-up cards behind the first. Her face darkened and her breathing grew shallow. Wolfe leaned closer.

"What do you see?"

"Your mission is more dangerous than you realize. If you succeed, many innocent people will suffer. Even you will be horrified by the outcome."

He snorted contemptuously. His hit list contained the names of seven psychics living in New York that he'd been ordered to kill. Killing seven people wasn't the end of the bloody world, was it?

"Try again," he said.

"You're not satisfied?"

"No. You're way off."

"The cards don't lie. There are consequences for everything in life."

Wolfe didn't want to hear about consequences. His missions were cloaked in secrecy; even he didn't know the reasons why he was sent to kill the people that he did. He traveled to a city with a list of names, and when he left that city, everyone on that list was dead.

Before they could continue, the front door banged open, and a couple of wildly drunk college kids wearing NYU sweatshirts staggered into the parlor.

"What do you want?" Madame Marie demanded.

"Tell her, Bobby," the drunk girl said.

"Katie wants to know if I'm screwing around on her," her boyfriend replied.

"Oh, Bobby," the drunk girl giggled.

"Go away. I have a customer," Madame Marie said.

"Come on, lady. She doesn't believe me," the boy said.

"You heard me! Get out! Both of you!"

The college kids laughed to themselves. Madame Marie came around the table, grabbed them by the arms, and ushered them outside. Slamming the door, she deadbolted it. She returned to her chair.

"Now, where were we?"

Wolfe glanced out the front window. The college kids were standing beneath the awning, making out. He needed to kill time and wait for them to leave.

"Sorry, I don't remember."

"Perhaps we should start over?"

"That would be good."

The cards were gathered and re-mixed. Then, another row was dealt onto the table. Cards representing the Devil, Death, and the High Priestess stared up at them. Panic filled Madame Marie's eyes, and she drew back in her chair.

"I know who you are," she muttered under her breath.

"You do?"

"Yes. You're going to kill all those people in Times Square."

"What are you bloody talking about?"

"You're the Devil, and must be stopped."

"Me? Come on. Get real."

She drew a small-caliber pistol from her dress, and aimed it at Wolfe's chest. Her breathing had grown accelerated, and he realized she was going to shoot him without caring about the consequences. He had a few seconds to save himself, and his mind raced.

It was difficult to own a legal handgun in New York, and, as a result, there were few firing ranges in which to practice. That was to his advantage. As he upended the table and sent the cards into the air, she fired, the bullet missing him by a foot and lodging in the ceiling.

He knocked the old Gypsy out of her chair, and jumped onto her chest. A feeble scream escaped her lips. On the other side of the curtain, Wolfe heard footsteps. He was not surprised when the curtain brushed back, and an elderly man charged into the parlor clutching a baseball bat, which he waved menacingly at Wolfe's skull.

"Let her go," the man declared.

"And who might you be?" Wolfe asked.

"I'm her husband. Now release my wife."

"Whatever you say."

Wolfe grabbed the rug the husband was standing on, and pulled his feet out from under him. The man flew backward through the curtain and disappeared. The sound of his body hitting the floor was loud and painful. Wolfe resumed looking at his wife.

"Tell me about Times Square."

"I didn't see it," Madame Marie said.

"Who did? Tell me, and I won't make you suffer."

"No."

Wolfe picked up the bat and tapped it against her skull.

"Who was it?" he asked.

"Please, don't hurt me."

He tapped a little harder. "Tell me, damn it."

"No."

He smashed the bat onto the floor, making her scream.

"Last chance," he said.

"It was Peter," she whispered.

"The magician?"

"Yes. He saw you during a séance. He said you were going to kill thousands of people in Times Square on Tuesday night."

"How?"

"He didn't know."

Wolfe wasn't buying it. He didn't have the means to kill that many people. Even if he had, he wouldn't have done it. The only people he killed were the names on his list. That was what he got paid to do. There were no freebies in his line of work.

The husband groaned behind the curtain. It was time to go.

Wolfe put his hands around Madame Marie's throat, and squeezed the life out of her. She shuddered once, and the life seeped out of her body.

"Have a nice hereafter," he whispered.

Retrieving the pistol from the floor, Wolfe went into the back room. The husband lay on the floor in a daze. Wolfe inserted the pistol into his mouth, and squeezed the trigger. It made a loud popping sound, and the husband died instantly.

Let the police draw their own conclusions, he thought.

He slipped out of the parlor. The college kids were gone and the street was quiet, save for the steady beat of the rain. He fired up a cigarette and filled his lungs with smoke. Each time he killed, he was overcome with revulsion. Buried deep within his psyche there were still the small remains of a conscience. Someday, he guessed, it would be gone, and the Devil Madame Marie had seen in her cards would be all that remained.

7

Peter barely slept. His parents' abduction kept playing in his head like a trailer for a bad movie. He couldn't turn the damn thing off, no matter how hard he tried.

He opened his eyes the next morning to the smell of toasting bagels. The spot beside him on the bed was empty, and he could hear Liza downstairs in the kitchen. Tossing on his clothes, he barreled down the narrow staircase to the first floor.

Liza was a wonderful cook who did magic in the kitchen. He found her standing by the sink, wearing one of his dress shirts and a pair of fuzzy Garfield slippers. His eyes grew wide at the spread of food on the table. Sliced lox, cream cheese, tomatoes, chives, and a basket filled with sliced bagels. New Yorkers held bragging rights for many things, and that included the world's best bagels. Some claimed it was the water they were boiled in; others said it was the dough. Whatever the reason, a New York bagel was a delicacy found nowhere else.

"This is awesome. What's the occasion?" he asked.

"After last night, I thought you deserved a treat," she said.

"You're the best."

"Have a seat. The show is about to begin."

The food gave him an idea. He went to the basement, and grabbed a bottle of vintage champagne given to him by the Sultan of Brunei after a private show at the Waldorf. Liza oohed and aahed when he brought the bottle to the table. The cork hit the ceiling with a distinct *Pop!* He served her, and raised his own glass in a toast.

"May we never have a repeat of yesterday," he declared.

"I'll drink to that," she said.

They drained their glasses and began to eat. As he bit into his bagel, he noticed Liza looking at him out of the corner of his eye. "Something wrong?"

"I just wanted to make sure you were okay."

"Don't I look okay?"

"You talked during your sleep last night."

"Really? What did I say?"

"You were calling for your parents. I never heard you do that before."

He swallowed hard. There were so many things that he wanted to tell Liza about himself that he didn't know where to start. And now he had more to add. He shouldn't have waited this long, not with Liza. He put his bagel onto his plate.

"There are some things I need to tell you," he blurted out.

"Really? About what?"

"About what happened last night. I know this is going to sound strange, but that guy who attacked me is somehow related to my parents' deaths."

Her eyes grew wide. "He is? How?"

"The cult he belongs to was responsible for their murders."

"But I thought you told me the police didn't know who murdered your parents."

"They don't know. But I do. I saw it last night."

"Oh, my God, Peter. Is that what you were dreaming about?"

It was the perfect explanation, only it wasn't the truth. He had to start being honest with Liza if this was going to work. He took a deep breath. "No. I went back in time, and saw the men who killed them. One of them had a shimmering tattoo on his neck. It was the same tattoo as the man who attacked me at the theater."

"You mean you had a flashback," Liza corrected him.

"No, I mean I went back in time."

"Come on, that isn't possible. Not even for you."

She laughed at him with her eyes. Why couldn't this be easier? He tried to continue when his eyes were drawn to the paper bag the bagels had come in. The Order of Astrum's shimmering symbol had appeared on its side with bright red blood oozing from its center.

"Please give me that bag."

"Don't tell me you saw a roach crawling out of it. Yuck."

"No. It was something else."

By the time the bag reached his hands, the symbol had vanished, and been replaced by the bagel store's cartoon logo. It was a sign from the other side. He needed to act quickly.

"I need to make a phone call."

"But you hardly touched your food," Liza said, sounding put out.

"I'm sorry, but this is important."

A hurt look crossed her face. "Whatever you say."

"I'll explain everything later."

"You're acting weird, Peter."

He hurried upstairs to the bedroom. Snatching Schoch's card off the dresser, he punched the detective's number into his cell phone. "This is Detective Schoch of the NYPD," a cheery recorded voice answered. "Please leave a message at the tone and I'll get right back to you." Straight to voice mail. Damn it. He told Schoch it was urgent and hung up.

He was pacing the floor when his cell phone vibrated.

"Hello, Peter. How are you doing this morning?" Schoch said.

"I need to speak to you about the Order of Astrum."

"What about them?"

"I know the real reason you came to see me last night."

"Really."

"Yes. I had a vision."

"You don't say."

"I mean it. My parents' murders play into what's going on. The Order had them killed, and now they're after me. That's why you and your partner came to see me, isn't it?"

"Don't say any more. I'm driving in to work right now with Dag. Give me your address, and I'll come by, and we can talk."

"I live at three hundred and twenty East Sixty-second Street."

"I'll be there in ten minutes."

"I'll be waiting," he said.

He returned to the kitchen to find Liza rinsing the breakfast dishes in the sink. His plate of food sat on the table, covered in plastic, while the other delicacies had been put away. When he came up from behind and tried to touch her, a plate slipped from her hands and broke.

"Shit," she swore.

"I'm really sorry," he told her.

She faced him. "I don't like it when you keep things from me. You do that a lot."

"I'm sorry."

"You need to be more open with me. All of this secrecy is driving me crazy."

He'd never seen her this angry, and mumbled "Okay" under his breath.

"Is that a promise?" she asked.

"Scout's honor," he said.

"Were you ever a Boy Scout?"

"What do you think?"

"Damn it, Peter, I'm trying to be serious."

She was boiling mad, ready to walk out. He'd stepped over a dangerous line.

"I promise to start acting normal," he said.

"I'm going to hold you to that."

The conversation had turned awkward. It was hard to live a lie, harder still when it was with the woman you loved. The doorbell rang, saving him.

"I'll get it."

He sprinted down the hallway and opened the front door. Schoch stood on the stoop wearing a beige raincoat and looking straight out of the pages of a glossy women's magazine. Behind her, Dagastino was parked at the curb. He still looked angry about last night.

"We got here as fast as we could," Schoch said. "Now, tell me about your vision."

Peter stepped outside and shut the door. "I know you'll think this is crazy, but I went back in time last night. I saw the three men who killed my parents. One had the Order of Astrum's tattoo on his neck."

"Hold on. You went back in *time*? How does that work?"

"The spirits do it. It's how they reveal things."

"The spirits."

"That's right. This morning over breakfast, the Order's symbol appeared to me. There was blood coming out if it. The presence of blood is a sign that someone's about to die. Wolfe's getting ready to kill again."

Schoch blew out her cheeks. "Assuming I buy in to this, who's his next victim going to be?"

"I wish I knew."

"Where will it happen?"

"I don't know that, either."

"In that case, I'd say we're plumb out of luck."

"You don't believe me."

"It has nothing to do with believing you. I need something solid."

"It's the best I could do. I thought you should know."

Schoch eyed him skeptically. "Let me ask you a question. Were your parents involved with dark magic? Did they practice witchcraft or anything like that? It's important that you be up front with me."

Peter had never discussed his parents' psychic abilities with anyone outside of his Friday night group. Telling Schoch was going to feel strange, yet he knew it must be done.

"They were both psychics," he said. "They held séances in my father's study with a group of their friends. I stumbled upon them one night when I was a kid."

"Could your parents have been involved with the Order?"

He thought back to his father's study. Astrological symbols on the table, white candles, and the five-pointed star used to ward off evil spirts. He had not seen the Order's symbol.

"No," he said.

"Your parents were from England. Could they have been involved with the Order when they lived there?"

"We left England when I was little."

"But you still have memories."

"We lived in a flat in London. My parents taught at a small college. On weekends we went to the park, and I played while my parents read books. If they were members of the Order, I never saw any evidence of it." He paused. "But you already knew most of this, didn't you? You knew these things when you came to see me last night."

"Most of it, yes," she admitted.

He hated when people deceived him, and he felt himself grow angry.

"Who told you about my parents?" he asked.

"Please lower your voice."

He took a deep breath to calm himself.

"I'm sorry. Please. Who told you?"

"I can't tell you who gave me the information," she said. "But I will tell you this. There are a lot more people besides the police looking for Wolfe. With any luck, they're going to find him, and we can get to the bottom of this." She consulted her watch. "I'm late for work. Call me if you have any more visions."

"I'll do that."

Schoch got into the Volvo and her partner drove away. Peter shook his head. Why was it that whenever he talked with her, he felt like he knew less than when he'd started?

He opened the front door, and went inside the brownstone. Liza awaited him in the foyer. If looks could kill, he would have been six feet under, pushing up daisies.

"Why are you looking at me like that?" he asked.

"Figure it out. You're the mind reader," she said.

He shut the door behind him. The intercom was covered with wet fingerprints. She'd heard their conversation. He leaned against the door, and shut his eyes.

"You were listening," he said.

She punched him in the arm. "Stop climbing into your shell. Look at me."

He opened his eyes and looked at his beloved.

"Damn you, Peter! We've been living together for two years. When were you going to tell me you had these strange powers?"

"I tried to over breakfast."

"You really can travel back in time?"

"I can do a lot of unusual things."

"Like have visions?"

"Yes."

"And read minds?"

"Uh-huh."

"What am I thinking about right now?"

He gazed into her eyes. "You're thinking about spending the night at your girlfriend's."

"That's a no-brainer. Which one?"

"Amber."

She brought her hand to her mouth. "Oh, my God. You really can. It's not a trick."

"Yeah."

"Damn you, Peter. That's not fair."

She was pulling away from him. If he didn't come clean with her now, it was over. Tell the truth, and maybe he had a chance.

"Do you remember my friend Nemo?" he asked. "We ate oysters at Balthazar while he told you jokes. He made you laugh the whole time."

"What about him?" she said.

"Nemo is also psychic, and can see into the future. The CIA found out about his powers, and whisked him away to a farm in Virginia. He's in their employ now, so to speak. They're never going to let him go. That's what happens to people like me. The government gets ahold of us, and we never come home."

"There are more of you?"

"Yes. We have these gifts that we keep hidden."

"You still should have told me."

"I wanted to, but I was afraid."

"Of what?"

"That you'd think I was a freak, and leave," he said, the words pouring out. "I didn't want to lose you. I know that's selfish, and I'm sorry."

The truth had a way of cutting through just about everything else. Liza crossed the foyer, and put her hand under his chin. Their eyes met.

"I would never do that," she said.

"Is that a promise?" he asked.

"Scout's honor."

"Then I'll never hide anything from you again."

They kissed. Liza still loved him. He had been saved.

They returned to the kitchen. Peter sensed they were not alone. His eyes scanned the room, spying the Order's shimmering symbol on the refrigerator. The oozing blood coming out of its center had been replaced by a face.

Peter got up close to stare.

It was Wolfe. The assassin sat at the counter of a diner, eating a breakfast of steak and eggs. Taking the knife off his plate, Wolfe tested the knife's sharpness. Satisfied, he stuck it up his sleeve, and hopped off his stool.

The symbol vanished, leaving a menu for Chinese takeout.

"He's going to kill someone," Peter muttered.

"Who? What are you talking about?" Liza asked.

The diner looked familiar. It was on the Lower East Side, and served a mean breakfast. He had to alert the police, and grabbed his leather jacket off the back of a chair.

"I have to go out."

"What? You can't be serious. Didn't you just promise me—"

"I'll explain everything later."

"I'm sure you will."

He tried to kiss her, and Liza pulled away.

"You have to trust me," he said. "The man who attacked me last night is about to strike again. I have to stop him."

"How can you possibly know that?"

"I just do."

"You're treading on dangerous ice, Peter."

Liza followed him down the hallway. He went outside, and turned up his collar to the annoying rain. The front door slammed angrily behind him.

He hurried down the sidewalk, hoping she'd understand.

8

The greasy spoon on East 11th Street had no name. Wolfe sat at the counter, gazing at a dingy storefront across the street. THE SACRED PLACE—PSYCHIC READINGS FOR ANY OCCASION. He pulled a slip of paper from his wallet to make sure he had the right place. Lester Rowe, owner of The Sacred Place, was number three on his hit list.

Wolfe resumed eating his steak and eggs. A police cruiser passed by, splashing water onto the sidewalk. It was the third cruiser he'd seen in the past ten minutes. That wasn't normal, and he guessed the law was looking for him. That was the tricky part of his work. It was classic cat and mouse, and he relished his role as the mouse.

Wolfe glanced at his waitress, a young woman with spiked hair and a ring in her nose. She was flirting with another customer, a punked-out boy about her age. Picking up his steak knife, he slipped it beneath the rubber band on his wrist, and pulled down his sleeve. His captain in the army had taught him the usefulness of rubber bands. They came in handy in so many situations, he always wore one.

The rain was spitting as he crossed the street. The weather was worse than London. The front door was locked, and he rapped loudly on the glass while peering inside. It was a toilet, with cheap furniture and even cheaper wall coverings. Hundreds of psychics worked out of storefronts in New York. Except for the names on his list, they were all fakes. There were so many fakes that the real ones were forced to scrape by giving readings out of places like this. A greeter wearing a turban unlocked the door, and ushered him inside.

"Welcome to The Sacred Place. My name is Habib."

Wolfe was good at placing accents. Habib was from the southern region of Turkey.

"I'd like a reading with Lester Rowe," Wolfe said. "Is he available?"

"Yes, he is. You will need to make a one-hundred-dollar donation. Cash or credit?"

A donation. That was a new one. Wolfe paid in cash, and Habib handed him a clipboard and a pencil.

"Please fill this out. I will return shortly."

Wolfe parked himself on a cheap plastic chair in the reception area and read the printed form on the clipboard. It asked for his name, date of birth, astrological sign, and personal things about himself, including his fears, beliefs, likes, and dislikes. The last question was the kicker. Why had he come for a reading today?

He laughed to himself. He'd been given a similar form to fill out in psychic parlors before, and knew what it meant. The Sacred Place was a scam. There was a hole in the wall behind his chair which Habib was staring through at this very moment. Habib would copy down his answers, and share them with Rowe before their session began.

Taking out his Zippo lighter, Wolfe stared into its reflection, and found the hole in a framed picture hanging behind his chair. Rowe was a bloody fake, and shouldn't have been on his hit list. Something wasn't right here, and he decided to find out what was going on.

Wolfe scribbled down his answers. Soon, Habib returned.

"All done?" Habib asked cheerfully.

"I believe I am," Wolfe replied.

"Very good. Take the form off the clipboard and put

it in your pocket. We ask you to write down your answers so you can better channel your thoughts during
the reading."

Sure you do.

"Please follow me, and watch your step. The carpet
needs to be replaced."

They passed down a narrow hallway to a small parlor with Persian rugs hanging on the walls. A white-
bearded Turkish man sat in a wheelchair strapped to an
oxygen tank. The apple had not fallen far from the tree.
Habib looked just like him.

The elderly Turk motioned toward an empty chair.
Wolfe sat down.

"Are you Lester Rowe?" Wolfe asked.

"Do I look like a man whose name is Lester Rowe?"
the elderly Turk replied.

"I've never met the man. But I'm guessing you're not
him."

"You are a good guesser. My name is Akan. I bought
the business from him a few month ago."

"Do you have Rowe's address? I need to get in touch
with him."

"Why do you want to contact a man you've never
met?" Akan asked pointedly.

"It's a personal matter," Wolfe replied.

Wolfe heard someone breathing. Behind the wheelchair was a door with light streaming through the bottom. A pair of shoes lurked on the other side. Son
number two, he guessed.

"You are a liar," Akan said. "Sedat! Come out here!"

A dark-skinned man built like a Greco-Roman wres-
tler marched into the parlor. He pulled Wolfe out of his
chair, and patted him down.

"He's clean," son number two said.

"What's the meaning of this?" Wolfe demanded.

"I think you know," Akan said.

"No, I don't. I'm not a mind reader. Then again, neither are you."

"Do not make fun of my father." Sedat had a voice like a bear. "You're the man in the BOLO. The police say you're extremely dangerous."

"What's a bloody BOLO?" Wolfe asked, trying to buy time.

Sedat removed a flyer from his pocket, and held it out for Wolfe to see. Wolfe's photo was printed on the paper, along with the words BE ON THE LOOKOUT, courtesy of the NYPD.

"That doesn't look anything like me," Wolfe said indignantly.

"I will be the judge of that. Take off your hat."

"And what if I say no?"

Sedat ripped off Wolfe's baseball cap, and compared his face to the one in the photo.

"You bear a strong resemblance to this man," Sedat said. "I am going to call the police. If you are innocent, then there is no harm done."

Wolfe's mind raced. He needed to keep several steps ahead of the police if he was going to have a chance to complete his mission.

"By all means, do call them," Wolfe said. "Because I plan to tell the police there's a bloody hole in the wall in your front room that you're using to spy on customers. Once they hear that, they'll take your license away, and shut you down."

The parlor fell silent. Akan shifted uncomfortably in his wheelchair.

"Perhaps we can come to some kind of arrangement," the elderly Turk said.

"You mean a bribe to keep your mouths shut? How much do you have in mind?" Wolfe asked.

"How about a thousand dollars?"

"That sounds reasonable enough. Do you take traveler's checks?"

"Of course."

"Gentlemen, you have a deal."

Sedat held his hand out for the money. It was the opening Wolfe had been waiting for. He kicked the big man in the chest, and sent him tumbling onto his father's wheelchair. Habib came next. Drawing the steak knife, Woolfe slashed son number one across the face.

"Stand against the wall," Wolfe ordered him.

Habib cowered against the wall, his hand pressed to the gushing wound. Wolfe pointed his knife at Sedat, who was trying to rehook the oxygen tank to the tube hanging around his father's neck. The crying sound of escaping oxygen filled the air.

"Give me Lester Rowe's address, and I'll leave you alone," Wolfe said.

"I don't have it," Sedat replied.

"You bought his bloody business. You must have some idea where he went."

It was Habib who answered him. "Lester Rowe moved his business to Second Street, between First and Second Avenues. He works out of an apartment house on the bottom floor."

"What's the address?"

"He didn't give it to us. He has a steady stream of clients. You won't have a problem finding him."

"That wasn't so hard, now, was it?"

Sedat had pulled his father into his lap, and was trying to revive him. It was touching to see the son's devotion to his father. Had it been his own father, Wolfe would have taken his head and smashed it against the floor, then given it a twist for good measure.

Wolfe backed out of the parlor. Stopping in the doorway, he pulled out his trusty Zippo, and grabbed a promotional flyer off a table. He crushed the flyer into a ball and began to ignite it.

"No!" Sedat said.

"The police offered you a reward for turning me in, didn't they?" Wolfe said.

Sedat nodded his head fearfully.

"How much for my head?"

"Does it matter?" Sedat asked.

"It does to me."

"Twenty thousand dollars."

"That's a lot of money. Why settle for a thousand?"

"We are illegals. If the police found out, they'd throw us out of the country."

"Makes sense. Have a nice hereafter."

Wolfe lit the flyer with his Zippo, and tossed the flaming paper directly at the tank. The escaping oxygen made a distinct *Pop!* as it ignited and caught fire. He went into the hallway and slammed the door, then braced himself. He could hear the Turks yelling in their native tongue. Seconds later the tank exploded, and the whole building shook.

It was still raining as he went outside. Eleventh Street was deserted, although it would not be that way for very long. He fired up a cigarette, and smoke filled his lungs as he started to walk. It was strange: The more times he killed, the harder it was for him to calm down. Madame Marie had called him the Devil, only he didn't think the Devil had a conscience. He still did, no matter how small it might be.

Soon he reached Second Avenue, and began to hunt for Lester Rowe.

9

The lobby of the 19th Precinct was filled with people. Located on East 67th Street between Lexington and Third Avenues, the precinct served one of the most densely populated areas of the city, which included many foreign missions and consuls. Peter sifted his way through the mob, and caught the eye of a gruff female desk sergeant. He sidled up to her desk.

"Good morning."

"You always take a shower with your clothes on?" she asked, working a piece of gum.

Everyone in New York was a comedian. Especially the cops.

"I'd like to see Detective Schoch," he replied. "Is she here?"

"Depends who's asking. Hey, I know you. You're that magic guy. I saw your show last year. Not bad. There's something I've always wanted to know. Is that your real name?"

"Warlock is my stage name."

"I didn't think so. Show me a trick."

Peter made it a rule to never walk out of his brownstone without a trick in his pocket. Only today he'd forgotten, so he had to improvise. He told the desk sergeant to think of a card, and when he attempted to read her mind, hit a wall. It happened sometimes. Borrowing a pen and a piece of paper, he wrote down a prediction and placed it face down on the desk.

"Name your card," he said.

"Queen of hearts," she replied.

"Want to change your mind?"

"Nope."

"Happy with the mind that you have?"

"Very funny."

"Turn my prediction over."

She flipped over the paper. Written on it were the words QUEEN OF HEARTS.

"Wow. How'd you do that?"

There were only five playing cards that people ever thought of—the ace of spades, queen of spades, queen of hearts, king of hearts, and seven of spades. Most middle-aged women chose the queen of hearts. He smiled and shook his head.

"Not going to tell me, huh?" The desk sergeant slid a form toward him. "Fill this out so I can sign you in. Is Detective Schoch expecting you?"

"She was at my home earlier, discussing a case," he said.

"Is that a yes, or a no?"

"No, she's not expecting me."

"I'll give you a pass this time." She made a quick call, then hung up. "Detective Schoch will be down in a few minutes. Have a seat in one of those chairs. Nice meeting you."

"You, too."

He sat on a hard plastic bench bolted to the wall. A copy of today's *New York Post* lay on the seat beside him. No one did headlines like the *Post*. KIDNAPING SUSPECT TO GO FREE—COPS OUT-RAGED! By the time he'd finished the story, Schoch had come downstairs. She was all business, and wore a sidearm strapped to her side.

"Hey, Peter, what's up?"

He rose from the bench. "I had another vision. Wolfe's on the Lower East Side, stalking his next victim. He was eating breakfast in a diner that looked familiar."

She shot him an exasperated look. "That's it? You can't give me an address, or a name?"

"No. Sorry."

"Thanks for the heads-up. I'll put out an alert."

Schoch started walking toward the elevators. He hurried to catch up.

"Please tell me what you know about Wolfe," he said.

"I already told you, I can't do that."

"I have something to trade."

"What are you talking about?"

He pulled the *Post* out from under his arm. "I can help you solve this kidnaping case."

"Exactly how do you plan to do that?"

"The newspaper ran a photo of the ransom note. I saw something in the note that told me who the kidnaper is."

"Our handwriting expert looked at the ransom note, and didn't see a thing."

"He must of missed it."

She rolled her eyes.

"I see things that other people miss. I can help you crack this."

"Is that part of your psychic abilities?"

"Actually, it comes from being a magician. We look at things differently."

Schoch gave him a long, searching look. She shrugged her shoulders as if to say what the hell, and punched the elevator button.

"Follow me," she said.

Homicide was a sea of cubicles and ringing phones. Dagastino's cubicle was a pigsty, his desk covered in dead coffee cups and dog-eared reports. Dag was on the phone, and had his feet propped on the desk. He ended the call as they entered, and shot Peter a hostile look.

"We've got company," Schoch said.

"I see that," Dagastino said. "To what do we owe the pleasure?"

"Peter thinks he can help us solve the Bunny Ruttenberg kidnaping."

"Be my guest."

"He wants something in return," she said.

"A horse trade?"

"That's right."

"I want to know about the guy who tried to stab me last night," Peter jumped in.

Dagastino scratched his chin, and gave it some thought.

"You go first," the detective said.

"Do we have a deal, or not?" Peter asked.

"We have a deal. Now, start talking."

"The ransom note spray-painted on the wall of Bunny Ruttenberg's apartment was put there by her husband, who the *Post* said was going to be let out of jail," Peter said.

"You figured that out just by reading the *Post*?" Dagastino snorted. "Give me a break, for Christ's sakes."

"It's right there in the ransom note," Peter said defensively.

"The note was spray-painted on the wall of the apartment. Our handwriting expert studied it. There was nothing to see," Dagastino shot back.

"Your expert missed it. The clue was right there."

"What clue?"

"Magicians call it the familiar-name principle. I'll show you." Peter turned his back to the desk. "In random order, write the name of someone important to you on a piece of paper, then write the names of four people you don't care about on the same piece of paper."

Dagastino's pen scratched across a legal pad. "Done."

Peter turned back around. Dagastino handed him the pad, which he studied. Five names were written across it. A quick glance told him everything he needed to now.

"The second name on the pad, Maryann Magliaro, is someone you care deeply about," Peter said. "Am I right?"

Dagastino's mouth opened, but no words came out.

"Is she your wife?"

"Jesus H. Christ. How'd you know *that*?" the detective asked.

"You wrote her name differently," Peter explained.

"I did?"

"Yes. You've probably written your wife's name hundreds of times, maybe more. You wrote her name without having to think about it, and used the subconscious part of your brain. The other names you had to think about, and therefore used the conscious part of your brain. The difference shows up in the handwriting. It's an old magic trick."

Peter had the copy of the *Post* under his arm. He laid the paper on the desk and pointed to the ransom note in the story. "Look at the words in the note. They all have paint dripping down them, except Bunny Ruttenberg's name. Her kidnaper spray-painted her name without having to think about it. It's her husband."

Dagastino studied the ransom note printed in the newspaper. "That's brilliant. Now how do we get him to admit it?"

Peter had thought about that while sitting in the lobby. The *Post* article said the Ruttenbergs had been married forty years. He guessed this was a crime of passion, and that there were other clues in the apartment that the police had missed.

"Let me see the file," he said.

Dagastino went and got the file. "Find something to incriminate the husband, and I'll tell you everything we know about the guy who tried to cut your heart out."

"Deal," Peter said.

10

The Ruttenberg file was an inch thick. It included a stack of black-and-white crime scene photos taken at the Ruttenberg's multi-million-dollar Park Avenue penthouse. Even by New York standards, the dwelling was spectacular, and filled with the finest things money could buy. The panoramic view of Central Park was enough to take a person's breath away.

Peter sat at Dagastino's desk. He quickly sorted through the photos, and found himself drawn to a shot of the master bedroom, which was bigger than most apartments in the city. Something about the walk-in closet struck him as odd, and he showed the photo to Schoch.

"This doesn't look right," he said.

"What do you mean?" Schoch replied.

"Look at the way the clothes are hung. Bunny Ruttenberg's dresses are in the back of the closet, behind her husband's suits and sport coats. A woman wouldn't let her husband put his clothes in front of hers, would she?"

"You've got a point. What do you think it means?"

"The husband knows his wife isn't coming back. He killed her, and is feeling guilty about what he's done. He moved her clothes so he doesn't have to look at them."

"So his conscience is eating at him."

"Yes. He probably wanted to throw the clothes out, only he knew it would look suspicious, so he moved them instead."

"Hey, Dag, take a look at this," Schoch said.

Dagastino was schmoozing with another detective. He hustled over, and Schoch pointed out the discrepancy in the photo.

"That's good. Give me more," Dagastino said.

Peter spread the photos across the detective's desk, and looked for more evidence of the husband's guilt. One photo showed a dresser in the master bedroom with the couple's wedding photo on it. Bunny's face was blocked by an alarm clock.

"Here's another. The husband can't bear to look at his wife's face, so he stuck an alarm clock in front of it. He's guilty as sin."

Dagastino stuck a stick of gum into his mouth. He vigorously chewed while staring at the photo of the dresser.

"What are you thinking?" Schoch asked.

"I want to pull the husband out of the holding cell in the basement, and grill him while making him look at Bunny's picture," her partner said.

"Think he might crack?" Schoch asked.

"Could happen."

"I'll go get him." Schoch slipped on her jacket and went to retrieve the husband.

"I'd like to watch," Peter said. "I might see something else."

"The more the merrier," Dagastino replied.

* * *

Henry Ruttenberg was moved from the holding cell to an interrogation room on the third floor. The room was small, and had a desk and two chairs. A distinguished-looking man with silver hair, Ruttenberg sat with a blank look on his face and examined his fingernails.

The door banged open, and Dagastino came in. In his hand was a photo of Bunny Ruttenberg printed off the Internet. She was an attractive woman, and could have passed for an aging movie star. He slapped the photo on the desk.

"You didn't mean to kill her, did you, Henry?" Dagastino asked.

Ruttenberg stared at his wife's lovely visage, and his eyes grew moist.

"It was an accident, right?" Dagastino barked.

Ruttenberg shut his eyes, and did not respond.

"Look at me when I'm talking to you," Dagastino said.

The suspect opened his eyes. The blank look had returned.

"I don't know what you're talking about. There was no accident," Ruttenberg said.

"Then it was a fit of rage."

"Stop it."

"Here's my question, Henry. How soon after you murdered your wife did you decide to move her clothes to the back of your closet?"

"I have no idea what you're talking about."

"You knew she wasn't coming back, but you couldn't part with her things without people getting suspicious." Dagastino put his fists on the desk. "You gave yourself away, Henry."

Ruttenberg stared at the photo of his wife, and remained silent.

"You even moved your wife's picture on your dresser so you wouldn't have to look at it. You still love her, don't you?"

A long minute passed. Ruttenberg's chin dipped, and tears rolled down his face. Dagastino handed him a tissue, and the accused man loudly blew his nose.

"You figured it out," Ruttenberg said.

"Yes, we did. But some of the details are sketchy. Why don't you fill us in? It will go a long way with the judge."

Ruttenberg dabbed his eyes with the tissue. "Bunny found out I was having an affair with my personal trainer. It was nothing, just a fling, but Bunny wouldn't hear it. She told me last Saturday night that she wanted a divorce. I blew up, and we started to fight. By accident, I knocked her down. Bunny hit her head on a coffee table, and cracked her skull."

The memory was too much, and he started to shake. "I tried to revive her, but she was gone. I didn't want to kill her. You have to believe me. I loved my wife."

"Keep talking," Dagastino said.

"I was afraid to call the police, so I carried her to the car in the basement garage and drove to our farm in Connecticut. I buried her in the woods. It was her favorite spot."

"Will you show us where?" Dagastino asked.

Ruttenberg nodded solemnly.

"If I give you a confession, will you sign it?"

Ruttenberg again nodded.

Dagastino looked at Peter and Schoch through the two-way mirror. He grinned.

* * *

They met up in Dagastino's cubicle ten minutes later. Dagastino had the signed confession and was beaming from ear to ear.

"Nice work," Dagastino said. "Let me know if you ever want to change careers."

"I'll do that," Peter replied. "Now, it's your turn. Tell me about Wolfe."

Dagastino parked himself on the edge of his desk. A toothpick appeared in his mouth as if by magic. "Two days ago, a customs agent at JFK got spooked. He thought a guy coming into the country might have lied to him. The agent pulled the guy's photo off a surveillance video, and ran a facial recognition scan against their database. Turns out it was Jeremy Wolfe, a member of the Order of Astrum. Every intelligence agency in the world wants to have a sit-down with this guy. Whenever he's around, dead bodies show up."

"He's an assassin?" Peter asked.

"Yes, and a damn good one," Schoch jumped in. "While Wolfe was in the army, he was nearly blown up by a roadside bomb, and came out of it with a heightened sense of hearing that made him invincible on the battlefield. His superiors called him a killing machine."

Every person was born with some psychic ability. It was not uncommon to have these abilities awakened after traumatic events. Wolfe sounded like a classic late bloomer.

"Now, here's where it gets interesting," Dagastino said. "The FBI got involved, and interviewed a twelve-year-old girl who sat next to Wolfe on the flight over. Turns out, the girl saw Wolfe reading from a list of names. With her parents' consent, the FBI put the girl under hypnosis. The kid responded to the hypnosis, and said the list contained seven names. The only name she remembered was yours. Seems she's been to your show, and is a fan."

"So I was on a hit list," Peter said.

"Correct," Dagastino said. "The FBI asked us to alert you, since you live within our jurisdiction. My partner volunteered, since she knew you. We went to your theater, only Wolfe had attacked you by the time we arrived. That's the story."

"But why did he attack me?" Peter asked.

"Don't know."

"What did the FBI say?"

Dagastino glanced at his partner. "You tell him."

"The FBI told us the Order of Astrum were linked to your parents' deaths, which was news to us," Schoch said. "When we asked them to explain, they refused."

Peter was dumbstruck. "The FBI *knew*?"

Both detectives nodded. They didn't like it any more than he did.

"Damn them," Peter said.

Schoch walked Peter to the elevators. Her face was filled with sorrow.

"I'm sorry, Peter. I know this has been hard on you. I'll call you if we learn more."

"Thanks," he mumbled.

Schoch squeezed his arm before leaving. Peter punched the elevator button in anger. The idea that he might someday find his parents' killers was never far from his mind. That the FBI had known who was behind their deaths and not told him was unthinkable.

He took several deep breaths, and forced himself to calm down.

He had to find Wolfe. Wolfe could lead him to the three men who'd abducted and shot his parents in cold blood. Wolfe was the key.

No elevator. He glanced at the display above the door. It was stuck on the seventh floor. He hit the button again.

"Come on."

He felt himself grow cold. He spun around, sensing Nemo's presence. His friend was reaching out to him. But from where?

A rectangular mirror hung on the wall opposite the elevators. In its glass, a swirling white cloud had appeared. Within the cloud, a number took shape.

Seven.

"Seven?" he said aloud.

The number began to flash.

"Seven *what*?"

The cloud vanished, and the number disappeared. The air temperature returned to normal. Peter turned around. The elevator was still stuck on the seventh floor.

Then it hit him what Nemo was trying to say.

There had been seven names on Wolfe's list.

His name was at the top of the list.

There were seven people in his Friday night séance.

He was the leader of the séance.

The Order had sent Wolfe to kill him and his friends.

He turned around to face the mirror. "Thank you," he told it.

He started back to Homicide, only to stop. He had told the detectives enough about himself. Any more, and they'd find out about his friends. Secrecy was the bond that kept the Friday night séance intact, and he'd sworn never to break it.

He took the stairwell to the lobby, and ran outside. In the middle of Third Avenue, he was nearly run over by a bus. Unfazed, he hailed down a cab, and hopped in.

"Where to?" the driver asked.

"Just drive," he said.

11

Peter had never asked to be the leader of the Friday night séance. Nor had the group ever voted on it, or held a discussion, or anything like that. It had just happened, largely because the spirits seemed comfortable communicating through him, just as they'd channeled through his mother years ago.

He'd become the group's leader as a teenager. The fact that he'd been doing it for so long now seemed odd to him. It would have been nice to have shared the responsibility.

He called Max, Madame Marie, and Reggie Brown, got their voice mails, and asked them to call back as soon as possible. His next call was to Holly, whom he caught going into a study group at Columbia University. She quickly detected the apprehension in his voice.

"What's wrong?" she asked.

"I just came from seeing the police. Something bad is about to happen to a member of our group. You must go to your aunt's apartment. Stay with her until I call you back."

"What's going on?"

"An assassin named Wolfe is trying to kill us. Don't ask me to explain, because I can't."

"Do the police know?"

"Yes, they're hunting for him."

"I mean about us."

"No, I didn't tell them."

"What can I do?"

"Do you have Lester Rowe's cell phone number? It's not in my address book."

"Lester doesn't have a cell phone. He's a Luddite. He doesn't have a phone in his apartment, either. I think he uses his neighbor's phone when he wants to call."

"Do you know his address? I have to warn him right away."

"He lives down on the Lower East Side. You sound scared."

He *was* scared. Not for his own life, but for one of them, his secret family, and it came through with every word he spoke. "I am scared. Call me when you reach your aunt's, okay?"

"But I thought you said the police were hunting Wolfe."

"You don't understand. Wolfe's a member of a cult of dark magicians. They murdered my parents, and now they're trying to murder us."

"Oh, my God, Peter. Oh, my God."

"I know. Now go stay with your aunt."

"What about you? Where are you going?"

"I have to warn the others."

"You're putting yourself in harm's way. Come to my aunt's, and hide with us."

Hiding was the last thing on his mind. "I need to go," he said.

"I love you, Peter. I always have."

The words struck him like a thunderbolt. "You do?"

"Yes. Ever since I was little, and you did magic tricks for me. I'm sorry to be telling you this now, but I just have to."

He stared out the rain-soaked window at the street. Babysitting Holly while practicing his magic were some of the fondest memories he had, and now seemed like another lifetime.

"You're not mad, are you?" she asked.

"Happy," he said.

"Really?"

"Yes, really."

"That's so wonderful. I'll talk to you later."

He folded his phone, his heart doing a strange flip-flop inside his chest. The driver tapped his meter. They had just crossed 14th Street, and the fare was over twenty dollars.

"Gimme a hint," the driver said.

Madame Marie's fortune-telling parlor wasn't far, and he decided to go there, and alert her. He gave the driver the cross streets and soon they were heading west.

Peter shut his eyes and leaned back in his seat, trying to make sense of it all.

He opened his eyes to the sight of an ambulance and a police cruiser parked in front of Madame Marie's parlor. The cruiser's bubble cast a sickly red glow over the scene.

He was too late.

He paid the driver and got out. On the sidewalk were a gathering of spectators and a uniformed cop talking into a walkie-talkie. Two grim-faced medics wheeled a body draped in white sheets through the front door of the parlor. Peter felt a dagger pierce his heart.

"What happened?" he asked a woman in the crowd.

"An old fortune-teller and her husband were murdered late last night."

"How?"

"Strangled and shot. I tell you, the neighborhood's falling apart."

He fought back the tears. Madame Marie had taught him how to the read the Tarot cards when he was a little boy. He'd sat on a phone book in the back room of her parlor, and learned what the cards stood for in the spirit world. A giving teacher, she'd never once reprimanded him when he got one wrong. And now she was gone.

A second body followed, and was loaded into the ambulance with the first. Marie and her husband were inseparable, and it was fitting they left this world together. The back of the ambulance was closed, and it drove down the block with its bubble still flashing.

The spectators dispersed, leaving Peter and the cop.

"They were my friends. Can you tell me what happened?" Peter asked.

"Looks like a murder-suicide," the cop explained. "I'm sorry for your loss."

"You don't think someone murdered them?"

The cop gave him a funny look. "Can't say that I do."

Peter saw movement inside the fortune-telling parlor. A group of old friends had gathered inside to pay their last respects.

"What are you looking at?" the cop said.

"Nothing," Peter replied.

"You can't go in there, if that's what you're thinking. I'd suggest you move along."

"I'll do that."

The cop's walkie-talkie came to life, and he stepped

away to take the call. Peter went straight to the parlor's front door. He broke yellow crime scene tape, and stuck his head in.

It looked like a wake. All of Madame Marie's spirit-world acquaintances were crammed into the small space. There was the ridiculous-acting Fool; the Hermit in his threadbare clothes; the always-aloof High Priestess and High Priest in their flowing robes; the Lovers, whose bodies were forever entwined; the Hanged Man with his grotesquely twisted neck and bubble eyes; and the other spirits who made up the major arcana of the Tarot cards that Madame Marie used to peer into the future. These spirits had inhabited the earth since the beginning of time, and were the archetypes of human existence, embedded in the collective unconscious of every human being. They represented life, death, and everything that fell in between.

Their mournful wails filled the parlor. Peter knew of nothing sadder than hearing the spirits cry. He wanted to comfort them, but the words had not been invented to make their pain go away. The Fool shuffled over.

"How's tricks?" the Fool said with a raspy voice.

"Hello, Fool," Peter replied.

"This is a sad day. I will miss her."

"She was very fond of you," Peter told him.

"And I of her. Who would do such a thing?"

"A monster named Wolfe. I'm going to find him, and make him pay."

"Be careful. This is the Devil's work."

"Didn't you hear what I just said," the cop's voice rang out.

"I must be going," the Fool said. "Be safe."

"And you as well."

The Fool disappeared before his eyes, as did the other spirits crammed inside the parlor, leaving only Madame

Marie's worn deck of Tarot cards spilled across a worn rug on the parlor floor. Peter shut the door, and turned to face the irate cop.

"Sorry," he said.

"Who the hell were you talking to?" the cop asked.

"Myself."

"Come again?"

"She was a special person. I had to say good-bye."

"I told you to stay out of there. Let me see some ID."

Peter handed him his wallet. The cop gave his identification a cursory inspection, and flipped the wallet back to him. "Get out of here. Don't let me see you hanging around."

"Yes, sir."

He walked to the next block and ducked beneath an awning to get out of the rain. When a psychic died, there was a void felt on both sides of life, a tear in the fabric of existence. There was no one waiting in the wings to fill Madame Marie's shoes, no apprentice who could jump in and pick up where she'd left off. Her gifts had been unique, and could never be replaced. She'd helped thousands of people, and done countless good deeds, none of which would ever be recorded. She had made a difference, and her loss would forever haunt him.

He wanted to scream. The monster inside of him had woken up. He could only keep it contained for so long. Eventually, it would come out. When it did, Wolfe would pay for what he'd done.

12

Lester Rowe gave psychic readings out of a building on Second Street on the Lower East Side. Once a haven for the homeless, the area had been transformed by upscale apartments and trendy restaurants. Rowe's building was run-down, and stood out like a sore thumb.

Wolfe sat in the reception area waiting his turn. The room was hot, and he was sweating. Beneath his coat was the hand axe he'd purchased at a hardware store on First Avenue. It was not the kind of thing he wanted to be showing off.

Beside him sat a crazy woman with beautiful rings on every finger of each hand. In her lap sat a fluffy toy dog with hair covering its eyes. Both had pink ribbons tied in their hair like characters out of a warped fairy tale.

"Are you going on a trip?" the crazy woman inquired.

Wolfe stared at an imaginary point in space, and said nothing.

"I always come to see Lester before I take a trip," she said, ignoring his snub. "Lester always knows what the weather will be like where I'm going, and which restaurants are good, and all the places to avoid. His prescience is extraordinary."

Wolfe wanted to tell her that she could get the same information off the Internet, but remained mute.

"Excuse me? Did you say something?" the crazy woman asked.

Wolfe shook his head, and kept looking straight ahead.

"I swear I thought you said something."

Such a pest. Wolfe hoped she didn't get in the way, and force him to give her a whack with the axe. He'd been raised a Catholic, and the church's teachings had been pounded into his skull at an early age. Not a day went by when he didn't think about the special place awaiting him in hell. It would have been easier to be an atheist, but those people were boring.

A red light above the door began to flash.

"Lester's ready," the crazy woman said breathlessly. "Why don't you go next? You look like a man who has a lot on his mind. I'll go take Buttercup for a walk."

Wolfe glanced at the dog in the old woman's lap. The animal appeared mortally afraid, and would not stop shaking.

"Take him for a long walk," he said, breaking his silence.

"Excuse me?"

"I said, take your dog for a long walk. It will be good for him."

"You must have a great deal to talk to Lester about."

Wolfe rose from his folding chair, and led her to the door. "Have a nice walk."

"Why, thank you. I will. I didn't catch your name."

"It's Jeremy."

"Mine's Alice. Enjoy your session with Lester. He knows *everything*."

She left, and Wolfe locked the door behind her. He waited a spell to make sure she didn't return, then headed for the back room, the axe rubbing against his leg.

Lester Rowe gave his psychic readings in a bright pink room that was hard on the eyes. Framed pictures of the Zodiac hung on the walls, and dark blinds covered the windows. In the room's center was an antique table where Lowe sat, gazing into a crystal ball as big as a cantaloupe. He was the size of a leprechaun, and sported a mane of red hair.

"Hello," Wolfe said.

"You're not Alice," Rowe said.

"No, I'm not. She gave me her slot." Wolfe sat down in the other chair.

"How considerate of her. And who are you? No, wait, don't tell me."

Rowe gazed into the depths of his crystal ball and scrunched up his face. "I'm seeing it clearly. Your name is Robert."

"Jeremy," Wolfe said.

"Damn. I get a lot of hits with Robert."

"I'm sure you do."

"To answer your question, the place used to be a bordello," Rowe said. "I haven't gotten around to repainting the walls just yet."

Wolfe was impressed. He had planned to ask Rowe about the pink walls before he hacked him to death, only the little fellow had beat him to the punch. Slipping his fingers beneath his jacket, he grabbed the axe handle, and started to pull it free from his belt. Oblivious to the danger he was in, Rowe continued to gaze into his crystal ball.

"I'm afraid I have some bad news," the psychic said.

So do I, Wolfe nearly replied.

"The people you work for are about to betray you."

Wolfe grew hot under the collar. He pulled his hand out, wanting to hear more.

"Is that so? What are they planning to do?"

"A hundred dollars. Cash or credit?"

The crummy little bastard had hooked him. Wolfe took out his wallet, and tossed the bills onto the table. He noticed that Rowe was unshaven and wore a satin blue bathrobe. Rowe probably lived in the building, and had a short commute.

"Now, tell me what you saw," Wolfe said.

"Your employer is not happy with how things are going," Rowe said, peering intensely into his crystal ball. "Something happened recently which has caused them to lose faith in you."

Through their psychic prowess, the Order followed Wolfe's every movement when he was on assignment, and would have known about the botched hit on Peter Warlock.

"Go on," Wolfe said.

"Your employer is convinced you will not succeed with your current assignment, and is making arrangements to make sure they're not dragged down if you fail." Rowe lifted his eyes. "Am I getting warm?"

"Very." Wolfe choked on the word.

"Would you like some water?"

Wolfe was dying for a drink, and nodded.

"Bottled or sparkling?"

"Bottled."

"That's another five dollars."

Wolfe wanted to kill him. "Forget it. Continue."

"Let me see your palm."

"Which one?"

"Either will do."

Wolfe placed his upturned right hand on the table. Rowe pointed at a puncture wound that had been caused by a bullet that had been meant for Wolfe's face. Rowe made a clucking sound with his tongue as if the wound held deep and significant meaning.

"More trouble lies ahead," the psychic proclaimed.

"What do you mean? What kind of trouble?"

"Do you really want to know? It's not why people come to me."

Wolfe felt a fist tighten in the pit of his stomach. "Yes—tell me."

Rowe gave him a funny look. Reaching behind the table, he opened a small lacquered cabinet, and removed a bottle of The Glenlivet single malt Scotch whisky and two shot glasses. Filling the glasses to the brim, he slid one in front of his visitor.

"On the house," Rowe said.

"The news must be bad," Wolfe replied.

"I'm afraid it is."

They knocked back their drinks. Rowe put his elbows on the table, and dropped his voice. "I'm not in the business of causing trouble. In fact, causing trouble is bad for business. But I've got to call them the way I see them."

"I understand," Wolfe said.

"I don't want you to get angry with me. Some people think it's necessary to kill the messenger, if you know what I mean."

His choice of words was prophetic, and Wolfe hid a macabre little smile.

"I won't get mad," he promised.

"Very well. Your employer has maintained a distance from you, which you've always found troubling. Only one thing connects you, and that thing is now being wiped out."

"My bank accounts?"

"I'm afraid so."

"How many?"

"All of them."

The Order paid Wolfe by wire transfers to offshore bank accounts that he kept all over the world. Besides himself, they were the only people who knew the accounts' locations, and how to access them. A bead of sweat rolled down Wolfe's nose and hit the table.

"They see it as a business decision," the psychic explained.

"Have they wiped me out?"

"The process has started. You need to save whatever's left."

Wolfe's chair scraped the floor as he pushed himself away from the table. "Where's the closest coffee shop with Internet access?"

"Try the Coyi Café on Avenue B and Third Street," Rowe said. "It's where I go."

"Much obliged."

Wolfe slipped his hand into his overcoat and grabbed the axe. He really didn't want to kill Rowe. After all, the little man had done him a huge favor. Only Rowe knew too much about his life for Wolfe to be comfortable with.

"I think we should set up another appointment," Rowe suggested.

"Why's that?"

"Your future is filled with surprises."

"What kind of surprises?"

"I see a ravenous, dark-haired lady in your future."

Rita. Wolfe hadn't believed he was capable of falling in love until he'd met Rita. She'd stolen what little was left of his heart, and he longed to see her again.

"What about her?" he asked.

"You sent her a letter a month ago."

"Yes?"

"She only just received it. She misses you terribly, and is in the process of responding to you. Look, we can discuss this later. Go take care of your business. I have a cancellation at three this afternoon. Come back then, and we can talk in more detail."

"All right," Wolfe heard himself say.

His head was spinning as he left the building. He'd never spared a victim before. It told him that there were still things more important than money. On the sidewalk he ran into the crazy lady and her precious mutt. She had her skirt pulled up by her waist, and was kneeling down with a plastic bag covering her hand. Only in New York did masters clean up after their bloody dogs.

"I hope you weren't disappointed in Lester," she said.

"Hardly," Wolfe replied, and hurried up the street.

13

Max was bending minds for a table of lovely la-dies as Peter came through the front door of Perilla in the West Village. Although technically retired, Max still performed in trendy restaurants around the city, and delighted in making patrons shriek at his miracles.

Seeing his student, Max nodded, and continued his trick. Getting Max to quit during the middle of a show was like asking the pope to give up religion, and Peter took a seat at the bar to watch. With his shock of snow white hair and dated tuxedo, Max looked more like a harmless old kook than a master magician, which was part of his wonderful charm.

"Your name, please?" Max asked a lady seated at the table.

"Anita," she replied.

"A beautiful name. Have we ever met before, Anita?"

"I think I'd remember if we had."

"That makes two of us. With your help, I'd like to try a little experiment in thought transference." Max picked up a large pad of paper from a chair, and held it for his audience to see. "Ladies, I am going to write a long number on this pad. Anita, as I write, I want you to call out whatever numbers come to mind. Sound easy enough?"

"Whatever you say," Anita replied.

"Wonderful. Here we go."

Using a black magic marker, Max wrote a long number on the pad that soon ran off the page. At the same time, Anita turned around in her chair so she could not see what Max was writing, and began to call out the exact same numbers that were appearing. It was a miracle for which Peter had no explanation, and by the time they were finished, he was clapping along with everyone else inside the restaurant. Max hadn't lost his touch. The great ones never did. Moments later, his teacher sidled up beside him at the bar.

"Peter, what a surprise. What are you drinking?"

"I'm not." He dropped his voice. "Someone is trying to kill us, Max."

The bar was noisy, and his teacher broke into a smile.

"I slayed them, dead, didn't I?"

Peter spoke in his teacher's ear. "Someone is trying to kill us. He already got Madame Marie and her husband."

"*What?* I just spoke to Marie yesterday."

"I just came from her parlor. She's gone, Max."

The bartender placed a shot of bourbon and a beer chaser on the bar. Max downed the shot, chased it away with the beer, and wiped his mouth on his sleeve. His face was filled with anguish, and he shook his head. "Who would do such a thing?"

"His name is Wolfe. He tried to kill me last night at the theater."

"He attacked you during your show?" Max asked incredulously.

"He gave new meaning to the phrase 'Knock 'em dead.'"

"That's not funny, Peter."

"And this isn't either. He was sent by the Order of Astrum to kill our group."

Max's head snapped. "Who told you about the Order of Astrum?"

"A police detective. Have you heard of them?"

"Yes, although not in a long time. They're a cult of dark magicians out of the UK. Have you warned the others?"

"I've left messages for everyone but Lester. He doesn't have a phone."

"I know where Lester lives. We'll go there right now, and make sure he's all right." Max addressed the bartender. "Good sir, how much do I owe you?"

"Sixteen dollars," the bartender replied.

A cocktail napkin was taken off the bar and turned into a crisp twenty-dollar bill.

"Keep the change," Max said.

The world outside the restaurant was loud and unfriendly. Max hailed a cab by whistling so shrilly that he stopped traffic in both directions. They hopped in, and his teacher barked an address to the driver. Soon they were racing across town.

"That was a wonderful trick you did with the woman at the table," Peter confessed. "You fooled me."

"That's high praise, coming from you," Max said.

"Will you tell me how was it done?"

"You don't know?"

"I wish."

"The number I wrote on the pad was the stops on the subway line Anita takes each day."

"How did you know which line she rode?"

"I overheard Anita talking with her friends. She mentioned living on Christopher Street. The Number One Line services that station. I cued her to start with the next station, which is Fourteenth Street, and work her way up. Since she hears those stops every day, I knew the numbers were burned into her memory. I have all the stops of the subway system memorized. The trick is finding out which line the spectator rides. The rest, as they say, is showmanship."

"You cued her?"

"Of course I cued her. We spoke earlier at the bar."

"So she was a stooge."

"Exactly. I can't read minds like you."

"Tell me about the Order of Astrum," Peter said.

Max stared out the window at the passing scenery. It was still raining, and the buildings had taken on a gloomy gray color that only sunlight would erase.

"We'll talk about this later, all right?" his teacher said after a moment.

"I'd prefer now," Peter said.

"This is not the right place. Please don't challenge me, Peter."

It had been a long time since Max had raised his voice to him. It made Peter feel like he was a child again, and not a young man battling demons whose origin and motives he did not understand. He nodded his head compliantly.

"Of course, Max. Whatever you say," he replied.

14

~~~

The Coyi Café was in an area of the city called Alphabet City, the avenues named after the first letters of the alphabet. The axe was rubbing Wolfe's leg,
and he ditched it in a trash bin.

The café had red brick walls and a menu of organic
loose-leaf teas from the Far East. Wolfe ordered a cup
of Lung Ching tea and a grilled pork sandwich called a
Banh Mi. When his waitress was gone, he leaned back
in his chair. The place was crowded. Everyone on a laptop or smart-phone. He needed to get one of these
people to let him use their laptop so he could get on the
Internet, and check his bank accounts. He could have
done this with a smartphone, only he didn't carry a
smartphone for fear of it being traced. And his laptop
was in his hotel room on the other side of town.

He listened to the people around him. When he put
his mind to it, he could hear just about anything, even
an insect crawling up a wall. He didn't think that
someone in his profession could have asked for a better
gift.

The college girl at the next table was a good candidate. With a laptop open in front of her, she ate lunch
while instant-messaging a friend. He listened to her
breathing, which told him a great deal about her personal state of mind. Her breathing was slow and normal. Not a hint of excitement or stress was going on in
her life as of this moment. Wolfe tugged her sleeve.

"Sorry to bother you. I'm here on holiday, and just
got a call from my bank saying I may have been robbed.
I need to get on the Internet, and make sure everything's

okay. I know this is a terrible intrusion, but may I use your laptop?"

She studied him for a few moments. Her breathing did not change. That told Wolfe she had bought his story.

"What's your name?" she asked.

"Jeremy. What's yours?"

"Blair. How long will you be?"

"A few minutes at most. I'd like to pay for your lunch."

"That's not necessary."

"Please. I insist."

"Well, all right."

She spun the laptop around so it faced him. Wolfe pulled his chair up to her table. From his wallet he removed a slip of paper containing the access codes to his different accounts and began to type. The Web site for his bank in the Caymans appeared. He entered his user name and password, and waited for his account to come up.

Even monsters had dreams. Wolfe's dream was to one day move to the Seychelles Islands in the Indian Ocean, and start up a business. He had his eye on a small ferry that took people out to the coral reefs in the outer islands. It was a two-person operation, which was where Rita came in.

His account appeared and he checked the balance. To his surprise, all of the money was still there. It gave him hope that maybe he hadn't taken such a bad hit.

Exiting the screen, he pulled up the Web site for his bank account in Guernsey, a tiny island in the English Channel. The money in Guernsey was still there as well.

"What the hell," he said under his breath.

"Did you get robbed?" Blair asked.

He'd forgotten all about her. He shook his head and smiled.

"Good," she said.

He checked his bank accounts on the Isle of Man, Luxembourg, and Andorra. Not a penny had been touched in any account, and a numbing sensation crept over him.

Rowe had tricked him. The little psychic had figured out Wolfe was an assassin. Instead of panicking, Rowe had looked into Wolfe's black soul, and found the things which Wolfe was afraid of. The expression "played like a fiddle" came to mind.

Rowe had been wearing a bathrobe during the reading. More than likely, he'd retreated to his apartment, and would be easy to hunt down.

Wolfe stood up. His waitress came over and told him his food would be right out.

"Keep it," he told her.

He started to leave, and caught Blair looking at him.

"You offered to pay for my lunch," she said.

"Piss off," he said.

He hit the sidewalk. He checked the trash bin for his axe. It had already been pinched.

He started to run. If he'd learned anything on the battlefield, it was that every second counted when it came to dealing with the enemy. Rowe's apartment was three blocks away. A two-minute run, if he caught the lights right. He passed a courier holding a delivery envelope. Parked by the curb was a Suzuki motorbike with a helmet resting on the seat.

Wolfe stopped. "That a Razor?"

"Sure is," the courier replied.

The courier stared at the addresses on the storefronts. He looked lost. His breathing reflected this. It was slightly accelerated.

Wolfe glanced up and down Avenue B. The street was filled with delivery trucks and yellow cabs, while the sidewalks were filled with people holding newspapers over their heads. Some of his best killing had been done in the middle of busy cities like this. People assumed they were safe in crowds, and that no harm could possibly come to them. Wolfe knew otherwise.

Wolfe got up next to the courier. Raising his arm, he chopped the side of the man's neck. The courier's eyes rolled up into his head, and he crumpled into Wolfe's arms. A quick search of his pockets turned up a key ring. Wolfe laid the courier onto the sidewalk as two punked-out teenagers walked past.

"My friend's feeling a bit under the weather," Wolfe explained. "He'll come round."

Wolfe straddled the Razor. The bike lived up to its name. It was sleek and made plenty of noise. Soon he was racing crosstown with revenge on his mind. Lester Rowe was going to pay for messing with Wolfe's dreams.

15

Peter and Max could not get into Lester Rowe's apartment.

Max tried the intercom in the lobby. When there was no response, his teacher went outside to the sidewalk, and shouted Rowe's name through cupped hands. Four floors up, a window opened, and Rowe's red head popped out.

"Who is it?" Rowe called down suspiciously.

"Max Romeo. I'm here with Peter. Let us in. We need to speak with you."

"I'm in a bit of a hurry, Max. Can it wait until some other time?"

"No!"

"He's already been here," Peter said, looking up and down the street.

His teacher turned to stare at him. "Who's been here?"

"Wolfe. I can feel it in my bones."

"What do you mean? Feel what?"

Peter's body had gone cold, and the very tips of his fingers felt like cubes of ice. With the sensation had come the knowledge that Wolfe had recently been here.

"I can't explain it," Peter said.

Rowe buzzed them in. They climbed the creaky staircase to Rowe's apartment. At the third floor landing, they stopped so Max could catch his breath. His teacher's cheeks had turned pink, and he seemed on the verge of collapsing.

"Still smoking those cheap cigars?" Peter asked.

"I've cut back," Max replied. "Now, I only smoke one at a time."

"I know this great program to help you quit. Every time you want a smoke, you dial a phone number, and a guy comes over and gets drunk with you."

"Your jokes are getting worse all the time."

"I had a good teacher."

"Touché."

They climbed the last flight of stairs. Upon reaching the fourth floor, Rowe stepped out of his apartment wearing a suit and snappy bow tie.

"Hello, Max. Hello, Peter," the diminutive psychic said.

"Hello, Lester," Max replied. "Sorry to barge in, but there's a madman running around the city trying to kill our group. He's already done away with Madame Maire and her husband."

Rowe's face sank at the news of Madame Marie's death. "He visited my parlor a short while ago. He was going to cut my head off with an axe! I saw it in my crystal ball. This is horrible news about Marie, the poor thing. Come inside, I'm just finishing packing."

Rowe dead-bolted the door behind them. The apartment was a reminder of what dwellings in New York once looked like, with high-ceilinged rooms, dark wood floors, and ornate crown molding. Rowe entered a bedroom where an open suitcase lay on the bed.

"Any idea why he's after us?" Rowe asked, tossing clothes into the suitcase.

"He was sent by the Order of Astrum," Max explained.

"The Order of Astrum. I haven't heard that name in years." Rowe closed the suitcase and locked the clasps. "The man's pure evil. I looked into his future, and saw scores of people dying because of him. Is this the same fellow Peter saw during the séance?"

"Same man," Peter said.

"Egad. What's he up to?"

Peter shook his head. That was the frustrating part of seeing into the future. Often, he had no idea what the things he saw meant. A buzzer in the hallway rang.

Rowe looked alarmed.

"Ignore it," Max suggested.

The buzzer rang again. It had a harsh, angry edge to it. Peter went to the bedroom window and gazed down at the street. A motorbike was parked at the curb with a helmet resting on its seat. The bike's owner stood on the stoop, hidden from view. The only people who used motorbikes in the city were couriers and drug dealers.

"Are you expecting a delivery?" Peter asked.

"My travel agent is sending a ticket over," Rowe said. "I have a cousin in Ireland that I haven't laid eyes on in twenty years. I thought it was time we became reacquainted."

"Don't let him in until you get confirmation," Peter said.

"Good idea."

Rowe walked out of the bedroom and went down the hallway to where the intercom was located. He looked shaken by what had happened, and was muttering to himself. Peter turned to his teacher. "You'd better watch him, Max."

"Right," his teacher said.

Peter returned to the window and gazed down. The man on the sidewalk was gone. The icy feeling returned to his bones, and made him shiver.

Beside Rowe's bed was a bookshelf. For a person who was against technological progress, Rowe had a large collection of DVDs, with labels like LIVING DEAD/BOMBAY 1/19/76, FIRE BREATHERS/BALI 3/16/88, WITCH DOCTORS/JAMAICA 9/07/94. One title caught his eye, and he pulled it from the shelf. CLAIRE & HENRY WARREN 12/10/92. His parents, filmed right before their deaths. On the cover, Rowe had scribbled a note which Peter now read aloud. "First encounter with the Order of Astrum. Claire and Henry showed us things that were beyond the realm of our imaginations."

A yell sent him an inch off the floor.

"Peter!" Max called out. "Come here. Hurry!"

"I'm coming!"

He slipped the DVD into his pocket with a promise that he'd return it once he'd had a look. Then, he rushed out of the bedroom and down the hallway. Max and Rowe stood with their shoulders to the front door.

"What's going on?" Peter asked.

"It's Wolfe," Max explained, frantically dialing his cell phone. "One of Lester's neighbors mistakenly buzzed him in. I'm calling 911."

"He's in the building?" Peter asked.

"Yes!" they both said.

Peter's vision clouded over. A burning rage swelled his chest and made his breathing shallow. Since he was a boy, he'd wanted to meet up with someone connected to his parents' deaths. How he would act had played itself out countless times in his imagination. He knew exactly what he was going to do.

Entering the kitchen, he grabbed an empty whiskey bottle from the trash. It made a harsh sound against his palm. Returning to the hallway, he placed his hand on Max's shoulder.

"Stand aside," he said.

"Peter, don't be foolish," his teacher said. "I just spoke with an operator. A cruiser is on its way."

"I said, stand aside."

"Peter, no."

"Do it. Both of you. *Now.*"

Peter had been told that he looked like a demon when he became enraged. It must have been true, because Rowe and his teacher backed away from the door.

"You going to fight him?" Rowe asked.

"That was the idea," Peter replied.

Rowe grabbed a walking stick out of a bucket by the door, and thrust it into Peter's other hand. It was made of walnut, and felt good and solid.

"Take this. It's got some heft to it."

"Thanks. Don't come out until I say so."

Max grabbed his arm. "Peter, please be careful."

"I will, Max."

"Make sure you hit him first, and hard."

"Good idea."

"Good luck, my boy."

Rowe did him the courtesy of throwing back the

dead bolt and opening the door. Peter squared his shoulders and stepped outside the apartment. He supposed he should have felt apprehensive, yet for some reason, he felt more confident than he ever had in his life.

He walked onto the landing, ready to slay the dragon.

16

Everybody had a history.

Peter had read that in a book whose author had survived the Holocaust. The book's message had been clear. Every person had events in their past which were painful, and hard to bear. It was part of life, and there was no getting around it.

Deal with it.

He had been dealing with his parents' deaths for as long as could remember. So long that it had become a fabric of his life. He had learned to cope during holidays, birthdays, and when he needed a shoulder to cry on, or an ear to listen. He had accepted that the two people who loved him most were gone, and that there was nothing he could do about it.

Deal with it.

He had, as best he could. Becoming a magician had let him escape to a make-believe world where he could manipulate reality, and pretend nothing bad had ever happened to him. But the anger was still there, and always would be. It rumbled inside of him like a volcano, bubbling just below the surface, hidden to everyone but himself.

Until now.

His footsteps sounded like cannons going off as he ran down the apartment stairwell. The coldness had returned to his joints, and he could not stop shivering. He stopped to look over the railing. Wolfe was on the landing below, holding a metal pipe in his hand.

"Hey, asshole," Peter shouted.

Wolfe looked straight up. His mouth dropped open in surprise.

"Remember me?"

Peter threw the whiskey bottle at the wall behind Wolfe's head. It shattered into a hundred pieces, spraying tiny shards of glass into his enemy's face. Wolfe let out a startled yell, and bolted down the stairs.

"Coward!"

Peter hopped over the railing, and landed on the steps below. Wolfe was already to the next landing, and running hard. The young magician hopped over the railing again, then again. He'd never been much of an athlete, yet now he felt like he could have won a decathlon. Reaching the first floor, he stopped and looked around the empty lobby. Wolfe was gone. His breathing grew short, and his vision narrowed. In the theater of his mind, he saw Wolfe hiding outside the apartment house on the stoop, waiting to strike when he emerged. He could see the tiny cuts on Wolfe's face, and even smell his foul breath. It was like having a target in his sights.

He clutched the walking stick. He'd never been able to project his thoughts like this before. A new gift, courtesy of the spirits. How long it would last, he had no idea.

Kicking open the front door, he came out of the apartment swinging. Wolfe was right where he'd expected, and he caught him on the side of the face with the stick. The cry of pain was worth savoring. He chased Wolfe into the street, and began to strike his enemy at will. Every blow found its mark, and produced howls of excruciating pain. Each time Wolfe attempted to counter or strike back, Peter saw the blow or kick coming seconds before it was delivered, and parried it. Wolfe was bigger and stronger, yet hopelessly outmatched. His eyes took on a desperate look.

"No more," Wolfe said.

"You quitting?"

"Yes. Stop hitting me."

"Put your arms in the air."

Wolfe raised his arms in surrender. Blood was pouring out of his mouth and nose. Peter fought back the urge to strike him again, and finish the job. Looking into Wolfe's soulless eyes, he saw a little boy who'd been tortured by his father, who'd grown up to be a torturer and killer himself. He had a history, too, only it was no excuse for who he'd become.

"Start talking," Peter said.

"What do you want to know?"

"Tell me about the Order."

"No thanks."

Peter raised his stick and took aim. One blow was all it would take to send him straight to hell where he belonged. Wolfe recoiled in fear.

"All right, all right, I'll tell you the little that I know. There are three elders of the Order. I've never seen their faces, nor do I know their names. They send me jobs to do, and pay me well. That's the arrangement."

Peter thought back to the three men he'd seen whisk his parents away. Were those the elders? Something told him they were, and he said, "One of the elders has crooked teeth and a twisted nose. What's his name?"

"Like I told you, I've never seen their faces," Wolfe said.

"You must have some idea."

A spark of recognition sparked Wolfe's eyes. *He knew something*. Peter whacked him in the kneecap. His enemy let out a muffled cry and sank to the ground like he was melting. Peter brought the tip of the stick beneath Wolfe's chin, and raised his head so their eyes met. Wolfe's life flashed before his eyes.

"Last chance," Peter said.

Wolfe blinked. He was not ready to die.

"I don't know who the elders are," Wolfe said. "But the other members of the Order might. There's one here in New York. A spy. I'll bring him to you."

"What do you mean, a spy? What does he do?"

"He gathers information. Before I arrived he emailed me the list of names of people I was supposed to kill."

"What's his name?"

"I don't know his name. Just his cell number."

"Would he know who the elders are?"

"He might. He's been with the organization for a while. Longer than me."

"Give me his cell number."

"It's in my wallet."

"Get it. And no funny stuff."

Wolfe pulled out his wallet and extracted a slip of paper from his billfold. Peter leaned forward in anticipation. It was just the opening Wolfe had been waiting for. Springing up, he shoved Peter and sent him backwards, then hobbled over to his motorbike and jumped on. The engine barked to life.

"Bastard!" Peter shouted.

The bike sped away. Their eyes met in the motorbike's mirror.

Wolfe was laughing at him.

The rage swelled up inside of Peter. The walking stick flew out of his hand and gyrated through the air, slicing the raindrops like a scythe. He hadn't thrown it; it had just *gone*.

The stick smacked Wolfe in the back of the skull.

Wolfe lost control of the bike, and it went down in the intersection of Second Avenue and Houston. Several Good Samaritans got out of their cars to give help. Wolfe jumped into an idling vehicle, and sped away.

The slip of paper with the phone number lay at Peter's feet. He picked it up, and unfolded it. It was a receipt from a restaurant.

"Damn you," Peter swore.

Max had appeared on the stoop. He hurried over to his student.

"Peter, come with me."

"Did you see that, Max?"

"Yes. You gave him a hell of a fight."

"I mean the walking stick. It left my hand on its own accord. Did you see that?"

"Yes, Peter, I saw it."

"How did I do that?"

"You did it very well. Now come with me, before the police arrive."

Max pulled his student beneath a shop awning across the street, and hid in the shadows. Two police cruisers pulled up, and the sidewalk in front of Rowe's apartment turned into a crime scene in the blink of an eye. Max suddenly looked afraid.

"I must get you out of here," Max said.

"But I need to talk to the police, and tell them what happened," Peter said.

"No, you don't. You've got to stay away from the police. Let me deal with them."

"Are you sure?"

"Trust me, it's for your own good." His teacher pushed him down the sidewalk toward First Avenue. He did not stop pushing until they'd reached the busy intersection.

"Now go home. I'll call you later, once the dust has settled," Max said.

"All right, Max. But first answer my question. How did I do that?"

"I think you know."

"With my mind? But that's not possible."

"For you it is, Peter."

Peter didn't understand what Max meant. A psychic's powers were limited, and did not include mind over matter, or the ability to instantly anticipate what a person was going to do, as he'd done with Wolfe. He'd never heard of such powers before. Across the street he spotted a uniformed cop taking a statement from an eyewitness, who kept pointing in their direction.

Max pushed him. "Go. Before it's too late."

Too late for what? Peter had more questions, but the tone of Max's voice was enough for now, and he hurried up First Avenue, away from the chaos he'd just created.

PART II

THE CHILDREN OF MARBLE

17

With his ears ringing and his vision blurred, Wolfe staggered into his seedy hotel room. He'd ditched the car he'd stolen, and made his way back to where he was staying, through a series of alleys and crowded sidewalks. The police were everywhere, and he'd been lucky to escape their manhunt.

He kicked off his shoes and collapsed onto the bed. For a few minutes he stared at the water stains on the ceiling while trying to collect his wits. He was staying in the Hotel Carter on West 43rd Street. A search on Google had shown it to be the worst-rated hotel in Midtown. So far, it had lived up to its reputation. It wasn't the kind of place where the police would come looking for him. At least, not right away.

His head was throbbing and he went to the bathroom and downed two aspirin with a glass of water. Then he gazed into the mirror above the sink. As a soldier, his speciality had been hand-to-hand combat, although he never would have known it by his reflection. His face was cut up, his left eye nearly shut. On the back of his head was a lump that made him wince every time he touched it, while his left ear looked like a blood sausage. He'd come out on the losing end of this one, that was for sure. The question was, why?

Everything had been on his side, from the element of surprise, to the fact that his opponent didn't know how to fight. So why had he lost? He could blame it on bad luck, only that was a weakling's excuse. Something else was going on here, and he was determined to find out what it was.

Sitting on the bed, he pulled his laptop from its case, and powered it up. It was noon, which made it five o'clock back home in England. The British lived for traditions. Tea at four, pubs closing at the stroke of midnight, and other strange rituals that were ingrained in the genes, and would never die. The Order was no different. He was required to contact them every day, rain or shine, come hell or high water, at five in the afternoon their time, regardless of what part of the world he was in, or what he was doing. Sometimes a phone call would do; if he was embedded in a city, as he was now, then it was over the Internet using Skype, which let the Order see and talk to Wolfe via the Web cam on his laptop. A loud beep signaled the connection had gone through. A minute passed.

"Come on, lads, I haven't got all bloody day," he grumbled.

A blue light flickered across his laptop's screen. It expanded until he was staring at the Room of Spirits, a darkened chamber whose walls were covered with mystic signs from ancient Babylon. The room boasted several aquariums filled with poisonous reptiles and venomous snakes that snapped at the glass. Flanking the aquariums were life-size marble statues of the Oracle of Delphi, and the Greek sorceress Medea. It was here that the elders of the Order held séances, and peered into the future.

Three men dressed in black robes sat at a glass table encrypted with Zodiac figures, kabbalistic emblems, and algebraic symbols that pulsated with a life of their own. Each man wore a white plastic mask which covered his face. The elder in the middle addressed him.

"Hello, Major Wolfe. How are we today?"

"I've had better days," Wolfe replied.

"Is something wrong?"

He tilted the laptop so the Web cam captured his damaged face. "See for yourself."

The elders leaned forward in their chairs to study his face.

"You look rather beat-up," the middle elder said.

"That would be an understatement. I nearly got bloody killed."

"By who?"

"That little bastard Peter Warlock did this to me."

"Did he catch you by surprise?"

"On the contrary. I had him right where I wanted him." Wolfe paused to let the words sink in, then said what was on his mind. "He's one of you, isn't he?"

Clearly upset by his remark, the elders stirred in their chairs.

"What is that supposed to mean?" the elder on the left asked.

"Peter Warlock is more than just a psychic," Wolfe replied. "He anticipated my every move, and knew exactly what I was thinking. I didn't stand a chance."

"You're making excuses," the middle elder said accusingly. "Admit it. You blundered."

Wolfe brought his face inches from the screen. "Listen up, gents. I know when someone's got my number, and Peter Warlock has it. He got into my head. Every time I tried to take him down, he anticipated what I was going to do. It was like trying to fight against myself."

"You're saying he's different than the others," the middle elder said.

"Much different."

"Excuse us for a minute, Major. We need to discuss this."

"Be my guest."

The elders began to talk amongst themselves. Not knowing their names, Wolfe had learned to differentiate them by their accents. The elder on the left had attended either Oxford or Cambridge, and spoke like an aristocrat; the middle elder had worked in broadcasting and had what was commonly called a BBC accent; while the elder on the right was a commoner, and spoke with a Cockney bite. Finished, the elders resumed looking at him through the Web cam.

"What about the other names on your list?" the middle elder asked.

"I took out Madame Marie last night," Wolfe replied. "Afraid there was some collateral damage. Her husband attacked me. No choice but to blow him away."

"And the others?"

"I had a go at Lester Rowe this morning. That's when I ran into Warlock."

"Did you dispose of Rowe?"

"Afraid not."

"Do you mean to say you've only eliminated one psychic so far?"

"That's right."

"You've been in New York three days. This is taking too long."

"Have I ever let you down?"

"Not yet, Major. But there's always a first time."

"I'll get them all. You have my word."

"Even Peter Warlock?"

"I'll run a bloody bus over him if I have to."

"Glad to hear it. Give us a timetable for your mission's completion."

"I'll be done in forty-eight hours," Wolfe replied.

"No sooner?"

"What do you have in mind?"

"How about thirty-six hours?"

Wolfe didn't like this. Killing people by committee never worked. He made his own decisions, which was why he'd lasted as long in his profession as he had.

"I could, but it would mean a lot more collateral damage."

"Squeamish?" the elder on the left asked.

"If you want a butcher, go to the meat market."

"Is that an attempt at sarcasm, Major?"

"Take it any way you please."

The elders fell silent, clearly displeased.

"Is forty-eight hours the best you can do?" the middle elder asked, breaking the silence.

"Yes, it is," Wolfe said.

"Very well."

A breeze passed through the Room of Spirits, causing the elders' robes to flutter. The circular table began to rotate, and the strange signs etched on the glass glowed like night flies. The elders studied the signs while mumbling to themselves. Finally the table stopped spinning, and the signs lost their glow.

The middle elder addressed Wolfe. "We have reached a decision. It is imperative that you finish your mission. Find the remaining psychics on your list, and do away with them. A forty-eight-hour window is not preferable, but is acceptable. Once you are done, get out of there as fast as possible. Is this understood?"

"Understood." Wolfe's finger touched the mouse on his laptop.

"I'm not finished. We are bothered by your lack of resolve, and your defiant attitude. You were recruited into the Order because you're a soldier, and soldiers do not run in the heat of battle, or question their superiors. Your mettle needs to be tested."

"There's nothing wrong with my bloody mettle," Wolfe snapped.

"We feel otherwise."

A hissing sound came out of the laptop. Behind where the elders sat, an aquarium wall had lowered, and a giant Burmese python spilled out, and slithered across the floor. Wolfe had encountered a Burmese python while in the army, and knew it was lethal. Jumping into the air, the python burst through the laptop's screen, courtesy of the elders' dark magic.

The python landed in his lap. Wolfe grabbed the snake before it could wrap its body around his throat. It was six feet long, and incredibly powerful. Falling onto the floor, he wrestled with the beast, knocking down furniture and causing all sorts of noise. Finally he got the python's head between his powerful hands, and squeezed until it went limp.

The laptop had fallen on the floor. Its screen was facing him, and he saw the elders nod their approval.

"Good-bye, Major Wolfe," the middle elder said. "Stay in touch."

The picture became a pinprick, then disappeared. Wolfe stared at his hands. The python had vanished. In its place was one of his shoes, which had been lying on the floor.

"Bloody arseholes," he said.

18

Liza was furious. Peter had been gone for hours, and hadn't responded to her calls or texts. She knew that her boyfriend had mood swings, and often took long walks to clear his head. There was nothing wrong with that, but it wasn't right that he didn't stay in touch, especially after the attack at the theater last night.

Fuming, she sat at the kitchen table. Peter was a psychic, and he was also a flake. He hardly seemed to care about her feelings, or what she thought about their relationship. There were times when she wondered if he'd been raised by wolves.

A pad of paper sat on the table. On it she'd written the words *Order of Astrum*. The man who'd attacked Peter was a member of the Order, and she'd overheard Peter and Detective Schoch talking about them on the stoop. They were the key to the puzzle.

She pulled out her BlackBerry to try and learn more. To her surprise, her Google search turned up nothing but a vague reference on Wikipedia. She decided to call in reinforcements, and dialed Snoop.

"Hey, it's me," she said. "You at home?"

"I'm sitting at the bar at the Waverly Inn watching the beautiful ladies," Snoop replied.

"I have a favor to ask. Can you meet me at Peter's place?"

"I'm game. The girl I was hitting on just blew me off."

"Her loss. Do you still have that hot laptop you told me about?"

"Hot isn't the word. It's steaming."

"It can't be traced back to you, can it?"

"Not in a hundred years. What have you got in mind?"

Liza stared at the pad. If the Order of Astrum was sending assassins out to kill people, then some government agency had to know about them.

"I want you to hack a government mainframe," she replied.

"Yipes. Which one?"

She had to think. Secret Service? No. CIA? Not them, either.

"FBI," she said.

"Now you're talking. I'll grab the laptop from my apartment."

"Thanks, Snoop. I owe you big time."

Liza ended the call. She assumed that breaking into the FBI's computer was a federal offense, punishable by jail time, waterboarding, and who knew what else, yet she had no qualms about doing it. Peter was in danger, and she was going to find out why.

She fixed a pot of coffee while waiting for Snoop. When it came to hacking, Snoop had few peers. At fourteen, he'd gotten caught downloading a hundred thousand music files off the Internet, which he'd distributed to his entire high school class. At sixteen, he'd been tagged for breaking into a dozen Fortune 500 companies. At nineteen, he'd hit for the cycle, and been arrested for hacking three government servers deemed impenetrable. When a judge had asked him why he'd done it, Snoop had replied, "Because they're there, Your Honor." Snoop had never hidden his past. If anything, he was proud of his accomplishments, and boasted that there wasn't a computer in the world whose defenses he couldn't penetrate. Liza hoped he was right, because it was the only way she was going to find out what was going on.

The front buzzer rang. She bounded down the hall and opened the door.

"That was fast."

Snoop entered with a shoulder bag draped over his shoulder. His hair hung in his face like a shaggy dog's, and his purple sneakers were untied. They walked down the hall to the kitchen. Taking a Dell Latitude laptop from the bag, he placed it on the table.

"So who's our target?" he asked.

"I told you—I want you to hack the FBI."

"I thought you were kidding."

"Afraid not. Is that a problem?"

Snoop picked up the coffee mug Liza had set for him, and sipped the steaming brew. "Depends on what your definition of problem is. Is spending ten years of your life making license plates inside a federal prison a problem?"

"You can back out if you want to."

"Me? Back out? Never. But we need to take precautions. The FBI doesn't screw around. Once they realize we've hacked their computer, they'll come after us."

"I thought a hot laptop couldn't be traced."

"It can't be traced to me, but it still can be located. The FBI has developed a special tracing system which allows them to lay an invisible thread into a hacker's computer," Snoop explained. "That thread lets them pinpoint a hacker's location anywhere in the world. I found out the hard way when I was in college. I wanted to find out what the FBI knew about Roswell, so I hacked their computer. Ten minutes after I'd signed off, an SUV with tinted windows pulled up to my dorm, and four guys in black suits came and arrested me."

"The men in black ran you down? Come on, be serious."

"I am being serious."

Liza drank her coffee. Snoop looked nervous. That was hardly like him.

"Look, I don't want you to get in trouble because of me," she said. "Just show me how to get into the FBI's mainframe, and I'll take care of this myself."

"That could take years. I'll get us in, but on my terms. Deal?"

"Deal."

Snoop drained his cup and returned the laptop to his shoulder bag. "There's a sports bar on Second Avenue called Ball Four that has Wi-Fi and roasted peanuts. We'll go there."

"Why not use the Internet here? It's secure."

"Nothing's secure on the Internet. Besides, I like peanuts."

He left the kitchen before Liza could reply. A moment later, the front door banged open. She got the hint, and hurried to catch up.

B all Four had all the charm of a college frat house. Liza got two Cokes and a bowl of roasted peanuts from the bar, and brought them to the corner booth where Snoop sat typing. His boyish features were a study in concentration, his fingers a blur.

"Someday, you're going to have to explain how you hack a computer," she said.

"Hacking isn't as hard as you think," he said. "Most passwords use lowercase letters, and the numbers zero through nine, or thirty-six total characters. A five-character password has a total of sixty million possibilities. I can run a sixty-million simulation on my software program in five minutes."

"It can't really be that simple."

"It just takes practice."

He fell silent, and continued to work his magic on the laptop.

"Okay, I've broken through the FBI's firewall and bypassed the security system," he said. "With one click, I'll be inside the mainframe. Now, what are we looking for?"

"The Order of Astrum."

"Didn't the guy who attacked Peter belong to that group?"

"Yup. I need to find out who they are."

"Does Peter know about this? You know how he gets when we do things and don't tell him."

Liza thought back to Peter's shocking revelation of this morning. It had felt like a betrayal, and she had to know what else her boyfriend was hiding.

"Do it anyway," she said.

"Whatever you say. Once I log in, you've got ten minutes to find what you're looking for. Then we get out of here. Agreed?"

"Agreed."

Snoop clicked his mouse. "Okay, we're in the FBI's system. Nice home page. I'm typing the Order of Astrum into the search engine. You hit pay dirt. They've got a file on them." He spun the laptop around, and slid it across the table. "The clock's running. Go!"

Liza started reading. Her skin was tingling, and she felt like Alice jumping down the rabbit hole. The first paragraph practically knocked her sideways.

"Holy cow," she said. "It says the Order of Astrum has been linked to several ruthless dictators who are enemies of the United States, and they are considered a threat to national security."

"You were expecting the Boy Scouts of America?"

She tossed a peanut at Snoop, and continued reading.

"This is amazing," Liza said a few minutes later. "According to this, the Order of Astrum wasn't always bad. There are five members, four boys and one girl. In 1942, when they were little kids, they used their psychic powers to help the British fight the Nazis. It says a group of American generals asked for a meeting, and were taken to a town called Marble in southern England. The children conducted a séance, and made furniture move around the room. When the séance was finished, the children told the generals which towns the Germans were stationed in. It says this information was used to plot the Normandy invasion."

"Sounds like there's a movie here," Snoop said.

Another peanut hit Snoop in the face.

"Better hurry. You've only got a couple of minutes left," he cautioned.

"Afraid of the men in black running you down again?"

"You think I'm kidding? Just wait."

Liza went back to reading the file.

"Oh, my God," she said. "It says that the Order of Astrum went silent after the war. In 1988, the FBI's New York field office was contacted by a British couple who claimed to be members of the Order, who had fled England with their son to escape the other members. The couple's names were Claire and Henry Warren."

"So?" Snoop said.

"Those were Peter's parents."

"What? Are you sure?"

"Positive. Peter showed me their pictures."

"Let me see that."

Liza slid the laptop across the table. Snoop found the spot, and read aloud.

"'The Warrens claimed the other three members of the Order were selling their services to the highest bidder, and were in league with the Devil. When the Warrens were asked to rejoin the group, they refused, and were threatened by the other members.'

"The FBI protected the Warrens for six months. Right after the protection was lifted, the couple were abducted and murdered after attending a show in New York. The FBI believes the Order was behind the killings."

Snoop looked up from the laptop. "Wow. Do you think Peter knows any of this?"

Liza shook her head. Peter had confided in her that he knew little about his parents. Now, she thought she understood why.

"Who's going to tell him?" Snoop asked.

"I guess it's up to me."

Snoop looked at his watch. He slid out of the booth, and made a bee-line for the front door. Going outside, he looked back at her through the window and rapped loudly on the glass.

"Damn it," Liza swore.

She wanted to read the file again. There were still many things she didn't understand. The town of Marble had produced five psychic children. Two of those children had produced Peter. She tried to imagine what could have happened in that small town to cause such an amazing thing to occur. Had something mysterious happened that had caused the children to become psychics? And if something had happened, what was it?

Snoop was jumping up and down, waving at her. He'd already been arrested by the FBI once, and she didn't want him to get arrested again. She joined him outside.

"Did you turn the laptop off?" he asked.

"No—was I supposed to?"

"Yes. Leaving it on makes it easier for them to find us. We need to get out of sight."

They crossed Second Avenue and ducked into an alley where they stood hidden in the shadows. Soon the ground was littered with peanut shells.

"Maybe they're not coming," Liza said.

"Fat chance."

A black GMC Terrain sport-utility vehicle braked across the street. The doors sprang open, and four figures wearing hoodies piled out, and entered Ball Four.

"Is that the FBI?" she asked.

"Sure is. They always drive GMC vehicles. The hoodies are new."

A deafening noise came out of the sky. A black chopper without visible markings hovered over the office buildings on Second Avenue like a giant insect waiting to strike.

"Chopper's new, too," he added.

A minute later the four figures emerged from the bar. There were three men and one women. The man in charge was a stocky African-American, mid-forties, with graying temples and a deep scowl. Cradled against his chest was Snoop's laptop. He talked into a cell phone while staring across the street into the alley where they were hiding.

"He sees us," Liza squeaked.

"Maybe not. Just be still," Snoop replied.

The four FBI agents got back into the van. As it drove away, the chopper rose into the sky, and was swallowed by the dark clouds. The air trapped in Liza's lungs slowly escaped. She wouldn't have believed this if she hadn't seen it with her own eyes.

"Sorry I doubted you," she said.

They emerged from the alley. Liza checked both ends of the street. Something didn't feel right, only she couldn't get a handle on what it was. The city seemed almost *too* quiet.

They headed up Second Avenue, ducking raindrops.

"That was intense," Snoop said.

"I really didn't mean to get you involved with this."

"You don't have to apologize."

She squeezed his arm. "Thanks."

They had reached 62nd Street. As they came around the corner, they both stopped dead in their tracks. The black Terrain was parked by the curb, and the four FBI agents stood on the sidewalk, wearing laminated badges around their necks. The man in charge pointed an accusing finger.

"You're both under arrest," he declared.

"Shit," Snoop swore. "Busted again."

19

Peter had walked from the Lower East Side to his brownstone uptown in the rain. It had given him time to think about what had happened outside Lester Rowe's apartment. As a kid, he'd never been much of a fighter, preferring to talk his way out of tight situations, or take off running. So how had he managed to beat Wolfe to a bloody pulp? And how had the walking stick flown out of his hand like it had a mind of its own? He didn't know. But Max did. He'd sent his teacher several texts, and had not heard back. Max was avoiding him.

The front door to his brownstone opened. Peter bounded up the steps, thinking it was Liza. She'd sent him several texts, and he needed to apologize to her for not responding. A man built like a baseball umpire came out, his body thick and solid.

"Who are you?" Peter asked.

"Special Agent Garrison, FBI. You must be Peter Warlock."

Peter froze. What was the FBI doing inside his house? He decided to make light of the situation, for no other reason than he didn't know what else to do.

"That's right. I'd invite you in, but I see you've already made yourself at home."

"Cut the comedy. I'm not in the mood."

Garrison looked as mean as a junkyard dog. Peter entered the brownstone, and the snarling FBI agent slammed the door behind him.

"Start walking," Garrison said.

Peter went down the hall with Garrison on his heels. He entered the kitchen to find Liza and Snoop sitting at the breakfast table with three grim-faced FBI agents hovering around them. His friends flashed brave smiles.

"You guys okay?" Peter asked.

"Not really," Liza said softly.

"Having the time of my life," Snoop replied, his voice filled with false bravado. "You're not going to believe this, but one of these agents actually arrested me when I was in college."

"That's amazing. Which one?"

Snoop pointed at the lone female in the group. "Special Agent Nan Perry. We're buds."

Garrison stood in the doorway with his arms folded. "Both of you, cut the conversation. Your friends have been illegally accessing classified information, and are in serious trouble."

"What kind of classified information?" Peter asked.

"The Order of Astrum."

Peter glanced at Liza and Snoop, and saw his girlfriend lower her eyes. This was her doing. *Damn,* Peter thought. Liza knew about the Order, and now the FBI were here. He needed to regroup, and figure out a way out of this mess.

"If you don't mind, I'm going upstairs to throw on some dry clothes," Peter said. "Help yourself to some coffee and whatever's in the fridge. I'll be right back."

"Not so fast. I've got some questions to ask you," Garrison said.

Peter went to the doorway where Garrison stood. "This is my home. I'm not going to be told what to do by you, or anyone else. If you don't like that, arrest me. Or, you can let me change my clothes, and then we can have a nice, friendly conversation. It's your call."

Garrison scowled at him. He looked like he just might take Peter up on his offer, and haul him off to jail. Then his face softened.

"All right. You can change your clothes, but I'm coming with you."

"I can change myself. Really."

"Shut up, kid."

Peter walked out of the kitchen with Garrison breathing down his neck. The other three agents remained behind, and continued to watch his friends as if they were dangerous criminals.

Upstairs in the bedroom, Peter pulled fresh clothes from the closet, and went into the bathroom to change. Garrison stood by the window, looking down at the courtyard.

"Make it fast," the FBI agent said.

"Are you going to time me?"

"I just might."

Locking the bathroom door, Peter sat down on the toilet, and buried his head in his hands. This was bad. He didn't want Liza and Snoop to go to jail. He loved

Liza, and Snoop was the closet thing to a brother he'd ever had. He was ready to fall on his sword before he let anything happen to either one of them. After a minute had passed, Garrison banged on the door.

"Hurry up."

Peter got undressed. In his pocket was the DVD he'd taken from Lester Rowe's apartment. If Garrison did arrest him, he didn't want the FBI agent seeing what was on the DVD before he did. He hid the DVD in the cabinet beneath the sink.

His cell phone sat on the washstand. It began to vibrate, and he picked it up. Max had sent him a text. It was about time his teacher got back to him.

U OK? Max asked.

YEAH   WHERE R U?

JFK   JUST PUT ROWE ON PLANE

FBI IS HERE

!!!!!!!   SAY NOTHING!

HAVE TO TALK TO THEM

WHY?

LONG STORY

TELL ME!

MY GIRLFRIEND KNOWS ABOUT ME

THIS IS BAD

NO KIDDING

"What the hell are you doing in there?" Garrison said through the door.

"My hair," Peter called out.

"Fifteen seconds before I break the door down."

Peter told Max he'd talk to him later, and folded his phone. Throwing on dry clothes, he opened the door to find Garrison standing outside. The FBI agent pointed at the doorway.

"Move," he said.

They returned to the kitchen. Garrison added a chair to the table, and told Peter to sit down. Peter parked himself in the chair while staring at Liza and Snoop. They both looked petrified. It was now or never if he was going to save his friends.

"I have a proposition for you," Peter said.

Garrison stood at the head of the table with his arms crossed. "How come you keep talking when you're not supposed to?"

"Sorry. Want to hear it?"

"Go ahead."

"You obviously want to talk to me. If that wasn't the case, you would have run Liza and Snoop to the station house, and booked them. Correct?"

"Correct."

"I'll be more than happy to talk to you, but you have to let my friends go."

"I don't think so. They've already admitted to hacking our computer."

"That's half the story. I told them to."

"Doesn't matter. They still broke the law."

"They both work for me. I would have fired them if they said no."

"Is that so? Why did you do that?"

"Let them go, and I'll be happy to tell you."

Garrison did a slow burn. "I don't like your attitude."

"And I don't like the FBI."

The special agent came around the table, and got in his face. "What did you say?" Garrison acted like he might rip Peter's head off. The young magician held his ground.

"My mother and father were murdered when I was a kid," Peter said. "This morning, I discovered that the FBI knew the Order of Astrum was responsible for their deaths, but never shared the information with the police. Like I said, I'm not a big fan of your employer."

The words hit Garrison hard. He stepped back, unsure of how to respond. Liza caught Peter's eye, and mouthed the word *Wow!* Snoop nodded approvingly.

It was hard to admit when you were wrong. Harder still when you had to do it in front of a roomful of people. The words that came out of Garrison's mouth were a surprise.

"Sounds like the FBI owes you an apology," Garrison said.

"It would be a good start," Peter said.

"I'm sorry we never spoke to the police about the Order of Astrum's involvement in your parents' murders," Garrison said. "They had a right to know. And so did you."

Nothing was going to change the way Peter felt about his parents' deaths. But it was still nice to hear Garrison say the FBI had not handled things right.

"Thanks," Peter said. "Now how about letting my friends go?"

20

"You win," Garrison said. "Your friends can go."

Liza and Snoop broke into smiles. Garrison wagged a finger in their faces.

"Keep your noses clean," the FBI agent said.

Snoop walked out of the kitchen with a lift in his step. Liza came around the table, and kissed Peter lovingly on the cheek.

"You're a star," she whispered.

"Get out of here before he changes his mind," Peter whispered back.

Liza hurried out of the kitchen. Moments later, Peter heard the front door open as Liza and Snoop left the brownstone. He breathed a sigh of relief, knowing his friends were safe.

Garrison turned to his team, and told them to wait in another room. The three agents filed out.

"I need some coffee," Garrison said.

Peter fixed a fresh pot. Soon they were facing each other at the table, the hostility between them all but gone.

"You go first," Garrison said.

"I'd never heard of the Order of Astrum until last night, when one of their members tried to kill me during a show," Peter said. "A British guy named Wolfe."

"Who told you Wolfe was a member of the Order?"

Peter sipped his drink. Detective Schoch had told him Wolfe was part of the Order. He wasn't going to give her up any more than Liza or Snoop.

"Wolfe had the Order's tattoo stamped on his neck," Peter said. "One of my assistants recognized the tattoo, and told me about the Order."

"How did you make the connection between the Order and your parents' deaths?"

"I saw it in a dream last night."

"What do you mean?"

"I was there the night my parents were abducted, and repressed the memory. It came out last night, and I saw the men who did it. One of them had the Order's tattoo on his neck."

"You were there."

"That's right. So what's Wolfe's deal? You must have some idea."

The ball was back in Garrison's court. When the FBI agent did not respond, Peter gazed into his guest's troubled eyes, and read his thoughts. *He knows something horrible is about to happen, and doesn't know how to stop it.*

"Tell me what you're afraid of. Maybe I can help," Peter said.

"Who said I was afraid of something?"

"It's written all over your face."

"Is that so. Are you psychic?"

"I don't have ESP, but I do have ESPN."

"Ouch. Just answer the question."

"I see things that other people miss." He paused. "I can help, if you let me."

Garrison drummed the table. He had a face like an open book. Now it was saying, "What the hell do I have to lose?"

"All right. I'll tell you what I know," Garrison said.

Peter refilled the special agent's mug. Garrison appreciated the gesture, and dipped his chin.

"I run a special division of the FBI called the Pattern Recognition Unit," Garrison said. "We solve cases through data mining and information analysis. You familiar with this?"

"I think *CSI* did an episode about it," Peter said.

"I'll give you an example. There was a serial killer in Boston who was slashing women the third Friday of every month. The Boston police were stymied, so the case was handed to us. We mined several thousand pieces of data to see if anything popped. Turns out, a movie theater in Boston was showing splatter flicks every third Friday. We contacted the mental hospitals to see if any patients got turned on by that stuff. Wouldn't you know, there was a guy who did, and he'd been missing for months. We caught him."

"Did a pattern lead you to the Order of Astrum?"

"Yes, it did," Garrison said. "Last year, an oil field in Riyadh, Saudi Arabia, was mysteriously blown up. The next day, the price of crude oil skyrocketed, and a ruthless dictator in Africa named Big Daddy made a killing in the oil futures market. It looked real suspicious, so my group decided to investigate.

"We looked at thousands of pieces of information. Based upon our investigation, Big Daddy wasn't connected to the bombing in any way. But we found something else. Big Daddy had recently unveiled a new flag with the Order of Astrum's symbol replacing the country's national emblem. That bothered me, so I decided to have a look at the Order.

"There wasn't much information available about the Order, except for a file on the FBI's computer, which said the Order had killed your parents, who were both psychics. I wondered if there could be a link to their killings, and the case in Riyadh."

The words went off in Peter's head like a bomb. *The FBI knew that my parents were psychics.* Did they know about him, and the Friday night séance group as well?

"Was there?" Peter asked.

"Yes, there was. Don't get ahead of me."

"Sorry."

"I contacted the Saudis, and asked them if there had been any unusual killings in Riyadh before the pipeline attack. Guess what I found?"

"There were."

"Right again. There were three suspicious deaths the week before the bombing. One victim was a woman who had occult stuff hidden in her house. The second victim was an old man who claimed to be two hundred years old, and gave spiritual guidance to his neighbors. The third was a teenage boy who was shunned by everyone who knew him."

"Why?"

"The boy's neighbors claimed he used to sit on the sidewalk, and stare into the sun while predicting the future." Garrison paused. "We think they were all psychics."

"How were they killed?"

Garrison gave him a hard stare. "Why is that important?"

"Wolfe used a knife. I read somewhere that knifings are rare."

"They are rare. Most murderers use a firearm. To answer your question, the victims in Riyadh were stabbed, strangled, and beaten to death."

"It has to be him. Wolfe likes using his hands." Peter paused to think about what Garrison had told him. "You think Wolfe was sent to Riyadh to bomb the pipeline. But before he did that, he killed these three psychics so they wouldn't tip off the police."

Garrison took another sip of coffee. "You're very perceptive."

"Like I said, I see things other people miss."

"You sure you're not a psychic like your parents?"

Peter stared into the depths of his drink and said nothing.

"My father had an expression," Garrison said. "He used to say, 'I may have been born late, but I wasn't born late last night.'"

"What does that mean?"

"I think you're lying to me."

"Why would I do that?"

Garrison put his elbows on the table. "I'm going to share a little secret with you, Peter. For the past ten years, the FBI has been getting anonymous letters warning them about disasters that haven't happened yet. The letters are all postmarked from New York, and they're written in different sets of handwriting. About, say, seven different sets. You wouldn't happen to know anything about those letters, would you?"

Peter thought he was going to be sick.

"Because something tells me you're one of these psychics," Garrison went on. "I can't prove it, but then again, I really don't want to. I just want to know what you know, and stop whatever terrible attack the Order is planning for New York. Will you help me?"

Peter leaned back in his chair. If he told Garrison what he knew, his life would never be the same. But if he didn't, thousands might die. He needed to come clean with Garrison if he wanted to stop that from happening. Seen in that light, he really had no other choice.

"Here's the deal," he said. "I'm part of the group that's been sending you letters. I was about to contact you about Wolfe, who I saw during a séance. He's planning to attack Times Square this Tuesday night after the shows let out. He's got some kind of weapon that doesn't make any noise. People will just drop on the sidewalk, and die. I can't figure out what it is."

"You saw this?" Garrison asked incredulously.

"In a manner of speaking, yes."

"Could you be wrong about the timing, or location?"

"I've never been wrong before."

"Really."

Peter nodded. "Really," he added for emphasis.

"Do you think Wolfe knows that you know?"

It was an idea which Peter hadn't considered. If true, it would explain why Wolfe had come to the theater and attacked him, and why he was trying to kill the others as well.

"He might," Peter said.

Garrison abruptly stood up from the table. A new look had sparked the special agent's eyes. Hope. He came around the table, and pumped Peter's hand.

"This will help us find him. You did the right thing telling me."

Peter wasn't so sure. The authorities had never understood psychics, and he doubted they ever would. He walked Garrison to the front of the brownstone. The rest of the team was in the living room, playing with the illusions. Special Agent Nan Perry was sitting cross-legged on a Magic Carpet while floating in space. Her two partners had taken a liking to the Arm Chopper, and were taking turns cutting off each other's hands.

"Playtime's over," Garrison announced.

The three agents filed out of the room and went outside to the street. Garrison stopped at the door, and again shook his hand.

"Your secret is safe with me," Garrison said.

No, it wasn't, Peter thought. A secret was never safe once too many people knew it. He'd opened Pandora's box, and did not know how he'd ever get it closed.

Garrison handed him a business card. "Call me if you have any more visions."

"I'll do that."

"Thank you."

Garrison walked down to the sidewalk and got into his vehicle. Peter shut the door and pressed his forehead against the cold wood. He could not help but wonder if he was doomed.

21

One West 72nd Street was the address of the most legendary apartment building in New York, the famed Dakota. Home to celebrities, rock stars, and the fabulously wealthy, it was a secretive place that had inspired graphic novels, television shows, and a movie about a coven of witches.

As Max Romeo got out of the cab, he glanced nervously up and down the street. Wolfe was still on the loose, and Max needed to stay on his toes. Seeing nothing out of the ordinary, he passed through the Dakota's main entrance, a porte cochere large enough for a horse-drawn carriage, where he found a uniformed attendant at the front desk. The attendant was new, and cast a suspicious eye at the aging magician.

"What can I do for you?" the attendant asked.

"I'm here to see Millicent Adams," Max replied.

"Name please."

"Max Romeo. I've been coming here for thirty years."

"Reason for your visit."

"That's none of your business, good sir."

The attendant raised an eyebrow. "I'd like to see some identification."

"My good man, is that necessary?"

"We have rules, sir. If you won't follow them, I'll have to ask you to leave."

Max didn't like the attendant's snippy attitude. In his closet was a pair of shoes older than this young man. Drawing back his sleeves, Max plucked an egg out of thin air and cracked it against the desk, pouring the yolk into a glass filled with mineral water that the attendant had been drinking. "Allow me to introduce myself. I'm Maximilian Augustus Romeo, Master of the Impossible, available for private parties, birthdays, weddings, and bar mitzvahs. Would you like to see some more?"

The attendant stared at his ruined drink. "No."

"Very well. Please call Millicent Adams. She's expecting me."

"What about my drink? Can you fix it?"

"I haven't figured that part out yet."

Soon Max was riding an elevator to Milly's floor. The shocked look on the attendant's face was a keeper, and he found himself wishing he'd snapped a photo on his cell phone. The doors parted, and he walked down a hallway to Milly's front door, where he rapped softly.

"It's open," a voice called from within.

He entered and headed for the living room. Milly stood by a large picture window facing Central Park. On the other side of the glass, a flock of crows were performing an aerial ballet. The birds' movements were perfectly synchronized, and bordered on poetry.

Milly gazed at him in the glass. She wore an embroidered red robe of Oriental design, and a red sash in her silver hair. A tiny woman at five feet tall, she weighed no more than ninety pounds. But her presence could fill a stadium, and Max always felt puny around her.

"How bad is it, Max?"

"Bad," he replied. "The Order of Astrum has sent an assassin to kill us. He did away with Marie and her husband last night, and tried to kill Lester and me this morning. Luckily, Peter came to our rescue, and beat him up. It was something to see."

Milly blanched at the news that Marie was gone. In a subdued voice she said, "Peter saved you and Lester? How wonderful."

"Yes and no."

"What do you mean?"

"Peter is changing, Milly. Something has triggered his powers to a new level. I've never seen anything quite like it. He seems astonished by it all, and is begging me to explain. On top of that, he's talking to the FBI."

"Is that it?"

"Isn't that enough?"

"I'm certain that Peter will know how to deal with the FBI. My main concern is what you told Peter about himself."

"Nothing, so far."

"Are you planning to speak with him?"

"Yes, I am. Once Wolfe is caught and the dust settles, I plan to tell Peter about who he is, and who his parents were."

"Why, pray tell?"

"Because he deserves to know. We've kept it from him for too long."

Milly spun around. Max felt the unbearable weight of her stare. He shifted his feet uneasily, and gazed at the floor.

"I'm being a terrible hostess. Sit with me on the couch," she said.

Together, they made the couch sag. The crows hovered outside, flapping their wings furiously. They were the small, pigeon-sized jackdaw variety, black from head to toe, and as feisty as pit bulls. They had migrated from Milly's hometown of Ipswich, Massachusetts, when she'd relocated to New York, and now resided in a stand of oak trees across the street. Ipswich's loss had been New York's gain, with the birds providing regular entertainment for Milly and her guests. Witches held a powerful sway over animals, and the crows were as obedient, and loyal, as any domesticated pet.

"No, Max," Milly said firmly.

"No?" he replied meekly.

"No."

"I will always bow to your wishes, Milly."

"Thank you. Let me explain. It is not your place, or mine, to tell Peter about himself or his family history. He must have the curiosity and desire to seek self-discovery. Once he goes down that road, he will learn quickly enough who he is, and what he's capable of. It's how the process works, and we must abide by it."

"Should I lie to him?"

"If you must, yes."

"But why? I'm closer to him than my own son."

Milly placed her hand on Max's forearm, and gave it a gentle squeeze. "I know that. Be there for him. He's a grown man. Stop treating him like a child."

"Very well." Max paused to gaze out the window, then looked back at his hostess. "Not to change the subject, but have you given any thought to how to deal with Wolfe?"

"I have," she said. "Holly is moving in with me for the time being. The building is quite secure, and is wired into the local police. We'll be safe here. You're welcome to stay in one of the guest bedrooms, if you'd like. They're quite comfortable."

"Thank you, but I'm staying put in my apartment," Max said. "I live across the street from a police precinct. It's one of the safest areas of the city. Have you spoken to Reggie?"

"We talked earlier. Reggie wishes to remain in his apartment as well. You two should consider staying together. There's safety in numbers, you know."

"That's not a bad idea. I'll go over and see him right now."

Max rose from the couch. Outside, the crows levitated in the air, hanging on their master's every word. *Such wonderfully obedient creatures,* he thought. Perhaps in his next life, he could come back as a witch, and have a flock of birds follow him around as well.

"Good-bye, Max. Be safe," Milly said.

"And you as well," he replied.

"He's gone," Milly called out after the front door had clicked shut.

"Are you sure?"

"Positive. You can come out now."

"Did he leave his wallet on the couch? He does that sometimes."

Milly glanced at the indented cushion beside her. "No. The coast is clear."

Holly slipped into the living room from the butler's hallway, and joined her aunt. She was dressed in her school uniform of faded blue jeans and a brown turtleneck, her hair pulled back in a bun. Her cheeks were flushed, and she seemed filled with nervous energy.

"Do you think Max knows I was spying on him?" Holly asked.

"It wasn't spying," Milly said sharply. "We need to know if Max is trying to protect Peter. Since you're close to Peter, I thought it was best if you heard what Max had to say."

"It certainly felt like spying."

"Very well. You *were* spying on him. Now tell me, is Max trying to protect him?"

"I don't think so, Aunt Milly."

"Good."

Holly gazed out the window. In profile, she bore a striking resemblance to her aunt. Witches carried powerful genes, and it was not unusual for descendants hundreds of years apart to look nearly identical. Milly was a direct descendant of Mary Glover, who'd been hanged during the Salem witch trials. Glover's powers had included the ability to see into the future, cast spells that only she could break, and a strange sway over dogs, cats, farm animals, and birds. Holly had seen a portrait of Glover in an old book entitled *Memorable Providences Relating to Witchcraft and Possessions*. The resemblance had been uncanny, right down to their hairstyles, and the birthmarks on their chins.

"I have a question," Holly said. "Are you really going to let Peter go it alone?"

"You heard what I told Max," her aunt replied. "Peter must take this journey by himself. That's how the process works, and there's no getting around it."

"I suppose you're right."

"I am right."

"I wonder what he's told the FBI."

"There's only one way to find out."

Holly looked at her aunt. "Do you want me to spy on Peter, as well?"

"I most certainly do. When was the last time you spoke with him?"

"This morning. He called to warn me about Wolfe. Oh my, look at the crows."

Milly shifted her gaze. The crows were hovering in perfect rows, flapping their wings like the Radio City

Music Hall Rockettes. There were times when she did not find their antics amusing. She flipped her hand, and they dispersed to the trees across the street, where they began to squawk up a storm. Even birds did not like to be dismissed.

"You seem distracted," Milly said. "Is something wrong?"

Holly bit her lip and shook her head.

"You're red in the face. Are you getting sick?"

"I feel perfectly well, Aunt Milly. Thank you for asking."

"Good. Now here's what I need you to do. I want you to contact Peter, and find out what he's said to the FBI. Loose lips sink ships, as they say. Make certain that he isn't talking to anyone else. He has a girlfriend, doesn't he?"

"You mean Liza?"

"Do you know her?"

"She's Peter's assistant. I saw her at his show. She's very beautiful."

"Do you think he's sleeping with her?"

"Aunt Milly!"

"Don't act so shocked, my dear. It's a perfectly legitimate question."

"I would think so. They live together."

"Damn."

"Is that a problem?"

"Men are idiots when it comes to sex, and I'm sure Peter is no exception."

Her niece was blushing. They'd talked about sex before, and it had been perfectly comfortable. Something was on her niece's mind.

"Look at me," Milly said.

Holly turned from the window to look at her aunt. A long moment passed.

"Oh, my God. You're in love with him."

Holly swallowed hard and nodded. "He loves me too. He said as much over the phone this morning. I've been in love with Peter ever since I could remember, and I think he's always loved me. It just took something dreadful to happen for us to both acknowledge it."

"But he has a girlfriend."

"This is different."

"You think he'll leave her for you?"

"I'm not thinking that far ahead. Peter will decide when the time is right."

Milly rose from the couch and crossed the room. She put her hand on her niece's shoulder and looked her straight in the eye. "You are heading down a dangerous path, my dear. For your own good, please reconsider."

Holly's face clouded. "No."

"Not even for my sake?"

"No. I won't turn him away. Not even for you."

Milly felt the air escape from her lungs. She had no one to blame but herself. It was her doing that Peter and Holly had formed a bond when they were young; what had she thought was going to happen? This was real, and there was no changing it.

Milly stared out the window. Of late, it seemed like so much of her time was spent here, gazing at the lush oasis of the park across the street. The habits of an old woman, she supposed. In the glass's reflection, Holly slipped her arm around her aunt's waist.

"Are you mad at me?" her niece asked.

"Never," Milly replied.

"Disappointed?"

"Ask me after the shock wears off."

Holly let out a little laugh, then her face grew serious. "Do you believe that things happen for a reason?

Or is life just a random series of events that we have no control over?"

"Everything on this earth happens for a reason," Milly said. "It is the nature of the order of the universe, whose mysteries we are forever trying to fathom."

"I agree. Everything *does* happen for a reason. There is a reason why the Order of Astrum sent someone to kill us, and why Madame Marie and her husband have died. There's also a reason why Peter is discovering the true extent of his psychic powers at precisely the same time. And there's a reason why Peter told me he loved me. These things are connected."

"But how? What is the link?"

"If I knew that, I'd be the smartest person in the world." Holly gave her aunt a squeeze. "What I do know is, we must let the good things happen, and make sure the bad things don't happen. You told me that when I discovered I was a witch, and I've always believed it."

"And you think your being in love with Peter is a good thing," Milly said.

"How could it not be?"

Her niece had never been in love. If she had, she would have known how destructive a force it could be. Milly would have given anything to be so young and naïve again.

"Let's hope you're right," Milly said.

22

*P*eter told Liza everything.

He took her to Sojourn on East 79th Street, whose interior was filled with warm oak and red tones, and sat at a corner table where they split a carafe of the house Chablis. In a subdued voice, he explained how as a boy he'd gotten a surprise visit by Hecate, spirit of magic, who'd come to his family's apartment in response to a séance being held by his parents, but ended up in his bedroom instead. Hecate had been talking to him ever since, along with a variety of other spirits and ghosts. Their waiter delivered a plate of roasted figs and prosciutto to the table.

"You're going to have to bear with me for a minute here," Liza said when the waiter was gone. "What exactly was a ghost doing in your bedroom?"

"I think her GPS was broken."

"Come on, be serious. I'm having a hard time grasping this."

"She mistook my bedroom for my father's study, which was down the hall," he explained. "She hovered over my bed, and woke me up, and we ended up having a conversation."

"You weren't afraid?"

"I'd been seeing ghosts since I was little. Late at night they'd come into my bedroom, and make a nuisance of themselves. There's nothing scary about them."

"I'm finding this hard to believe."

"It's true. You have to understand the spirit world, and the beings that inhabit it."

"Since I don't, why don't you explain it to me?"

He paused to gather his thoughts. It was hard to explain a place that Liza had never seen, let alone imagined, and he chose his words carefully. "There are two worlds. The physical world which we inhabit, and the spirit world which spirits, ghosts, and castaway angels inhabit. At one time, the inhabitants of the spirit world were human, and as a result, are just as flawed as humans are. They make mistakes and get lost, and sometimes do really stupid things. In that regard, they're no different than we are."

"What's a castaway angel?"

"A demon."

"Oh. Do you ever speak with them?"

"No. They're dangerous, and in league with the Devil."

"So you're telling me there really is a Devil."

"Of course. He's responsible for just about every bad thing in the world."

Liza was having a difficult time believing him. She ate a fig while staring into his eyes. "Okay, so how did your parents summon this ghost to their apartment? E-mail?"

"They used symbols, which they placed around my father's study before the séance began. Specific symbols call specific spirits. The symbol for Hecate is three moons. One is waxing, one is full, and the third is waning."

"Do all psychics talk with the spirits?"

"No. Most just glimpse into the future, and try to interpret what they see."

"But you do talk to them. What makes you different?"

"My charming personality."

"Seriously, Peter."

"I wish I knew. My mother was a channeler; so maybe I inherited it from her."

"What's a channeler?"

"It's a medium whose body is actually inhabited by a spirit during a séance. The channeler is under the spirit's influence while inhabited. The spirit will often send the channeler back and forth in time to witness things."

"You've done this?"

"Many times."

"Tell me what's it like."

"It's not as much fun as it sounds. The only thing I can compare it to is an out-of-control roller-coaster ride. I'm exhausted when the séance is over."

"What do the spirits try to tell you?"

"The spirits care deeply about the physical world, and want to save it from the Devil, who's intent on destroying it. Usually, the spirits reveal disasters that haven't happened yet, in the hopes of stopping them from occurring."

Liza speared another fig and offered him a bite. "Can you actually change the future?"

"Yes. That's the psychic's greatest power. It's what makes it worthwhile. No thanks."

"Do you channel when we're at home?"

Peter picked up his glass of wine and took a healthy sip. He'd not been looking forward to this part of their conversation. Liza wasn't going to like his answer. "No. Never at home."

"Then where?"

"I channel during a weekly séance with six other psychics. We meet on Friday nights at an apartment on the West Side where one of them lives."

A hurt look spread across his girlfriend's face. "Hold on a minute. You told me you were getting together with some magic buddies at a restaurant, and trading tricks. That isn't true?"

"I'm sorry."

"There's no restaurant where magicians meet?"

"There is. I just don't go there."

"So you've been lying to me all this time."

He put down his wineglass and nodded. Her eyes had not left his face.

"That's so wrong," she said.

"Everyone in the group is sworn to secrecy. It's part of being a psychic."

"That doesn't make me feel any better."

Her voice was trembling. Peter had to do something, and he pulled up a photo of the Friday night group on his cell phone, and showed her. It had been taken in Milly's living room before one of the séances. Liza studied the group and zeroed in on Holly. "Who's *she*?"

"Holly Adams. I've known her since she was an infant. She's a witch."

"Oh really. And I suppose there are vampires in your little group too?"

"Vampires don't exist anymore. There were a few in Arizona, but they got wiped out."

"Seriously?"

"Everything I'm telling you is true. Please believe me."

She pointed at Holly. "Should I be afraid?"

Nothing like getting everything on the table, Peter thought. He loved Holly, and he loved Liza, but he loved Liza differently, and he didn't see that ever changing.

"No," he said.

She handed him back the cell phone. "Here's something I don't understand. Why did you become a magician if you already had these amazing powers? I mean, why do fake magic when you can do real magic? What's the point?"

"It was an accident. After my parents died, I lived with Milly Adams. One day, Milly got a call from a teacher at my school. My teacher wanted to know how

I could be calling out answers to questions before she asked them. Milly panicked, and told my teacher it was a trick, and that I was a budding magician. My teacher thought that was great, and asked if I'd do a show for the class. Milly was stuck, so she called Max Romeo, a magician from our group, and asked him to teach me. I became Max's student, and fell in love with magic. I guess you could say it became my cover."

"That's sort of ironic."

"I know."

They ate the rest of the figs and the prosciutto in silence. When the plate was clean, Liza leaned forward, and dropped her voice. "Now, it's my turn."

"You have something you want to tell me?"

"Yes, and it isn't good. I read something on the FBI's Web site that you should know. Your parents were part of group of psychic children in a small English town in the 1940s that helped beat the Nazis, and win the war."

"Really? That's incredible."

"Here's the bad part. They called themselves the Order of Astrum."

Peter felt the blood drain from his head. He stammered as he spoke. "That's not possible. The Order of Astrum practices dark magic, and are cold-blooded murderers."

"They weren't always that way," Liza explained. "In the late 1980s they started hiring themselves out, and your parents fled to New York because of it. The Order tracked them down, and did away with them. The Order has been doing bad things ever since."

He took a deep breath. His parents were good people. This couldn't be true.

"Are you sure this came from the FBI?" he asked.

"Positive."

"Maybe you read it wrong."

Liza reached across the table, and rested her hand atop his. "It was all there. Your parents were original members of the Order of Astrum. I didn't read it wrong."

He felt himself growing angry. What he knew about his parents' past, he'd learned from Milly and Max. Had they known all of this, but never told him?

"Damn them," he muttered.

"Peter, what's wrong?"

"They've been holding back on me all this time."

"Your friends?"

"Yes, my friends."

He slapped the table with the palm of his hand. Heads turned throughout the restaurant. He suddenly was being bombarded with thoughts, and knew what every person in the restaurant was thinking. He'd never experienced anything like it before. It was unnerving, and he threw down money and stood up.

"Let's get out of here," he said.

"Please sit down, and tell me what's wrong."

He shook his head. The room was changing, the red tones and warm wood turning the color of bright red blood. The angry beast buried deep inside of him was taking over.

"I'll meet you outside," he said.

He stood beneath an awning and waited for her to come out. Cars and yellow cabs raced past on the rain-soaked street. He didn't really know who his parents were, which meant that he didn't really know who he was. It was like becoming an orphan all over again. Moments later, Liza came through the front door, and saw that he was weeping.

"Oh, Peter, I'm so sorry," she said, and hugged him until the aching pain went away.

23

Langston Turnbull was a retired shopkeeper from Wales who'd had the misfortune of being the same height and build as Wolfe. Wolfe had spotted Turnbull on the beach in sunny Spain while on vacation, and later drowned him so he could steal the Welshman's passport. The passport contained the only photo Wolfe had of the dead man. Physically, they shared much in common. Facially, not as much. Turnbull had sandy hair, a round face with flared nostrils, and wrinkles. Wolfe looked nothing like him.

That was about to change.

Wolfe waited until dusk before leaving his hotel. The police knew what he looked like, and would eventually track him down. By turning himself into Turnbull, he could check into another hotel under his new identity, and stay out of the law's grasp.

There was a Duane Reade drugstore on every block in New York. Entering the branch on Eighth Avenue near his hotel, Wolfe glanced at his reflection in the window. His face was swollen and bruised, and would only draw further attention to himself.

He grabbed a shopping basket and started his search. The aisles were jammed with merchandise. How anyone could find what they were looking for was beyond him.

He heard the tiniest of noises. Someone had crept up behind him. Based upon the sound their feet had made, the person stood about five-two, and weighed a hundred pounds.

He spun around. "Yes?"

A diminutive Hispanic woman in a blue store uniform stood behind him. The last time someone had snuck up on him like that, he'd punctured their windpipe.

"I'm Carmella, the store supervisor," she said. "Can I help you?"

"Your store's layout is confusing."

"Tell me what you want, and I'll help you find it."

Carmella guided him up and down the aisles. It was like having his own personal shopper, and he grabbed a tube of hair dye, a pair of barber shears, nail polish, a tub of makeup, hair spray, and a pair of cheap reading glasses.

"All done?" she asked.

Wolfe had to think. He'd turned himself into Turnbull before, and there was always one item he forgot to purchase before he made the transformation.

"I need a piece of plastic tubing," he remembered. "A half inch wide, and a few inches long. My wife asked me to pick some up."

"Do you know what she needs it for?"

"Love, we've been married twenty years. You learn not to ask questions."

"Smart man. Let's ask our pharmacist."

Carmella talked a bearded man in a white lab coat into selling Wolfe a piece of plastic tubing. Wolfe paid for the items at the checkout with Carmella ringing him up. Behind the checkout was a cork board covered in flyers. One flyer had Wolfe's face plastered on it with the word WANTED. If Carmella saw the flyer, he was done.

He nervously glanced around the store. The other employees were out of earshot. He sized Carmella up. She looked frail, and would be easy prey.

"Forget something?" she asked.

"Do you have the time? My watch has stopped running."

She consulted her watch. Wolfe lifted his arm, prepared to chop her windpipe with the side of his hand. It was a trick he'd learned in the army. Without her windpipe, she couldn't cry for help, and would die without anyone being the wiser.

Motion caught his eye. Outside the store, a pair of uniformed policemen walked past, swinging their night sticks in unison. He covered his mouth as if coughing, and watched them pass.

"It's a few minutes past six," she said.

He backed away from the counter, and moved toward the exit. He wanted to tell her to buy a lottery ticket. It wasn't very often that one of his victims got away.

"Have a nice day," she called after him.

Bathrooms in hotels were ludicrously small, and hardly big enough for a grown man to stand in. Hugging the sink in his room, Wolfe unscrewed the bottle of clear nail polish, and began to coat his face with the tiny brush. Facial recognition technology was used by most law enforcement agencies to catch fugitives, and was considered infallible. Wolfe knew otherwise. The software used in these programs recognized twenty-five different points on a person's face. If four of those points were changed, the program could be fooled into thinking the person was someone else.

Soon the bottle of nail polish was empty. He dried his face with a hair dryer, then crinkled his cheeks, and made dozens of wrinkles appear. He looked ten years older already.

The next step was his hair. The hair dye he'd bought was called Just For Men, and he generously brushed the product into his scalp. Before his eyes, his hair turned from black to sandy blond. He didn't look good as a blond, but neither had Turnbull.

Then came his face. Turnbull's face was decidedly smaller than his. Wolfe solved that problem by brushing his hair onto his forehead, and carefully molding it into place with hair spray. It made his face look smaller than it really was.

His nose also needed work. Turnbull had flared nostrils. This was where the plastic tubing came into play. Cutting off two small pieces, he slit them open and stretched them out, then shoved them into his nostrils, causing both to expand.

The last item of business was the Order's tattoo on his neck. Wolfe sported multiple tattoos, and they'd all faded over time. Not the Order's. It was still as vibrant as the day he'd joined, something he'd never quite understood. He covered it with pancake makeup, and made it disappear.

He was done. Picking up Turnbull's passport, he held it to the mirror, and compared his face to the dead shopkeeper. It wasn't a perfect match, but no one ever looked like their passport photo, and he knew it would pass muster.

Something didn't feel right. He stared long and hard at the photo before realizing what it was. Turnbull had worn a dark suit and necktie in the photo, and looked dignified. He needed a new outfit, and the transformation would be complete.

Eighth Avenue was a potpourri of discount stores run by Middle Easterners. He picked a store called The Gent that sold men's clothes. Shaking off the raindrops, he went inside.

Behind the counter sat a man wearing a purple Nehru jacket straight out of the psychedelic sixties. Wolfe had a theory about people who dressed in period costume: They were not happy with their lives, and wished to be living another one. An old Beatles song blared out of a boom box on the counter.

"My name is Fami. Welcome to my store," the proprietor said.

"I'm looking for some business attire," Wolfe said.

"What price range do you have in mind?"

"The cheaper the better."

"How cheap is cheap?" Fami had a voice like a bird. *Cheep cheep.*

"I don't plan to wear the clothes more than a few times."

"Try the bins in the back. Those are the cheapest clothes in the store."

The sixties motif followed Wolfe down the aisle. Posters of Hendrix, Joplin, Lou Reed and the Velvet Underground, and Jefferson Airplane covered the walls. Wolfe's memories of the music were as faded as the art work, and he wondered why people like Fami wouldn't let go.

The clothes in the back were knockoffs. He grabbed a fifty-dollar suit, a nine-dollar dress shirt, a five-dollar plastic belt, and a three-dollar striped necktie. The Beatles song ended, and he heard Fami making a phone call. The proprietor dialed only three numbers.

Wolfe's radar went up. Fami could have been calling information, but hardly anyone used that service these days, preferring to look up phone numbers on the Internet.

An automated voice answered the call.

"You have dialed 911 of the New York City Police Department. Your call is very important to us. Please hold on."

Wolfe cursed under his breath. Had Fami made him? It didn't seem possible, yet that was the only explanation. He returned to the front of the store with the clothes. As Wolfe neared the counter, Fami drew a .38 Special from beneath the register, and aimed it at him.

"Put your arms where I can see them."

"Hey, look, I just want to buy some clothes."

"Do as I say—right now!"

Wolfe dropped the clothes onto the counter, and lifted his arms into the air.

"Mind telling me what I did?"

"You are a wanted man. The tattoo on your neck gave you away."

A smokey mirror hung behind the counter. In its reflection, Wolfe saw how the Order's tattoo had bled through the makeup. The elders were tracking him like a damn dog.

"Hey, be careful with that thing," Wolfe said.

Fami's hand was shaking. People who never handled guns were more dangerous than those who did. Wolfe prayed Fami didn't shoot him.

No such luck.

The sound of the .38 discharging sent Wolfe an inch off the floor. The bullet ripped a swatch of fabric clean off the arm of his coat. The startled look on Fami's face said he hadn't meant to squeeze the trigger; it had just happened.

"You shot me," Wolfe gasped.

His hand went to his side. The bullet had only grazed him. He pretended it was much worse, and started to moan.

"Help me . . ."

Fami took the bait. He came around the counter wearing a stricken look. Wolfe waited until he was close before knocking the gun away. He threw his hands around Fami's throat, and began to choke him with the gold peace symbol hanging around his neck.

"This is 911. What's your emergency?" came a voice out of the cordless phone on the counter.

"Help! He's killing me," Fami screamed.

"Hold on! We're on our way," the operator replied.

Two quick blows and Fami was lying on the floor. Wolfe grabbed the clothes off the counter and fled.

The gunshot was ringing in his ears as he entered his hotel room. Every soldier had a preference of how he wanted to die. Getting shot to death by a bloody hippie was not his.

He sat on the bed, and waited for his head to clear. His laptop sat on the dresser. The screen saver was of the beach in the Seychelles where he planned to retire with Rita. Just looking at the cobalt-blue ocean made him feel better. Without warning, the picture morphed into the Order's shimmering symbol. It was the elders.

He grabbed the laptop and logged in. The elders had sent him an e-mail with an attachment, which he opened. It contained photographs of the remaining people on his hit list. The photograph of Millicent Adams had a bright red circle drawn around it, and he guessed they wanted him to take her out next. Bloody idiots. Next they'd be picking his meals for him.

He signed out of e-mail. To his surprise, the Order's symbol remained on the screen. When he tried to retrieve the Seychelles screen saver, he discovered that it had been erased. He grabbed the laptop and shook it in a rage.

The elders were going to harass him until he got the job done. They didn't care if he lived or died. He was just another dog they were keeping on a psychic leash.

Wolfe decided that he'd had enough. This would be his last contract for the Order. It was time for him to start a new life.

He put on his new clothes, feeling better about his situation already.

24

Peter and Liza cabbed it to the theater. Peter did not feel like talking, content to hold his girl-friend's hand while staring out the window at the gusty winds that now accompanied the rain. The weather had been foul for days, and he wondered if the spirits were trying to tell him something. Instead of coming out and saying what was on their minds, the spirits always made it a puzzle, and challenged him to figure it out. It was as if he weren't good enough for them, and had to prove himself whenever they made contact.

"Your fingers are ice cold," Liza said. "I hope you're not getting sick."

He looked down at his hands. The skin had turned blue, and he cupped his hands and blew into them. He was reminded of how cold he'd gotten while confronting Wolfe outside Lester Rowe's apartment. Was this a sign telling him that Wolfe was lying in wait at the theater? He wasn't going to take any chances, and he called Zack on his cell phone.

"Hey Peter, what's up?" his head of security answered.

"I'm five minutes away from the theater," Peter said. "How we looking?"

"The place is packed. Your fan club from New Jersey is here."

"I thought that was next week."

"Nope. It's tonight. Hope you're ready for them."

Peter sank into his seat. His fan club consisted of six hundred starry-eyed teenage girls who'd created a Web site where they posted their favorite stories about his shows. Dealing with them was almost as scary as the prospect of the assassin on the hunt for him.

"Any sign of Wolfe?" he asked.

"He hasn't shown his ugly face," Zack replied. "I tripled security inside the theater, and we're giving everyone a pat down before they come in."

"Is that causing any problems?"

"Yes. But there's nothing I can do about it."

"Stay on your toes. Something tells me he's nearby, hiding under a rock."

"I'm all over it like a cheap suit," Zack said.

"I know you are. See you soon."

Five minutes later, the cab pulled up to the theater. A line of New Jersey tour buses hugged the curb. As Peter and Liza got out, a squealing teenager slipped out from beneath the canopy in front of the theater, and shoved a giant greeting card into Peter's hands that had been signed by every member of his fan club.

"We love you, Peter," she said breathlessly.

"What's your name?" he asked.

"Sophia. I'm the president of your fan club. Your tricks are so cool."

Sophia had braces and looked no more than fifteen. She had braved the elements to meet him, and deserved a reward.

"Would you like to see a trick, Sophia?" he asked.

"Would I! That would be totally awesome."

What kind of trick would she like to see? Something with lots of color and flash, he determined. Cuffing his sleeves, he plucked a blue scarf out of the air, and made it magically tie itself in knots while held at arm's length in front of his chest. Rolling the scarf into a ball, he tossed it into the air, where it turned into confetti that scattered harmlessly at her feet.

"You're amazing! Wait until I tell my friends!"

Squealing with delight, the teenager hurried inside. Peter remained on the sidewalk with Liza. The coldness in his bones had not gone away, nor had the feeling that danger was lurking nearby. He looked up and down the quiet block. Wolfe was preparing to strike. But where?

"You're shaking," Liza said. "Are you sure you're all right?"

"I'm fine," he said.

"Let's go through the back entrance. Don't want your fans to see you like this."

They walked around the theater to the rear entrance. At the back door Liza stopped, put her arms around his waist, and brought her face up so their noses were nearly touching.

"Please tell me what's going on," she whispered.

"Something's happening to me," he whispered back.

"What do you mean? You have to open up."

"I'm changing. My powers were never like this. I didn't anticipate things, or feel strange premonitions coming on. It seems like my powers are out of control."

"I've known you for two years. You've never acted like this before."

"I've never felt this way before," he admitted. "It started when Wolfe attacked me on stage the other night."

"*What* started? Come on. Be more specific."

How could he explain the strange metamorphosis taking place inside him? It took a moment before the right words came out. "I used to be a bystander. I would do séances, and see things in the future, and try to figure out what they meant. The mind reading was the same way. I'd read people's thoughts, and try to make sense of them. I'm not a bystander anymore."

"Then what are you?"

"I'm part of it."

Liza didn't understand. Her frightened eyes pleaded with him to explain.

"The spirit world is like a river with an unbelievably strong current," he said. "It's always moving, and never slows down. Before, I was standing on the side of the river, watching things flow past."

"What are you doing now?"

"I've been pushed into the river against my will, and I'm being pulled along by the current, heading downstream to some strange place that I've never been to before."

"Is it scary?"

"It's scary as hell," he said.

"Do you think it's permanent?"

"I wish I knew."

His cell phone vibrated, and he pulled it out of his pocket. It was Snoop.

"Hey, you lovebirds, we've got a show to do," his assistant said.

Peter looked into the eye of the surveillance camera perched over the back door. "Are you spying on us?"

"How do you think I got the name Snoop?"

"We'll be right in."

He folded his phone and put it away. Liza did not let him go.

"I'm so sorry you're going through this," she said.

He had made it a point to never read Liza's mind. It was not fair to their relationship, or to her. But now he cheated, and took a tiny peek at her thoughts. What he saw made the cold leave his bones and his heart race. Liza loved him with all her heart, and all her soul. If he was going to survive this, it would be with her by his side.

They kissed, and headed inside.

The curtains rose to a theater filled with squealing teenage girls. For the next forty-five minutes, Peter put everything he had into making his young fans happy. It wasn't easy. He could not rid himself of the haunting feeling that Wolfe might strike at any moment. The first half ended to a long ovation, and he stood in the wings as the stage was prepared for the next portion of the show. Zack spoke to him through his earpiece.

"No sign of Wolfe."

"Did you check outside the theater?" Peter asked.

"Sure did. The security company I hired has two guys patrolling the street. They radio in every few minutes. Everything's quiet."

"Tell them to be on the lookout."

"Peter, he's not here. Trust me."

"I can feel him in my bones, Zack. He's out there, waiting for me."

"If Wolfe enters the building, he's mine. I've got a score to settle with that guy."

Zack was ticked off. Peter had never questioned his head of security before, and realized how strange it sounded. "Sorry, Zack. Guess I'm just being paranoid. Thanks for checking in."

"Talk at you later," Zack said.

The second half began with Peter standing on the empty stage, ready to take requests from the audience. It was the most difficult part of the show, for he never knew which routines his audience might ask him to perform. The house lights were raised, letting him get a clear look at the sea of eager young faces. A dozen hands shot into the air.

"I see that we're all ready," he said with a laugh. "The pair of twins sitting in the second row, please stand up, and tell us your names."

A pair of identical twins rose in their seats. Both had pigtails and faces filled with freckles. In a squeaky voice, one of them said, "Hi. My name is Lorna, and this is my sister Lauren. We've been to your show ten times."

"Ten times? Then I bet you know how every trick is done," Peter said.

"I wish!" Lorna replied.

"What would you like me to do, Lorna and Lauren?"

"Read our futures."

"At the same time?"

"Yes," they chorused.

"That's quite an unusual request. I've never read two people's minds at the same time. Let's give it a try. I want you to hold hands, and concentrate. Are you ready?"

The twins clasped hands and squinched up their faces. Reading the minds of children was easy compared to adults, children having experienced so little in their lives. Peter looked into their minds and saw two futures filled with hope and promise.

"You both wish to become fashion designers and create your own line of clothes, although one of you also would like to be an actress on Broadway," he began. "I'd tell you which one, only you look too much alike for me to be sure. You have an aunt who lives in the south of France who would like you to come visit this summer. One of you wants to go, the other doesn't. I see you both going, and having a wonderful time. How am I doing so far?"

"Incredible," Lorna said.

"Awesome," her twin chorused.

Peter wished he had a dollar for every time a teenager told him his magic was awesome. As he started to continue, he noticed that the twins looked different. Their faces had changed, and were now bruised and bloodied, while their cute pigtails had grown into full heads of hair. He swallowed hard. They had turned into Milly and Holly.

It was a sign from the other side. But what did it mean?

Then, he noticed their eyes. Lifeless.

They were both dead. Something dropped in the pit of his stomach. Wolfe was about to kill his friends. He had to get off the stage.

"That's all I'm seeing. Thank you very much," he said.

"Tell us more," the twin that looked like Milly begged.

He couldn't concentrate, and shook his head. "Sorry."

"Please!" they chorused.

"Come on, everyone. Let's give them a big round of applause," he said.

The audience started to clap. The applause had a strangely hollow sound. To his horror, he realized that every member of his fan club had also changed. Rows of dead Millys and dead Hollys confronted him, their clapping motions stiff and awkward.

"What's wrong?" Liza asked through his earpiece.

"The spirits are communicating to me," he whispered into the mike in his shirt collar. "I've got to get off the stage."

"But this is your fan club. You can't let them down."

He wasn't thinking straight, and couldn't have continued if his very life depended on it.

"I can't."

"*Peter*. These are teenage girls. They'll be crushed."

"I'm freaking."

"Do it anyway. Finish the routine, damn it."

He gave it his best, and stepped to the foot of the stage. "Who'd like to be next?"

"Take me!" A young man wearing a ridiculous fake moustache stood in the aisle in the very back of the theater. Snoop to the rescue. When tricks in the show broke bad, his assistant had been trained to jump in, and salvage the routine. It was an old ploy developed by Houdini, and had stood the test of time.

"Your name," Peter said.

"Jerry Smith, and I want my future read," Snoop said.

"Very well, Jerry. Please concentrate. I see a shiny race car. Is it yours?"

"Why, that's amazing. Yes, it is."

"Formula One?"

"Yes—how did you know that?"

"You don't look like a NASCAR kind of guy. You race cars for a living, which is something you've wanted to do since you were a little boy. You're visiting New York with your family, celebrating a race you just won. In a few days you'll fly off to Europe, where you plan to race in all the major events."

"That's impossible. How did you know *that*?"

It was crude to use Snoop as a plant like this, but Peter had no other choice. The sea of dead faces stared at him with morbid fascination.

"I see a long future for you in car-racing. One day,

you may own your own team. I'd tell you good luck, but I don't think you're going to need it."

The hollow clapping began. Peter signaled that he wanted the stage lights turned off. Hurrying into the wings, he spent a moment composing himself. Then, he pulled out his cell phone. Holly's number was the first he called, Milly's the next. He left messages on voice mail, telling them their lives were in danger.

"What are you doing?" Liza appeared beside him.

"Wolfe is going to attack my friends, Milly and Holly."

"What are you talking about?"

"I just had a vision. I have to warn them. Please go out there, and make up some story that I've fallen ill, and that the show is cancelled."

"You can't be serious."

Peter took his girlfriend by the shoulders. "The face of every girl in the audience turned into Milly and Holly. They were both dead. He'd killed them."

"No, they didn't. It's just a bunch of giggling teenagers."

"I saw it. You have to believe me."

"Do you know where your friends are?"

"No. I need to go find them."

"You're leaving right now?"

"Yes."

"Peter, this is insane. Call the police. They can protect them better than you can."

The police hadn't protected his parents, or Madame Marie and her husband, and Peter knew they wouldn't be able to save Milly and Holly. When it came to dealing with the spirit world, the police were always one step behind.

"Offer everybody a rain check," he said.

Liza stepped back. The look in her eyes bordered on pure disdain.

"Please don't do this."

"I have to go. If that doesn't work, give them a full refund."

"Whatever you say, Peter." And then she was gone.

25

Wolfe waited until dark to hunt Millicent Adams. According to the information he'd found on the Internet, she was considered *the* psychic in New York, and counted many of the city's rich and famous as her clients. She worked out of a luxurious apartment building called the Dakota on the Upper West Side across from Central Park. Finding her would not be difficult, even in a city as big as this one.

Still wearing his elaborate disguise, he left the Hotel Carter at nine o'clock, and walked to the busy Times Square subway station at 42nd Street. Soon he was packed in a subway car with a mob of people hooked into iPhones or reading a newspaper.

Just north of 59th Street, the car hit a bump in the track, and the lights went out. The smell of fear emanated from his fellow passengers like cheap perfume. The day his hearing had changed, so had his other senses, and his sense of smell was better than a dog's. Human beings threw off a variety of smells depending upon the mood they were in, and Wolfe knew what each smell meant. It had saved his life many times.

He exited at the 81st Street station. At the top of the stairs was a man hawking the *New York Post*. He bought a copy. Splashed across the front page was his picture with the words HAVE YOU SEEN THIS MAN? Everyone in the bloody city was looking for him.

He found an isolated spot outside of the station and opened up the newspaper beneath a dim street light. There was a long story explaining his various misdeeds. The police had upped their reward to $100,000 for his capture. The captain of the NYPD was quoted as saying, "We're going to nail this son of a bitch, so help me God!"

Wolfe did not scare easily. But the *Post* story was troubling. It mentioned the tattoo on his neck and included a drawing of it. It was like having a scarlet letter stitched to his chest. He had to get the damn thing removed.

Stuffing the paper into a trash bin, he headed south on Central Park West, walking along the wide sidewalk beside the park. The smells emanating from the park were more varied than in the subway. Joggers panting, lovers in between breaths, a baby needing its diaper changed, someone smoking a joint. At the corner of 72nd Street, he caught another smell coming out of the oak trees inside the park. It made every hair on the back of his neck stand up.

A waist-high concrete wall separated the sidewalk from the park. Wolfe pressed his stomach to it. A mob of black crows stared back at him from the tree limbs. As a soldier, he'd learned about crows. They were meant to guide spirits into the afterlife, and were considered dark omens on the battlefield. He tried to put their presence out of his mind.

A more pleasant smell invaded his head. On the corner, a vendor sold roasted chestnuts from a metal cart.

Wolfe bought a bag, and asked for directions to find the famed Dakota.

"You must be from out of town," the vendor said.

"Is it that obvious?" Wolfe said.

"It's across the street."

He had a look. The Dakota took up the entire block, and was as imposing as a medieval fortress. He spotted no less than a dozen security cameras secured to the front, a doorman, and more security people inside the lobby. No wonder the city's elite chose to live here. Breaking into the building would be difficult, if not downright impossible.

He thought back to the articles he'd read about Millicent Adams. Milly, as her friends called her, was a creature of habit, and dined each night at a quaint French restaurant on West 86th Street, where she sat at her own table, often in the company of a friend, ate a simple meal of broiled fish and vegetables, and drank a single glass of white Chablis. She'd been following this routine for forty years, and had ventured out every night, regardless of the weather. Would tonight be any different? Something told him it wouldn't.

He ate his bag of warm nuts. To throw off any curious passersby, he glanced at his watch every few minutes, as if awaiting someone's arrival. He also regularly took out his cell phone, and pretended to be having a conversation.

He repeated the charade until nine-thirty. By now, the vendor had gone home, and the block was deserted. He was soaked to the skin, and his cheap suit had started to fall apart.

Then, his luck changed.

A taxi pulled up to the Dakota, and Milly Adams climbed out, wearing a mink stole and a mink hat. With her was a young woman in jeans and a sweater. The second woman was Milly's spitting image. This had to be Holly Adams, the last name on his list.

Wolfe smiled through chattering teeth. What was the expression? Kill two birds with one stone. Or two psychics with one pair of hands.

He started across the street.

His victims stood beneath the building's awning, oblivious to the danger they were in. That was good, because he planned to snap them both like twigs.

The front door opened, and a doorman stepped out. Beneath his blazer was something substantial, perhaps a gun, or billy club. Wolfe decided to take the doorman out first, just to be safe. The element of surprise was his. It was all he'd ever needed.

A new person came through the door. Wolfe instantly recognized him. It was Peter Warlock, dressed in his magic-show outfit. *Three birds with one stone,* he thought.

"Where have the two of you been?" Warlock said. "I've been looking *everywhere* for you."

Milly Adams dismissed him with a wave, and went inside. Her niece gave the young magician a kiss on the cheek, and followed her aunt through the front door.

Wolfe stopped in his tracks. These women were not stupid. They knew their lives were in danger, yet had chosen to venture outside. Had he missed something?

Rain poured down the back of his collar. He heard a noise that was louder than the rain. Like a tornado bearing down on him. He slowly turned around. The army of crows was flapping their wings and shrieking at him in a mad chorus. The power of their wings was so great that the rain was blown sideways. They looked ready to rip him apart.

Wolfe was not fond of animals. A tiger had nearly torn him to pieces in Kenya, and a monkey had chewed off a piece of his ear in India. The crows looked particularly formidable. And there were lots of them.

He who runs away, lives to fight another day.

A soldier had said that. A very smart soldier. He turned away from the building, and headed up the street. The crows' shrieking was so loud that he couldn't think. He had experienced fear many times in his life, but nothing like this.

He took off at a dead run. He heard a sound like a page being torn out of a magazine, amplified a thousand times. He glanced over his shoulder.

The crows were after him.

He looked for a restaurant to duck into, or an alley, but there was nothing. At the next corner, a cab pulled up, and a well-dressed couple disembarked. Wolfe grabbed the door before it closed, and hopped in.

"Go north," he told the driver.

The cab sped away, and Wolfe fell back in his seat. The idea of retirement had never seemed more inviting than it did right now. A banging sound broke his concentration.

"What was that?" the driver asked.

Wolfe turned around. A single crow had caught up to them. It slammed its beak against the glass while its bloodred eyes tore a hole into his soul.

"Something's attacking my cab!"

The driver drifted over to the curb and hit the brakes. As he opened his door, the crow flew into the cab. Flying through the open partition into the backseat, it bit Wolfe's face. Wolfe grabbed the bird with both hands, and pulled it away. Clutched in its beak was a piece of his disguise, the rest of which hung off his face like dead skin. The bird shrieked like an angry schoolteacher before going limp in his hands.

Wolfe was shaking as he got out of the cab, and tossed the dead bird into the gutter. The driver stood a safe distance away, looking at him fearfully.

"You're a zombie!"

Wolfe decided to steal the cab. He'd broken so many damn laws that it didn't really matter. Soon he was speeding north on Amsterdam, wondering how he was going to explain this to the men who employed him.

Movement in his mirror caught his eye. Two blocks behind him, Peter Warlock was running down the middle of the street, chasing him. He'd seen a lot of strange things in New York, and the notion that the young magician might somehow outrun the cab did not seem as crazy as it might have a few days ago.

He punched the gas, and watched Warlock disappear.

26

"Coward!" Peter yelled at the fleeing cab.

He stopped in the middle of Central Park West as the cab's taillights faded away. He'd caught the license plate, and pulled out Special Agent Garrison's business card from his wallet, and punched the FBI agent's number into his cell phone. Garrison picked up on the first ring.

"Who's this?" Garrison asked suspiciously.

"This is Peter Warlock. Wolfe just tried to attack two of my friends. He's now heading north on Central Park West in a stolen yellow cab, license plate number 9AH 4B7."

"How's he dressed?"

"He's wearing a cheap dark suit and some kind of fake skin that makes him look like an old man. I didn't recognize him at first. A bird tore most of it away."

"A bird?"

"I'll explain later."

"Right. Was anyone hurt?"

Peter looked at the cab driver, whom Wolfe had knocked to the ground, being helped to his feet by a well-dressed couple. People were always saying that New Yorkers were cold and unfriendly, yet in fact the opposite was true. The driver was shaken up, but no worse for wear.

"The driver got knocked on the head, but it looks like he's going to be okay," Peter said.

"What about your two friends? Did Wolfe hurt them?"

"No, but he got close."

"I'm alerting the NYPD. Hopefully, they've got a patrol car in the area, and can run him down. I need to know your friends' names, so the police can get a statement from them."

"I can't tell you that."

"You're playing a dangerous game. Your friends are in danger, and so are you."

"Telling you their names won't change that," Peter said.

He hung up the phone and started walking back to the Dakota. A black object lying in the gutter caught his eye. It was one of Milly's crows, its body broken and lifeless. He picked it up, remembering all the times he'd seen the crows perched in the oak trees across from the building. Every psychic had secrets they did not share, or a past they did not talk about. The crows were part of Milly's past, and he knew little of their history.

Holly was waiting inside the lobby. The shock of what had happened had sunk in, and her face was ashen. Seeing the dead bird, she let out a tiny sob.

"Oh, no."

"You weren't supposed to go out," Peter said.

"My aunt thought it would be okay if we went to dinner together."

"It wasn't okay. Damn it, Holly. Wolfe came *that* close."

His voice was trembling, and he tried to control himself. Seeing into the future was often terrifying. It was more terrifying when no one would listen.

"Please don't be angry," Holly said as they rode the elevator upstairs.

"I have every right to be angry," he said. "You're behaving like a child."

"Peter, please stop. I can't stand when you act like this."

Holly had never had her loved ones taken away from her. Hopefully, she never would.

"Just listen to me," he said. "We have these amazing powers, but in reality, we're no different than anyone else. We can still get sick, still die. We're mortal. Stop acting like you're not."

Her lower lip trembled. "Is that how I'm acting?"

"Yes."

"All right. I'll stop. Now please calm down."

"Right."

"I mean it. Your face is so *angry.* I hate when you get like this."

"When did I ever get like this?"

"When we were young, and you babysat for me. Sometimes, you just boiled with anger."

"Did you listen to me then?"

"Stop it. Please."

He stared at the elevator door. The anger had been buried inside of him for as long as he could remember. When it reared its ugly head, there was no getting out of its way.

"I'll try," he said.

Milly met them at the front door to her apartment. She took the dead crow out of Peter's hands and held it protectively against her chest. With her free hand, she touched the side of Peter's face, and brushed back an errant strand of hair.

"Thank you for bringing him," she said.

"He died trying to protect you and Holly," Peter said.

"I know he did. Please come inside."

She took them to her study. It was a small room with floor-to-ceiling bookshelves lined with musty-smelling volumes on the occult. Milly had them sit on a leather couch, then wedged herself between them. She stroked the dead bird's feathers while staring into space.

"These crows have been a part of my family for three centuries," Milly said. "They first appeared when my ancestor, Mary Glover, was hanged for being a witch. Mary called out to the crows right before she was put to death, and the crows replied by making a terrible cawing sound. They've been making that sound ever since. Holly, would you fetch a towel from the kitchen?"

Holly rose from the couch and walked out of the room. Peter had been waiting for this opportunity, and placed his hand on Milly's sleeve. "I need to speak with you in private."

"Not tonight, Peter. I'm tired and upset, as I imagine you are as well."

"You and Max can't avoid me forever," he said.

"Are we avoiding you?"

"It's beginning to feel that way."

Holly returned with a dish towel, which Milly used to wrap the dead bird. Peter sensed she was not looking forward to this conversation any more than he was. Milly spoke to her niece in a quiet voice. "Holly, be a dear, and leave us alone. Peter and I need to speak in private."

"About what?" Holly asked, sounding annoyed.

"The past."

"How can you be keeping secrets at a time like this?" Holly asked.

"I'm sorry, my dear."

Holly's shoes clomped across the wood floors. Milly laughed under her breath.

"I would give anything to be her age again," she said.

Peter took the dead bird from her and placed it on the desk. Returning to the couch, he sat down beside the woman who'd help raise him, and took her frail, liver-spotted hands in both his own. "I want you to tell me about the children of Marble, and how my parents became part of the Order of Astrum," he said.

"Who told you that?"

"My girlfriend. She and my assistant hacked the FBI's computer. There was an article about the Order that claimed my parents were founding members. Is this true?"

His words had a powerful effect on her. Or perhaps, it was the memory being dredged to the surface after being buried for so long that caused her to pause. Her eyes took on the faraway expression of a person lost in a daydream.

"I don't know the entire story, and I'm not sure that anyone does," Milly said. "But I will tell you what your mother told me. Perhaps you will be able to figure out the rest."

"Please," he said.

"One day when your parents were small children, they were playing with three boys from their village. It was the dead of winter, and they were making a snowman in a field. Suddenly they heard a noise that sounded like a baby crying, and decided to investigate. They left the field and entered a forest, where they walked down a path until they came to a frozen pond where the townspeople sometimes ice-skated. Stuck in the middle of the pond was a black cat, which appeared to be having a problem standing on the ice, and was crying for help.

"I suppose your mother had heightened sensibilities at a young age, for she immediately became suspicious. She had never seen the cat before, and couldn't understand how it had reached the middle of the pond, yet could not get back. Your mother suggested that they find a grown-up, and let them deal with the situation. The other children scoffed at her, and said they didn't need an adult, they could save the animal themselves.

"The four boys ventured onto the pond, and tried to rescue the cat. Your father turned to your mother, and asked her to join them. I suppose the attraction between them had already begun, for your mother agreed, and walked onto the ice.

"Then, a peculiar thing happened. The cat stopped crying, and became deathly still. Your mother remembers that it began to make a strange sound, as if snorting at them. The next thing she knew, the ice began to crack all around her. The children screamed. One by one, they fell into the icy water. Your mother was the last to go into the drink. She had not taken her eyes off the cat, which proceeded to run away, and disappear into the woods."

"It wasn't hurt," Peter said.

Milly shook her head.

"Was it a trap?"

She nodded.

"But by who?"

"Whoever owned the cat, I suppose."

"I'm sorry. Please go on."

"The children were heavily clothed, and quickly sank to the bottom of the pond," Milly continued. "Your mother said it was very dark, and quite surreal. She could feel the others thrashing about in the water, but could not see them. She tried to save herself, but soon ran out of energy. Finally, she had no choice, and gave up."

Peter swallowed hard. "What happened then?"

"That, as my generation used to say, is the sixty-four-thousand-dollar question. Your mother said they should have died. None of them could swim, nor were they wearing anything that would have helped them float. They should have died, and that would have been the end of their short, uneventful lives. Those were the exact words that your mother used when she told me the story. Only the children of Marble didn't die. Something happened in the depths of that pond which forever changed them. They floated to the surface, and climbed out through the holes in the ice, and hurried back to the village."

"How did they climb out if they couldn't swim?"

"Your mother never explained that part."

"You must have some theory."

Milly shrugged and did not reply. Peter felt himself growing frustrated.

"Did they know they were psychic at that point?" he asked.

"That is a question I asked your mother," Milly said. "She told me that it happened a short while later. Your father was pillaging the attic in his house when he found a chest that had belonged to his great-grandparents. The chest contained a talking board carved out of old wood with a matching planchette."

"You mean a Ouija board?" Peter asked.

"A Ouija board is a game for children and drunk adults," Milly said. "A talking board is used when speaking with the dead. The talking board in the attic of your father's house was such a device. It had been carved from a single piece of wood, and contained the twenty-six letters of the alphabet, the numbers one through ten, and the arching sweep of a crescent moon with a black cat sitting within the moon and wearing a pentacle pendant around its neck. The cat bore a striking resemblance to the cat that had drawn the children to the pond, hence your father's interest in it.

"Your father took the talking board from the attic, and went down the street to where your mother lived. He showed it to her, and she agreed that the cat on the board matched the cat they'd seen. She suggested they play a game with the board, and ask it a question. They sat at the kitchen table, placed their hands on the planchette, and asked the board if it was sunny or cloudy outside. To their surprise, the planchette raced across the board under its own power, and answered them. That was the beginning of the séances. Later, they invited their other three friends to join them."

Peter stared into space. For some reason, he'd always assumed that his mother and father had been born psychic, just as he had, and never considered that something might have happened during their childhoods which made them this way. It put a spin on things which he did not completely understand.

"How did they become the Order of Astrum?" he asked.

"I asked your mother that very question," Milly replied. "She said it was your father's idea. Your father felt they needed a name for their little group. He had read a story about Aleister Crowley, who had practiced dark magic during the turn of the century. Crowley called his group Argentium Astrum, which in Latin means silver star. Your father thought this was just splendid, so he named their group the Order of Astrum."

"So it was all a game."

Milly leaned into him. "Yes! Your parents never meant for it to be anything more than that. The horrible things came later, when the children grew up."

"Do you know why?"

"Money." She let out a deep breath, and seemed suddenly fatigued. "The other three were all failures at the work they did. They banded together, and decided to use their powers for financial gain. Your parents were against it, and left England and came to New York."

"Is that why my parents were killed? Because they wouldn't play along?"

"That was always my assumption." Milly rose from the couch, signaling that she was done. "It's been a long night. I need to get my rest."

Peter rose as well. There was no doubt in his mind that his parents had sworn Milly to secrecy, and breaking that vow had not been easy for her. He put his arms around her, and rested his chin on her head. "Thank you," he whispered. "Thank you so much."

"You're welcome, my dear boy," she said.

27

It had grown late, and Milly was tired. She bid Peter goodnight and headed off to bed. Peter passed through the living room on his way out. He sensed the presence of a third person.

"Holly?"

He saw an indentation in the cushion of a love seat. Had Holly been sitting in the living room, waiting for him? If so, then why had she left? He wanted to speak with her, and headed down the hallway to the kitchen, where he pushed in the swinging door.

Holly sat at the round kitchen table with a sullen look on her face. On the table was a plate of her aunt's homemade chocolate cookies.

"Still mad at me?" he asked.

"What do you think." She sulked.

They had never fought well, even as kids. He grabbed a quart of skim milk out of the fridge and retrieved from the cupboard two glasses, which he placed on the table before pulling up a chair. Holly eyed him sullenly as he filled the glasses to the brim and slid one toward her.

"Who said I wanted a glass of milk?"

"I did."

"But I don't."

"You always drink milk with your cookies."

"Stop treating me like a child. I hate when you do that."

"Pardon, madame."

Peter picked up his glass and made an imaginary toast. When he put it down, his lip was covered in a white moustache. Holly forced herself not to smile, and looked away. He bit into a cookie and made an *mmmm* sound. She couldn't help herself, and was soon eating one as well. The unhappy look would not leave her face.

"I'm sorry for upsetting you in the elevator," he said. "I was out of line."

"You were mean. And ugly. I didn't like it."

"I was out of my mind with worry. When I saw Wolfe come after you and your aunt, I lost it."

"Did you have to take your anger out on me?"

"You were the closest target."

"That's no excuse, Peter."

He was not going to win this argument, so he just finished his cookie. He glanced at Holly out of the corner of his eye, hoping her anger would fade. She still looked furious.

"I want you to explain something to me," she said after an excruciatingly long minute had passed. "How can you tell me that you have feelings for me, and then treat me so rudely a few hours later? How does that work?"

"You know what they say. You always hurt the one you love," he said.

"Is that supposed to be a joke?"

"It's a song by the Mills Brothers. 'You always hurt the one you love, the one you shouldn't hurt at all.' Never heard of it? Well, it's true, and I'm sorry I hurt you."

"That moustache on your lip looks ridiculous."

Peter found a towel and cleaned his face. The conversation had turned awkward. He'd spent a lot of time with Holly growing up, less so as an adult. She seemed a different person than the one he'd known as a kid. Had he a few hours to spare, he might have been able to get to the bottom of what was bothering her, only he needed to call Liza, and hear how his fan club had reacted to his bolting from the show. Hopefully, she had kept the damages to a minimum.

"I need to go," he said. "When this is over, and Wolfe is caught, I want to take you out to lunch. We need to talk."

"I'll have to check my calendar."

"Please say yes."

"Can I pick the restaurant?"

"Of course you can."

She met his gaze for the first time. "All right, yes."

"Thank you. Good night." He rose from his chair and went to the door.

"I want to help," Holly said out of the blue.

The words caught him by surprise. He turned around slowly.

"What do you mean?"

"I want to help you catch Wolfe," she said. "I have powers, too. We could work together, and track him down. Two heads are better than one."

Holly still didn't get it. Wolfe was a monster, and so were the men who employed him. The best way to deal with monsters was to stay away from them.

"Do you really want to help me?" he asked.

Her face lit up. "Yes!"

"Good. Convince your aunt to stay indoors until we find him. Also, go find Reggie, and convince him to stay inside as well. Something tells me Reggie is still wandering around Central Park at all hours, conversing with the statues."

"Damn it, that's not what I meant! I want to help you. We could be a team."

"I don't think that's a good idea."

She made another of her faces. He had seen people run away from her when she made faces, they were that powerful. He held his ground without flinching.

"Why not?" she seethed.

"Because you could get hurt, that's why."

"I'm willing to take that chance."

"Well, I'm not. I couldn't live with myself if anything happened to you."

"When did this just become about you? Wolfe's trying to kill all of us."

"Let me deal with him. I have a bead on him. I see signs before he's going to strike, and can react to what he's doing."

"What are you saying? That I'll only slow you down?"

She had taken the words right out of his mouth. He gave her a tired smile.

"Good night. I'll call you tomorrow first thing."

"Go to hell, Peter."

He waited until he was outside before turning on his cell phone. It was still raining, and a howling wind was blowing down Central Park West. He called Liza, and got voice mail. He didn't leave a message, hoping his girlfriend wasn't still angry with him. He tried the number at the brownstone. Still no answer.

A cab pulled up, and the driver looked at him through the windshield. Peter hopped into the back, and gave the driver his address. Soon they were driving toward the east side of town. Then he called Snoop. His assistant sounded more than a little upset when he answered.

"Peter—where the heck have you been? You had me worried, man," Snoop said.

"Sorry. I've had my hands full. What happened after I left?"

"Well, I've got good news, and bad news. Which do you want to hear first?"

Peter braced himself. "I could use some good news. Give me that first."

"Sure enough. Liza saved the day after you split. She walked onto the stage, and told the audience that you'd been battling the flu, and could no longer continue. She made it sound like you'd dragged yourself from your deathbed to do the show. She was awesome."

"My fan club didn't revolt?"

"On the contrary. They totally understood, and gave you a standing ovation. Liza rescheduled the date for the end of next month. Everyone left happy."

"Whew. That's great."

"I thought you'd like it."

"So, what's the bad news?"

"You sitting down?"

"Uh-huh."

"Liza quit."

Peter brought his hand up to his face. "You've got to be kidding me."

"I wouldn't kid you about something like that. She came up to me after we closed the theater, and said she was leaving the show. She's giving you two weeks' notice so you can hire another assistant, and train her. I tried to talk her out of it, and she shut me down. Did you two have World War III or something? She was totally pissed."

"She's mad at me. I didn't realize she was that mad."

"Mad is an understatement. You need to talk to her, man."

"Any idea where she is?"

"She went back to your place. I think she's packing her things."

Peter cupped his hand over the phone, and addressed the driver. "Can you go any faster? I'll double the fare." The cab sped up, and he lowered his hand. "Did she say anything else?"

"I asked her if you two guys were done," Snoop said.

"And?"

"She turned away and started crying."

"Thanks, Snoop. I'll call you later."

"I'm here if you need me."

Peter folded the phone, wondering if he could still get Liza back. They'd had fights before, but never anything like this. The cab entered Central Park, and began to race down the twisting roads. He stared out the window, wishing he could turn his life back forty-eight hours, and erase everything that had happened. *What a trick that would be,* he thought.

L iza was in the living room when he entered the brownstone.

"Are your friends all right?" she asked through clenched teeth.

"Yes. I got to them in time," he replied.

"Glad to hear it."

"Please don't leave."

"Who told you I was leaving?"

"Snoop did. Say it isn't so. Please."

"My mind's made up. If you'll excuse me, I was in the middle of something."

Taking out her cell phone, Liza snapped a photo of a stuffed panda named Butch that sat on the mantel over the fireplace. Butch could find playing cards, blow perfect smoke rings, and tell the future by banging on a drum. It was all a trick, courtesy of some amazing radio-controlled devices, but Liza had fallen in love with the little guy anyway. She hoisted her suitcase off the floor, and headed for the door, brushing past him. He wondered how he'd managed to ruin two relationships in one day.

"At least give me a second chance. I deserve that, don't I?"

The suitcase fell from her hand. She crossed her arms in front of her chest, and gave him a soulful stare. "Tell me something. How can someone who can read people's minds be so clueless about their feelings?"

"I don't mean to be."

"But you are. You ran out on those kids. You should be ashamed of yourself."

"I had to save my friends."

"You couldn't have called the police? Come on, Peter, when did you turn into a superhero?"

"I'm not a superhero."

"You're sure acting like one. Anytime you think something bad is going to happen, you go flying out the door without caring about the people you leave behind."

"I'm sorry."

"Stop saying that."

"But it's true. Look, this will be over soon, and things will go back to normal."

"Things will never be back to normal," she said, sounding ready to cry. "You're not the person I thought you were. Let me rephrase that. Half of you is the person I thought I knew; the other half is a strange dude with psychic powers who's been leading a secret life none of his friends knew about. That's the guy I'm having a problem with."

"I didn't want to keep secrets from you."

"But you did. And you're still doing it. I don't know who you are."

"I haven't changed that much, have I?"

"Yes, you have. You act like someone possessed."

"You're exaggerating. It's not that bad."

"Yes, it is. You're changing, and I don't know why. Do you?"

He thought back to what Milly had told him. His parents had fallen into a lake with three of their little friends, and been miraculously saved by a spirit from the other side. But had it been a good spirit, or a bad spirit? His parents had changed the course of a war, yet had also been founding members of a murderous cult. He had no way of knowing what type of spirit had guided them. And if he didn't know what spirit had guided his parents, he couldn't know which spirit was guiding him. Liza wasn't the only one who was confused.

"No," he said quietly.

"No what?" she said, sounding exasperated.

"No, I don't know why I'm changing. But I'm going to find out."

"Well, send me a postcard."

"You're not going to give me another chance?"

"You've run out of those."

He followed her out of the brownstone. The rain was coming down so hard that it made it difficult to see. At the corner she waved frantically for a cab. It was as if she couldn't get away from him fast enough.

"I'll do anything you want," he shouted over the storm.

She spun around. "Anything?"

"Yes."

"Do you really mean that?"

"Yeah. Just name it."

"Stop doing these crazy séances, and come back to the real world."

"I can't do that. It's who I am."

"Then good-bye."

A cab braked at the curb, splashing them both. Liza rammed her suitcase into the backseat, hopped in, and slammed the door. Kneeling down, he gazed at her through the window. He mouthed the words *Please don't go*. She shook her head.

The cab sped away. He walked back to his empty brownstone, wondering if his heart might break. Liza had made him feel *whole*. Without her, he was nothing.

He looked to the sky. Was this his reward for doing the right thing? It hardly seemed fair, and he let out a frightening yell.

"God damn it!"

A car alarm pierced the air. It was quickly followed by another car alarm, and then another. Within seconds, every vehicle parked on the street was blaring.

He looked up and down the street in fear. His powers had made those alarms go off. He concentrated, and tried to turn them off.

Nothing doing.

He hurried inside his brownstone before his neighbors came out, and saw what he'd done.

28

Lying in bed that night, Peter stared at the side of the bed where Liza normally slept. Her leaving hadn't seemed real a few hours ago. Now it did, and the pain was tearing a hole in his heart.

He rolled onto his back and gazed at the plaster ceiling. Tomorrow was Monday, and the theater was dark. Normally, he and Liza would sleep in, and spend the afternoon plundering an uncharted area of the city. New York had hundreds of neighborhoods, thousands of shops, and even more restaurants, and they'd tried to visit them all.

He retrieved his cell phone from the night table. He'd

sent Liza several text messages, and apologized in every conceivable way he knew how. Still no response.

A clap of thunder shook the walls. He threw on a bathrobe, and went to the window which looked out on the courtyard. Some of the best séances he'd ever conducted had occurred during bad storms, and he'd assumed it had something to do with the air being filled with electricity. Now, he found himself not caring about the spirits, or anything associated with them. He just wanted her back.

He thought about her request. *Stop doing these crazy séances, and come back to the real world.* Up until two days ago, he would have said yes; his love for her was that great. Up until two days ago, he would have been able to walk away from it. But now he couldn't. The spirit world had taken over, and he couldn't have run away from it if his life depended upon it. But Liza deserved better than what he'd given her. She'd committed herself to him, and he'd repaid her by keeping her in the dark about who he was. There was a name for what he'd done. It was called being a shit.

His cell phone was vibrating. His heartbeat quickened as he grabbed it off the night table. Liza had sent him a text message.

"Thank you," he whispered.

He returned to the window, and read her message by the light of the storm.

P,

I'm sorry to run out on you, but you gave me no choice. You're scaring me. I don't know this person you've become.

Do you?

L

It was a good question. He'd done things in the past couple of days that he would never have dreamed of doing before, and the answer was as obvious as it was frightening.

No, he didn't.

He didn't know this person at all. This person had powers and feelings that were brand new to him. If he wanted to get back together with Liza, he needed to find out who this person was. For her sake, and for his own.

But how? He supposed it had to start with knowing who his parents were. The family tree, as it were. Then he might understand himself a little better.

He went into the bathroom. Reaching beneath his bathroom sink, he removed the mysterious DVD that he'd taken from the bookshelf in Lester Rowe's apartment. Maybe the DVD had the answers he was looking for, or could point him in the right direction.

His bedroom had a large entertainment unit built into the wall. Slipping the DVD into the player, he pulled up a chair, and sat a foot away from the giant screen. He had no films of his parents, just scrapbooks filled with aging photographs, and the ghostly images he carried in his head. He wondered what it would be like to see them again.

Moments later, he had his answer.

His mother's lovely face filled the screen. Her eyes were expressive, and her smile could light up a room. She said hello to the camera.

"Hey," he whispered back.

The camera pulled back. His mother was dressed as if going to the theater, and wore a strapless black evening gown and a string of white pearls. She sat at a table covered in black cloth with occult symbols painted on the fabric. Symbols were an important part of the spirit world, and every psychic worth his salt knew what they represented. The symbols on the cloth were new to him, and appeared to be a cross between a unicursal hexagram used to summon the spirits, and a common pentagram.

The camera pulled back even farther. His father sat to his mother's right at the table. The quintessential college professor, he favored rumpled sports jackets and never combed his hair. Now he wore a tailored suit, a white shirt with a button-down collar, and a tie with a gold stickpin. His goatee was neatly trimmed, and the part in his hair was as straight as an arrow.

They both looked like royalty. He hit pause with the remote, and spent a long moment staring at them. His eyes grew moist. It was an image that he would forever savor.

He hit play, and the film resumed. Out of the shadows appeared four other people, who took their places at the table. Two men, two women, all dressed in formal attire. It was Lester Rowe, Milly, Reggie Brown, and Madame Marie, all looking twenty years younger.

On the screen, his mother said, "Let's begin."

The other participants nodded agreement.

His father struck a match, and lit three white candles in the table's center. The lights in the dining room were dimmed. Everyone at the table joined hands.

His mother began to chant. She was soft-spoken, and he strained to pick up the words. Unexpectedly, things started to happen. First the candles' flames flickered, then various pieces of furniture began to move around, with a painting on the wall crashing to the floor. In a mirror hanging behind the table, a ghostly reflection appeared. It was a man whose face had melted on one side. The man was laughing, and appeared to be enjoying himself.

"What the hell," Peter said aloud.

His mother stopped chanting, and the face vanished from the mirror.

Everyone at the table seemed to relax.

Peter did as well.

His mother said, "Henry?"

His father reached beneath the table, and came up with a rectangular wood board. He moved the candles off to the side, and placed the board on their spot. The board looked ancient, and was covered in numbers, letters, and astrological signs. It was a talking board.

His mother said, "Ready, everyone?"

The others bobbed their heads. His father removed a heart-shaped planchette from his jacket pocket, and placed it onto the talking board. Everyone placed their fingertips onto the planchette, and scrunched up their faces. The planchette moved deliberately across the board, stopping briefly to touch on different letters and symbols, before moving on. Suddenly, his mother jerked in her chair as if being shocked by a cattle prod, while her face made horrible contortions. The other participants drew back in their chairs, clearly alarmed.

His father said, "Claire!"

His mother shook her head wildly, causing the pearls to flop around her neck. Her eyelids fluttered, revealing nothing but white. She had become possessed, and was no longer in control of herself. A stiff wind blew through the room, sending everyone's hair on end. The candles went out, throwing the room into darkness.

Peter squirmed in his chair. He tried to remind himself that it was just a film, but it didn't calm him down. His father relit the candles. Everyone was standing at their places except his mother, who'd collapsed onto the table and appeared to be passed out. His father gently lifted his mother's head, and spoke in her ear.

"Are you all right?"

His mother sat up straight in her chair. Her eyes were now bloodshot, her beautiful face dark and ragged with age. Her fingernails had grown several inches, and resembled talons. An evil spirit had invaded her body.

Jumping up, his mother tossed her husband across the room with a flick of the wrist. He crashed against a wall, and winced in pain.

His mother clawed viciously at the air, causing the others to coil away in fear. She was like a wild animal, and appeared fully capable of killing someone. This was not the same woman who'd nurtured and raised him; it simply couldn't be.

He tore his eyes away to look at the mirror behind the table. The visitor had returned to the glass, and was again laughing at everyone's expense.

He looked back at his mother. She was wrestling with Reggie, who was attempting to grab her by the wrists. Reggie was a foot taller and outweighed his mother by a hundred pounds. It didn't matter. His mother tossed poor Reggie over a chair like a child.

Lester Rowe was up next, grabbing his mother from behind in a bear hug. Lester was strong for his size, but no match for her. His mother broke free, and raked her fingernails across Rowe's face. Ribbons of blood appeared, prompting her to laugh wickedly.

His father returned to the picture. In his hand was a small brown bottle. He uncorked the bottle and tossed several drops of clear liquid his mother's way. She screamed, and protectively covered her head with her arms. His father calmly corked the bottle, and returned it to his pocket. Then he placed his hand comfortingly on his wife's shoulder.

"Claire," he said.

His mother struck out at him. The demon was slowly leaving her body, and the blow bounced harmlessly off her husband's chest.

"Claire," he said again.

His mother's body trembled. Then, slowly, she lowered her hands. Her face had returned to normal, and she looked beautiful again. She seemed bewildered by what had happened, and glanced nervously at her friends.

"What's going on?" his mother asked.

His father smiled thinly. So did the others in the room, who'd gathered around to comfort her. In the mirror, the demonic face faded away.

It was here that the film ended.

P eter lay in bed trying to make sense of what he'd seen. Before his very eyes, his mother had turned into a monster. Had the others not restrained her, there was no telling what she might have done. It didn't seem possible. His mother had been the most gentle person in the world, and had never hurt anyone, as far as he'd known.

He felt himself becoming one with the darkness. Was he also turning into a monster? Would he at some point start to physically change like his mother had, and become out of control? He shuddered to think how his friends would react. He had wanted to know the truth about his parents, and now he did. His mother and father and their three little friends had struck a deal with the Devil. In return for their lives being spared, they'd allowed the Devil to inhabit their bodies, and give them psychic powers. There was no other explanation for the things he'd just seen. This was the origin of the Order of Astrum. Its members were in league with the Devil, and had been since they were children.

Which made him what? A child of the Devil? He wasn't sure. All he knew for certain was that he was changing, and those changes had driven away the woman he loved.

He slipped out of bed, and threw on his robe. His body had grown cold again. He could feel evil nearby, stalking him. He looked around his darkened bedroom. He was alone.

Or was he?

He turned on the light and had another look. In the mirror above the dresser he saw the face from the séance. It was hideous to behold, burned so severely that one eye was gone. He had seen many horrible things in the spirit world, but none quite like this.

"Go away. Leave me alone."

The face began to laugh at him.

He picked up a shoe from the floor, and threw it at the mirror. The face vanished the moment the glass broke. He had sent it back to wherever it came from.

He sat on the edge of the bed. His heart was pounding out of control.

He thought back to Liza's text.

You're scaring me.

You and me both

PART III

THE WICKED ONE

29

"**D**o you have the money?"

Big Daddy, the ruthless dictator of Somaliland, nodded. He'd said little since arriving at the Order of Astrum's magnificent estate in the south of England a short while ago. Wearing a black leather cowboy hat and denim jacket, he looked more like the villain in an Italian spaghetti Western than the despot of a tiny African nation. According to the newspapers, his country's economy was in a shambles, and his people were close to revolting. He was a desperate man, and it showed on his face.

"I brought cash," the dictator said. "Now give me the information. I am anxious to know when the attack on New York will take place."

"You know the rules. I must first have the money."

Big Daddy made a call to his driver on his cell phone. The driver appeared at the front door of the mansion with a bulging suitcase. Big Daddy brought the suitcase into the parlor, and dumped stacks of fifty-pound-sterling notes around his host's feet.

"There is your money. Now tell me about the attack."

His host visually counted the money before proceeding.

"Very good. Now here is your information," his host said. "On Tuesday night, at a few minutes past ten o'clock, New York will experience a major attack in Times Square that will effectively shut down the city. Thousands will perish."

Big Daddy's eyes glistened. "Go on."

"I'm afraid that's all I can tell you."

"That is unacceptable. It is not enough."

His host did not like to be challenged, and his eyes narrowed. "I beg to differ. This information will serve two purposes, both being beneficial to you. It will send the stock market into a tailspin, as these types of events tend to do. You will benefit by shorting the market, and reaping huge financial rewards. Second, it will show the world how vulnerable the United States is. Both of these things serve your purposes, yes?"

"I must know more."

"Sorry, but that was our deal. It's not like you haven't done business with us before."

"Give me something, anything."

"I can't."

"Will the attack be a bomb? Guns?"

"I can't tell you that."

"How many men will be involved? A dozen? More?"

"Sorry."

"What organization are they affiliated with?"

"I can't share that information with you, either."

Big Daddy fumed. A long minute passed.

"Tell me where your powers come from," the dictator said.

His host leaned forward. Rarely did their clients ask them to pull back the curtains, and show them how things worked. "Do you want to know how we see into the future?"

"Yes—it fascinates me."

"Have you ever visited the spirit world?"

"No."

"There is a price of admission, if you will."

"I will pay."

"Are you sure?"

Big Daddy nodded, having no idea what lay in store.

"Very well. Come with me."

They walked outside the mansion. The sun was shining, and it was a spectacular day. The Order lived on a sprawling estate in a remote area of England not far from the Chiltern Hills. The area was not on a map, nor could it be found on Google Earth.

The property had been run down when the Order purchased it. Tapping into its vast fortune, the Order had transformed the grounds into an occult appendage of Versailles, with each building more ornate and spectacular than the next. One building housed a Pagan temple, where the elders could indulge in every sexual fantasy known to man. Another was a museum which stored their vast collection of rare paintings and artwork. Then there was the castle, complete with drawbridge and moat filled with brackish water, called the Palace of the Occult. It was here that the elders conducted séances and communicated with the Devil.

The two men crossed the bridge to the palace. By the entrance stood a pair of stone-faced guards with submachine guns. For security purposes, guards were strategically placed around the estate, with orders to shoot intruders on sight.

Inside the palace were a maze of twisting, dimly lit vestibules. They passed rows of Carrara marble statues and walls covered in gold leaf. On marble benches sat a trio of beautiful dark-skinned girls in diaphanous white and green garments. Plucked off the mean streets of India, they served as concubines for the elders and their guests.

The host stopped, and pointed at the girls.

"Pick one."

Big Daddy pointed at the middle girl. "Her."

His host waved his hand. The chosen girl's eyelids grew heavy, and she fell into a trance. She rose and followed them as if sleepwalking.

"Is she hypnotized?" Big Daddy asked.

His host did not reply.

"At least tell me where we're going. I don't like to be kept in the dark."

"Be patient. You'll understand soon enough."

At the end of the vestibule, a door opened by itself, and they entered a chamber whose walls were covered with burning white candles. In the room's center sat a wooden table with carved astrological signs. The girl climbed onto the table, and lay facing the ceiling.

His host opened a drawer on the table. A gold knife with sparkling jewels encrusted in the handle was taken out. He handed the knife to his guest.

"What do you want me to do with this?" Big Daddy asked.

"You don't know?"

"No. Tell me."

"I want you to plunge it into her heart."

"*What?* You can't be serious."

"If you want to be like me, then you must pay the price."

"Killing her is the price?"

His host laughed. "No. Giving up your soul."

"And if I do that, will I be like you?"

"If you kill her, you *can* be like me. It's how the process works."

Big Daddy stared at the sacrificial girl lying on the table. Many times he'd ordered his army to kill citizens of his country that he did not like. It was not the same as killing himself.

The dictator shook his head.

"Suit yourself. Give me the knife," his host said.

"Are you going to do it?"

"Yes. There is no going back with the Devil."

Big Daddy handed him the knife. His host raised the knife above his head, and plunged it into the girl's chest. She struggled briefly, her blood soaking her clothes. The candles on the walls flickered and died, plunging the room into darkness.

"What is happening?" the dictator asked.

"Be quiet," his host replied.

A cold wind passed through the chamber. The candles sparked back to life. The table was now empty, the dead girl gone.

They walked back to the mansion, where a limo waited in the drive. Big Daddy did not speak a word, and was visibly shaken. He climbed in, and the limo sped away.

His host waved good-bye. His name was Harold Webster, and he was a founding member of the Order. Webster was well into his sixties, yet looked like a man in his twenties. As part of his pact with the Devil, he had not grown old. In fact, he looked exactly as he had in the prime of his life. It seemed like the perfect arrangement, only his back, which he'd injured playing soccer, always ached. The Devil was funny that way—he never let his subjects forget who was in charge.

Webster walked back to the castle. A hallway took him to the Room of Spirits, an octagon-shaped chamber with an elevated platform on which sat three swivel chairs. Two of the chairs were occupied by the other founding members, Charles Gill and Edward Eastgate. Both looked as they had in their twenties. Gill's curse was a Cockney accent that he detested, while Eastgate's nose and teeth remained crooked from when he'd wrecked his car.

Webster took the third chair. It was strange, not growing old. The world around them changed, but they did not. It often made him wonder what would happen if they fell out of favor with the Devil. Would they all suddenly grow old and frail? There was no way of knowing. The Devil held all the cards, while they had nothing.

"How did it go?" Eastgate asked.

"He paid in full," Webster replied.

"Cash?"

"Of course. Now we just need to make sure that nothing goes wrong Tuesday night. The last thing we need is an angry African dictator after us."

"Do you think he'd do that?"

"Yes. His country is a shambles. He's a desperate man."

They fell silent. Taking risks was part of the game, and so was taking insurance.

"I'm thinking we should help Wolfe with his mission," Webster suggested.

It was Gill's turn to speak. "Help him how?"

"We could trick the police into thinking Wolfe is dead. That would give him some breathing room," Webster said.

"You mean a decoy?"

"It's worked before. I was in touch with our spy in New York. He found a subject we can use. The man is the same age as Wolfe, and shares the same physical characteristics."

The elders employed spies on every continent. The

operative in New York had provided the information on Wolfe's hit list, and was reliable.

"Then let's do it," Eastgate said.

"I agree," Gill said.

"Good. We're in agreement. Are you ready?"

His partners nodded. Webster fingered the control pad on the arm of his chair, causing the domed roof above their heads to slowly part. A hydraulic lift raised the platform into the air until they were outside of the palace, staring at a pale blue sky sprinkled with puffy white clouds.

"Face east toward New York," Webster instructed them.

They faced the pastoral countryside. Astral projection had been a part of the psychic's arsenal since the beginning of time. The elders had played with various forms, most recently the use of fiber optic cables to transmit themselves to various parts of the world. But the best way was still the old way.

"Manhattan, Museum of Natural History, Seventy-ninth Street and Central Park West," Webster said. "The decoy works as a night guard, and has just ended his shift. He's about to begin his commute home. He's driving a pale green van with black masking tape covering the rear window. It's a real junker."

The elders projected themselves across the ocean to the island of Manhattan. The sensation was like traveling in a bullet train, with scenery rushing past in a blinding blur of color and sound. It was still nighttime in New York, the city being drenched by a storm. The West Side was being hit hard, and traffic was at a standstill. A green van was not among the vehicles.

"I don't see him," Eastgate said.

"Perhaps he got off early from work," Webster said. "Let's check the Henry Hudson Parkway on the West Side."

They projected themselves onto the eleven-mile highway which ran from 72nd Street to the Westchester County boundary. Traffic there resembled a parking lot as well.

"I see him," Gill said. "He's at the toll bridge over the river with the strange name."

"You mean the Harlem River," Webster said.

"That's it. The decoy is about to pass through a tollbooth."

They projected themselves up the parkway to the tollbooth where the van waited in line. The decoy was at the wheel, eating a submarine sandwich dripping with mayonnaise.

"That's him. Are we ready?" Webster asked.

"Ready," Eastgate said.

"Ready," Gill said.

"On the count of three. One . . . two . . . three!"

The elders projected themselves inside the van. Using the collective power of their minds, they created an image inside the van that was not real. The driver became Wolfe, who was also eating a submarine sandwich. The false image lasted only a few seconds. Just long enough for the surveillance camera above the tollbooth to capture it, and transmit it back to the New York Police Department, the FBI, and every other law enforcement agency that was hunting for Wolfe. Then, the image disappeared, and the decoy was back.

Webster fell back into his chair. "Done."

"How long do you think it will take?" Gill asked.

"Hard to say. The weather being what it is."

They watched the van head into Westchester County. Traffic had thinned out, and the van got onto the Saw Mill River Parkway, and picked up speed. Within minutes, a pair of highway patrol cars began to follow. The officers inside the patrol cars wore body armor, and cradled automatic rifles in their laps. They did not seem in any hurry to pull the van over.

"There's must be a roadblock ahead," Webster said. "We can't let the police take him alive. Who wants to handle this?"

"It's your turn," Eastgate said.

"I think he's right," Gill said.

Webster projected himself up the parkway. Just as he'd expected, the police had created a roadblock by parking a pair of cruisers sideways in the middle of the road. Four officers with rifles were crouched behind the cruisers. The trap was ready to be sprung.

The van pulled up to the roadblock. Webster projected himself behind the wheel, and slammed his foot on the gas pedal. The van rammed the two vehicles in the roadblock. A bullet came through the windshield, scaring him half to death. Webster didn't know if bullets could kill him while he was projecting himself, and was in no mood to find out. He departed, and watched the resulting carnage from the safety of his perch above the palace.

Bullets ripped through the van and turned the driver into a quivering mass. The van veered off the parkway, and rolled down a steep incline. The gas tank would have exploded on its own, but Webster helped it along with a murderous glare. Soon the vehicle was a mass of flames, the driver burned beyond recognition.

"You haven't lost your touch," Eastgate said.

"Or your sense of timing," Gill said. "Good show."

Webster fingered the arm of his chair, causing the platform to lower back inside the palace, and the domed roof to close. He took a moment to collect himself. He found himself wondering if the driver had a wife, or children, and just as quickly dismissed the thought. In making a pact with the Devil, he had accepted that something was due the Devil, the rest of the world be damned. This was the nature of the Order of Astrum, and let no man stand in its way.

30

His vibrating cell phone snapped Peter's eyes open. Only bad news called this late at night. He sat up in bed, and brought the phone to his face. Caller ID said it was Snoop.

"Don't you ever go to bed?" he answered.

"Sorry to be calling this late. Someone's looking for you," his assistant replied.

Lightning flashed through the bedroom window. He'd been dreaming he was a little kid again. It had seemed like such a long time ago.

"No need to apologize. Have you talked to Liza?"

"She's crashed on our couch. She thought she had a bed at a friend's apartment, but it fell through, so she came here. Zack fixed her a hot toddy, and she fell asleep."

"Thanks for taking care of her. Is she still mad at me?"

"To put it mildly. I don't mean to switch subjects, but someone's trying to get ahold of you."

"I'm more concerned about Liza."

"She's fine. Trust me."

"Promise me you'll keep an eye on her."

"You have my word."

"Thanks. So who's looking for me?"

"He says he's an old friend, wouldn't give me his

name. He sent me an e-mail, and said he's been trying
to find you. He sounds desperate."

"Sounds like a kook."

"I don't think so. He knew a lot about you."

"How am I supposed to contact him?"

"He said go to your computer, and he'll Skype you."

"You're not just saying Liza's okay, are you?"

"Stop worrying about it. I'll talk to you in the morning."

Peter ended the call and breathed a sigh of relief.
He didn't want Liza out by herself with Wolfe still on
the loose. If she was staying at Snoop and Zack's place,
she was safe. Soon he was in his study, parked in front
of his computer. His e-mail account had over two hundred messages. So much for his spam filter. He scrolled
through them, starting with the most recent. One message popped out. It said, *Hey Superstar, Where you
been? We need to talk! Omen.* Omen? Who the heck
was Omen? As he started to erase the message, it hit
him. Omen was Nemo spelled backwards. He typed a
reply to his friend, and hit send.

Nemo's real name was Hector Rodriguez. A street
kid from Spanish Harlem, Nemo was a gifted psychic
who did not need the help of other psychics to communicate with the spirit world. His ability to see into the
future was unparalleled, which was why the government had made him their prisoner. Nemo was also a
petty thief, and had been in and out of trouble most of
his life. He and Peter had met in Max's magic shop
when they were kids. Each had instantly recognized
that the other was psychic, and they became close
friends. Outside of having to bail him out of jail several
times, Peter missed having Nemo in his life.

Nemo quickly responded to his e-mail. He wanted to
talk, and sent Peter a Skype ID to call on his computer.

Peter's fingers raced across the keyboard as he called Nemo.

Technology was a wonderful thing. A split second later, Nemo appeared on Peter's computer screen. He'd grown a scruffy beard, and wore a sweatshirt with the words PROPERTY OF UNITED STATES GOVERNMENT stamped across the front. At least he hadn't lost his sense of humor.

"Hey, stranger," Peter said by way of greeting.

"I've been looking for you," Nemo replied.

"I'm sorry I've been out of touch. Did you escape?"

"Nope. I'm still on the funny farm in Virginia."

"How did you get your hands on a computer?"

"I'm using one of the guard's laptops. I got my hands on some sleeping pills, and slipped him a few. He's passed out in front of the TV."

"You're going to get caught."

"What are they going to do? Take away my HBO? Listen, Peter, I've got something I have to tell you. That's why I took the risk to make contact."

Peter smiled at the image on the screen. "Thanks, man. Lay it on me."

"The government is on to you. One of my handlers mentioned it yesterday. He said the FBI had gotten a tip from a psychic in New York that an attack was going to happen in Times Square on Tuesday night. My handler said the psychic was a young guy who held séances with a group of other psychics. I knew right away who they meant."

Peter shook his head in disbelief. Special Agent Garrison had promised to keep their deal a secret. This sounded like a betrayal if he'd ever heard one.

"Did your handler mention me by name?" Peter asked.

"Nope. I think the FBI is keeping you under wraps

for now. You know how these law enforcement guys are. Always fighting for turf."

Peter relaxed. He was safe, at least for a little while.

"Thanks for the heads-up," he said.

"There's more."

"What do you mean?"

"Your life is in danger. My handlers asked me to look into the future, and see if I could visualize the attack. I put myself into a trance, and transported myself to Times Square on Tuesday night. It was a flipping nightmare. There were bodies everywhere. I saw you standing in the middle of it. You were fighting with some guy dressed in black."

"Wolfe," Peter said.

"You know him?" Nemo asked.

"He's an assassin. Tell me what happened."

"Well, I hate to be the bearer of bad news, but you lost."

Peter swallowed hard. "I did?"

"Yeah. This Wolfe dude was choking the crap out of you."

"What happened then?"

"You started to die."

"You sure?"

"On my mother's grave."

"What happened then?"

"I came out of my trance."

"You don't think I could have saved myself?"

"Naw, man, you were toast. That's why I had to warn you. You need to take a trip, and get out of the city. Otherwise, you're going to be pushing daisies soon."

In a day filled with bad news, this was the cherry on top of the cake.

"I'm not running," he heard himself say.

"But you're gonna croak," Nemo said.

"I have to stop Wolfe. Too many people will die if I don't."

"You sure about this?"

"Positive. Did you see anything else?"

"Yeah. My handlers asked me how the attack was going down. I put myself in a trance three more times. Each time, I went to different parts of the city. It was bad."

"It wasn't just isolated to Times Square?"

"Nope. It was everywhere. East Side, West Side, Midtown, even the Village. It was hard to figure out what was going on, being nighttime and all. I saw lots of dead people. One of my handlers called it a hell storm. I looked it up. It's what people who chase tornadoes call a monster storm. Chances of surviving one are slim."

"The city's going to be turned into a hell storm."

"Looks like it. Sure you don't want to bolt?"

"I'm staying."

"Would you mind doing me a favor then?"

"Name it."

"I have a cousin that lives in Spanish Harlem. She doesn't own a computer, otherwise I would have contacted her. Could you warn her?"

"Of course."

"Her name's Juanita. She lives at 1743 East Ninety-seventh Street, apartment 37D. Phone number is 925-4781. She tends bar. Best time to get her is in the day."

Peter wrote the information down. "Got it. I'll call her in a few hours."

"Thanks. One more thing. She doesn't have any money. And she's got a little boy. Could you help her out? Buy her a bus ticket or something?"

"Does she have someplace to go?"

"We've got relatives in Jacksonville."

"I'll buy her and her son plane tickets."

"You don't have to do that."

"Don't worry about it. Anything you want me to tell her?"

"Tell her I think about them every day."

"I'll do that."

"Thanks, man. I'll pay you back."

"You already have."

Peter heard the front door buzzer. He lived in one of the quietest neighborhoods in the city, and no one ever came calling this late.

"I've got to go," Peter said. "Be safe."

"And you as well," Nemo said.

Peter shut down the computer. Moments later, he was standing at his front door. Turning on the outside light, he stuck his face to the peephole. Garrison stood outside with raindrops dancing on his shaven skull. He was alone, and wore a tired smile on his face.

Peter opened the door, praying that he brought good news.

31

"Where's your entourage?" Peter asked, ushering Garrison inside.

"Home in bed, which is where I'm heading once we're done," the FBI agent said, stamping the cold out of his feet in the foyer. "It's been a long couple of days."

"You're going home?"

"Damn straight. We nailed the son of a bitch."

"You caught Wolfe?"

"Better."

"He's dead?"

"He's deader than a church social, as my pappy used to say."

Peter rocked back on his heels. It was like a giant invisible weight had been lifted from his shoulders, and he slapped Garrison on the arm. "That's the best news I've heard in a long time. You want a cup of coffee?"

"Dying for one."

Garrison finished his story at the kitchen table with a steaming mug clutched in his hand. "The Westchester police spotted Wolfe on a surveillance camera at a tollbooth early this morning. They set up a roadblock, and had a cruiser with a SWAT team come up from behind. Wolfe tried to run, and got shot to bits. His vehicle went down a ditch, and the gas tank caught fire. He got burned like a marshmallow at a weenie roast."

Peter leaned against the counter. He wanted to be happy, only what Garrison was describing didn't sound right. Wolfe had impressed him as someone who knew all the angles, not a guy who'd get taken down by a bunch of local cops.

"The last time I saw Wolfe, he was wearing an elaborate disguise," Peter said.

"So?"

"If the Westchester cops spotted Wolfe on a surveillance camera, it meant he wasn't wearing a disguise. Don't you think that's odd?"

"Look, Peter, it was definitely him."

"How can you be sure?"

"Because I saw the tape myself."

"Was he carrying any ID?"

"Like I told you, he got burned up."

Peter thought back to what Nemo had said about the government knowing who he was. Garrison had betrayed their confidence, and he felt himself grow angry as he gazed at the FBI agent.

"You told your superiors about me, didn't you?" Peter said.

"I didn't have a choice," Garrison replied.

"I thought we had a deal."

"Too many lives were at stake."

"Well, you just ruined mine."

"No, I didn't. I protected you. I didn't reveal your name."

"But you told them I existed. They'll start to look for me."

Garrison placed his mug down. "The FBI already knew you existed, and that you'd given them valuable information in the past. I simply told my bosses that you'd made contact in order to warn me about Wolfe. It worked like a charm."

"You mean you used me as leverage," Peter said.

"Your predictions are highly regarded within the FBI."

"But you didn't give them my name."

"No, sir."

"What about your team?"

"Sworn to keep quiet. Told them you were our secret weapon. Which you are."

Talking to Nemo had reminded Peter how precious his freedom was. "I'm not your secret weapon," he said.

"Don't you trust me?"

"You, I trust. Not the people you work for."

"That's a low blow, man. The people I work for are cool."

"You think so?"

Garrison's eyes grew wide. "What's that supposed to mean?"

"How many people did you tell about me?"

"Just my immediate superior, who swore he'd stay silent. Why?"

"He broke his promise to you, that's why," Peter said. "The CIA is holding a psychic friend of mine at a farm in Virginia. They use him to look into the future. My friend made contact, and told me the CIA was on to me. He heard it from one of his handlers."

Garrison looked crushed, and stared at the table. "I don't know what to say."

"Start with 'I'm sorry' and work your way up."

"I'm sorry. Really, really sorry."

Peter pulled up a chair, and sat down beside his guest. His life was about to become a living hell, courtesy of the man sitting across from him. He had to deal with this right now, or risk losing everything. "Erase me," he said.

"What is that supposed to mean?" Garrison asked, clearly perplexed.

"I heard it in a spy movie. I want you to make me disappear."

"How am I supposed to do that?"

"Tell your boss I've vanished, or died, or went to Nepal to live with the monks. Whatever you think he'll buy, tell him."

"Erase you."

"That's right. Poof."

"You're not going to help me anymore?"

"I didn't say that. But you're going to have to tell your boss that the information is coming from some-where else." He paused. "Is that possible?"

Garrison gave it some thought. "I don't see why not," the FBI agent said.

"Good."

They shook hands. It wasn't a perfect solution, but it was the best Peter could think of. Now, if he could just figure out how to win Liza back, his life would return to normal.

Garrison smothered a yawn. "I need to head out. I've got a long drive home."

"Where do you live?"

"Out on Long Island. Little burg called Greenlawn."

"Want another cup for the trip?"

"You're a mind reader," Garrison said, and burst out laughing.

Garrison soon left. Peter sat in the kitchen and drank more coffee. The ordeal was over, only he didn't feel relieved. Too many questions were still unanswered. It was like a jigsaw puzzle filled with holes, and he wondered if he'd ever know the whole story.

Through the kitchen window the sky was starting to lighten. He wondered if Liza was awake. He wanted to call her, and share the good news. It might be a good way to start over, and get their relationship back on track.

Then, he had a better idea. He'd get dressed, and take her out to breakfast. Telling her in person was better than over the phone, as was asking her to forgive him.

He headed upstairs and took a hot shower. There were other people he needed to contact as well. Holly, Milly, Max, and Reggie. He guessed they were probably all asleep, and he decided to wait another hour before making the calls.

He dressed while watching the morning news. The main story was Wolfe's capture in Westchester County. A perky blond newscaster read the story while a photo of the burned-out van Wolfe had been driving was shown. *No one could have survived that,* Peter thought.

The story ended. The newscaster announced that a video of Wolfe was coming after a commercial break. Stay tuned, she said.

Peter found himself shaking his head. The story didn't add up. Why had Wolfe decided to go to Westchester County? And where had the van he'd been driving come from? His body was growing cold, the feeling seeping out from his bones. He put on a wool sweater, and when he didn't get warmer, put on a pair of wool socks as well.

The promised video clip arrived. It showed Wolfe pulling up to a tollbooth, and dropping a handful of coins into the hopper. He was eating a sub, which he clutched in the same hand which held the wheel. There was no doubt it was him, yet something still didn't feel right.

The clip was shown again. Peter drew closer to the screen to get a better look. His eyes were drawn to Wolfe's neck. The collar of Wolfe's shirt was open, the flesh plainly exposed.

Peter cursed.

He pulled up Garrison's cell number, and called him. Voice mail picked up, and he called again, and again. On the fourth try, the FBI agent answered, his voice heavy with sleep.

"Hello?" Garrison grumbled.

"Hey, it's me, Peter. You make it home okay?"

"Yeah, just climbed into bed. What's up?"

"I've got some bad news. Wolfe isn't dead. That wasn't him in the van."

"I told you, I saw the tape. It was Wolfe. Now, if it's okay with you, I'm gonna get some sleep."

The cell phone went dead in Peter's hand. Garrison needed convincing. Peter surfed the other stations. He found one showing a story on Wolfe's apprehension.

The same video was being shown, and he hit redial. Garrison practically barked at him this time.

"This is getting old," Garrison said.

"You're going to be a lot angrier once you realize I'm telling you the truth," Peter said. "Turn on the Channel Eleven news."

"Why should I do that?"

"Because I'm going to prove to you that Wolfe isn't dead."

Garrison growled at him. Peter could hear a TV being turned on in the background. He stared at the screen in his bedroom. The clip of Wolfe pulling into the tollbooth was on.

"This is the same clip I saw," Garrison said.

"Did you look at his neck?" Peter asked him.

"Why should I?"

"The Order of Astrum tattoo is gone. What you're seeing is an illusion, courtesy of the Order. They tricked you into thinking Wolfe was dead to bring your guard down."

"So who's driving the van?" Garrison asked.

"Some poor guy who never knew what hit him. You need to marshal your troops. Wolfe's going to strike soon."

"How do you know that?"

"Because I'm cold."

"You're *what*?"

"I'm freezing from the outside in."

"What the hell's that supposed to mean?"

Peter grabbed his leather jacket off the back of a chair, and headed down the stairs with the cell phone jammed into his neck. There were some things that couldn't be explained; the feeling that he got in his bones whenever Wolfe was about to strike was one of them.

"You still there?" Garrison asked.

"Still here."

"Come on, man, you've got to work with me."

"I am working with you. Wolfe isn't dead, and he's getting ready to kill one of my friends. You need to alert the police that he's on the streets."

"Tell me where your friends live," Garrison said.

"One lives in the Village on Mercer Street, two live on Seventy-second Street and Central Park West, and the third lives in a hotel on Central Park West and Fifty-eighth Street. Ask the police to stake out those areas, and they might apprehend him."

"Why won't you give me names? It will help us protect them."

"Because I promised them I wouldn't."

"You've got to trust me, Peter. That's the only way this can work."

The CIA already knew that Peter and his friends existed. If Peter gave Garrison his friends' names, there was a chance the CIA would find out, and their lives would be ruined.

"Later," Peter said, and ended the call.

Peter stood in the foyer. He tried to put himself in Wolfe's shoes. He didn't think Wolfe would want to tangle with Milly's crows again, which left Max or Reggie as his next victims. He placed calls to both men on his cell phone. Voice mail. Leaving a message wouldn't do. They had to be warned before it was too late.

He went outside. Herbie was parked at the curb in the limo, reading the sports section of the paper. He could not remember ever being more happy to see his driver.

"Morning, boss," Herbie said as he hopped in.

"You're a sight for sore eyes, Herbie."

"You need glasses, boss. Where to?"

"Max's apartment on Mercer Street."

"Got it."

"Do you mind turning the heater on? I'm freezing."

The limo pulled away from the curb. Warm air invaded the backseat, yet Peter could not get the aching feeling out of his bones. He dialed Holly's number, and heard her pick up. He hoped she wasn't still angry with him after last night.

"Hello, Peter," she said coldly.

"Hi. I need a favor. Call Reggie until he picks up. Tell him to stay indoors."

"Didn't you see the news? Wolfe's dead."

"Wolfe's not dead. It was a trick. He's getting ready to attack. I'm going down to Max's place to warn him. You need to do the same with Reggie."

"Let me come with you. We can catch him together." The ice had melted from her voice.

"That's not a good idea, Holly," he said.

"I have powers, Peter. Aunt Milly's been teaching me how to use my gifts."

"Can we talk about this later? Please?"

"Suit yourself. I'll make sure Reggie gets the news."

"Will you call me once you hear from him?"

Holly didn't answer, and Peter realized she'd hung up on him. He stuck his head through the opening in the partition that separated him from his driver.

"Faster, Herbie," he said.

32

Holly slipped her cell phone into her pocket. She sat at the dining room table in her aunt's apartment, enjoying a breakfast of fresh fruit salad and an omelette au fromage that Milly had prepared for her. Her aunt sat across the table, eyeing her intently.

"Is something wrong?" Milly asked.

"Peter said the story on the news isn't true. Wolfe's alive, and he's gunning for us."

"You make it sound like we're in a Western, my dear."

"I didn't know what other expression to use."

Milly put her fork onto her plate, and wiped her mouth with a napkin.

"What did Peter suggest we do?" her aunt asked.

"He wants me to warn Reggie. Peter also wants us to stay in the apartment, and hide like defenseless women."

"You sound put out with him."

"I hate when he talks down to me."

"There is no shame in hiding, especially when someone is trying to kill you. Perhaps we can watch a movie together, or play canasta."

Holly folded her napkin, and placed it beside her plate. "We can help catch Wolfe, if Peter will let us."

"How do you propose doing that?"

"We could set a trap for him, and use one of us as bait."

"I don't think that's a good idea. Wolfe is a monster, and so are the people he works for. Peter is correct in telling us to stay out of sight. It's for our own good." Milly rose from the table, her own breakfast barely touched. "Now, if you'll excuse me, I'm going to take a hot bath. Invite Reggie over for lunch, will you?"

"Of course, Aunt Milly."

"And stop being in a huff with Peter. He's just doing what he thinks is right."

"Yes, Aunt Milly."

Her aunt walked out of the dining room, leaving Holly to stew by herself. She didn't like being treated like a child. She supposed being the youngest in the Friday night group had something to do with it, but that still didn't mean that her ideas didn't have merit. She could catch Wolfe. She was absolutely sure of it. She rang Reggie on her cell, but got no answer. Maybe he was still asleep, or taking a shower. She called again. Still nothing.

"Damn it," she swore to herself.

What was she supposed to do if he didn't pick up? Sit here, and bite her fingernails to the quick? She was a witch. She didn't need to rely on a stupid cell phone to contact him.

She quickly came up with a plan. It was sneaky, and made her skin tingle with excitement. Her aunt was going to be furious with her if she found out. *Better to beg for forgiveness than ask permission,* she thought. She rose from her spot at the table and headed down the hallway. Reaching the master bathroom, she stopped, and stuck her ear to the door. She heard water running, while her aunt sang an opera to herself. *Perfect,* she thought.

Her next stop was the kitchen. From the refrigerator, she removed a plastic container filled with black dirt. The dirt had come from the root and herb garden of Mary Glover, the witch from whom she was descended. Dirt was an important part of a witch's ritual, and provided a spiritual connection to the earth. She placed a small handful onto a paper towel. Pouring a glass of water, she picked up the towel by the corners, and headed for her aunt's study.

"Forgive me for stealing your precious dirt," she said quietly.

H er aunt's study was on the other side of the apartment. The blinds were always closed, the room in perpetual darkness. Holly positioned herself at her aunt's desk, flicked on the lamp, and placed her props in front of her. She gave Reggie another call; still no answer.

"Don't want to pick up your phone, do you?"

She went to work. Dipping her fingers in the water, she began to sculpt the dirt into a small figure, or poppet. Poppets allowed a witch to become connected to someone, even if the person was thousands of miles away. Holly was molding a likeness of Reggie. Reggie was built like a scarecrow, so she made the arms and legs unusually thin. He was also a dapper fellow, and liked to dress well. Grabbing a pencil, she used the point to add a bow tie, and lines for his perfectly combed hair. Finished, she placed the poppet on the blotter so it faced her.

"Hello, little fellow," she said.

Now came the hard part. Picking up the glass of water, she held it a few inches from her face, and focused on the water's shimmering surface. The ritual was called scrying, and would allow her see Reggie wherever he was. Long ago, witches had used large pools of water to scry on people, while today it was more common to use a glass of water like she was doing.

"Water, oh so bright, let me see Reggie Brown in your perfect light."

She waited for what seemed like an eternity. A bubble rose to the water's surface, then another. To her delight, an image of a man appeared inside the glass. It was Reggie, lying in bed in striped pajamas. He was yawning, and appeared to have just woken up.

"Wonderful, he's home," she said, feeling relieved.

She watched Reggie climb out of bed. A minute later, he was at his kitchen sink, sipping a hot drink. He was a confirmed bachelor, and the counter and sink were cluttered with dirty dishes. He went into his living room, and switched on the TV. The news came on, with Wolfe's death the lead story. Reggie pumped the air joyously with his fist.

"Oh, no," Holly said.

She called him again on her cell. In the glass, Reggie glanced at the ringing phone in his kitchen, but did not answer it.

"Pick up the phone, damn it," she swore.

Reggie still did not answer. Instead, he returned to his bedroom, where he selected a pair of dark slacks and blue blazer from the closet, and tossed them onto the bed. Next came a sporty dress shirt and solid blue necktie. He was planning to go out and celebrate, not knowing that danger might be lurking around the corner, ready to take him down.

Holly kept calling his apartment, and Reggie kept refusing to answer. Panic set in. She had to do something, and she was not about to call Peter and beg for his help. This was her time.

Rising from the desk, she crossed the room. In the corner of the study was a small closet. She flicked on the overhead light and entered. It was empty, except for the safe set into the wall. Many of the building's apartments had safes just like this one. Her aunt had entrusted her with the combination years ago, and she recited it from memory while spinning the safe's dial.

The safe clicked open, and she pulled back the door. The interior was lined with shelves filled with witch's tools: a human skull, a cracked mirror, a jar of chicken bones used to cast spells, a box of talismans for removing spells, and the most precious item of all, a braided lock of Mary Glover's hair. These items had been passed down among the Glover witches for centuries, and would someday be hers.

She decided upon the lock of hair. Shutting the safe, she hurried from the study.

33

Reggie Brown finished dressing. Now that Wolfe was dead, he was going to celebrate, and do a little gambling. Gambling was his passion, and always got his juices flowing. The question was, should he play the horse tracks in New York, or gamble at the Indian reservation casinos in Connecticut? Each was a pleasant car ride away. Each had nice accommodations, good food, and friendly service. None had yet to catch on that he'd been robbing them blind for years, and passing along his winnings to charity.

Decisions, decisions.

Most psychics would have looked down their noses at such behavior. Psychics were not supposed to steal, even if playing Robin Hood. Reggie saw the situation differently. The casinos and horse tracks were supposed to lose every now and then. Why not redistribute the wealth to the people who needed it most?

The phone continued to ring in the kitchen. He ignored it. The only people who ever called were the charities that he'd given money to. He didn't feel like talking to them right now, or anyone else.

He went to the window to check the weather. It was still raining like there was no tomorrow. That settled it. He'd dance with Lady Luck in Connecticut.

He pulled his overcoat off a hanger in the closet and started to put it on. He had company, and he heard himself gasp. The garment fell from his hand to the floor.

"Hello, Marie," he said. "How wonderful that you came by."

"Hello, Reggie," his guest replied.

Madame Marie sat on the couch in his living room dressed in one of her elaborate Gypsy costumes. She looked just like the last time he'd seen her. It was not uncommon for the newly dead to drift for a few days, as if in a spiritual fog, yet that didn't lessen the surprise.

"As they say in the old movies, fancy meeting you here," he said. "Are you all right?"

"I suppose so, considering I'm dead," she replied. "I've been saying good-bye to friends and loved ones. I wanted to make sure I didn't miss you."

"That was awfully nice of you."

"You were my favorite among the Friday night group. You always came wearing your best clothes. I like that in a man."

"Can I get you something?"

"There's nothing I need anymore. In that regard, being dead is rather pleasant. Were you going out?"

"Matter of fact, I was."

"Please don't leave just yet. We need to talk."

Reggie took a deep breath. Having a conversation with a ghost was the last thing he wanted to do right now. But this was his lifelong friend, so he dutifully sat down beside her. His weight made the cushion sag, yet Madame Marie did not move. He crossed his hands in his lap, and waited for her to begin.

"When you die, the unanswered questions that have bothered you don't go away," Madame Marie said. "They remain, begging for answers."

"Really," he said.

"One of those questions came to me right before I was murdered. I looked at my Tarot cards, and saw that the Order of Astrum had sent an assassin to kill us. I asked myself, 'What did any of us do to deserve this fate?' If the Order wanted us out of the picture, they could have been a little more subtle about it, don't you think?"

"They do seem to be in a bit of a hurry," Reggie conceded.

"Does that bother you?"

"Come to mention it, yes."

"What do you think's going on?"

Reggie had always left the Big Questions to the others, and preferred to dwell on life's more pleasant diversions, like picking the ponies and playing cards at the casinos.

"I haven't the faintest idea," he mumbled.

"Do we pose a threat to the Order?"

Reggie had never posed a threat to anyone in his life, and chuckled at the notion. "A threat? What kind of threat can we pose to a group of madmen? Not to belittle what we do, but in the vast scheme of things, it's rather insignificant, don't you think? We mean nothing to them."

"Until now."

"How so?"

"We hit a nerve, Reggie, and now they're afraid of us. Why else would they send an assassin to kill us?"

"I suppose you're right."

"And how did they infiltrate our group? We are all sworn to secrecy, yet somehow they knew who we were. How did they know?"

"I don't have the foggiest idea."

"You need to find out. If you don't, you'll be asking yourself later, like I did."

Reggie nodded solemnly. Madame Marie had come to say good-bye, and to warn him. A better friend he'd never had. It saddened him to think that she had departed this earth, and that he would not be seeing her again for a while. Without thinking, he leaned forward to kiss her on the cheek, then pulled back upon realizing his mistake. A smile crossed her face, and then she was gone.

Reggie kept a vintage 1971 Aston Martin DB6 parked in a private garage near his hotel. Keeping a car in the city was expensive, but he wouldn't have had it any other way. Of all mankind's inventions, the one he'd fallen in love with was the automobile. It was the only thing he'd found which made him feel young again.

He waited for the Aston to be brought up. The drive to Connecticut was two hours plus. He had to hurry if he was going to beat the casino, and be home for dinner. He thought about his encounter with Madame Marie. What a wonderful gift she'd given him. To sit and talk and look into her face again. Simple things, yet so precious when they were taken away from you.

"Reggie! Reggie!"

He snapped out of his daydream. Holly ran toward him with a frantic look in her eyes.

"Holly—Good Lord, what's wrong?" he asked.

Milly's niece put on the brakes, gasping for breath. "Oh, my God, I'm so glad I caught you. Please start picking up your phone."

"Was that you calling? I'm sorry, but I hardly answer anymore."

"I have terrible news, Reggie."

He grabbed her by the forearms. "Don't tell me another in our group has died."

"No, no, everyone's fine."

"Well, then how terrible can it be?"

"It's about Wolfe."

"I saw the news. Good riddance, I say."

"What you saw isn't true. Wolfe's still alive, and he's hunting us."

The Aston pulled up with a rubbery squeal, and the parking attendant hopped out. Reggie tipped him generously, and opened the passenger door for his young friend.

"Can I take you somewhere?" he asked graciously.

"You need to go back to your hotel, and lay low," Holly said.

"But why? Except for the rain, it's a beautiful day."

"Didn't you hear what I said? Wolfe isn't dead."

"Do you honestly think Wolfe's going to ambush me on the road? Let's be reasonable, shall we? Now, where to?"

She grabbed his arm, and tried to squeeze some sense into him. It was no good.

"Oh, all right. I'm staying with my aunt at the Dakota."

"The Dakota it is! Hop in."

Soon they were on the West Side, heading up Central Park West. Reggie wore kid gloves and a tan cap when he drove, and clutched the wheel like a professional driver. He looked comical, and other drivers slowed down to wave, or snap pictures on their cell phones.

"You should charge them," Holly suggested.

"Not a bad idea. So tell me, how can Wolfe be alive after the police shot him to death?"

"It was a trick, courtesy of the Order of Astrum."

"I'll be damned."

Reggie braked at a traffic light. A group of uniformed schoolchildren crossed in front of them. Seeing Reggie behind the wheel, several stuck out their tongues. Reggie turned in his seat to look at his passenger. "Why is the Order after us, Holly?"

"I don't know why," she replied.

"How do they even know about us? Could there be a traitor in our group?"

"Don't say that, Reggie."

"Think about it. Someone tipped Wolfe off. It's the only explanation."

Holly bit her lip. "But who, Reggie? Who in our group would betray us?"

"I hate to say it, but I think it's Max. He's been having money problems, lost a bundle on the stock market."

"But Wolfe tried to kill Max yesterday. Peter told me so."

"Really? Well, there goes that theory, I suppose."

"It's not one of us, Reggie, I'm sure of it."

The Aston rocked forward. Startled, they turned in their seats to stare at the delivery van that had tapped their bumper. The delivery driver shrugged his shoulders as if to say *Sorry*.

Reggie shook his fist at him. "Idiot!"

The driver shook his fist back.

"How dare he shake his fist at me," Reggie said furiously.

The light changed. The driver beeped his horn, mocking them.

"Think you're funny, do you?" Reggie shouted.

"Reggie, no," Holly said.

Reggie undid his seatbelt and hopped out of the Aston. He stood in the middle of the street, and put his dukes up, challenging the driver to a fight. The delivery van driver got out as well. Almost too quickly, Holly thought. He wore a baseball cap, and on his neck glowed a shimmering tattoo. From his jacket he removed a pipe, which he whacked against his palm.

The light changed. Cars slipped around them, avoiding the two men facing off in the middle of the busy street.

"Reggie—it's Wolfe! Run!" Holly yelled.

"Oh, my Lord," Reggie said.

Discretion was the better part of valor. Reggie ducked the traffic, and got on the sidewalk. He took off running, his arms and legs pumping like a comic strip character. He was fast for his age, but Wolfe was right on his heels, and the race's outcome was never in doubt.

Holly jumped out of the Aston and started to give chase. She did not look where she was going, and nearly collided with a professional dog-walker out with his pack. There were poodles, dachshunds, a drooling boxer, and several breeds she'd never seen before. The dogs gave her an idea. Taking Mary Glover's lock of hair from her purse, she waved it in the air.

"Little mongrels, oh so spry, do my bidding, or you will die!"

The dogs changed before her eyes. No longer were they a pack of domesticated house pets; now, they were vicious beasts, prepared to follow her every command. Holly pointed up the sidewalk at Wolfe.

"Stop him!"

The pack broke forward, throwing their handler to the ground. Up the sidewalk they went, trailing their leashes. They surrounded Wolfe, attacking from all sides. Wolfe waved his pipe frantically. *He doesn't like dogs.*

"Tear him up!" she commanded.

Within seconds, Wolfe's pants were shredded, and he was starting to look like a meal. Several of the smaller dogs had latched on to his shirt sleeves, and pinned his arms. Seeing Holly approach, he cursed her.

"Bitch."

"Try witch," she shouted back.

"You'll pay for this."

"Go for the throat!"

The dogs leapt into the air, trying for Wolfe's windpipe. Sheer panic filled Wolfe's face. The hunter had become the hunted.

"Say, lady, those are my dogs."

The handler had gotten to his feet, and stood beside Holly. He blew through a dog whistle that hung around his neck. The pack broke free of her spell, and ran back to him.

"Thanks for lending them to me," Holly said.

Wolfe still had his pipe. His arms and legs were bleeding, his eyes filled with pain. Holly waved the lock of hair.

"Evil man, oh so wicked, cast away thy weapon, or be stricken."

The pipe flew out of Wolfe's hand, and landed in the gutter. A smart man knows when he's beaten.

Wolfe staggered across the street, and melted into a crowd.

Holly breathed a sigh of relief. She tucked the magic lock of hair into her purse. She wasn't so defenseless after all. Too bad Peter hadn't been here to see her.

Reggie had parked himself on a bench, and was attempting to catch his breath. She sat down next to him. His cheeks had turned an alarming color.

"Are you all right?"

"Call 911," he gasped.

"What's wrong? Did he strike you?"

Reggie would not look at her, his eyes peeled to the sky.

"My heart," he whispered.

"Are you having a heart attack?"

He let out a deathly moan. "Oh, my."

"What's wrong?"

"I see them."

"Who?"

"The welcome wagon." He managed the weakest of smiles, and spoke to a presence only he could see. "Hello, Marie. Back so soon?"

"Reggie, you've got to hold on," Holly begged.

"Too late. Good-bye, my lovely friend."

Closing his eyes, Reggie slid off the bench to the ground, where he lay in a heap. Holly punched 911 into her cell phone with tears streaming down her face.

34

Peter's limo pulled up to the emergency entrance of Roosevelt Hospital on West 59th Street and Tenth Avenue, and he hopped out. Like many New Yorkers, he knew of Roosevelt Hospital through an episode of *Seinfeld,* where Jerry and Kramer had accidentally dropped a Junior Mint into Elaine's ex-boyfriend during an operation. The send-up of the inept hospital staff had seemed funny at the time. It didn't now.

The emergency room was loud and chaotic. He found Holly giving a statement to a uniformed policeman. Their eyes met, and Holly shook her head as if to say *Not now.* He backed away, and headed for the nurse's station. He wondered what story Holly was giving the police. Something that left out the Friday night psychics and the Order of Astrum, he guessed. That was the bad thing about living a lie. Once the lie got started, there was no turning back.

The nurse's station was also busy. The nurse in charge was a middle-aged woman with a kind face, and appeared to be the calm in the eye of the storm.

"May I help you?" she asked.

"A friend of mine named Reggie Brown was admitted a short while ago. I was wondering if you could tell me how he's doing."

She slipped on her bifocals and consulted a clipboard. The corners of her mouth turned down. "I'm sorry, but your friend didn't make it."

The words hit him like an invisible punch.

"You mean he's dead?"

"Yes. He passed away a short while ago."

He brought his hand up to his face. What good were his powers if he couldn't save the people he loved? He wanted to scream.

A phone on the desk rang, and the nurse answered it. Peter lowered his hand. The cup of coffee on the desk was boiling over, the black liquid running down the sides onto the blotter. He forced himself to calm down, and the coffee went back to normal.

She hung up the phone, and resumed speaking to him.

"I'm sorry for your loss," she said.

"Thanks," he whispered.

The hospital cafeteria was near the emergency room. Except for a group of nurses on break, it was empty. Peter sat at a corner table, and stared at the pale blue wall. It didn't seem possible that Reggie was gone. He'd been a part of Peter's life for as long as he could remember. The notion that he was no longer alive just didn't seem real.

Every psychic Peter knew was an eccentric; it seemed to come with the territory. But Reggie had been unique. He could look at any game of chance, and predict its outcome. Instead of turning himself into a billionaire, he'd used his gift to help others, and had supported many of the city's less fortunate through his generosity. Reggie's favorite quote had come from the Talmud. *He who saves a single life, it is though he has saved the entire world.*

Holly slipped into a chair across from him. In her hand was a Kleenex, which she used to dab at her eyes.

"What did you tell the police?" he asked.

"I told them Reggie got sick, and collapsed on the sidewalk."

"You didn't tell them Wolfe was chasing you?"

"How could I?"

"Tell me what really happened."

"I went to Reggie's hotel to warn him, and he convinced me to take a spin with him in his sports car. We were going north on Central Park West, when Wolfe rammed us with a delivery van. When Reggie got out, Wolfe came after him with a pipe."

"Did Wolfe beat him?"

"No. I cast a spell on a pack of dogs, and they went after Wolfe."

Peter drew back in his chair. "You did what?"

"Aunt Milly's been working with me on casting spells. I'm getting good at it."

"Then how did Reggie die?"

"Heart attack. I guess all the excitement got to him. I felt so helpless."

Tears cascaded down her cheeks. She'd had an innocent childhood, until now.

"Does Reggie have any next of kin?" he asked.

"A sister in California. The hospital is calling her to make arrangements."

"Good. I want you to go back to your aunt's apartment. None of us are safe."

"Are you mad at me for going out?"

"No."

"You're not just saying that, are you?"

He reached across the table, and took her hands into his own.

"You did the right thing warning Reggie."

She nodded and took a deep breath. "There's something I have to tell you. Reggie thought one of our group might be helping the Order of Astrum. I think he was right."

"You do? Why?"

From her purse she removed a folded piece of paper, and slid it toward him. "I found this on the sidewalk. One of the dogs pulled it from Wolfe's pocket before he ran."

Peter unfolded the paper and had a look. It was a list of the names of the seven members of Friday night psychics. Beneath each name was the person's address, home phone number, and, if they had one, cell phone number.

"This is Wolfe's hit list," he said.

"That's right."

"How did he get all of this information?"

"Someone in our group must have given it to him."

"You mean a spy."

"That's right."

"But all of our names are on the list."

"So?"

"If there was a spy in our group, do you think he'd want Wolfe to kill him as well?"

Holly bit her lower lip. "No, I guess not."

"There's a spy, but it isn't one of us. Someone else did this."

"But who could it be?"

Peter again studied the list. Something about it bothered him. After a moment, he realized what it was. The information included Max's cell phone number. Max had only recently crawled out of his cave and purchased one. Max had given Peter the number in case of emergency, and asked that he not share it. Max was a private person, and Peter didn't think the other members of the Friday night group had the number.

There was one way to find out.

"Do you have Max's cell phone number?" Peter asked.

"I don't know. Let me check."

Holly took out her cell phone, and went through the phone book. "No, I just have his apartment number. Is that significant?"

"Yes. I'm the only member of our group that has Max's cell number. The spy got this information from me."

"But how's that possible? I mean, this isn't stuff you talk about, is it?"

Peter never talked about his psychic friends. Nor had he put their names and phone numbers on his computer. The spy had gotten the information from *his* cell phone.

He slammed the table with the palm of his hand.

"For the love of Christ," he swore.

"What's wrong? You're getting all red in the face."

"I have to go."

"Peter, wait."

He rose from the table so abruptly that he knocked over his chair. The nurses stopped their conversation to stare at him.

"Go back to your coffee and gossip," he told them.

"Peter, get a hold of yourself," Holly said.

He hurried out of the cafeteria. Holly caught up with him in the hallway, and grabbed his arm. "Don't run away from me like that," she said furiously.

"I have to deal with this," he said.

"Do you know who it is?"

"I have a good idea. Go back to your aunt's apartment, and stay there until I call you."

"Don't order me around. I hate when you do that."

"Do it anyway."

"What's gotten into you?"

They came to the street entrance. Outside it was cold and nasty and wet. Peter zippered his jacket while staring at his reflection in the glass door. Not having a family growing up, he'd compensated by creating one as he'd gotten older. It made the betrayal that much greater.

"Please tell me what's going on," she begged.

"It's one of my assistants," he said.

35

The sidewalks on Broadway were an endless sea of umbrellas. Peter stared out the passenger window of his limo, trying to control his rage.

"You okay, boss?" Herbie asked.

"I'm fine," Peter replied, hearing the lie in his voice.

"You don't look fine. Sure you're not getting sick? There's a bad flu going round."

"When did you become a doctor, Herbie?"

His driver fell silent. Peter continued to watch the passing scenery. The anger he'd felt in the hospital had manifested into a burning rage that would not go away. First Reggie had died, then he'd learned one of his assistants had stuck a knife into his back. Bad news came in threes, and he wondered what was going to come next.

"You had anything to eat?" his driver asked.

"Just some coffee."

"That explains it." Herbie lifted a Philly cheesesteak sandwich wrapped in wax paper off the seat, and passed it through the partition. "Eat this. Make you feel better."

"You think so?"

"Always worked for me."

Peter quickly ate the sandwich. He was surprised at

how hungry he was. He caught Herbie watching in the mirror.

"Better?" Herbie asked.

"A little. Remember the guy who tried to stab me the other night during my show?"

"Sure. What about him?"

"One of my assistants is feeding him information."

Herbie frowned. "That's bad stuff. Who is it?"

"I don't know. He took the information off my cell phone, and passed it to him."

"I thought you kept your cell phone locked for security."

"I do."

"Then how did he get it open?"

That was a good question. Even if one of his assistants had gotten their hands on his cell phone, they couldn't have accessed the directory without knowing the password. Had he given the phone to one of them to use while it was unlocked?

"I must have let one of them borrow it," Peter said.

"Like when the power went out," his driver said.

A week before, there had been a power outage at the theater, and Peter had lent his cell phone so an electrician could be called. The electrician had not been able to find anything wrong with the fuse box, which had seemed odd at the time. Now, he knew why.

His third piece of bad news had just arrived.

"It's Zack," Peter said.

"You sure?"

"Yes. He had my cell phone. He's a spy."

"But I thought Zack fought with that guy who attacked you."

Zack and Wolfe *had* fought, or so it had seemed at the time. Now Peter realized what had really happened. Wolfe had tried to stab him. Peter had blinded Wolfe with a load of flash paper. Realizing Wolfe might be caught, Zack had leapt onto the stage, and pulled Wolfe through the trapdoor, allowing the assassin to escape. Peter marveled at the boldness of what Zack had done. Even he had been fooled.

"It was a trick," Peter said.

"So what are you going to do?" Herbie asked.

"Confront him."

"But Zack's a monster. He does mixed martial arts."

"I've still got to confront him. Liza's staying in his loft. She's not safe."

"Why don't you call the cops?"

"No cops."

"But boss—"

"I said, no cops."

"Whatever you say."

Peter resumed looking out the window. There were names for men like Zack. Traitor, spy, Judas. None of them adequately conveyed the harm he'd caused. All the cops could do was arrest Zack. Peter had something else in mind. He was going to make his assistant talk, and tell him about the men who ran the Order of Astrum. Then, maybe he'd call the cops.

"I hope you know what you're doing," Herbie said under his breath.

"Trust me," he said, hearing the rage in his voice. "I do."

Zack and Snoop shared a loft in SoHo, in what was once the heart of the New York art scene. They lived in an old factory with a cast-iron facade and a hundred and fifty years of history. Herbie parked by the front door. It was quiet, the rain keeping everyone inside.

Peter gazed up at the third floor where his assistants lived. Liza was up there, and had no idea that her life was in danger. He needed to get his girlfriend to safety before confronting Zack. He started to get out.

"You got something to defend yourself with?" his driver asked.

"Just my wits," Peter replied.

"Zack will kill you with his bare hands."

Peter thought back to his encounter with Wolfe. He'd been able to anticipate every move Wolfe had tried to make, and didn't see things being any different with Zack.

"We'll see."

"Be careful, boss. I got bills to pay," his driver said.

Peter climbed out of the limo. The building's front door was locked, with visitors needing to be buzzed in. If he called upstairs, he'd have to explain why he was here. He considered picking the lock, and even breaking the front door down. Before he could decide, the front door opened, and a female artist emerged, dragging a large canvas.

"Crummy elevator is out of service," she said.

Peter held the door for her, ducking inside when she was gone. He found the stairwell and started up, hearing the dull echo of his footsteps. A naked bulb lit his way.

He felt his rage build, and clenched his hands into fists. As a boy, his parents had forbidden him from fighting. After they'd died, he'd lived with a number of their psychic friends who'd continued to stress that rule. He could remember getting into a scuffle at school with an older bully twice his size. The next thing he'd known, the bully was in the nurse's office with a bloody nose and a pair of black eyes, while he was in the principal's office getting a lecture. Milly, his guardian at the time, had begged him never to lash out again. Now, he understood why. Milly had seen his mother turn into a monster, and was fearful that her son was capable of doing the same thing.

He stepped out of the stairwell onto the third floor landing. His assistants' loft was at the end of the hallway. Zack's racing bike was parked by the door.

He rapped on the door, and stood facing the peephole. The door swung open, and he stood face-to-face with Liza. She wore gray sweats, no makeup, and had her hair tied in a bun. His heart did the funny thing it did whenever he saw her.

"Hi," he said.

"What are you doing here?" She did not open the door all the way, and he sensed that there was something inside the loft she didn't want him to see.

"Am I disturbing you?" he asked.

"Sort of. We were just practicing one of the illusions in the show."

The words were slow to sink in. Last night, she'd told him she was quitting.

"You're not leaving?"

"No. Look, I'm still mad at you, Peter. You screwed up, big time."

"I know I did. I'm sorry."

"You're going to have to do better than that. Let's get together later and talk, okay?"

"Sure." He tried to look over her shoulder. "Is Zack here?"

"Didn't you hear what I just said?"

"Is he?"

"Of course he's here. Is something wrong?"

He brought his finger to his lips, and in a whisper said, "Zack set me up the other night at the theater. He's a spy. You and Snoop are in danger."

"Cut it out."

"I'm not kidding. I have proof."

"Oh, my God," she whispered.

"Please let me in."

"What are you going to do?"

"Send him to the nurse's office."

"What is that supposed to mean?"

His girlfriend looked scared. Zack's voice could be heard inside the loft. Snoop was with him, and they were discussing how to repair an illusion from the show. Peter pushed open the door, and entered the main living area, a large space with high ceilings and a succession of large, identical windows that faced the street. The furnishings were sparse, and consisted of several pieces of mismatched furniture bought from a thrift store.

The Sword Suspension illusion was in the center of the loft. Zack and Snoop were tightening the mechanism which let Liza rotate on the tip of a sword while suspended in midair. Peter had pulled the trick from the show after the sword began to wobble. Had Liza fallen, the sword's blade could have ended her life.

His assistants stopped what they were doing.

"Look who's here." Snoop crossed the loft, and slapped Peter on the arm. "To what do we owe the pleasure of your company?"

"Stand behind me," Peter said.

"Say what?"

"Just do it."

Snoop shrugged and slipped behind him so he was standing next to Liza.

"You and I need to talk," Peter said to Zack.

Zack put down the tool he was holding. His head of security wore a sleeveless black shirt that exposed his thick, muscular arms. He worked out every day, and had the ripped physique to show for it. "About what?" he replied.

"I think you know," Peter said.

"Afraid not. You got something on your mind, spit it out."

"I want to know why you betrayed me."

Zack started to answer, then thought better of it. He picked up the sword that held Liza in the air during the trick. He ran his finger down the blade, testing its sharpness. The look in his eyes was pure evil. Zack had known this day would eventually come, and he had already decided what he would do. Lifting the sword over his head like a samurai, he came forward.

"If it means anything, I didn't know they were planning to kill you," Zack said.

"How touching. Now put the sword down," Peter told him.

"Why should I?"

"Because if you don't, I'm going to kill you."

"You're funny."

"I mean it. Give up while you can."

"Right."

Peter looked into Zack's eyes, and plumbed his thoughts. He saw Zack inside a primitive hut made of mud and straw, choking the life out of an African witch doctor. Tossing the half-dead man to the ground, Zack lit a match, and tried to set the hut ablaze. Several tribesmen entered the hut, and began to fight with Zack. Zack panicked, and ran away. It was then that Peter understood.

"You're an assassin, too," Peter said. "You're just as evil as Wolfe."

A strained look spread across Zack's face, and he did not reply.

"You screwed up your last job in Africa, and they sent you to New York."

Zack said nothing.

"You don't like being a spy. You'd rather kill people."

Still nothing.

"How do you plan to kill us?"

Zack finally found his voice. "I can make it painless, or you can suffer. It's up to you."

Liza let out a little shriek, Snoop a soft moan.

"Bring it on," Peter said.

Zack let out a savage yell and charged him. Peter ducked as the sword sliced the air inches above his head. He danced away, and Zack chased him. Zack took another swing, and destroyed a lamp sitting on a table. He tried again, and demolished a chair. Each time, he was getting a little closer, and his eyes danced at the inevitable outcome.

Herbie had been right. He couldn't beat Zack with his bare hands. Snoop still had the screwdriver he'd been using to repair the illusion. Peter clicked his fingers, and Snoop tossed it to him. Peter held the screwdriver by the tip. The demon inside of him told him to strike.

"Last chance," Peter said.

"For what?" Zack replied.

"Give yourself up."

"No thanks."

"That's my final offer."

"Up yours, magic boy."

The demon said *Now*. Peter flicked his wrist and tossed the screwdriver. It did one complete revolution as it flew through the air, and hit Zack in the chest. The point went all the way in, where it became impaled in his heart. Zack froze, and gazed down at himself.

"That's not possible," he gasped.

"Wrong," Peter said.

Zack staggered around the loft. As the life drained from his body, he found the strength to pull the screwdriver out. A geyser of blood followed, and he pitched to the floor.

Liza let out a shriek, and covered her face.

Snoop let out a war whoop.

The demon in Peter said nothing.

Peter became himself again a few moments later. It was like snapping out of a daydream, and he gazed at the dead man lying on the floor. He'd killed Zack, as hard as it was for him to believe. He went to where Liza was standing, and put his arms around her protectively.

"I'm sorry you had to see that," he said.

"Oh, my God, Peter, this is so awful," she cried.

"Wow, Zack was going to kill us," Snoop said. "To think I roomed with the guy."

Zack had known everything about the Friday night psychics there was to know. More than likely, he'd stored the information on his computer. Peter needed to call the police. But first, he needed to find that information, and erase it from the computer's hard drive.

"Herbie is parked down front. Have him drive you to my place," Peter said.

"What about the police?" Snoop asked.

"I'll deal with them."

"You sure you don't want us to stay, and give them statements?" Snoop said.

"Just go. It's for your own good."

Snoop grabbed Liza and started out the door. His girlfriend came back inside the loft, and stood directly in front of him.

"Look at me," she said.

Peter looked into her beautiful face.

"Tell me how you feel," she said.

"Like I might get sick."

"You didn't want to kill Zack, did you?"

He shook his head. The demon had wanted to kill Zack, but he hadn't.

"Say it," she said.

"I didn't want to kill Zack, despite everything he'd done."

His answer seemed to satisfy her. She turned around and walked out of the loft. He shut the door with his head spinning. The shock of what he'd done had started to set in. He found a chair and sat in it. For several minutes he did nothing but stare at the floor.

36

Once he started to feel better, Peter went searching for Zack's laptop. There weren't that many places in the loft to look, and he tried Zack's bedroom first. Zack had been a minimalist, and the room had little in the way of furnishings save for a mattress on the floor, and a weight-lifting bench with barbells and dumbbells lying around it. A laptop lay on the floor beside the bed, an ultrathin Dell Latitude. Peter tried to see what was on it, only to discover he needed a password. He called Snoop, and his assistant's cheerful voice answered on the first ring.

"You don't know the password to Zack's computer, do you?" Peter asked.

"I know the passwords to everyone's computers," Snoop said proudly.

"You don't know mine."

"It's Houdini, spelled backwards."

"That's actually a little bit scary."

"I'm just that good. Zack's is BULLYBOY, in caps. Was Zack really an assassin for the Order of Astrum?"

The less Snoop knew about what was going on, the better. But at the same time, Peter couldn't keep his assistant in the dark forever. Trust ran both ways. "I'm afraid so. He would have killed us if I hadn't stopped him."

"But why? What does the Order of Astrum want?"

It was the same question Peter had been asking himself from the beginning.

"I wish I knew. I've got to go," Peter said.

"Call me if you need me. Liza says she loves you."

"Tell her that I love her. Talk to you later."

Peter returned to the main room of the loft, where he sat at the dining table with the laptop in front of him. Zack lay on the floor a few yards away. His assistant had died with his eyes wide open, staring lifelessly into space. Peter's stomach started to do strange things, and he looked away. He had come here with the intention of making Zack tell him the Order of Astrum's secrets, and knocking him around a little bit. He had never expected it would end like this.

He focused on the laptop. Its hard drive contained fifteen files, each named after a major city. He opened them, and scanned their contents. Zack had been gathering information on psychics in other cities, including Boston, Philadelphia, and Washington, D.C., and preparing hit lists. Strangely, there was no file devoted to the Friday night group, and he supposed Zack had erased the file from his computer after sending the information to his bosses.

He had to find that file. It would explain why Wolfe was trying to kill them, and what the Order of Astrum's reason was for sending Wolfe to New York. He knew enough about computers to know that nothing was ever permanently erased from a computer's memory. The New York file was still on the laptop, and needed to be retrieved, and studied.

It was time to bring Garrison into the loop. As he pulled up Garrison's number, something on the floor caught his eye.

He gasped.

Zack's neck was glowing like he'd turned radioactive. Peter had never seen anything like it before. He placed his cell phone onto the table, and went to have a look.

He stopped a few feet from the body. Zack looked dead. Just to be safe, he nudged him with his toe. His assistant didn't move.

He knelt down, and studied the glowing skin. It was the size of a half-dollar, and was shimmering. The Order of Astrum's symbol had been tattooed into Zack's neck, and covered with a piece of flesh through plastic surgery. Zack was dead, yet the Order's symbol lived on. Garrison needed to see this.

He went to the table and retrieved his cell phone. A voice was coming out of it. Had he put the call through without realizing it?

"Hello?" he said into the phone.

"Peter—is that you?" Garrison asked.

"It's me. You need to get over here, and see this."

"See what? What's going on?"

"I just killed one of my assistants."

"You did *what*?"

"His name was Zack, and he was an assassin and spy for the Order of Astrum. He's lying dead on the floor, only the side of his neck is glowing. I think the Order is somehow keeping tabs on him. It's freaking me out."

"Why did you kill him?" Garrison asked.

"He attacked me with a sword."

"Did you shoot him?"

"No, I used a screwdriver."

"A *screwdriver*?"

"It's a long story. I also found his laptop."

"Tell me where you are, and I'll be right over," Garrison said.

Peter looked back at Zack. The side of his assistant's neck looked like it was on fire. Zack had traded his soul to be a member of the Order, and was now burning from within.

He gave Garrison the address.

37

Wolfe sat in the corner of a West Side bar called The Gin Mill, tending to the dog bites that covered his arms and legs. None of the bites were particularly severe, yet they still managed to sting like the devil each time his clothing rubbed against them. Dipping a paper napkin into a glass of vodka, he cleaned the wounds to avoid infection.

Music played out of a jukebox. The Rolling Stones's *Some Girls*. Above the bar was the prerequisite flat screen TV; across the room, a foosball game. Wolfe found himself longing for a simple pub with a dartboard and a snoring dog. He'd had enough of bloody New York, and was ready to go home again.

He placed down his empty glass. His waitress hit the table like a shark. She'd told him her name while taking his order, but he'd promptly forgotten.

"Ready for another Stoli?" she asked.

"Yes. And a beer chaser," Wolfe said.

"You got it, cowboy."

He snorted contemptuously. He hardly felt like a cowboy. What he felt like was a battered and beaten soldier. Every job came with a price, he'd learned that long ago. Each time he took a life, a tiny piece of his soul was taken away, until he had no soul at all. He could live with that aspect of his work. What he couldn't live with was getting eaten alive by a pack of lunatic dogs. He was going to walk away, the elders be damned. He'd never done that before, and he supposed there was a first time for everything.

His drinks arrived, and he belted back the vodka. He wasn't sure how he'd get out of New York, or for that matter, the country. Using any mode of public transportation was out of the question. He needed a new identity. He supposed he'd have to kill some bloke.

He threw down money, and headed for the door. The pay phone next to the dart board started to ring. The waitress who'd been serving him answered it. "Hold on, I'll check." She cupped the receiver into the crook of her neck. "Is your name Jeremy?"

Wolfe's hand was on the front door. He shot her a murderous look.

"What if it was?"

"Someone's looking for you," she said, gulping hard.

"Who?"

"Some guy with a funny accent."

"Does he have a name?"

"He wouldn't give it to me."

Wolfe crossed the bar and motioned for the receiver. Lifting it to his ear, he felt the cold plastic seep into his skin. The waitress skipped away.

"What do you want?" he said.

"Hello, Major Wolfe," said the elder with the BBC accent. "When you didn't contact us at the usual time, we decided to track you down. How is your mission going?"

Wolfe parked himself onto the stool next to the pay phone. He had not decided how to break the news to his employer, and supposed now was as good a time as any.

"I've hit a bump in the road," Wolfe replied.

"How so?"

"I tracked down Reggie Brown this morning, and got attacked by a pack of dogs. There was a young woman with him, chanting some sort of spells. I think she's a witch."

"Will you be able to continue?"

Wolfe laughed to himself. Nothing like getting right to the bloody point, was there?

"No," he said flatly.

"You can't continue, or won't?"

"Does it matter?"

"Answer the question, Major."

"Won't. I'm finished. Game over."

"That's our decision to make, not yours."

"The police have circulated my photograph, and everyone and their brother is looking for me," Wolfe said, surprised at how calm his voice sounded. "It's just a matter of time before I'm caught, so I've decided to chuck it."

"We have an agreement," the elder replied. "You signed it in your own blood when you became a member of the Order. There is no quitting on our watch."

"Oh, piss off," Wolfe said, letting the alcohol talk for him.

"How dare you speak to me in that fashion."

"I'm hanging up now. Have a nice day."

"Wait!"

"Give me one good reason why I should."

The elder hesitated. "What if we change our deal?"

"What are you offering?"

"More money."

"I've got all the flipping money I want. It will have to be something fresh. Put your thinking cap on, and come up with something."

"I need to speak with the others."

"Do that," Wolfe told him.

The line went mute. Wolfe found himself staring at his reflection in the silver plate on the payphone. The tattoo on his neck had intensified in color. The tattoo was like a homing device which let the elders keep track of him. The day Wolfe had the tattoo removed, he would have to tell the doctor to cut very deep.

"Are you still there?" BBC accent said, coming back on the line.

"I'm here," Wolfe replied.

"We wish to make you a new offer in recognition of your present situation. This offer should more than compensate you for your trouble."

"I'll be the judge of that," Wolfe said.

"If I'm not mistaken, you are presently in a bar with several large-screen television sets. Walk to the nearest screen, and stare at it."

"Why the hell should I do that?"

"Major—just do it!"

Wolfe dropped the phone, the receiver banging against the wall. The nearest screen hung directly over the bar. He crossed the room and gazed up. A basketball game was showing, with men flying through the air like they had wings on their feet. In the blink of an eye, the picture changed to a tranquil bay with deep blue water, and a fishing boat tied to a dock. A sunburned man wearing a straw hat was cleaning the deck, while whistling to himself. The man looked happy, without a care in the world, and Wolfe's face grew warm as he realized that he was looking at himself, the picture on the screen his dream of one day retiring to the Seychelles. It upset him to know that the elders knew such intimate details about him, but that was the price you paid for working with men who practiced dark magic. He went back to the pay phone.

"No thanks."

"But—"

"I've got all the money I need to buy my boat and start my charter fishing business," he said. "You can't dangle that carrot in front of my face."

"You're a hard man to please, Major. You realize we could crush you like a bug, if we so choose."

"But then there would be no one to kill Peter Warlock and his friends."

"We could find someone else."

"Who can kill psychics like I can? Good luck."

"Perhaps we can sweeten the offer."

"Go right ahead," Wolfe said sarcastically.

Again the phone went mute. Wolfe could count on the fingers of one hand the number of times in his life he'd been in a position like this. He caught the waitress's eye, and mimicked chugging a beer. She got him a perspiring Heineken from the bar, and slapped it into his hand with a knowing wink. The elder with the BBC accent returned to the line.

"We have something else we'd like to put on the table," the elder said.

"I'm listening," Wolfe replied.

"Go back to the large screen TV you were looking at a moment ago."

"What for?"

"It's part of our offer."

Wolfe crossed the room. A commercial with a talking lizard was showing on the flat screen. Before his eyes, the reptile turned into a ravishing woman sitting on a prison cot in some godforsaken part of the world. It was Rita. He walked back to the pay phone.

"Where is she?" he said into the receiver.

"Turkey," the elder said.

"Don't tell me she's in Diyarbakir."

"It's a rather nasty place, isn't it?"

Diyarbakir was a hellhole. Torture by the guards was common, with prisoners dragged behind cars across a concrete courtyard until they died.

"How did they catch her?" Wolfe asked.

"Your girlfriend attempted to kill an Arab terrorist who was in Turkey on vacation. It seems she's employed by the Israeli Mossad. How ironic that both of you are in the assassination business."

"Shut up, you dirty swine."

"Now, now, Major, we didn't put her there, but we can get her out."

"You can? How?"

"Leave the details to us. Our offer to you is this. Stay in New York and finish your job. Rita will be sprung from prison, and flown to a city of your choice. First class, of course."

Wolfe took a swig of beer. Rita was the only woman he'd ever loved. Like him, she had no family or friends. He was the only person who cared about her, and she him.

"You have a deal," Wolfe said.

"You'll kill the rest by tomorrow?" the elder asked.

"You have my word."

"Tell me how."

Wolfe hadn't thought that far ahead. Killing the others in such a short amount of time would be hard, unless he set a trap. He had not forgotten the old witch and her niece going out for dinner, even though they knew their lives were in danger. They were naïve, and he would use them as bait to draw the others in.

"I'll have to get them all in the same room," Wolfe said.

"Is that possible?" the elder asked.

"They're a close-knit group. It shouldn't be difficult."

"When will this take place?"

"Right now."

"Splendid. I look forward to speaking with you soon."

"What about Rita?" Wolfe asked. "When will I know she's safe?"

"Don't worry about Rita. We'll take care of everything. Farewell, Major."

The phone went dead. Wolfe crossed the room and stared at the flat screen. The elders had left Rita's image there, just to torture him. His dream of running away to the Seychelles had always included her. Without Rita, the dream would die. He would not let that happen, even if it meant killing half the people in New York with his bare hands.

"I love you," he whispered to the screen.

His beloved began to fade away. A pitiful sound escaped his throat. Once during a mission he'd been captured and tortured in the Congo, and it hadn't been as painful as this.

He left the bar knowing what he had to do.

38

Nothing ever died on a computer. Every file left a history, even if had been erased. It was all there, recorded like a giant footprint for posterity, if you just knew where to look.

Garrison knew where to look. The FBI agent worked the keyboard on Zack's laptop, a study in concentration. Peter sat beside him, and tried not to look at Zack, who lay on the floor fifteen feet away. His assistant's neck had stopped glowing right before the FBI arrived.

"So what am I looking for?" Garrison asked.

"A file on me and my psychic friends," Peter replied. "Hopefully, it will help us figure out what Wolfe's mission is."

Garrison resumed his search. "I'm still having a hard time believing you killed Zack with a screwdriver while he had a sword. How does that work?"

"I got lucky."

"Lucky, my ass. What are you, a Jedi warrior?"

Peter did not have a good answer. How could he explain that the demon inside of him had killed Zack? Now that the demon was gone, he wanted to put the incident out of his mind.

"Found something," Garrison said several minutes later.

Peter leaned in to have a look. The file was called FNP. That had to stand for Friday Night Psychics. Garrison opened the file, and scrolled through the pages. It contained the names of the Friday night group, their phone numbers, and their addresses. There was no mention of Wolfe, or why he'd been sent to New York.

"Damn it," Peter said.

Garrison closed the laptop and slid it off the table. "I'm going to let our forensic team have a crack at it. Maybe there's more here I'm not finding."

"You're taking the laptop away?" Peter asked.

"I sure am."

Peter felt himself start to panic. He trusted Garrison, but not the people he worked for. He couldn't let the FBI get their hands on those names.

"You have to erase that file," Peter blurted out.

"No can do. This is evidence."

"You have to. Otherwise, everything falls apart."

Garrison gave him a healthy stare. "Explain yourself."

"If my friends' names get out, the Friday night psychics are no more."

"What are you talking about?"

"There are rules to conducting a séance that must always be followed. They have to be conducted at night, the participants have to dress a certain way, and certain props must be used, including occult signs and astrological symbols. It's part of the deal, and there's no getting around it."

"So?"

"One of the most important rules is secrecy. Each member vows to protect the identities of the other members of the group. If the group becomes exposed, its ability to talk with the spirit world ends. If you let that file out, our ability to conduct séances will die."

"You're saying you won't be able to help me?" the FBI agent asked.

"That's right."

"Why do you need a group? Why not just do it yourself?"

"The spirits don't often hear us. If one psychic calls out to them, they usually don't respond. If a group of psychics calls, they do. It's because of all the commotion in the spirit world."

"It's noisy on the other side, huh?"

Peter nodded. He'd been there, and it was as loud as a busy subway station.

"You're asking me to commit a crime," Garrison said. "As an officer of the law, I'm not about to step over that line. At the same time, I don't want to do anything that will diminish your ability to help me. So, here's what I'm going to do. I'm going to go over to the other side of the room. The laptop stays right here. If this file's gone when I come back, I'm not going to say anything."

"Got it," Peter said.

The FBI agent's chair made a harsh scraping sound as he rose from the table.

"See you in a few," Garrison said.

Peter texted Snoop, asking how to make the file disappear from Zack's laptop. His assistant replied with a detailed set of instructions, and Peter went to work. Garrison stood on the other side of the loft, talking to a member of his team.

Several excruciating minutes later, the file was gone.

Peter breathed a sign of relief. His cell phone vibrated in his pocket. It was Holly. He answered in a hushed voice.

"Hey."

"Are you all right?" Holly asked.

"I can't talk right now. I'll call you later."

"Wait. Did you figure out who the spy was?"

"I took care of it."

Garrison had finished his conversation, and began to cross the room.

Peter said, "I've got to go."

"Don't hang up," Holly said. "My aunt's had a change of heart, and wants to contact the police. She's afraid Wolfe will kill us if she doesn't do something. I tried to talk her out of it, but she won't budge. I called Max, and he's coming over to talk to her. We need you here, too. My aunt will listen to you. When can you get here?"

His loyalty was to his friends, and always would be.

"Give me twenty minutes," he said.

"I'll be waiting for you."

Peter ended the call as Garrison neared the table.

"Locked and loaded?" the FBI agent asked.

Peter wasn't sure what Garrison meant, and simply nodded.

"Glad to hear it. I need to get a statement from you about what happened." Garrison pulled up a chair and sat down. Taking a spiral notepad and a pen from his pocket, he began to scribble. "Okay. Now, start from the beginning."

"Can't you just make something up?" Peter asked.

"A man died here. No, I can't make something up."

Peter rose from his chair. He couldn't be in two places at once; giving a statement to the FBI would have to wait. He told himself that Garrison would get over it.

"Going somewhere?" Garrison said.

"There's someplace I have to be."

"Sit down. I'm not done with you."

The Sword Suspension illusion sat in the center of the room. Lying on the floor was a large white sheet that was used to cover Liza as she was suspended in midair. The sheet looked innocent, but in fact had stiff wires sewn into its fabric that resembled a human figure when held the proper way. Peter had made Liza disappear hundreds of times with it, and no one had ever discovered its secret. Picking the sheet up, he covered himself.

"Hey—what are you doing?" Garrison asked.

"I'm sorry," said his voice from beneath the sheet.

"Sorry about what?"

There was no response. Garrison grabbed the sheet, and whisked it away. The young magician had vanished like a puff of smoke. Garrison's trained eye gazed across the room. The door to the loft was wide open.

"Damn you!" the FBI agent exclaimed.

Peter was breathing hard by the time he reached the roof. Raindrops danced off the tar paper in a hypnotic ballet. He went to the edge, and looked straight down. Garrison and his team burst out the front door of the building. The last thing he needed right now was the FBI hunting for him, but he didn't see that he had any other choice.

"Hey!" Garrison shouted, looking straight up.

"I'll explain everything later," Peter shouted back.

"Get your ass down here, right now!"

"I can't do that."

"I'm going to throw you in jail."

"You'll have to catch me first."

"To the roof," Garrison said to his team.

The FBI agents hit the front door hard. They'd be on the roof soon. Peter turned around, and looked for an escape route besides the stairwell. He spotted an old-fashioned fire escape on the other side of the building, and hurried toward it. The roof was flat, and ran the length of the building. Many older buildings in the city were designed this way, and had once housed entire tent communities of people too poor to afford apartments, with residents traveling on catwalks from building to building without ever touching the ground below. Peter could feel their presence as he ran; this rooftop had been their home, and for many of their ghosts, still was.

He reached the fire escape. It was rusted with age, and hadn't been used in forever. He hoped it was strong enough to support him. As he took to the first step, Garrison and his team burst onto the roof, red-faced and puffing hard.

"I command you to stop!" Garrison shouted.

Peter glanced over his shoulder. "I'll call you later. I promise."

"I've had enough of your crap," Garrison declared.

The FBI agents rushed toward him. Peter started down the creaky stairs. Out of the corner of his eye, he spotted a man dressed in rags and wearing a broken top hat, sitting on the ledge. The man looked like a hobo, yet managed to have a dignified air about him. He was also transparent; half of him was there, and half of him wasn't.

It had been a while since Peter had seen a ghost. Back when he was a boy, they'd popped up fairly often, and he'd grown used to the late-night conversations with ghosts in his bedroom. As he'd grown older, their appearance had become less frequent. Now, if he saw a ghost every week, it was a lot. But that didn't mean they weren't there. Ghosts filled the earth, and resided in old houses and buildings they'd once called home. They continued to occupy these dwellings long after they died, and could not be driven out. Trying to remove a ghost from a house was a serious mistake, and could lead to all sorts of problems. The ghost sitting on the ledge had an impish look.

"I could use a little help," Peter said.

"I see that," the ghost said. "What did you do?"

"It's a long story."

"Most good stories are. Maybe someday you'll come back, and share it with me."

"You have a deal."

The ghost jumped off the ledge, and positioned himself in a crouch. As the FBI agents ran past, he stuck his leg out, and sent them flying through space. Later, the agents would say that they'd slipped, which was what everyone said who got tripped by a ghost.

"I owe you," Peter called.

The ghost flashed a crooked grin. He looked vaguely familiar, and Peter realized he'd seen his face in a book, and that he'd been someone important in his time. As Peter ran down the fire escape to the street, he promised himself to one day look up the building's history, and find out who the ghost was. It was nice to know who your friends were, even the dead ones.

39

"Please reconsider," Holly said.

"I've made up my mind," her aunt said stubbornly.

"That doesn't mean you can't change it."

"Are you lecturing me, my dear?"

"I most certainly am," Holly said. "Talking to the police is a mistake. Word will spread about who we are, and the government will swoop down, and take us away. They'll turn us into well-fed lab rats, like poor Nemo."

"Is the alternative any better?"

"We can catch Wolfe, if we put our minds to it."

They were in the kitchen in Milly's apartment, standing at the counter. Most people assumed that witches spent their free time riding broomsticks and causing warts to sprout up on people's noses, when in fact they liked to do normal things like everyone else. Milly's passion was cooking, and Holly helped her aunt knead the bread dough lying in a pan. Not that either of them were hungry, but it helped them get their minds off Reggie's death.

"So, tell me what's wrong between you and Peter," Milly said.

Holly worked the dough between her fingers. Her aunt had always been keen on her moods, and quick to offer advice, if she thought it might help. "Nothing," she said quietly.

"Then why does your voice go up every time you mention his name?"

"Is it that obvious?"

"Quite. It happens when people are in love. Tell me what's wrong. Maybe I can help."

Finding the words to describe her feelings was not easy, but Holly tried anyway. "I don't understand what's happening to Peter. One minute he's a dark, snarling person who's ordering me around like a slave, while the next he's the same wonderful boy I've always known. He's become two completely different individuals. I don't know how to deal with him anymore."

"Does his dark side frighten you?"

"Yes, and I don't like it."

"Nor should you," her aunt said. "Peter is a wonderful young man, and we must keep him that way."

"What do you mean? How can we influence who he is?"

"Simple. When his mood turns dark, you must continue to be kind to him. Do not become angry or upset. It will only make the situation worse."

Holly stopped what she was doing. "You've seen this side to him before?"

"Back when he was a child, yes."

"Is that how you treated him—by killing him with kindness?"

"That's exactly what I did. Max as well."

"Is there something wrong with Peter?"

"It's an inherited trait."

"His parents were like this?"

"Yes," Milly said quietly. "Peter takes after them."

"But I thought they were college professors, and very sweet."

"They were sweet, most of the time," Milly said. "But there was another side to them as well. I saw it once with his mother during a séance. I would liken it to watching Dr. Jekyll turn into Mr. Hyde. The transformation was frightening, to say the least."

"Where did it come from?"

Milly started to reply, then thought better of it. She removed an open bottle of Chablis from the refrigerator, filled two small glasses, and handed one to her niece. "Its origin is not important. What matters is that it's there, and you must be willing to deal with it."

Holly let the glass kiss her lips. "Why should I?"

"You love Peter, don't you?"

"Very much."

"And you're hoping that, one day, he'll leave his girlfriend, and be with you instead. It's entirely possible, considering that his girlfriend is not psychic, and will have a hard time dealing with Peter's powers once she learns about them. Every psychic has their heart broken at least once in their life, and I'm guessing Peter will not be an exception."

Holly sipped the wine. She didn't want Peter's heart to be broken, or have him end up with her just because someone normal wouldn't have him. It wasn't the scenario she envisioned for them at all. "Maybe he'll just grow tired of her," she said quietly.

"That's entirely possible," Milly said. "Whatever the case, you hope for the day when Peter will be yours. If that day comes, then you must be willing to deal with the dark side of his personality. That is the only choice you have, my dear. Don't make the mistake of believing that you can change Peter to suit your needs. That notion is what destroys most relationships."

Holly eyed her aunt coolly. "But why is it my only choice? Why can't Peter accept this isn't a good thing, and find a way to fix it? Men who have anger issues go to therapists and work out their problems. Why should Peter be any different?"

"Because he *is* different," Milly said.

"So am I. So are you."

"Not like Peter."

"Are you saying that he's special?"

"Yes. Henry and Claire Warren were not your ordinary, run-of-the-mill psychics, and neither is their son."

"I still don't like the way Peter's acting," Holly said, not backing down.

"It's a fight you cannot win, my dear."

Holly felt otherwise. She started to say so, when she heard the buzzer ring.

"That must be Peter," she said, and hurried from the kitchen.

* * *

Holly stuck her eye to the peephole in her aunt's front door.

"Hello, Max," she said, opening the door.

The old magician put his arms gently around her upon entering. "I'm so sorry about poor Reggie. It must have been horrible to see him go."

Holly stifled a tiny sob. Max lifted her chin with the tip of his finger, showed his hands empty, and made a beautiful red rose appear out of thin air.

"Thanks, Max," she said.

She hung his overcoat in the hall closet. In the living room Max took his usual spot on the couch. He looked exhausted, and took several deep breaths. Holly sat beside him and took his hand. "You're very warm. Are you feeling all right?"

"My heart has been racing all day," Max replied. "To lose two of your soul mates is brutal. Have you talked to Peter? Is he going to join us? We have to talk Milly out of this."

"Peter is on his way," Holly said. "Aunt Milly and I were just talking about him. Have you noticed how he's been acting lately? He's like a man possessed."

"We're all on edge," Max said defensively.

"That's not what I mean. Peter's changed."

"What do you mean?"

"Don't tell me you haven't seen it, Max. He's turned brutal."

"Not Peter."

"Yes, Peter. I want someone to tell me what's going on."

Max wiggled his fingers. A shiny silver dollar appeared, which he adroitly rolled back and forth across his knuckles. He split the silver dollar into two half-dollars, showed both sides of his hands, and split the half-dollars into four quarters. A smile lit up his face.

"Like it?" he asked.

"It was wonderful."

"Did I fool you?"

"Please stop avoiding the question."

He fished the various coins out of his sleeves and returned them to his pockets. "There is nothing going on, Holly, other than Peter is discovering certain things about himself that he will need to come to grips with. Our job is to be there for him, and help guide him."

"But—"

He shushed her with a finger. "You want to know why Peter's acting this way? That is something for him to tell you one day, not me, or anyone else. Do you understand?"

She shook her head helplessly. "No, I don't."

"Peter is evolving. Part of his evolution will be in the choices that he makes, and how he deals with these special gifts that he's discovering. The worst thing we can do is to interrupt this process, and make him question himself. Do you understand now?"

"No."

"What don't you understand?"

"Why I can't be let in on the secret."

Her aunt slipped into the living room, still wearing her apron. "Hello, Max. How are you holding up?" she asked.

"I've had better days. How about you, Milly?"

"If I could, I would make us all wake up from this horrible dream."

"If only that were possible. Come join us. We were talking about Peter."

Milly joined them on the couch, and sat to Holly's right. An uncomfortable silence followed. Holly hated when grown-ups went mute.

"For the last time, what is wrong with Peter?" Holly asked.

"She's like a dog with a bone," Max said to Milly.

"You're not being fair," Holly said.

"Life isn't fair," her aunt reminded her.

"Peter scares me," Holly said, raising her voice. "Is he some kind of demon? Should I be afraid of him? I have a right to know what's going on."

Another silence followed. Max cleared his throat.

"Would you like to tell her, or should I?" the old magician asked.

"Oh, why don't you," Milly replied.

Max faced Holly, and held her hands with both his own. "Since you asked, here it is. Peter is a warlock, and not just in name only. He's a real one."

An icy finger ran down Holly's spine. In books and the movies, warlocks were depicted as humans who had attained magical or mystical powers which they used for the betterment of mankind. Nothing could have been further from the truth. Warlocks were evil people who had entered into pacts with the Devil, and were the worst form of deceivers. Other psychics viewed them as heretics, and Holly was having a hard time believing that Peter was one.

"But he can't be," she said.

"But he is," her aunt corrected her.

"He *can't* be. I would have seen it long ago."

"Peter inherited it from his parents, who became warlocks as children," her aunt replied. "It's in his genes."

Holly shook her head in disbelief. She was in love with Peter, and had been for as long as she could remember. How could she have possibly missed this?

"How long have you known?" she asked.

"I saw it when Peter was a boy," Milly said. "He roughed up a bully at his school, and really hurt him. Max saw it as well. Didn't you, Max?"

"Afraid so," Max said. "There is a demon simmering just below the surface. I saw it several times when I was giving him magic lessons. I learned to give in, and never argue with him. Eventually, the demon would leave, and he'd go back to being his normal, fun-loving self. When he was searching for a stage name, I suggested Warlock because it sounded magical, but there was another reason as well."

"Because he is one." Holly rose and went to the window. The oak trees in Central Park were filled with her aunt's beloved crows, lined up in a military-like formation.

"Will he stay like this?" she heard herself ask.

"Only if we let him," her aunt replied.

"What do you mean? How do we play into this?"

"Every person, be they a witch or warlock or what-have-you, has a guiding force in their lives," Milly explained. "The guiding force in Peter's life is us. Our job is to surround Peter with positive influences. That was how we raised him, and it worked wonders. The same must hold true now. You cannot fight fire with fire."

"So when he acts like a monster, I should be nice to him," Holly said.

"Yes, my dear," her aunt said.

"That's going to be hard."

"Try."

The buzzer rang again, and Holly turned from the window. The burning sensation she felt when thinking about Peter had turned into a deep ache in her heart. Yet it did not diminish her love for him. If anything, her feelings for him were stronger than before.

"Would you like me to answer the door?" her aunt asked.

"No, I'll get it," Holly replied.

Holly stuck her eye to the peephole. In the hallway stood an older man wearing the camel-colored uniform that came with his security job. Clutched between his hands was a package with a UPS label. It was Ralph, who'd been working here since Holly was little.

"Who is it?" her aunt called from the living room.

"It's Ralph. He's delivering a package," Holly replied.

"I wasn't expecting anything. Were you?"

"No."

"He usually calls up first," her aunt said suspiciously.

"Maybe he forgot."

Through the peephole, Ralph gave the buzzer another jab. He was a good-natured man and friendly, but now had a troubled look on his face. Holly decided to err on the side of caution, and opened the front door without unfastening the security chain. "Hi, Ralph? What have you got for us?" She peered through the cracked door.

"Special delivery," Ralph said.

"Is something wrong? Who's that standing behind you?"

Ralph's eyes rolled up into his head, and he sunk to the floor still clutching the package. Behind him stood the man who'd attacked her and Reggie that morning. It was Wolfe, clutching a club in his hand.

"Aunt Milly, call 911," Holly shouted.

Wolfe kicked the door before Holly could shut it. The chain broke, and the door hit her in the face. Seeing stars, she fell to the floor. Wolfe entered and slammed the door.

"Hello, bitch," Wolfe said.

"It's witch," Holly whispered.

"I like bitch better. Stand up."

"I can't," Holly replied, fighting to stay conscious.

Wolfe grabbed Holly by the hair, and jerked her head so he was looking in her face.

"You're a difficult one, aren't you?"

"Go to hell."

Wolfe dragged Holly kicking and screaming into the living room like a caveman. Her aunt was waiting, and tried to hit Wolfe with an antique lamp. Wolfe lashed out, and sent her aunt sprawling to the floor. Max was next, and threw a clumsy punch at Wolfe's head. The old magician also ended up on the floor.

Holly pushed herself into a kneeling position. Blood was pouring out of her mouth, and one of her bottom teeth felt loose. She looked up at Wolfe.

The assassin was smiling at her.

"Your turn," he said.

Holly braced herself. She had accepted her own mortality long ago. It was part of being a witch. What she hadn't accepted was that she might be brutally murdered in the prime of her life. That wasn't fair, and she told herself she must fight back.

Through the living room window, she saw the crows dancing on the branches. They knew something was wrong, yet without Milly's direction, would not react.

Help me, she told them.

Wolfe raised his club.

40

There was no faster driver than a New York cabbie. Peter threw money at the driver and jumped out of the backseat. His shoulder hit the front door as he entered the Dakota.

The guard's chair behind the front desk was empty.

That was strange—there was always one guard behind the desk, and another standing in the lobby, ready to hold open the front door.

"Anyone home?"

A dull banging sound got his attention. The noise was coming from the coat closet behind the desk. He jerked open the closet door. A red-faced security guard stood inside. His wrists were bound together with wire, his mouth covered with duct tape.

Wolfe had beat him here.

Peter had felt it during the cab ride over, the coldness in his bones telling him that evil was knocking at his door. He ripped the tape from the guard's mouth. The man winced.

"How long has he been here?" Peter asked.

The guard gasped for air. "Just a couple of minutes. He came in pretending to be a delivery man, then jumped us."

"Us? Where's your partner?"

"He took him upstairs with him."

"Can you free yourself?"

"Yes, once I get out of this damn closet," the guard said.

Peter ran to the elevators and hit the call button. Nothing happened, and he stared at the LED displays above the doors. The building had three elevators, and each was stuck on the fifth floor. Milly's apartment was also on the fifth floor. He quickly found the stairwell, and flew up the stairs. The rage had returned, and he felt ready to take on an army.

He came out of the stairwell on the fifth floor, and ran the length of the hall to Milly's apartment. Outside her door the second security guard lay on the floor, moaning softly. The apartment door was closed, and Peter rammed it with his shoulder like he'd seen cops do in the movies. The door flew off its hinges, and he raced inside.

"Milly? Holly? Max?"

"Help," came a voice from the living room.

It was Holly, sounding hurt. He entered the living room expecting the worst. Milly lay on the floor in a pool of blood, while Max knelt beside her. Across the room, Holly was having her hair pulled out by Wolfe, who was preparing to strike her with a club.

"Stop!" Peter said.

Wolfe stopped what he was doing to look his way.

"You're an hour late, and a dollar short," the assassin said.

Peter grabbed a flower vase from a table and dumped its contents onto the floor. He'd ended Zack's life with a miserable screwdriver, and felt certain that he could arrange an equally inglorious demise for Wolfe as well. Flipping the vase over, he grabbed it by the neck.

He moved forward.

"Do you really think you can hurt me with that?" Wolfe mocked him.

He kept coming, halving the distance between them.

"Stop right there, or I'll crush her skull," Wolfe exclaimed.

Peter stopped on a dime. He heard a loud *Ping!* sound that reminded him of hail falling during a storm. There had been no hail outside, just a heavy rain, and he ignored it.

"Let her go, or I'll kill you," he said.

"I'm the one holding the cards here. Not you."

Wolfe was wrong. Peter had the power to hurt Wolfe, and bring this to an end. Call it a gift, or a curse; whatever it was, he'd had this power his entire life, and had just never known it was there. Now, he did, and he was going to unleash all its fury on Wolfe.

Peter raised the flower vase. "Last chance."

"You think you can take me down with that?" Wolfe said.

"Sure do."

"Take your best shot."

The pinging sound had not gone away. Peter glanced at the picture window that faced the park. Milly's crows were throwing their bodies against the glass, trying to get inside to save their mistress before it was too late. Or maybe they knew how evil Wolfe was, and were trying to stop him. Whatever their motive, they looked ready to die, just like him.

Peter threw the vase across the living room. He'd had lousy aim since childhood, and missed his enemy by several feet.

"Ha," Wolfe laughed.

The vase shattered against the wall. Instead of falling to the floor, the jagged pieces flipped backward through the air, and impaled themselves in Wolfe's neck.

"Ha, yourself," Peter said.

Wolfe screamed in pain, and let the club slip from his hand. With blood pouring down his neck, he staggered around the living room. With each step, his eyes grew more panicked.

"You tricked me," he gasped.

"Yes, I did," Peter said.

The living room had a working fireplace that got plenty of use during the winter. Wolfe fell to his knees in front of it, and looked ready to pass out. The tattoo on his neck began to glow, and his eyes snapped open. He pulled the poker from the ashes, and struggled to his feet.

Max and Milly had not moved from their spot on the floor.

Wolfe lunged toward them.

Peter stood on the other side of the living room. He thought back to the night he'd lost his parents. He couldn't live through that again, and looked at the birds.

"Get him!" he screamed.

The window imploded, allowing the crows to enter. In a mad flurry of beating wings, they crossed the living room and swallowed up Wolfe, biting at his clothing and his skin. He looked like a scarecrow having the stuffing pulled out of him. Within seconds, his clothes had been torn apart, and his face was a bloody mess. A pitiful sound escaped his lips.

"Help me," Wolfe begged.

Peter hesitated. The image of the dead and dying in Times Square had never been far from his thoughts. Wolfe had been in the center of the carnage, assessing his work like the merchant of death that he was. With Wolfe gone, there would be no massacre.

"No," Peter said firmly.

"Please!"

"No," he said again.

A gust of rain blew into the living room. The crows pulled Wolfe toward the broken window. Wolfe began to kick wildly as the birds lifted him cleanly off the floor.

Peter looked at Holly, now standing beside him.

"Are you controlling them?" he asked.

"I am," she replied.

"I didn't know you could do that."

"I'm learning."

The crows carried their prey through the window. Wolfe had stopped making any sound, and was frozen in fear. Once outside, he hung in the air, the sight both beautiful and horrifying at the same time. Peter crossed the room with Holly beside him, and stopped by the window. The crows pivoted Wolfe around so he faced them.

"Please spare me," Wolfe begged.

The words sounded strange coming out of his mouth. How many of his victims had he spared in his life? Not a single one, Peter guessed.

"Tell me about Times Square," Peter called to him.

"What about it?"

"How were you going to kill everyone? With a bomb?"

"I don't know what you're talking about," Wolfe replied.

Peter felt his blood boil. The coldness was gone, replaced by a hot wire that ignited his veins, and made him as capable of ending a life as the man hanging outside. He leaned against the windowsill, and stuck his head into the blowing rain. "You killed my friends, but I'm still going to give you a chance. Tell me what your mission is."

"To kill you, and your psychic friends," Wolfe said, his voice growing hoarse.

"Tell me the rest of it."

"There isn't any more."

"Liar."

Wolfe dropped a few feet in the air as the crows tired. He blinked wildly, and Peter wondered if his life was flashing before his eyes.

"They can't hold him any longer," Holly said.

"Tell them to bring him back inside," Peter said.

"I'll try."

The crows tried to bring Wolfe back into the apartment. His weight was too much, and he fell several more feet. A startled yell came out of his mouth.

"They can't do it," she said.

One by one, the crows released their grip, and disappeared into the night. Wolfe appeared to be hanging on an invisible thread as he floated in the air. The thread finally broke. He flailed his arms and legs while descending to the pavement below.

Holly turned away, unable to watch.

Peter stuck his head out the window just in time to see Wolfe tear through the building's awning. His body hit something on the sidewalk, and lay perfectly still. Peter didn't think anyone could survive such a fall, but was not willing to take a chance. He turned from the window to face Holly, and saw that she was crying.

"I just killed him," she sobbed.

"It had to be done."

"I'm not a monster, am I?"

"You did what had to be done. I'm going downstairs. Please stay here."

"Whatever you say."

Peter crossed the room to check on Milly and Max. The old magician was sitting on the floor, and had pulled Milly's head into his lap. A painful-looking welt had appeared on Milly's forehead, and Peter saw her eyelids flutter.

"Is she okay?"

"Just knocked out," Max said. "What about Wolfe?"

"I think he's dead," Peter replied.

"You think? Better make sure. We don't want another round of this."

"He fell five floors, Max. He's dead."

The old magician gave him a scornful look. Peter had learned everything he knew from Max, yet there were times that he wondered how much his teacher had really told him.

"He was sent by the Order. Five floors is nothing," Max said. "You need to check."

Peter nodded, and hurried from the apartment.

41

P eter took the stairway to the lobby and ran outside. Wolfe's crumpled body lay on the sidewalk.
His clothes were on fire, his face seared beyond recognition. Smoldering chestnuts littered the ground. In the
street sat the damaged chestnut cart he had landed upon.

Peter knelt down, just to make sure Wolfe was dead.
He was.

Beneath the damaged awning stood the security guard
Peter had freed from the closet. The guard had a cell
phone pressed to his ear, and a bewildered look on his
face.

"I could use a little help," Peter said.

With the guard's help, Peter patted Wolfe down until
the flames were extinguished. It was the perfect send-
off for someone going straight to hell, he thought.

"No one's going to believe this," the guard said.

"What do you mean?" Peter asked.

"He was being held in the air by a bunch of birds."

A siren pierced the air. No one had ever accused the
New York police of being slow. He needed to plant the
seed of doubt with the guard before the police arrived.

"What birds? What are you talking about?" Peter
asked.

"You didn't see them?" the guard asked.

"Afraid not."

"Come on. Don't tell me I'm seeing things."

"I don't know what you're talking about," Peter said.
"I went into Milly Adams' apartment, and found this
guy attacking my friends. We fought, and I threw him
out the window, and he fell to the sidewalk."

"You threw him out the window? What about the flipping birds?"

"You must have imagined them."

"No such luck. I stopped drinking twenty years ago. They were black and making this godawful racket. I think they were the crows that live in the oak trees across the street."

"I didn't see them."

The guard looked confused, just as Peter intended. If the guard doubted himself, the police would question his story as well, and hopefully not believe him. A white Crown Vic with a flashing bubble on its dashboard came racing up Central Park West. The cavalry had arrived.

"What are you going to tell the police?" Peter asked.

"That's a darn good question," the guard said.

The guard waved the vehicle down. It braked with a rubbery squeal, and four men wearing dark suits jumped out. Each sported a short haircut and had a Bluetooth in his ear. Not cops, but agents of some other law enforcement agency, Peter decided.

Two of the agents checked Wolfe to make sure he was dead.

"No life in this one," one of them said.

The man in charge nodded grimly. He was built like a linebacker, with broad shoulders and no visible neck. He confronted Peter and the guard.

"Which one of you called 911?" he asked.

"I did," the guard said.

"Come over by the car. I need to speak with you."

The guard stood by the Crown Vic and answered questions. Peter felt his cell phone vibrate, and slipped it from his pocket. It was Holly, sending him a text message.

U OK?

YES

I'M IN THE LOBBY   WHO ARE THOSE GUYS?

Peter glanced over his shoulder. Holly looked at him through a window, her breath fogging the glass. He turned back around, and resumed texting.

GOVERNMENT   THEY WILL PROBABLY QUESTION YOU

WHAT SHOULD WE DO?

LIE

I KNOW THAT!   SOMETHING WRONG WITH MILLY

WHAT?!

NOT TALKING RIGHT

CALL AMBULANCE

DID THAT   I'M SCARED

He again looked through the window. Holly looked very scared.

SHE'LL BE OKAY

HOPE SO

"Hey, I want to talk to you."

Peter looked up. The agent in charge was motioning to him. The guard stood to one side with a sheepish look on his face. He'd told him about the birds.

Peter walked over to the car, prepared for the worst.

"Who were you talking to on your phone," the agent in charge asked.

"A girl I know. Who are you?"

The agent flipped open his wallet. Chad Morningstar, CIA. The CIA had kidnaped Nemo, and Peter could not let the same thing happen to him, or Holly, or Max and Milly. None of them deserved to lose their freedom because of this.

"What's your name," Morningstar asked.

"Peter Warlock."

"Do you mind answering some questions, Peter?"

"Not at all."

"Good. Get in the car."

"Why? Where are we going?"

"To a secure place."

"What's wrong with right here?"

"You got a problem getting in the car?"

"Come to mention it, yes."

Morningstar grabbed his arm, and looked ready to get physical. A dark thought passed through Peter's mind, and he saw himself pounding Morningstar into the ground as payback for what his bosses had done to Nemo. He took a deep breath, and the feeling passed.

"Whatever you say," Peter told him.

Peter got into the back of the Crown Vic. As Morningstar shut the door, Peter gave the CIA agent a hard stare. The knowing look in his eye was all too familiar. *He knows who I am.*

Peter fell back into the seat. The game was over.

As the car pulled away from the curb, Peter glanced

at the front of the Dakota. Holly was watching, and had tears running down her cheeks. He wondered if he would ever see her again.

They hurtled downtown. *Out of the frying pan and into the fire,* Peter thought.

42

Morningstar took him to the 14th Precinct on West 35th Street, also known as Midtown South. It was here that the criminals of Times Square were brought to be booked. The precinct had a reputation for being a cesspool, and they passed an assortment of lowlifes on their way to the basement. Peter looked down as he walked, and tried to remain calm.

They entered a small room with a desk and two chairs. Peter sat in an uncomfortable wooden chair and put his elbows on the desk. There was another chair beside his, which he assumed was for a lawyer. Morningstar remained standing.

"Tell me about Wolfe," the CIA agent said.

Peter had already made up a story during the ride. Most of it was true, and he hoped Morningstar would buy the rest. He took a deep breath, and began. "A crazy guy attacked me three nights ago. Don't ask me why, because I don't know. This afternoon, I went to visit some friends at the Dakota, and this guy followed me there. He got into the building, and broke into the apartment. We fought, and I threw him through a window in the living room."

Finished, Peter leaned back in his chair.

"That's it?" Morningstar asked.

"Yes, sir."

Their eyes locked. The CIA agent wasn't buying his explanation one bit.

"Exactly what is your relationship with Millicent Adams?" Morningstar asked.

"She helped raise me," Peter replied.

"How about the other two people in the apartment?"

"Holly Adams is her niece, and my friend. Max Romeo, my magic teacher, also helped raise me. Max is a friend of Milly's as well."

"So you all know each other?"

"Correct."

"Why were you all together?"

No good answer came to mind, so Peter made one up.

"We were going out to celebrate my birthday," he said.

"Really. Give me your wallet."

"Why should I do that?"

"Just do it."

Peter dug out his wallet, and handed it over. Morningstar removed his driver's license, and held it up to the overhead light. "Your birthday was last month. Why are you lying to me?"

"I'm not lying," Peter said.

"Your birthday story is nonsense."

"No, it's not."

"Then why were your friends getting together so late?"

"I'm in show business, and work nearly every night. I miss a lot of holidays and anniversaries and stuff like that. We picked this afternoon because we were all available."

Morningstar tossed his wallet to the table. "What do you do?"

"Do?"

"For a living."

"I'm a professional magician."

"Do you read minds, and tell the future?"

Morningstar was trying to trap him. Peter told himself to stay calm.

"No, that's what a mentalist does," he said. "I do magic tricks, like sawing a woman in half and making things disappear."

"Are you trying to be funny?"

"No, that's what a comedian does."

Morningstar pulled the other chair out from the table, and sat backwards in it. He eyed Peter coolly. "You're the guy we've been looking for, aren't you?"

Busted! Peter thought.

"I don't know what you're talking about," he said.

"I think you do. Should I explain?"

"Please."

"You're the guy who can see into the future, and predict what's going to happen," the CIA agent said. "You know, the United States government could use a person with your talents. You could make the world a safer place. Think about it."

Peter shifted uncomfortably. "You've got me mistaken for somebody else. I'm not a psychic."

"Did I call you a psychic?"

"No, but that's what psychics do, and I'm not one."

"Why don't you admit it? It will make things a lot easier."

"Because then I'd be lying."

Morningstar rocked forward in his chair. "Tell me about the birds."

"What birds?"

"The flock of birds that helped you do away with Wolfe. The guard at the Dakota saw them fluttering outside the apartment window before Wolfe fell. Is that another one of your powers? Can you make animals do your bidding?"

"I can pull a rabbit out of a hat, if that's what you mean."

"You're not funny."

"I know. That's why I became a magician."

Morningstar came out of his chair faster than Peter would have liked. He pointed at the door. "I've got someone standing in the hallway that will identify you. Why don't you just admit who you are, and spare him the trouble of having to come in here?"

"There's nothing to admit," Peter said.

"Sure you don't want to change your mind?"

"I'm happy with the mind that I have."

Morningstar jerked the door open. "Come in."

Special Agent Garrison entered the room. He was the last person Peter wanted to see right now. Peter wondered if he could talk Morningstar into putting him on the same farm in Virginia where Nemo was being held. At least he'd have someone to talk to.

"Stand up," Morningstar said.

Peter rose from his chair, ready to face the music.

"Special Agent Garrison, is this the psychic you told the CIA about?" Morningstar asked.

Garrison popped a piece of candy into his mouth. He gave Peter a healthy stare.

"No," Garrison said.

Peter nearly hit the floor.

"*What?*" Morningstar exploded. "Are you sure?"

"Positive. It's not him," Garrison said.

"Hold on a minute. You told us you met with a psychic in New York who was dialed in to Wolfe. You said this psychic was in his twenties, slender, and good-looking. You're telling me this isn't the same guy?"

"The guy I met was thinner, and had brown hair," Garrison said. "This isn't him."

"Are you sure?"

Garrison shot him a nasty look. "What do you mean, am I sure?"

"You told the CIA you met this psychic in a dark bar, right?"

"That's right."

"Well, maybe he was wearing a disguise that altered his appearance."

"This isn't the guy I met."

"It has to be him. Everything points to him."

"What do you want me to say, that it's him when it's not?"

"Look at him again, will you?"

Garrison crushed the piece of candy in his mouth. "Sure, whatever you want." Taking out a pair of glasses, he fitted them onto his face, and leaned forward to stare at Peter. A long moment passed, with Peter doing everything in his power not to smile at the FBI agent. Finished, Garrison removed his glasses, and slipped them back into his shirt pocket.

"So what do you think?" Morningstar asked.

"Definitely not him," Garrison answered. "If you don't mind, I need to get back to work. You gentlemen have a nice day."

Garrison left without another word being spoken.

Everything got a lot simpler after that.

They went upstairs to an office, where Peter was given a cup of steaming hot coffee. Morningstar found a tape recorder, and made Peter recount his story again, which was then typed up by a police secretary, and given to Peter for his signature. The process took an hour, but seemed longer. By now, Morningstar had stopped treating him like a criminal. The crisis had passed, and Peter could not remember having ever felt more relieved in his life.

When they were done, Morningstar walked Peter to the front entrance of the precinct. He could not wait to set foot on the sidewalk, a free man again.

"Sorry for the mix-up," Morningstar said.

"You were just doing your job," Peter replied.

"No hard feelings?"

"Not at all."

Morningstar pumped his hand.

"Let me be the first to congratulate you," the CIA agent said.

"What for?" Peter asked.

"For bringing a dangerous man to justice. I don't know if you're aware of this, but Wolfe posed a serious threat to the entire city. By killing him, you saved a lot of lives."

"I'm glad to help," Peter said.

Peter walked down the front steps of the precinct. The weather was still miserable. Turning up his collar, he headed west on 35th Street toward Ninth Avenue on a sidewalk filled with people holding umbrellas. He waited until he was a safe distance away from the precinct before pulling out his cell phone. He checked for messages, but found none on voice mail, nor any texts. That was troubling, and he hoped Milly was all right.

He walked another block to Dyer Avenue in Hell's Kitchen before calling Holly. Voice mail picked up, and he left a message. As he ended the call, a black Lincoln pulled onto Dyer from 35th Street, and flashed its brights at him. His instincts told him it was Garrison, and he was proven right as the Lincoln's tires rubbed the curb, and the passenger window lowered.

"Need a lift?" Garrison called to him.

Peter hopped in. Garrison did a U-turn, and got on 34th, this time heading east.

"Thanks for the save," Peter said. "How are my friends doing?"

"The older lady took a whack to the head," Garrison said. "They rushed her to the hospital, and are treating her right now. I'm assuming that's where you want to go."

"You assumed right. Which hospital?"

"Roosevelt."

Peter felt himself shudder. They had taken Milly to the same hospital where Reggie had died. It was as bad an omen as he could ask for.

"How did it go with Morningstar?" Garrison asked.

"I survived," Peter replied. "I didn't realize the CIA was so intent on finding me."

"I told the CIA enough about you for them to get excited," Garrison said. "In hindsight, that was a mistake. I'm sorry."

"Morningstar would have taken me away to some secret location, wouldn't he?"

"Probably."

"And I never would have seen my friends again."

"Yeah," Garrison said under his breath.

"Do you mind my asking you a question?"

"Go ahead."

"Why did you lie to him? You're going to get in trouble if it comes out who I really am."

"Yes, I will. Might even lose my job."

"Then why did you do it?"

Garrison glanced at him out of the corner of his eye as he sped north on Eighth Avenue. Peter's life had turned into a cloak-and-dagger novel, and he needed to know who his friends were. Finally, Garrison replied.

"Like I told you the other day, you're my secret weapon."

"You're not going to share me with other government agencies?"

"Wasn't planning on it."

"What do you want in return?"

"Help. Not all the time, just when I'm stumped."

"That's it?"

"There's one other thing."

Peter braced himself for the worst. "What's that?"

"You and your friends have been sending notes to the FBI whenever you see something bad during your séances," Garrison said. "From now on, I want you to contact me directly. It will be quicker, and you can save yourself the postage."

"Anything else?"

"That's it."

Peter felt the air trapped in his lungs escape. He'd be more than happy to help Garrison if his life would return to normal and his friends were spared.

"You've got a deal," he said.

"Beautiful," the FBI agent replied.

A few blocks from the hospital, Peter's cell phone vibrated in his pocket. Caller ID said HOLLY. He felt his heart leap into his throat as he answered her call.

"Where are you?" he asked.

"At the hospital with my aunt."

"Is she all right?"

"No."

"Where's Max?"

"He's here with me. We're so scared."

Peter placed the cell phone against his chest. "Can you go any faster?"

Garrison hit the gas, and the car's wheels momentarily left the ground.

"I'm on my way," he said into the phone.

43

Holly was standing in the ICU as Peter came out of the elevator. Her cheeks were red and puffy from crying. Seeing him, she put her brave face on.

"Hi," she said.

Peter hugged her. "I got here as fast as I could. How's your aunt doing?"

"Oh, God, Peter, I'm so worried. She keeps slipping in and out of consciousness. One minute she's here, the next she's not. When she's awake, she babbles and doesn't make much sense. The doctor said she took a bad blow, and might have some permanent memory loss, and maybe some other side effects as well. He said the next few hours were critical."

"How are *you* doing?"

"I'm okay."

Holly didn't sound okay. Peter put his hands on her shoulders, and studied her eyes. Her anger was bubbling just below the surface, ready to erupt. An angry witch was a force to be reckoned with, as Holly had demonstrated at her aunt's apartment.

"Why don't you go back to the apartment, and get some rest," he suggested. "You've had a hard day, and need to take it easy."

Her eyes flamed. "No."

"It's for your own good."

"I'm not deserting her."

Peter looked around the ICU to make sure no one was listening. "All right, but don't let your anger get out of control. Please."

"Look who's talking," she said.

"Peter!" Milly called from inside the room.

"She's awake," Holly said in a hushed voice.

"Peter, is that you I hear in the hallway, conspiring with my niece?"

"Yes, it's me," Peter called into the room.

"Come here at once, young man. I wish to speak with you."

"She certainly sounds normal," Peter said.

Holly wiped away a tear. "Maybe she's coming out of it. Let's hope so."

"Where's Max, anyway?"

"He went to get a hot drink from the cafeteria for my aunt."

"Peter?"

"Coming."

"Go slow with her," Holly said quietly.

Peter slipped into room. Milly sat in a reclining position in bed, looking small and frail. A pillow was propped behind her head, while several tubes ran out of her arm to a gathering of beeping machines beside her bed. Her face sported a mosaic of bruises that would have seemed noble on a boxer or football player, but looked sickening on a seventy-year-old woman.

"There you are," she said.

He kissed her cheek. "How are you feeling?"

"Like I've been ground through a cement truck. You know what they say. All's well that ends well. And how are you, my dear boy?"

"I'm fine, Milly."

"Holly said that a government agent took you away."

"It worked out okay. We're in the clear."

"Leave it to you to make things right. It appears we have company."

Max came through the doorway holding a brown paper bag. He tore away the paper to reveal a large foam cup with a plastic lid. "Your drink, my lady."

Milly took the cup. She pulled back the lid and frowned. "It's empty, Max."

"Are you sure?" Max exclaimed.

"Yes. There's nothing in it."

"It must have vanished during the elevator ride up."

"More likely you drank it."

"Me? Perish the thought."

"If it vanished, then make it reappear."

"Your wish is my command." Max waved his hand magically over the empty cup. "Like a ghost passing through the wall of an Irish castle, I command your drink to reappear. One, two, three! Why, look what we have here—your cup of decaf."

The cup had filled itself with the steaming drink. Milly sipped it appreciatively. It seemed to lift her spirts, and the color returned to her face.

"How did you do that?" she asked him.

"Can you keep a secret?" Max asked.

"Of course," she said.

"So can I."

"How did he do that?" she asked Peter.

"I haven't a clue. He fooled me completely," Peter replied.

Max beamed at the compliment. Like all great magicians, he guarded his secrets like the crown jewels, and it would be a long time before Peter would be able to pry this particular trick out of him. Then, Peter had an awful thought. If Max were to die, he'd never know how the trick worked. The secret would die with him, along with all the other secrets that he possessed.

The thought gave him pause. Max had been present the night his mother had turned into a monster, and so had Milly. They'd seen the transformation, and understood its terrible meaning. The other people who'd been there—his father, Madame Marie, and Reggie—were gone. Lester Rowe had been there, but he was now thousands of miles away, and might never return.

Max and Milly were the only ones left who knew the secret of his parents' supernatural powers. Peter could wait for a better time to talk to them about it, but if he'd learned anything over the past few days, waiting was dangerous.

"I need to have a talk with you and Max," Peter said.

"This sounds serious," Milly said.

"It is."

"What do you say, Max?" Milly asked.

Max looked away, saying nothing.

"I'll take that as a reluctant yes," Milly said. "The floor is yours, Peter."

"Thank you. I have a demon inside of me, which I inherited from my parents, who had the same demon inside of them," he said, the words spilling out. "Both of you sheltered me from this demon when I was growing up, fearful of the harm I might cause. You tried to keep me from fighting with other kids because you worried I might hurt them."

"That's utter nonsense," Milly scolded him. "You had a nasty little temper when you were a boy, and were getting into scrapes with other children. We tried to curb it, just like any intelligent adults would do. Didn't we, Max?"

"He did have a temper," Max mumbled.

"Which he eventually outgrew as he became a man," Milly said.

"That he did," Max said.

"So you see, Peter, this is all in your head," Milly concluded. "If you'd had a demon inside of you, we would have had you exorcized, like that poor little girl in the movie. Only you didn't, so there was no need. Right, Max?"

"Right," Max said, laughing under his breath.

The hospital room fell silent, save for the incessant beeping of the machines. Peter might have been angry with Max and Milly, had he not loved them so much. He supposed that in their eyes he was still a child, and always would be. But that didn't change his desire to know who he was. If anything, it only made it stronger.

"I saw the demon in the film of my mother," he said quietly.

They both looked startled.

"What film?" Milly blurted out.

"The one taken during a séance many years ago at their apartment," Peter replied. "I found it in Lester Rowe's place."

Milly brought her hand to her mouth. "Lester filmed that?"

"Yes," he said. "And both of you were present."

"He knows," Max said under his breath.

A single tear ran down Milly's cheek. Max plucked a hanky out of thin air, and handed it to her. Wiping her eye, she said, "I seem to vaguely recall the incident."

"Tell me about it," Peter said.

"Max, you do it," Milly said.

Max moved closer to the bed, and dropped his voice. "Your mother never spoke about what happened that night, but your father did. We met in a pub for a drink, and ended up closing the place down. Your father told me that he and your mother had made a pact with a demon when they were children, and that it was this demon that had manifested during our séance, and taken over your mother's body. I asked your father if the demon had ever taken over *his* body. Your father said that it had, but only when he lost his temper. This was why your parents tried to avoid having arguments, for fear of bringing the demon on."

"And that's why you didn't want me fighting," Peter said.

"That is correct. I'm afraid the demon is in you as well."

"What is the demon's name?"

Max hesitated. "I told your father I would take this to my grave."

"I have a right to know who I am."

Max glanced at Milly in the bed. She nodded imperceptibly.

"The demon is one of Lucifer's sons," his teacher said.

Peter opened his mouth, but nothing came out. Max grabbed the room's only chair, and made him sit in it. Peter did. Leaning forward, he ran the fingers of his hands through his hair. Since the beginning of time, Lucifer's presence in the world had been a dark one. To do his bidding, he'd created seven demonic sons, whom he'd sprinkled around the planet. For thousands of years, these sons had vied to see who could cause more grief and destruction, and were responsible for many of mankind's atrocities. Their names were known to all in the spirit world, and they were the epitome of evil. Peter had never encountered one of these sons, and now shuddered to realize that he in effect *was* one.

"What's his name?" Peter asked.

"Your father never said," Max replied.

"He must have described him."

"In a manner of speaking. He called him the wicked one."

"How charming."

Peter rose and went to the room's solitary window. Cold air blew through the cracks, and slapped him in the face. "I don't understand. My parents helped the Americans and the British defeat the Nazis, and win the war. How was that possible, considering what you just told me?"

"They were children," Milly explained.

"So?"

"All children are born good. The corruption comes later, as they grow up."

"Are you saying that even this demon couldn't poison a child?"

"Children are pure," Milly said. "Your parents, and their three little friends, could not be corrupted by this demon until later on in life."

"But my parents weren't corrupted." He turned from the window to look at them. "They were wonderful people. Weren't they?"

"He doesn't understand," Milly said to Max.

"We're not doing a very good job explaining it to him," Max replied.

"Explaining what? What are you leaving out?" Peter said, exasperated.

"Come to me," Milly said.

Peter returned to her bedside. Milly took his hands, and held them tightly. "Yes, they were wonderful people. And so are you. Do you know why?"

"No," he said.

"It's simple, my dear child. It's called free will. The fact that you are possessed by a demon does not mean you must become evil. Being evil is a choice, just as being good is a choice. If you let the demon take over, it's because you choose to."

"You're telling me that if I control my emotions, the demon won't come out."

"That's right."

What Milly was asking was absurd. How could he not grow angry every once in a while? There were times when a person *had* to get angry.

"My temper isn't that bad," he said.

"Yes, it is," she corrected him. "Come closer."

He leaned over the bed. Without warning, Milly slapped him in the face. He shot her a murderous stare. The monitors she was attached to started to beep, and her vital signs began moving in the wrong direction.

"Milly!" he said.

Her eyelids fluttered, and she sunk into her pillow. Max came to her side, and put his hand on her forehead.

"Stop this right now," his teacher said.

Peter forced himself to calm down. Within moments Milly snapped to, and the monitors stopped their frantic beeping.

"Oh, my God, I'm so sorry," he said.

"Believe me now?" she asked.

"Yes, I believe you."

She again took his hand. This time when she spoke, he listened. "You must be stronger than the demon inside of you. Succumb to temptation, and you will lose your soul."

"I feel like I'm losing it already," he said.

"How so?"

"I killed a man who worked for me today. He was evil, and I suppose he deserved it, but I felt no regrets afterward. That's not normal, is it?"

"You are still one of us," Milly replied. "Isn't he, Maximilian?"

"Indeed he is," his teacher said.

"And you will stay one of us. Now, if you'll excuse me, I must rest. It's been a long day."

Milly's eyelids grew heavy, and just like that she was sound asleep. Peter glanced at the machines that she was attached to. The numbers had returned to normal.

"I'll stay with her," Max said. "Go home, and get some rest."

"What about Holly?"

"I sent her home earlier."

At least Holly listened to someone, Peter thought. He went to the door, turning to glance at Milly one more time. She looked so tiny and frail lying in that awful bed, and he could not help but feel that he was responsible for everything that had happened to her. He had accepted long ago that life wasn't fair, a sentiment that became more profound the older he became.

"Goodnight," he said.

"Be safe, Peter," his teacher said.

"And you as well."

44

Most New Yorkers were light sleepers. It came from living around so many people, and all the traffic. Peter was no exception. Any strange sound would lift him out of the deepest of sleeps, his radar on full alert. At three A.M., his eyes snapped open, and he stared into the familiar darkness of his bedroom. Liza stirred beside him.

"What's wrong?" his girlfriend mumbled.

"I heard a strange noise. It sounded like little kids playing. There it is again."

Falling silent, they listened to rain pelt the window.

"It's just the wind," she said.

"That's not what I heard. The noise was inside."

"Go back to sleep. You've had a hard couple of days."

Liza kissed him in the dark. Coming home to find her waiting for him had been the best thing that had happened to him in a long time. It had restored his faith in the world, and given him hope that things might be returning to normal.

He drifted off. He heard the sound again. He slipped out of bed without awakening his girlfriend, found his robe, and padded barefoot into the hall, listening hard while trying to block out the storm. The noise was coming from downstairs. It sounded like a small invasion.

He padded down the stairs, and followed the noise into his workshop. He flipped on the light, and was surprised to discover the room was empty, save for the clutter of tricks scattered about. Perhaps Liza was right, and his imagination was getting the better of him.

He turned off the light. The noise came back, softer than before, as if emanating from the bottom of a deep well. He let his eyes adjust to the darkness, and scanned the room.

He settled on the Spirit Cabinet. The noise was coming from there. It sounded like a gang of playful children. He'd never been visited by the ghosts of children before, and wondered why they were here.

He entered the cabinet, and shut the door. The tambourine used to summon the spirits lay on the stool. He picked the tambourine up, and sat down. The voices filled the small space, and were singing a nursery song he did not recognize. Something about making giant snow-men, and watching them melt. He banged the tambourine against his palm, wanting to know more.

His world changed. He stood in the middle of a barren forest. It was winter, and fresh-fallen snow covered the ground. Five children ran past him on a narrow footpath, laughing and screaming as they did. They were bundled up with hats and coats and mittens. The oldest was no more than seven, the youngest around five, and he counted four boys and a blond-haired girl with an angel's face. The significance of their number did not dawn on him until the little girl glanced over her shoulder, and waved to him as she ran.

"You'd better hurry," she said.

His heart nearly broke. It was his mother.

"Wait!" he called after her.

"Come along," she said, still running.

He chased her in his bathrobe and slippers. "Why are you running?"

"We're trying to catch the kitty," she said.

The cat. Milly had told him about the cat. It had strange markings on its forehead, and had lured his mother and father and their little friends to the frozen pond. The cat was evil.

"You have to stop," he said.

His mother ignored him. She ran out of the forest into a clearing with a large frozen pond. As Peter came into the clearing, he spotted her four little friends standing by the pond's edge, waiting for her. He tried to determine which one was his father. Then, he spotted the cat. It stood in the middle of the frozen pond, holding its leg as if injured. Jet black, it had a pronounced white star on its forehead. It emitted a shrill cry, begging to be helped. The children reacted as children do, and scurried onto the ice without thinking.

"No!" Peter shouted.

He ran onto the ice, desperate to pull them to safety. His life had been defined by what was about to happen here, and he wondered if he could change the outcome. Before he could find out, the ice gave way with a sickening crack. One by one, his parents and their friends dropped like stones, and vanished before his eyes. The cat skipped away, its injured leg miraculously healed. Then it was his turn, and he plunged into the icy darkness.

In many ways, living and dying were interchangeable, one unable to exist without the other. Peter knew he was dying as he sank to the bottom of the pond, yet felt remarkably alive, and not the least bit afraid. Perhaps this was because he knew what the future held, and that after this was over, he would one day live again.

His feet hit bottom. His mother was nearby, and looked like an angel floating in space. Nearby, her four little friends were thrashing about with bubbles exploding out of their mouths. He again tried to determine which of these boys was his father. The smallest had ruddy cheeks, just like his father had later in life, and Peter decided he was the one.

Peter shifted his attention to the other three. One day, these little boys would become the Order of Astrum, and cause widespread grief, including the death of his parents. It was hard to imagine that looking at them now, for they were young and totally innocent. He remembered what Milly had said about free will, and the choices he would have to make. Someday, these boys would choose evil, and never look back.

A bright light appeared in the water. It was perfectly

round, and looked like a portal to another universe. The little boys stopped thrashing, as did his mother. Peter could not help himself, and stared at the strange object.

A dark line appeared in the center of the light. It was followed by another dark line and then another. An inverted triangle appeared before his eyes as if drawn by an invisible hand. The triangle was balanced atop a large V with a line running across the top. It was a magical sigil. Sigils were as old as time itself. Made of complex symbols and geometric figures, they were used by occultists to communicate with the spirit world. The sigil being formed in the water was the Seal of Satan, and meant that one of Satan's sons was present.

Peter felt a tug on his body. A powerful force coming from the light was dragging him toward the sigil like an invisible current. He swam backwards, not wanting to be captured by it. The light's power was greater on the children. They drifted toward it, no longer filled with panic or fear. Three of the boys entered the light, and became one with it. Then, it was his father's turn. His father hesitated and turned to glance at his mother. Peter sensed that he didn't want to go without her. Without warning, his father vanished as well.

Peter continued to fight the sigil. As he did, his mother floated past. As the light began to swallow her up, she looked over her shoulder at him, her pale blue eyes beseeching him to join her. *Come with me,* they seemed to say.

Did she know what was on the other side? He didn't think so. But he did. He knew one of the Devil's sons was awaiting him if he joined her.

"No," he said, the bubbles escaping his mouth.

His mother gave him a sad look. Then, she was gone as well.

His world changed again. He was back inside the Spirit Cabinet, banging the tambourine against his palm. The afterimage of the sigil burned brightly in the darkness. He had to get away from it, and he placed the tambourine onto the floor, and stepped out of the cabinet.

He began to shiver. His bones had grown cold, just as they did when evil was present. He hadn't understood the significance, until now. The cold came from the pond's icy water, and had been passed down to him from his parents, along with so many other things.

He climbed the stairs and slipped back into bed. Liza had not moved. Outside, it was still raining, the gusting wind pushing at the window. Milly had called his parents wonderful people, and she was right, for they'd battled evil since they were young, and had not given in. They had set an example for him, one which he needed to follow for the rest of his life.

Pulling the covers up beneath his chin, he shut his eyes, but could not fall asleep.

PART IV

POSSESSED

45

P eter awoke the next morning to the sight of more promising weather streaming through his bedroom window. Liza's spot in the bed was empty, and he could hear her downstairs in the kitchen, fixing breakfast. Had his old life returned? He could only hope so, and hopped out of bed.

His blinking cell phone sat on the night table. He found a text message from Holly saying that her aunt was doing better, and would be released from the hospital soon, if her condition continued to improve. The news brought a smile to his face, and he put on his bathrobe, convinced the worst was over.

He bounded down the stairs. In the kitchen, Liza was scrambling eggs at the stove while scrolling through her own cell phone. She was dressed in baggy sweats and a Yankees baseball cap, clothes that would have looked drab on someone else. He affectionately wrapped his arms around her waist, and she craned her neck to kiss him.

"Sleep well?" she asked.

No, he hadn't, but he wasn't going to go there. This was a new day, and a new start, and he said, "Like a lumberjack. What's on the menu?"

"Why don't you sit down, and let me surprise you?" she said.

He took a chair at the kitchen table, and pored through the paper. Wolfe's demise was front-page news, and he was relieved to see the article did not mention him or the other members of the Friday night psychics, but simply said that Wolfe had fallen to his death on the Upper West Side, and the police were relieved that a crazed killer was now off the streets. He guessed Garrison had a hand in this, and made a mental note to thank him the next time they spoke.

Liza placed two plates on the table. Scrambled eggs, bacon, and toasted bagels left over from the other day. He dug in, and noticed that she was still playing with her cell phone.

"What are you looking for?" he asked.

"A relationship counselor," his girlfriend replied.

"For us?"

"Yes. Here's one. 'Dr. Ruth Berman, licensed New York therapist. Stop fighting, understand more. Connect deeply, love deeply.' This one sounds promising. 'Need help in improving your relationship? I'll show you how to be true to yourself, yet remain close to your partner in a passionate, caring relationship. Call today.' That sounds like us to a T."

Peter placed his fork onto his plate and wiped his mouth with a napkin. Liza was serious. He cleared his throat, causing her to look up.

"Is something wrong?" she asked.

"If it's all right with you, I'd like to talk out our problems first."

"Are you afraid of seeing someone? Be truthful."

"Yes, I am."

She reached across the table, and placed her hand on top of his. "I really want us to see a professional. You're different. I have to learn to deal with that."

"I'm not that different," he said defensively.

"Oh, Peter, please."

His cheeks burned, and he glanced down at his unfinished plate of food. "All right. I'm a lot different. But that doesn't mean we can't work this out ourselves. We need to try." He looked up, and saw her studying him. An uneasy silence filled the kitchen.

"Why are you so afraid of this?" she asked.

"I don't want to betray my friends."

"Therapists are sworn to secrecy. Something tells me that's not the reason."

Peter struggled with a reply. Liza was right. There was another reason, and it had to do with the dark side of his personality that he kept buried within him. That was something he didn't want to discuss with a therapist, or anyone else.

His cell phone began to vibrate. Liza frowned at the interruption. He pulled it from the pocket of his robe and glanced at the face. Garrison calling. He decided the FBI agent could wait, and placed the phone onto the table. It began to move around by itself, then went still.

"Guess it's not important," she said.

"Actually, it's probably very important," he replied. "You're just more important."

"Who is it?"

"Garrison."

"The FBI agent? Don't you think you should take it?"

He leaned forward on his elbows. "I can call him back. How about this? Let's talk before we go see someone, and set some ground rules."

"What kind of ground rules?"

"I don't want to talk about my parents except in general terms."

"Why not? Your parents are a part of this conversation."

There were places he didn't want to go right now, and his parents' history was one of them. How was he supposed to explain who they were without pushing Liza away from him?

"I have my reasons. Please respect them. That's all I want. Everything else is fair game."

"Is there something about your parents you haven't told me?"

"Yes," he said quietly.

Her frown grew. "More secrets, huh?"

"I only found out about it recently. I'm still not comfortable with it yet."

"How are we supposed to have a relationship if you hide things?"

His cell phone rattled on the table. He glanced at the face. It was Garrison, trying to track him down. Why couldn't he leave a voice mail like everyone else? Peter ignored it.

"I'm not hiding things," he said. "My parents died when I was seven. There are a lot of things I didn't know about them, and their past, that I'm only learning about now. It's making me see them in a new light and it's not easy."

Her eyes searched his face. It made him uncomfortable, and he resumed eating his food. His relationship with Liza had never been a struggle, and he wondered if they would ever return to the way things used to be.

"There's something I want to ask you," she said. "How does it work with psychics when it comes to relationships? How do they work these issues out? I'm assuming their partners are normal. Or aren't they?"

He gave her question some thought. Max's late wife had been psychic, and so had Milly's late husband. Reggie had been a confirmed bachelor, so he didn't count. Madame Marie's husband hadn't been psychic, but his parents had been, so he'd understood the drill. Peter didn't know about Lester Rowe, and as far as Holly was concerned, she rarely dated. There was Nemo, who'd changed girlfriends as often as he changed his socks. It occurred to him that none of his psychic friends had carried on a relationship with a normal partner. He wondered how he could tell Liza this, and not make her even more uncomfortable. Before he could answer, his cell phone did a slow crawl across the table. Garrison, calling again.

"Maybe you'd better answer it," Liza said.

"I want to talk about this some more," he said, ignoring the phone.

"Then answer my question. How do your psychic friends deal with their relationships? Or is that a secret too?"

"I don't know. I'll have to ask them."

"You don't know?"

"No."

Liza picked up her plate, went to the garbage disposal, and dumped her uneaten meal into the trash. Turning around, she gave him a fiery look. "How can someone with the gift of clairvoyance not know how to carry on a normal relationship? I just don't get it."

"You're the first normal relationship I've had," he said truthfully.

"Really. What about that Swedish supermodel you were dating, and the TV actress. Didn't those last a while?"

"I never got close to them. I couldn't confide in them like I have with you."

"You told me what you wanted to tell me, Peter. You didn't tell me the truth."

He rose from his chair. She was pushing him away, and he needed to come clean. "I was afraid that if I told you too soon, I'd damage the relationship, and you'd run away."

"You've already damaged the relationship. The question is, how do you plan to fix it?"

"I don't know."

"You know, I think that's the first honest thing you've said."

His cell phone did another little dance. Liza crossed the kitchen, and snatched it off the table. Flipping it open, she abruptly said, "Hello—are you looking for Peter? He's right here. Hold on," and shoved the cell phone into her boyfriend's hands. "Let me know when you're ready to have a real conversation," she said, and stormed out of the room.

Peter heard the front door slam as she left the house. He shook his head, wondering how he was going to make this right. He'd wanted to tell Liza about himself for the longest time, but had never been able to muster up the courage to do it. Now, he wondered if it was too late. A voice came out of the phone, and he raised it to his face.

"Hello?"

"You are one hard man to track down," Garrison said. "I've got a big problem, and I need your help."

"What kind of problem?"

"Wolfe isn't who we thought he was."

"What do you mean?"

"I don't want to talk about this over the phone," the FBI agent said. "I'll come by your place in ten minutes. Be outside on the curb waiting for me. I'll explain everything then."

Peter wasn't ready for this. He needed to find Liza, and talk things out with her. His personal life had taken enough hits in the past few days, and couldn't take much more.

"Hold on a second," he said. "I need to know what's going on. I have a life, you know."

"The city is still in danger," Garrison said.

Peter heard his own sharp intake of breath. He glanced at the window, and saw the rain coming down hard outside. The storm had returned with a vengeance.

"See you in ten," he said.

46

Peter threw on some clothes, grabbed an umbrella, and went outside his brownstone to wait for the FBI agent's arrival. His heart was pumping furiously, the images of the Friday night séance still fresh in his mind. Cars burning, people dropping like flies, and Wolfe standing in the middle of it like the Grim Reaper, assessing the carnage. That was the threat he'd seen during his journey to the other side; now that Wolfe was dead, the threat should have passed as well. For Garrison to be telling him otherwise made him shiver uncontrollably.

If there was one constant in his life, it was his ability to predict the future. He'd never been wrong, and could not understand how he'd called this one so badly. He glanced at his watch. "Come on," he said impatiently.

Garrison pulled up in his Lincoln, his eyes bloodshot from lack of sleep. Peter went around to the passenger side and jumped in. The car took off before his door was closed.

"How can the city still be in danger?" Peter asked.

"There's an envelope on the backseat you need to see," Garrison said. "Take a look at what's inside. Then I'll explain."

Peter retrieved a manila envelope off the rear seat, and dumped its contents onto his lap. Out fell a man's wallet, passport, an ancient Zippo lighter, and some loose change. The wallet and passport were darkly stained, and he realized they were covered in dried blood.

"Are these Wolfe's?" Peter asked.

"They are," Garrison replied. "The police found them on his body last night. I decided to take a hard look at them, in the hopes I might discover how Wolfe was planning to launch his attack on the city. The wallet contained a plastic hotel-room key. We're trying to track the location right now. There's also a snapshot of a woman named Rita Tomavich, who's an assassin for the Israeli government. We're looking for her, too. The thing that caught my eye was the passport. Open it up."

Peter flipped through the passport. Wolfe was well traveled, and the pages were filled with colorful stamps from a variety of foreign countries, including Spain, the Philippines, a number of countries in Africa, and Saudi Arabia. Wolfe had murdered three psychics in the Saudi city of Riyadh a few days before an attack on the city, and Peter wondered if that played into this.

"Is this the problem?" Peter asked, pointing at the stamps from Saudi Arabia.

"Very good," Garrison said. "How did you know?"

"I guessed."

"You're a hell of a guesser. Look at the dates when Wolfe arrived and departed from the Riyadh airport. They're next to the stamps."

The dates were printed in tiny letters, and Peter had to stare. "Let's see. It says here that Wolfe arrived in Riyadh on November third, and left on November seventh. Is that significant?"

"Yes. Want to take a stab at it?"

Garrison was making a game out of it, although not in a playful way. Peter thought hard, and finally gave up.

"I don't have a clue. What does it mean?"

"The attack on the oil pipeline in Riyadh took place on November ninth," Garrison said. "Wolfe was long gone before it took place."

"Maybe he slipped back into the country, and carried out the attack."

"Not likely. Flip the page."

Peter did as instructed. The next page contained a pair of colorful stamps for Rio de Janeiro. Wolfe had arrived in Rio on November ninth, and left on November fourteenth. Wolfe had been on the other side of the world when the attack in Riyadh took place.

"This doesn't make any sense," Peter said.

Traffic ground to a halt. Garrison threw the car into park, and turned in his seat. "My theory about Wolfe was that he killed three psychics in Riyadh, and then carried out an attack on the oil pipeline. That theory isn't valid anymore. Someone else attacked that pipeline."

"Who?"

"I don't know. That's why I called you."

"Maybe this is a mistake, and the dates on the stamps are wrong. Have you considered that?" Peter asked.

"Yes, I did."

"And?"

"I struck out. I stayed up last night checking all the other cities stamped in Wolfe's passport. In every one, prominent psychics were murdered during his time there, just like in Riyadh, and just like here. Wolfe was sent to those cities to murder psychics. And in every city, a horrible attack of some kind took place a few days after he departed."

"Are you sure?"

"Damn sure. Wolfe had nothing to do with the attacks in those cities, and wasn't going to conduct an attack on New York. Someone else was. The fact that Wolfe is dead doesn't mean the threat is over."

"But I already looked into the future," Peter said. "Wolfe was the one."

"The spirits gave you bad information," Garrison said. "Ask them again."

"It doesn't work that way."

"What do you mean?"

"The spirits tell you what they want, and that's it. There are no refunds."

The line of cars in front of them inched ahead. Garrison threw the Lincoln into drive, and the vehicle lurched forward. The veins were popping on the side of his forehead. He looked like a man ready to lose control. He took a right at the next intersection, and Peter realized he was circling back to the brownstone.

"Head south," Peter said.

"Why should I do that?" the FBI agent asked through clenched teeth.

"Because I'm going to help you figure this thing out."

"How? You just said the spirits wouldn't help."

"No, but I can."

"How do you plan on doing that?"

He'd told Garrison more about himself than he would have liked, but was never going to tell him about the demon. The men who ran the Order of Astrum had the same demon inside of them. In that regard, their powers were no greater than his. Peter suspected that if he put his mind to it, he'd be able to figure out what they were up to.

"I can't tell you that," Peter said.

"Why the hell not? We're talking about thousands of lives."

"I just can't."

"You like keeping secrets from people, don't you?"

Liza had accused him of the same thing over breakfast. Keeping secrets was part of who he was, and he'd never felt ashamed about it before, until now.

"Just go south," Peter said.

Garrison grunted under his breath. He punched his horn, and traffic began to move.

Garrison pulled up to the front of the Empire State Building on 34th Street, and parked in a No Parking space. He had calmed down, but only a little. He tossed an FBI sign on the dashboard before joining Peter on the sidewalk.

"So what's the plan?" the FBI agent asked.

"I'll tell you when we're in the observatory," Peter said.

"No offense, Peter, but the clock is ticking. I can't be wasting my time sightseeing."

"Indulge me, will you?"

They went inside. Of all the magnificent structures on the island of Manhattan, the Empire State Building was the best known. Considered one of the seven modern wonders of the world, it towered over every other skyscraper in the city, and offered spectacularly breathtaking views as far as the eye could see. Tickets to the 102nd-floor glass-enclosed observatory were expensive, unless you had an FBI badge you could pass in front of the ticket taker's face. They rode the elevator to the top with their ears popping.

The observatory was empty as they exited the elevator. Peter made his way toward the north side. He'd been coming to the 102nd floor since childhood, sometimes to think, other times to be by himself, and become lost in the puffy white clouds that often swallowed up the building. He sat down on a bench, and gazed at the storm that had engulfed the city. Garrison joined him.

"You still haven't told me how you're going to help me," the FBI agent said.

"You have a problem that you can't figure out," Peter replied. "Problems are mysteries, and I'm an expert at solving mysteries."

"How so? From being a magician?"

"That's right. It's how I learned the craft. Many of the great magicians, like Houdini and Blackstone, coveted their tricks, and refused to share them with other magicians. If I wanted to learn how Houdini and Blackstone's tricks were done, I had to figure out the method myself. That's why I'm good at solving problems that other people can't."

"And you did it up here," Garrison said.

"This was one of my favorite places."

"All right, so what's going on now."

"Let's start from the beginning. We know that Wolfe was going to cities around the world, and murdering psychics. A few days later, a horrific attack would occur. The Order of Astrum is selling this information to ruthless dictators, who are profiting from it. The FBI originally thought that Wolfe was behind the attacks, but that doesn't seem to be the case. Someone else is. Does that about sum it up?"

"In a nutshell, yeah."

Peter put his elbows on his legs, and stared into space. The storm was blocking the view, and he imagined the various buildings and monuments spaced out before him.

Several minutes passed before he glanced at the man sitting beside him. "It's something simple."

"Why do you say that?" Garrison asked.

"The greatest mysteries are always simple. That's what fools us. We're expecting something complicated, and don't realize the method is staring us in the face."

Garrison popped a candy into his mouth. "Give me an example."

"All right. There was a Dutch magician named Kaps. He was really great, and enjoyed fooling other magicians. He came to New York to perform on a TV show. Later, he got together with the best magicians in the city, and did a private performance. One of the tricks got everyone talking for weeks. Kaps borrowed a lit cigarette, and passed it through the center of a pocket handkerchief without causing it to burn. No one had a clue how he did it."

"Did they ever find out?"

"Eventually Kaps came back to New York, and one of the magicians begged him to explain. Kaps finally gave up the secret."

Garrison was on the edge of his seat. "Can you tell me how he did it?"

"Sure. There was a slit in the hanky."

"A slit? You mean a hole? Hell, I could do that."

"That's right, you could. Kaps knew that the magicians would never expect him to do something so brazen. It was brilliant."

"Do you think that's what's going on here?"

"Yes. There's a slit in the hanky, only we're not seeing it."

Garrison's frown said he wasn't buying it. "How can you be so sure? Maybe the Order of Astrum has another agent who's carrying out the attacks. Someone we all missed who's now here in New York, getting ready to strike. It's the only plausible explanation."

"It's the wrong explanation," Peter said.

"How can you be so sure?"

"How many pieces of information did you tell me your group looked at?"

"Thousands."

"If there was another agent, you would have spotted him, don't you think?"

Garrison started to reply, then thought better of it. He crossed the observatory and stood at the glass. With his hands shoved into his pockets, he watched the storm.

"You win," he said. "How long do you think you're going to need?"

There was no timetable when it came to solving a mystery, especially one which had the best brains in the FBI baffled.

"I have no idea," Peter admitted.

"Guess."

"A couple of hours. Maybe longer."

Garrison glanced at his watch. "I'm supposed to be giving the mayor a briefing at eleven. Call me if you come up with something."

"I will."

Garrison walked back to the elevators. He acted like he'd been expecting a miracle. Peter knew better. Figuring out the mysteries of the universe took time, especially when the forces of evil were involved. With the storm swirling around him, Peter shut his eyes, and soon became lost in thought.

47

Peter sat on the observatory bench with his eyes shut, and listened to rain pelt the windows. He felt like he was inside the belly of an enormous beast that had swallowed him whole. The only way out was to solve this mystery. Otherwise, he was a meal.

The minutes slipped by. The best way to figure out a trick was to pretend he was the person performing it. He'd done that with Houdini's Vanishing Elephant, which had fooled magicians for over a century. Everything in Houdini's show was based upon simplicity; what made the tricks great were the elaborate presentations. The secret of the Vanishing Elephant had also been simple. The elephant never left the stage. Houdini had performed an optical trick using mirrors and special lighting that made his audience *think* the elephant had disappeared, then sold it using superb showmanship.

He decided to try this approach with the Order of Astrum. On his fingers, he counted the things he knew about them. The Order had paranormal powers, and could see into the future. Each member had made a pact with Satan's son, and dedicated their lives to causing harm and destruction to the human race. They were pure evil, and always would be.

Then he examined the mystery. The Order had sent Wolfe to different cities to kill psychics. A few days after Wolfe finished his assignment, an attack would occur, harming the city. The Order was somehow connected to these attacks. That was the mystery, and if he didn't solve it soon, New York would be attacked as well.

He went to the window. Placing his hand against the glass, he felt the storm's power surge through his body. He was looking for a slit in the hanky, something so obvious that it would have bit him, had he gotten any closer.

But what was it?

He thought back to the Friday night séance when he'd seen Wolfe standing in Times Square among the dead and dying. He still did not understand how Wolfe had killed so many people without any visible weapon. The spirits could be vague that way, and there was no way to get them to change.

Lightning flashed around him, and he instinctively pulled his hand away from the glass. As he did, a strange thought went through his mind. The spirits did not play favorites, and treated all psychics the same. The Order of Astrum were seeing the same things during their séances that Peter was seeing during his.

It took a moment for the thought to sink in. When it did, he let out a shout. That was the answer to the mystery. *We're seeing the same things.*

He'd found the slit in the hanky.

He pulled up Garrison's number on his cell phone, and heard the call go through.

"Where are you?" Peter asked.

"Out front. Some jackass is trying to tow my car," the FBI agent said furiously.

"I figured out what the Order is doing. You're not going to believe this. It was right in front of our faces."

"Hold on. I'm on my way."

Peter waited by the elevators. It was so incredibly obvious that he couldn't believe he hadn't seen it sooner. *They're no different than me,* he thought. The elevator doors parted, and Garrison came out like a racehorse exploding out of the gate. A pair of foreign tourists were also in the elevator, hoping to take pictures. Peter guided Garrison away from them.

"Tell me," the FBI agent said breathlessly.

"It's simple. The Order isn't behind the attacks."

Peter thought the FBI agent might hit him.

"Are you crazy? Of course they are!" Garrison practically shouted.

The tourists were watching them. Peter pulled Garrison farther away.

"Listen to me. The Order is conducting séances, and looking into the future. When they see a horrific event taking place, they figure out where it's occurring, and send Wolfe to the city to kill any psychics before they see the same thing, and alert the police. The Order doesn't know who's behind the attacks, nor do they have to. All they know is that an attack will happen, just like I knew the attack on New York was going to happen. Get it?"

Garrison's face turned blank as he absorbed the information. Then, his eyes lit up. "And the Order is selling the information, instead of alerting the authorities."

"Exactly. In a way, they're coconspirators, since they know the attacks will take place. But they don't know who's behind them, or any of the details."

"I thought Wolfe was involved in the attack you saw."

"Wolfe was there. I'm guessing he was just a spectator."

Garrison swore under his breath. "So we're back to square one. We don't know who's going to attack the city, and have no way of stopping them."

Peter had come to another hurdle. He'd been sworn to secrecy the night he'd conducted his first séance, and vowed never to break the confidences shared by those who regularly visited the spirit world. But there were exceptions to every rule, especially now, when the lives of so many innocent people were at stake. New York was his home, its people his family, and he was willing to break his vows in order to save it.

"Yes, we do," he said.

Garrison grabbed his shoulders. "Then tell me how!"

The clouds were swirling around them, the city's skyline eerily visible as it came into view. He struggled to find the words to explain. "It's like this. Evil doesn't pop up overnight. It takes a long time to grow inside of a person. First there's anger, then rage, and finally evil appears. Over time, the evil creates an aura that's seen by the spirits. If the aura becomes too great, the spirits make it known during a séance that something horrible's about to happen."

"Describe this person," Garrison said.

"His soul has been poisoned, and he's teetering on the brink of insanity. He's a loner, and has pushed away whatever friends he once had. He'll stop at nothing to cause death and destruction."

"I hate to say it, but that describes a lot of people."

"He's also extremely intelligent."

"How do you know that?"

"During my séance, I saw scores of people die, but no evidence of a bomb or guns. Whatever took those people down was invisible to the naked eye. That tells me that the attack he's planning is extremely sophisticated."

"You mean like chemical warfare."

"Yes."

"Could he be some kind of scientist or engineer?"

"That would be my guess. He's got some kind of weapon he wants to unleash on the city. It's too deadly for him to have built here without people knowing about it. I'm guessing he built it somewhere nearby, and plans to bring it in. You need to alert every cop in New York and surrounding areas to be on the lookout. Have them check the subways, the bridges and tunnels. With all the security cameras in this city, they might just spot him."

"So what we're looking for is a crazed scientist who's carrying some type of dangerous weapon. That's a helluva piece of detective work. Sure you were never a cop?"

"Maybe in another lifetime I was."

Garrison stepped away and started making calls on his cell phone. Very soon, every law enforcement officer in the city would be on the lookout for their attacker, and, hopefully, bring him to justice. Peter had done his job, and felt a monumental sense of relief that he'd solved the mystery. Yet at the same time, he felt like he should do more. This was his city, and his home. When his parents had needed a place to run to, they'd fled to New York, just as millions of desperate people had come before them. It was a city that took in the needy, no questions asked. When the people who lived here said they loved New York, it was not a casual remark. They loved the city with all their heart, and all their soul, and so did he. It was the greatest place on earth, and he could not help but feel angry at anyone who'd want to cause it harm.

48

A stiff wind blew off Long Island Sound, sending a chill through Dr. Lucas Carr's body. Standing on the crest of a hill, he shielded his eyes with his hand, and watched a fishing boat make its way toward Connecticut's distant shores, its bow cutting a perfect V through the chop. It was the kind of day meant for being on the water, battling the elements. It was not the kind of day meant for bringing untold suffering to thousands of innocent people, yet that was precisely what was on Carr's mind.

Katie and Joanie are in the ground.

The thought brought stinging tears to his eyes. Carr was a fifty-six-year-old physicist, small of stature, with wire-frame glasses, graying hair, and a razor-sharp mind. Two years had passed since the car accident that had sent his wife and daughter to their graves. It was more than enough time for him to heal, yet no matter how hard he tried, he could not let go of them.

Katie and Joanie are in the ground.

He headed down a dirt path to the Shoreham nuclear plant where he worked. Shoreham had been built to generate power to two million Long Island residents, but shoddy construction had kept it from opening. That had been two decades ago. The state kept the plant operational in the hopes that one day its generators would be put to use. Carr's job was to keep the generators from falling apart. After the accident, he'd considered turning the generators on and causing a meltdown, but had been afraid the staff would have stopped him. Better to come up with a careful plan, and stick with it. That was how smart killers worked.

He'd spent a year planning for this day. Now that it was finally here, he felt strangely calm. Soon it would be over, and he would be reunited with his loved ones.

Katie and Joanie are in the ground.

And then Dr. Carr started to cry again.

Two black Doberman pinschers met him at the gated entrance. Carr swiped his plastic key against the security pad, and let himself in. He headed up the driveway with the dogs sniffing his heels. He had been coming to the plant on weekends, and had grown fond of the dogs. Being around them calmed him down, if just for a little while.

Reaching the front entrance, he stopped to have a look around. One of the staff was having a going-away party at a local tavern, and the last cars were leaving the parking lot. The lab would be empty. That was good, because he didn't want to talk to anyone right now. In fact, he didn't want to talk to anyone ever again.

His footsteps echoed down the hallway. His coworkers had been acting strange lately, watching him out of the corners of their eyes like a bunch of spies. They must have guessed he was plotting something, but were too afraid to confront him. Stupid them.

He entered the lab, and went to his desk. Standing with his back to the security camera in the ceiling, he opened the center drawer, and removed a Sig Sauer he'd bought at a gun show, and slipped it into his jacket pocket. There were security cameras everywhere inside the plant, and they were all operational. Big Brother was watching, but were they paying attention? He didn't think so. People broke the rules all the time, and no one said anything.

The refrigerator hugged the far wall. His coworkers used it to store their lunches in. Carr didn't think they would have done that, had they known what he was keeping in there. He pried open the double doors. A small blue knapsack that had belonged to his daughter was stuffed inside. He clutched it to his chest.

"Damn you all," he whispered.

He'd come to the lab every weekend for the past year to prepare for his attack. Except for the maintenance people, there had been no one in the building except him. It had given him the freedom to experiment, and create a device that, once unleashed, could not be stopped.

He glanced around the lab a final time. It would have been easier to have shot his coworkers to death while they sat at their desks. He could have just gone postal, and gotten the whole thing over with. But he wanted to make a statement, and leave his mark on the world. He wanted to go out in style.

"No backing out now," he said through his teeth.

A harsh laugh escaped his throat. It didn't even sound like him. Before the accident, he wouldn't have harmed a fly. But two years was a lifetime when the ones you loved were dead, and the blackness was festering inside.

He carried the knapsack to the garage where he'd parked his Ford Windstar. That morning, he'd removed the backseat, and replaced it with a stainless-steel footlocker filled with packets of dry ice. Sliding open the side door, he carefully placed the knapsack into the footlocker, and packed it down. Then he got behind the wheel.

His hands were trembling as he stuck the key into the

ignition. He'd read in a book about ancient warfare that fear was only for those who were uncertain about their life's path. A person should never be fearful of their destiny, no matter where it took them.

This was his destiny, and he told himself not to be afraid.

H e drove out of the garage into the late-afternoon sunshine. He needed to hurry if he wanted to miss the rush-hour traffic on the Long Island Expressway.

"Carr! Hold on!" a voice called out.

A physicist named Dr. Stan Skarda ran over. An aging hippie, Skarda wore his long white hair pulled back in a ponytail, and an annoying gold earring. Before the accident, the Carr family had socialized with the Skardas, and taken several skiing vacations together in Vermont. Carr hit the brakes to avoid running over him.

"Aren't you going to the party?" Skarda asked.

"I'm heading home. I'm not feeling well."

Skarda put his hands on the door of the car, wanting to talk. "If you don't mind my saying, you really need to get out more, and start socializing again. You can't grieve forever. It's not healthy."

Carr gripped the wheel and looked straight ahead. "I need to go, Stan."

"I know the anniversary of the accident is right around the corner. This must be a difficult time for you."

"It's today. The anniversary's today."

"It is? I'm so sorry."

An awkward silence followed. Skarda glanced into the backseat of the Windstar.

"What's in the footlocker?"

"Just some things," Carr said.

"What things?"

Carr did not like the tone of Skarda's voice. "That's none of your business."

"I heard you've been coming around on weekends, and doing work in the lab," Skarda said. "One of the maintenance people mentioned it to me."

"Really. Which one?"

"It was José. He said you were cooking up something using biohazardous materials."

"José said that?"

"Yes. He told me he found them in the garbage. What have you been up to?"

"Nothing, Stan. I have no idea what José is talking about. I need to go."

Carr started to drive away. Skarda reached through the open window, and grabbed his colleague by the arm.

"You're not acting right, Lucas. Tell me what's going on. I'm your friend."

"Let go of me."

"Not until you explain. I want to help."

Carr's rage bubbled up inside of him like so much poison. He threw the Windstar into park, and drew the Sig. It felt powerful in his hand, and he aimed at Skarda's forearm.

"This is what's going on, Stan."

He squeezed the trigger. Blood splattered the windshield and the wheel. Skarda grabbed his arm and staggered back. His face was a mixture of pain and surprise.

"You shot me," Skarda gasped.

Carr stared at the gaping wound that he had caused. The bullet had taken a small piece out of Skarda's arm, and the wound was bleeding profusely. Not that long ago, the sight of blood had sickened him. Now, it had the opposite effect, and sent adrenaline coursing through his veins. He pointed the Sig and took careful aim.

"What are you doing?" Skarda gasped.

"What does it look like I'm doing?"

"Please, Lucas. Don't do it."

"I read that there are three deaths. The first is when the body ceases to function. The second is when the body is consigned to the grave. The third is that moment in the future when your name is spoken for the last time. Do you believe that, Stan?"

"I'm begging you."

"Is that a yes, or a no?"

"I don't know."

"I think it's true. Let's find out."

Skarda tried to run away. Carr pumped three bullets into the man he'd once called his friend. The gunshots echoed across the property long after the Sig had gone silent.

Carr gazed at the dead man lying on the driveway with a strange sense of detachment. He waited for some feeling of remorse, or regret. There was none.

He was doing sixty when he took down the front gate. Five minutes later, he was weaving through traffic on the westbound LIE, his vehicle pointed toward the city.

49

Long Island was one hundred and forty miles in length. The distance from the city to the Shoreham nuclear plant was half that length, and took ninety minutes to reach without traffic. Or, you could take a helicopter, as Garrison chose to do, and land on the lawn in just forty minutes. Garrison exited the chopper wearing a navy windbreaker with the letters FBI stenciled prominently across the back. A Suffolk county homicide detective ran out to greet him.

"Any reporters snooping around?" Garrison shouted over the engine.

"There's a pack of them on the other side of the building, including a team from CNN," the detective shouted back. "The story hit the wires thirty minutes ago."

"Can you keep them contained? I don't want them photographing us."

"Not a problem," the detective said.

Garrison cupped his hand over his mouth. "Coast is clear. You can come out."

Peter climbed out of the backseat of the chopper. Garrison had asked him to come to see if he could determine if Dr. Carr was their attacker. Peter didn't know what he was supposed to be looking for, but felt compelled to help, no matter where it took him. To protect his identity, he wore a baseball cap, Ray-Bans, and an identical windbreaker.

"Lead the way," Garrison said.

The detective escorted them inside the plant. It was the size of a large warehouse, and had tiled floors that magnified the sound of their footsteps. During the flight, Garrison had explained to Peter how Carr had shot a co-worker to death an hour ago, and that Carr had been acting suspiciously for quite some time. It sounded as if Carr had lost his mind. Worse, Carr was a physicist, and had access to a variety of dangerous materials.

They entered the lab. Desks and computers took up most of the space. A team of CSI techs were searching Carr's equipment. Garrison pulled aside the tech in charge, a moustachioed man named Tricarico. Tricarico was sweating, and appeared to know the danger Carr posed.

"FBI," Garrison said, flashing his badge. "Show me what you got."

Tricarico pointed at a table covered in plastic evidence bags. "Carr's garbage can had plenty of good information in it. We found a map of Manhattan with a bull's-eye painted on Broome Street, near the heart of the financial district. A coworker said Carr has been acting weird lately. This morning, Carr came to work with a child's knapsack, which he put into the refrigerator, and asked everyone not to touch."

"Is there nuclear material stored here?" Garrison asked.

"Yes, there is," Tricarico replied. "They keep the generators operational. From what one of the physicists told me, you can never really shut one of these babies down. I guess there's always some residue of nuclear power left."

"What's Carr's motive?"

"Carr lost his wife and daughter after a drunk teenager hit them one Saturday night," Tricarico said. "Seems the kid's lawyer conned the judge into putting him on probation. Carr was dragged out of the courtroom, vowing revenge."

"On who?"

"The system. Today's the two-year anniversary of the accident."

"Show me his desk."

Carr's desk was in the corner, covered in framed photos of his family in happier times. He'd left his laptop. It was powered up, the screen saver showing a picturesque shot of Long Island Sound at dusk. Garrison touched the keyboard, bringing the screen to life. He dragged the mouse over the Favorites tab below the browser, and clicked on it. The tab scrolled down to reveal the different Web sites that Carr liked to visit. The site at the top of the list said RDD. Garrison clicked on it. A drawing of a homemade bomb filled the screen.

"For the love of Christ," the FBI agent said.

Garrison ripped out his cell phone. Unable to get reception, he hurried out of the lab. Tricarico crossed the room and spoke in a hushed voice to the other techs.

Peter had never heard of an RDD before, and studied the picture on the screen. It had six sticks of dynamite wrapped together along with a crude timing device. He read the accompanying text. An RDD, also called a dirty bomb, was a powerful explosive used to disperse radioactive material on densely populated areas. Although the dispersal of radiation wouldn't kill many people, it would cause a huge public disruption, and destroy the economy and living conditions in the contaminated area, with radioactive dust spreading on people, buildings, and roads. Life in the contaminated area would cease to exist as we know it.

He thought back to the Friday night séance. Whatever had caused all those people to perish in Times Square hadn't been radioactive material. They had died too quickly for it to have been that. Something else was going on here.

His eyes fell on the photos of Carr's wife and daughter, both of whom were strikingly beautiful. They'd been gone two years. Had Carr been plotting his revenge all that time? Something told him that the demented physicist had, and this was all a trick.

He ran out of the lab.

Garrison was on the lawn, talking on his cell phone. During the chopper ride in, Garrison had stationed teams of FBI agents at the entrances to all the bridges, tunnels, and railroad stations into the city.

Garrison was now alerting those teams to the deadly package that Carr was carrying. Peter grabbed the FBI agent's arm, causing him to jump.

"Don't do that!" Garrison said.

"Sorry. You need to hear this."

"You found something?"

"I sure did."

"Hold on." Garrison placed the phone against his chest. "Lay it on me."

"Dr. Carr is trying to trick us. He purposely left those clues around his desk, and even left his laptop on. Whatever's inside his knapsack is not a dirty bomb."

"How can you possibly know that?"

"I saw the attack, remember? People were dying on the spot. According to what that Web site said, a dirty bomb isn't capable of doing that."

"Then what's inside the knapsack?"

"I don't know, but I'm sure there's evidence inside the plant. He made the bomb here."

Garrison shot him an exasperated look. He wanted Peter to be wrong, but deep down, he knew that Peter was right. They went back inside, and Garrison cornered Tricarico in the lab.

"Did Carr have another work area inside the plant?" Garrison asked.

"Carr kept a desk where the generators are kept," Tricarico replied.

"I need you to take us there."

It took a minute for Tricarico to get them through the security checkpoints leading to the plant's powerful generators. As Peter moved deeper into the plant, he found himself thinking about Carr. The doctor's descent into madness had begun with the loss of his family, a feeling he knew all too well. There was no excuse for the path Carr had chosen, yet he still understood it.

A domed area housed the massive generators. The machinery was monolithic, and looked like props from an old science fiction movie. Carr's desk contained more family photos. On it sat another computer, this one a PC. Garrison sat down in front of the PC, and attempted to gain access. A red security warning flashed across the screen, stopping him.

"Damn. All the files are encrypted," the FBI agent said.

"Can't you break the code?" Peter asked.

"Not these. The files are encrypted with the TrueCrypt program, and use an algorithm at the AES 256 level. It's the same algorithm the government uses to keep its top-secret computers secure. Nobody can break it except the National Security Agency."

"Can't you call them?" Peter asked.

"It's not the kind of information they're going to give me over the phone."

Garrison shook his head gravely. He was beaten, and didn't have another plan.

"You guys need me for anything else?" Tricarico asked.

Garrison said no. Tricarico left the room. When he was gone, Peter said, "My turn."

"Don't tell me your psychic powers work with computers as well?" Garrison asked.

"Anything's possible," Peter said.

Garrison gave up his chair. Peter sat down at the computer, and stared at the gibberish on the screen. He was no genius when it came to technology, but he didn't have to be. Picking up the phone on the desk, he hit a button for an outside line, and punched in a ten-digit number.

"You're calling that hacker who works for you," Garrison said.

"I sure am."

"You can't be serious. No one can bust the AES 256 level."

"Don't tell Snoop that. He's done it before."

"What? I knew I should have busted that guy when I had the chance. He's a threat to national security," Garrison said.

Peter covered the phone's mouthpiece, and shot Garrison a wicked look. "Snoop is part of our deal."

"What's that supposed to mean?"

"You can't arrest him, no matter how many laws he breaks."

"Your friend's a public menace."

"Yes, he is. Now nod your head, and agree."

Garrison scowled, then nodded almost imperceptibly. Peter heard Snoop's ever-cheerful voice say, "Hey, Peter, what's shaking?"

"Stop whatever you're doing," Peter said. "I've got a job for you."

50

The AES 256 level algorithm was more important to national security than Peter could have ever imagined. According to Snoop, the complicated encryption device was used to protect the Pentagon, the CIA, and the National Security Agency, as well as the computers of every major bank and financial institution on Wall Street. The keeper of secrets, AES 256 was considered impenetrable.

"Ready when you are," Peter said to the intercom.

"Let me explain a few things," Snoop said. "Any password can be cracked if you give a hacker enough time. The software I use will run through all possible permutations of numbers and letters given the password's size. If the password has five characters, no sweat. Six, and I'll need more time, because there are two billion possibilities. Seven, and it jumps to seventy-eight billion possibilities. Any larger, and we'll be here all night. Make sense?"

"Loud and clear," Garrison said.

"How can you know the size of the password before you start?" Peter asked.

"Magic," Snoop said.

"Come on, be serious."

"It's actually pretty straightforward," his assistant explained. "A password must be easy to remember if it's used every day. Is the computer you're trying to hack being used often?"

"We think so," Peter said.

"Good. Then the password won't be complicated. I'll need information about the person using the computer. Name, date of birth, phone numbers, that sort of thing. Most passwords consist of familiar letters and numbers. Is that information available?"

"I'll go check," Garrison said.

The FBI agent beat a path to the door. Valuable time was slipping away, and Peter felt a growing sense of panic. Sometimes, it was murder to know the future.

"Is Papa Bear gone?" came Snoop's voice out of the box.

"He's gone," Peter said. "What's up?"

"Have you talked to Liza in the past couple of hours?"

No, he hadn't. Peter shut his eyes, fearing the worst. "Is something wrong?"

"She called me earlier, asked if she could rent Zack's space from me," Snoop said. "Are you guys Splitsville again? I thought you were getting things worked out."

"I don't want to be talking about this," Peter said.

"I'm in the middle of this, Peter," Snoop said. "I work for you, and your soon-to-be-ex-girlfriend wants to live in my place. That puts me in a delicate situation, as they say."

"Yes, we're Splitsville. I've been holding back on her about some things in my life."

Snoop let out a whistle that sounded like a bomb falling through space.

"Spare me the sound effects," Peter said.

"You shouldn't have done that," Snoop said, his tone mildly scolding. "You should have confided in her from the start. It's what women want from us."

"I realize that. If there was any way to undo it, I would."

"You really hurt her."

"You're really cheering me up, you know that?"

"I'm sorry, man. Somebody had to tell you."

Peter stared at the screen of Carr's computer. Talking to Snoop about his personal life was torture, and he wanted the conversation to end.

"You can't run away from this forever," Snoop said.

"Who said I was running away?"

"It's what you do when you don't like how things turn out in your personal life. You run away, instead of facing reality."

"Thank you, Dr. Phil. Next caller, please."

"You're my best friend. I just want to see you happy. Okay?"

Peter swallowed the lump in his throat. "Okay."

Garrison returned with a copy of Carr's personnel file, which he began to read into the intercom. "Here's the information you asked for. Doctor Lucas Carr. Age fifty-six. Height, five-foot-nine. Weight, one hundred and sixty pounds. Home phone number—"

"Hold on a second," Snoop said. "What kind of doctor is he?"

"He's a nuclear physicist at the Shoreham plant on Long Island."

"Holy crap! Why didn't you tell me that in the first place," Snoop said. "If he's working with classified information, the government requires him to encrypt his files with a password that's a minimum of twenty characters. We could be here all week."

Garrison tossed the file on the desk in disgust. "That wasn't the news I wanted to hear."

The intercom went silent. Peter could almost hear Snoop thinking.

"Has Carr been in trouble recently?" his assistant asked.

"He's been acting weird," Garrison said. "Lost his family. Why?"

"Did the people who supervise him notice?"

Garrison retrieved the file, and looked through Carr's records. "Matter of fact, they did. His supervisor noted Carr's erratic behavior on three separate occasions in the past year."

"Bingo! He's got a key-logger!" Snoop said triumphantly.

"How do you know he's got a key-logger?" Garrison asked.

"Because all government employees handling classified information who display erratic behavior in the workplace have key-loggers put on their computers without their knowledge."

"How do you know *that*?"

"I read it on a government Web site that I hacked."

"I pray to God you're right." Garrison got on his knees, and crawled beneath the desk. "Well, I'll be damned, there's a key-logger plugged into the power cord." He came out holding a device the size of a pack of cigarettes with wires attached to it. "I need another computer to look at this. I'll be right back."

Garrison did another sprint to the door. Peter checked his watch. They were creeping toward nightfall. Simple logic told him that it would be harder to catch Carr when the sun went down. That gave them only a few hours to find him. That was one scenario. The other was that they wouldn't find him, and whatever he was carrying in his knapsack would be unleashed.

"I need you to do me a favor," he said to Snoop. "Find Liza, and tell her to stay inside. Same for you. You don't want to be outside right now."

"Liza is at the theater. I was just heading there. What about tonight's show?"

"Cancel it."

Garrison returned to the room. In his hand was a pad of paper containing the password to Carr's computer that he'd lifted off the key-logger. He typed the password into the computer. On the screen appeared a page of complicated chemical equations. There was also a photo of a vaned spherical device the size of a bowling ball. Garrison let out an exasperated breath.

"We need to evacuate the building," he said.

"Later," came Snoop's voice over the intercom.

They ran down the hallway to the lab where the CSI techs were gathering evidence. Garrison made the techs strip down to their shorts, and ushered them outside, where he found a garden hose, and proceeded to spray them down. The techs knew the drill, and did not protest. When Garrison was finished, the techs went to their van, and put on spare uniforms.

"Tell me what's going on," Peter said.

"The strange-looking thing you saw on Carr's computer is called a bomblet, and is used to unleash biological weapons." Garrison ripped out his cell phone, and began punching in numbers. "Our government stopped making them in the seventies, but there are some still around. When the bomblet is dropped, its outer shell shatters, and the agent is sprayed out of the top."

"What kind of agent?"

"Based on what I saw on Carr's computer, I'd say it was Novichok, the most deadly nerve agent ever made. Exposure to Novichok will cause the involuntary contraction of every muscle in your body. That leads to cardiac arrest and immediate death. If Novichok is released into the atmosphere, tens of thousands of people will die. That's what you saw during your séance."

Garrison started talking into his cell. His eyes were filled with dread. This was it, Peter thought. If they didn't figure out a way to stop Carr, the game was over. He looked helplessly at the sky, as if the answer were hidden in the clouds. A flock of birds passed overhead, and it made him think of Holly, and the power she had over the crows. It gave him an idea, and he stepped away from the FBI agent, and called her. Holly picked up on the first ring.

"Where are you?" he asked.

"At my aunt's apartment," Holly said. "The doctor let her come home this afternoon. Max is making his famous chicken noodle soup to cheer her up."

The Dakota was thirty blocks from Times Square. The apartment would be infected if Carr detonated his bomb. What had Nemo called it the other day? A hell storm. And his three closest friends were about to be caught up in it.

"I have some bad news," he said, hearing the fear in

his voice. "The attack I saw during our séance is about to take place. A madman is going to release a biological weapon. He's on his way into the city right now. I don't know if the police can stop him."

"Oh, my God," Holly said.

"The madman's name is Dr. Lucas Carr. I was hoping you might be able to cast a spell on him, and slow him down."

"I can try. Do you think he's on Facebook? I need to know what he looks like to cast a spell."

"He's a physicist, and works at the Shoreham nuclear plant on Long Island. Try Googling him. There must be a photo somewhere."

"I'll do it," Holly said.

"Don't go yet. Did your aunt fix the broken window in the living room?"

"The maintenance people replaced it today."

"Good. Don't go near the windows, and shut the air vents. And for heaven's sakes, don't go outside, no matter what happens."

"Don't you trust me?" Holly asked.

"Damn it, Holly. My life is falling apart. I don't want to lose you, too."

"You're shouting at me."

"Am I? Maybe it's because you don't listen."

"Peter!"

"Just say it."

"I promise not to go outside."

"Thank you. I'll call you once I know something."

He said good-bye and ended the call. Garrison had finished his call as well. There was a spark of hope in the FBI agent's eyes.

"We just got lucky," Garrison said. "Carr's van was just found at the Hunters Point train station. A man resembling Carr bought a one-way ticket into the city.

He gets in to Penn Station at four-forty-five. The police are going to apprehend him when he steps off the train. I want to be there when that happens. Come on."

A break. It had been a long time since Peter had caught one. Perhaps the spirits were trying to help him. They hurried across the grass to where the FBI chopper was parked. The pilot stood outside his aircraft. Seeing them approach, he crushed out his cigarette.

"What's the fastest way to Penn Station?" Garrison asked the pilot.

"The Thirtieth Street Heliport is the closest," the pilot replied. "I'll have you there in thirty."

Soon they were airborne, flying just below the clouds. Peter sat in the front seat beside the pilot, his eyes peeled to the horizon. New York's jagged skyline was visible in the distance, the mass of tall buildings like a pirate's upturned treasure chest. Dark storm clouds continued to hang over the city, sending down heavy rain. In the storm's swirling mass, he made out the faces of his mother and father, Madame Marie and Reggie, the hobo he'd seen on the rooftop in SoHo, and many other ghosts that he communicated with during his séances. It was rare for so many spirits to come together at once, and he realized they were trying to protect the city by causing it to rain. They knew, just as he knew, that a deadly nerve agent was about to be released, and were doing everything within their supernatural powers to stop it from occurring.

But could the spirits stop the nerve agent from spreading by causing it to rain? Something told him they couldn't, and that the gesture was futile. That was the terrible part about battling evil. Sometimes, evil won out, and innocent people perished. It was how the universe had been created, and could not be changed. The only thing he could do was fight the battle, and push back at the darkness. No matter what the outcome, he had to try.

In the end, he supposed that was all that really mattered.

51

Holly folded her cell phone, and stared into space. She wanted to cry, but fought back the tears. Peter had sounded so *brutal*. It wasn't the person she knew, or loved.

"What's wrong, my dear?" Milly murmured.

Holly glanced at her aunt lying in bed. "I thought you were asleep."

"One can't sleep one's life away forever." Milly pulled herself into a sitting position, and leaned against the headboard. "You look upset. It's about Peter, isn't it?"

"How did you know?"

"Call it intuition. What's wrong now?"

Rain pelted the windows and sounded like tiny drumbeats. One of the wonderful aspects of living in the Dakota was that every room had windows, and made the apartment feel bigger than it really was. It was an illusion, just like everything else in her life.

"The doctor said you should stay quiet, and get plenty of rest," she replied.

"Is that a nice way of telling me to shut up, and mind my own business?"

"I'm sorry if it sounded that way. There's nothing you can do."

"Try me. You may be surprised."

"Very well. A mad scientist is about to attack the city. Peter wants us to stay inside, away from the air vents. He asked me to cast a spell on him to see if I can slow him down."

"Is this the same attack Peter saw during the séance Friday night?"

"Yes, it is."

"That's old news, my dear. Now tell me what's really wrong."

Holly rose and went to the window to stare out at the park. The crows had crowded the tree limbs, and not moved since her aunt's return home. How nice it was to have things so settled in your life, she thought. Perhaps that was one of the advantages of growing old.

"Peter's changed," she said quietly. "He's not the same person anymore."

"Tell me what's different about him," her aunt said.

"Peter never used to have a bad bone in his body. Now, he's angry and bitter about everything, especially his girlfriend. He told me his life's falling apart. She's upset with him, and he doesn't know how to deal with it."

"But that's good. At least for you. Peter will be all yours now."

Her aunt wasn't seeing the big picture, and Holly turned from the window. "But I don't want Peter like this. I want the wonderful boy I've always known, not some angry person who feels cheated by how his life's turned out. It's not fair."

"Life is rarely fair, my dear."

"That's not what I mean. We've put Peter in an awful position. We put all sorts of pressure on him, and made him lead two different lives. Now it's all come crashing down on his head, and you have the nerve to say that life's not fair."

"Are you blaming me?"

"Yes, Aunt Milly, I am. And Max as well. You're both responsible for this situation."

"What on earth did I do to Peter?"

"You raised him."

"Oh, I see," her aunt said quietly.

Max entered the bedroom holding an empty tray in one hand, and a dish towel in the other. He had his performer's face on, and said, "Allow me to present my mother's famous homemade chicken noodle soup. Guaranteed to cure whatever ails you."

He showed the towel on both sides, and draped it over the tray. A form mysteriously appeared beneath its folds. Whisking the towel away, he proudly displayed a steaming bowl of chicken noodle soup, which he placed upon Milly's lap along with the tray.

"Bon appetit, dear friend," he said.

"Well done," Milly said. "Did you see how he did it, Holly?"

"I don't have a clue," Holly confessed.

"I learned it from the famous Chinese magician, Long Tack Sam," Max said proudly. "Long Tack performed a complete somersault before making a bowl of liquid appear. I'm afraid that in my advancing years, such gymnastics are out of the question."

"We were just talking about you," Milly said, tasting her soup. "Holly believes you and I are responsible for Peter's current problems with his girlfriend, among other things. She feels we didn't raise him properly."

"We did our best," Max said stiffly.

"You did one thing wrong," Holly said, unwilling to back down. "You pounded it into Peter that he should never talk about his powers. That was harmful. Everyone has to confide in *someone*. Didn't both of you confide in someone when you were young?"

Max looked at the floor. "Well, there was a woman I

told once. Actually, there were several women I've told. A moment of weakness, I suppose."

Holly looked at her aunt. "And you?"

"I've told certain friends as well," Milly admitted.

"And so have I," Holly said. "You see, we've all confided in someone. Except poor Peter. Now look what it's done to him. His girlfriend doesn't trust him, and he's become bitter about it. He's not the same person he used to be."

"Peter has been out of sorts lately," Max admitted.

"I've noticed it as well," Milly said.

"And what were you going to do about it?" Holly asked. "Besides watch him suffer?"

Her words had shamed them, and they both fell silent. Outside the apartment, a police car's siren pierced the air. There was work to be done, and she excused herself from the room.

H olly went into her aunt's study and shut the door. A seldom-used Mac sat on the desk. Powering it up, she got onto the Internet. She'd read somewhere that one day the entire world would be owned by Google. She didn't doubt it; she did a search for Carr, and found a short profile posted on Wikipedia. Carr was a physicist of some renown, and had published several papers about the dangers of nuclear proliferation. A photo showed a man with soft blue eyes and a gentle mouth, and she wondered what had caused him to turn into a madman. Maybe when this was all over, Peter would explain what had happened to him.

She went to the closet and opened the safe. From it, she grabbed several of her aunt's magical potions and herbs. She supposed she should have asked her aunt's permission, but felt put out with her. Aunt Milly and Max had made a mistake, and needed to own up to it.

She returned to the desk. From her purse, she removed a bottle of water, and emptied it into a glass. Pouring equal measures of magical potions into the water, she stirred them gently with the tip of her finger. Always clockwise, never counter-clockwise, unless she wanted to upset the spirits, and lose her ability to talk with them.

> *"Dr. Carr, with eyes so bright, where are you on this ominous night?*
> *Are you hiding in a car, or a bus, or a train?*
> *Do you wish us harm during this terrible rain?*
> *Show your face to me, Dr. Carr,*
> *So that I may see the man you really are."*

It was not the best spell she'd ever recited, but it would do. The water inside the glass grew cloudy, then cleared. She found herself looking inside a railroad car filled with passengers. Dr. Carr was jammed into a seat in the front of the car. On the rack above his head was a bright blue child's knapsack. His eyes darted nervously from side to side like a caged animal. *The poor man's lost his mind,* she thought.

A man wearing a dark raincoat walked past Carr and kept going. Reaching the back of the car, the man pulled a walkie-talkie from his pocket, and began to whisper into it. Holly guessed the man was a policeman, and was watching Carr.

She had a thought. If the man watching Dr. Carr was a policeman, there would be other policemen. They always worked in teams. Again, she stirred the water with her fingertip.

"Like a bird from high above, let me see where this
*   train is going.*
Who is waiting on the other end?
Friend or foe?
Please show me, for I must know."

The water went through another transformation.
When it cleared, she found herself looking at an enclosed railroad platform inside Penn Station. The platform was filled with people waiting for a train to arrive.
She studied the crowd, and spotted more men talking
into walkie-talkies, waiting for Dr. Carr's train to pull
in. Carr couldn't escape from that many policemen. He
was going to be apprehended, and have his knapsack
taken away from him. Case closed.

Or was it? It wasn't over until it was over. Someone
famous had once said that. It wasn't over until the madman was led away in handcuffs. She twirled the water
again.

"Take me back inside the railroad car,
To see the doctor, whose name is Carr."

She was going to have to work on her rhyming skills.
The water inside the glass went clear, and Carr reap-
peared. Rising from his seat, the doctor pulled the back-
pack down from the rack, and clutched it against his
chest. He was carrying on a conversation with himself,
and being watched by the other passengers. He looked
ready to explode.

"Because you are an evil man,
I now must raise my hand.
May your eyes grow blurred,
And your feet feel like lead.

May your stomach grow so nauseous,
That you wish you were dead."

"Why, there you are," her aunt said, standing in the doorway in her bathrobe.

Holly looked away from the glass long enough for the spell to be broken, and the water to turn clear. "Aunt Milly, what are you doing out of bed? You could fall, and hurt yourself."

"All of those things are true," her aunt said. "Yet none are as important as this." From her pocket, she removed a gold locket in the shape of a heart, which she displayed to her niece.

"Do you recognize this? You coveted it as a child."

Holly crossed the study to get a closer look. "It's Mary Glover's locket. You showed it to me once. I never forgot it."

"The time has come for you to have it."

"Oh, Aunt Milly, I don't know what to say."

"Do you remember what I told you about this locket?"

"I certainly do. You said it contained the most magical of potions, and had the power to change a person's life forever."

"That is correct. With it, you will be able to help our beloved Peter, and give him back the things which Max and I have so unfairly denied him."

"The locket will help me do that? But how?"

"Easy, my dear child. I will explain."

Before the words had left her mouth, Milly's eyelids began to flutter, and her head sagged to one side. She sank noiselessly to the floor, her fingers clutching the locket.

"Max, come help me!" Holly called into the apartment.

52

As the train pulled into the platform at Penn Station, the interior lights flickered as the car bounced across the high-voltage electric tracks. Dr. Lucas Carr looked at the faces of the other passengers in the eerie strobe light.

"The time is here," he announced loudly.

The train came to a screeching halt, and the lights returned. Carr felt the weight of his fellow passengers' stares as they tried to determine if he was a threat. New York was filled with threats. Punks, street people, crazies. He wanted to tell them that he wasn't any of the above, just mad as hell. They'd find out soon enough.

Rising from his seat, he removed his knapsack from the overhead rack, and shoved himself into the aisle now filled with people.

"I was like you once," he said. "Just like you."

The doors to the train parted, and everyone filed out. Carr felt himself being caught up in their movement as if being pulled out to sea by a powerful tide.

"Stop pushing me," he said angrily.

His fellow commuters ignored him. It made his rage that much greater. He considered removing the bomblet from the knapsack, and throwing it against the nearest wall, causing the deadly Novichok to come spraying out in all directions, and take down every single one of them.

He didn't do it. He would not deter from his plan. He was going to take a subway to Times Square, get a bite to eat, and wait for the theaters to let out. When the sidewalks were packed, he'd toss the bomblet in front of a moving vehicle, the impact causing the nerve agent to dispel through the air. He'd done the math, and knew that he'd created enough of the deadly nerve agent to kill tens of thousands of people, not just in Times Square, but all across the city. Even this dreadful rain was not capable of containing it.

He'd targeted the theater district for a reason. The night before the accident, he'd taken his wife and daughter to see a musical in Times Square. Thinking about it broke his heart, and it was only fitting that he stage his attack in a place that held so many painful memories.

He followed the crowd up the stairs to the main level. Penn Station was the busiest train station in the country; during rush hour, hundreds of thousands of people were moved through its terminals. It was a microcosm of the city it served, and always hectic.

"Dr. Carr," said a man's voice.

The voice had come from behind him. Carr did not turn around. It might have been an old friend, but something told him that it wasn't. In his haste to get up the stairs, he shoved the burly construction worker in front of him, causing him to stumble.

"Watch it, buddy," the construction worker warned.

"Excuse me, but I'm in a hurry," Carr explained.

"Ain't we all."

"Dr. Carr," the voice called again. "Please stop!"

Carr stole a glance over his shoulder. The man was a few steps behind him, and had a policeman's badge clipped to the lapel of his overcoat. He was not alone. There were a dozen other men with badges clipped to their coats coming up the stairs, as well.

Carr sprinted around the construction worker. He would not to let himself be arrested. This was his last stand, and he was going to make the most of it.

Reaching the top, he looked for an exit. He was inside

the Long Island Railroad terminal, a claustrophobic space filled with food concessions and newspaper stands. Rush hour had started, and long lines of commuters stood outside the gates. More men with badges emerged from the crowd, circling around him.

Carr was trapped.

The rest of the cops appeared from the stairwell. They fanned out, and created a tight circle around him. The cop who'd been calling his name stepped forward.

"My name is Detective Emener," he said in a measured tone. "I need to talk with you, Dr. Carr. Please don't make this any more difficult than it already is."

Carr raised the knapsack above his head. "Don't come any closer."

"Don't do that, Dr. Carr."

"Don't you dare tell me what to do!" Carr bellowed.

"Calm down, Dr. Carr. Do as I say, and no one will get hurt."

"That's where you're wrong. Lots of people are going to get hurt."

"Please, Dr. Carr."

Carr was determined to go down fighting. He was surrounded by cops, who in turn were surrounded by mobs of anxious commuters watching the scene unfold. The presence of so many people gave him an idea. Drawing the Sig Sauer from his jacket, he aimed at the ceiling, and let off a round. It sounded like a cannon in the enclosed space. Women in the crowd screamed. It was exactly what Carr wanted, and he fired the Sig again. The commuters headed for the exits, knocking through the circle of policemen in a mad stampede for safety. Detective Emener started to move toward him, only to be swept aside by the rush of people. Slipping the Sig into his pocket, Carr joined the fleeing mob, the knapsack clutched protectively to his chest.

* * *

Carr ran out of Penn Station with a mad rush of adrenaline. He hadn't felt this good in forever, and wondered why he'd waited so long to seek his revenge. A long line of yellow taxi cabs were parked at the curb. Their drivers, mostly Russians, stood outside their vehicles, smoking cigarettes and talking in their native tongue.

Carr hurried toward them. Then, he stopped. His legs felt like they were made of lead. Worse, there was something wrong with his bowels, which felt ready to explode.

"Which one of you is available?" Carr stammered.

"You sick?" A Russian wearing an I LOVE NY tee-shirt eyed him suspiciously.

"Not sick," he managed to utter.

"Get away from my cab, you stinking drunk," the Russian declared belligerently.

A taxi appeared, and cut in front of the line of parked vehicles. The driver flashed his brights, signaling he was free. Carr poured himself into the back seat. He was on the verge of passing out, and struggled to speak.

"Times Square, and hurry," he gasped.

The taxi practically leapt off the ground. As it did, a small army of policemen burst out of Penn Station. Carr went low in his seat. Within moments he was out of danger. He sucked down air, and gradually started to feel better.

The taxi hurtled down Seventh Avenue. Carr had taken his share of dangerous cab rides in New York, but nothing like this. His driver swerved between lanes like a stock car driver.

"Where are you going? This isn't the way to Times Square."

The driver ignored him. Carr tried to get a look at his face. The partition separating them was covered in advertisements and public service announcements.

"Slow down. You're going to hit someone."

The driver gazed at Carr in his mirror. His eyes were a sickly yellow, and looked jaundiced. Something was clearly wrong with him.

"Didn't you hear me? I said, slow down!"

Instead of slowing down, the taxi picked up speed. Cars and buildings flew past at breakneck speed. Carr heard a noise from the trunk. A loud banging sound.

"What's that sound?" he asked.

The driver ignored him. At the intersection of 27th Street, he blew the red light. The banging sound grew louder. It was accompanied by another sound. A voice.

"Somebody help me . . ."

The voice sounded Chinese. Carr looked at the driver's license posted on the dashboard. Wei Lin. Only the man behind the wheel was clearly not Wei Lin.

"Who the hell are you?" Carr shouted at the driver.

At the intersection at 26th Street, a truck was stopped at the light. The driver swerved to avoid a collision, and went into the opposing lane. A city bus was coming right at them. The bus's driver hit his horn. They were going to crash. The irony was not lost on Carr. His wife and daughter had died in a wreck, and now, so might he. But he didn't want to die just yet. That would come later tonight, when he released the nerve agent. Remembering the instructions they gave on airplanes, he curled himself into a ball, and tucked his head in to his chest.

The bus sideswiped them. The crash was deafeningly loud. The cab pitched sideways, and began to roll. It did a complete revolution before landing upright in the middle of Seventh Avenue. The tires deflated, and it sank into the earth.

"I'm hurt bad," said the voice in the trunk.

Carr quickly examined himself. He should have been dead as well. The impact that had taken his wife and daughter's lives had been far less severe. Yet nothing on his body felt broken or even badly bruised except for the cut in his tongue.

"You're insane," he said to the driver.

The driver was slumped over the wheel. His head was twisted at an unnatural angle, his neck obviously broken. Carr snorted derisively.

"Serves you right," he said.

The driver stirred, and snapped his head back into place. Before Carr's disbelieving eyes, the dead man climbed out of the taxi, and came around to the passenger side. Throwing open the door, he reached in, and pried the knapsack from Carr's hands.

"You won't be needing that anymore," the driver said.

Carr looked at the driver's face. The skin was a violent purple, and his eyes had no life. Carr knew that the dead did not walk, or talk, or crash vehicles on busy city streets, and that this was a horrible illusion, courtesy of his poisoned mind.

People had started to gather around the cab. The driver pushed his way through them, and staggered away. Carr watched him leave, thinking surely he'd seen the Devil.

Then he broke down, and wept uncontrollably.

53

The West 30th Street heliport was located next to the Hudson River on the west side of Manhattan. The rain let up long enough for the FBI chopper to land. As Peter and Garrison jumped out, they were greeted by the female agent on Garrison's team who'd arrested Snoop years ago, a no-nonsense blonde named Nan Perry, who spoke with a thick Boston accent. Perry briefed them as they crossed the asphalt with the rain whipping in their faces.

"Dr. Carr arrived at Penn Station on the four-forty-five from Hunters Point," Perry said. "Although a gang of undercover NYPD detectives was waiting for him, Carr managed to escape by causing a riot outside the boarding gates. He got outside, and grabbed a cab. The cab got into an accident on Twenty-sixth Street, and Carr was apprehended."

"So we got him," Garrison said, sounding relieved.

"Yes. The doctor's in custody," Perry said.

The tension left Garrison's face, and he looked like a normal person again.

"Ready for the bad news?" Perry said.

"What do you mean? What happened?" Garrison asked.

"The person driving the cab wasn't the driver. It was an imposter, who hijacked the cab, and threw the driver in the trunk. Right after the accident, the imposter snatched Carr's knapsack and took off. You know what they say. Only in New York."

"Please tell me someone saw this person," Garrison said pleadingly.

"We've gotten a couple of eyewitness accounts, most of them sketchy. Our thief was a six-foot-tall male. He was walking stiffly, and may have been hurt in the accident."

A town car with tinted windows was parked at the curb, its engine spitting black fumes. They finished the conversation driving into Midtown.

"What shape is Carr in?" Garrison asked.

"He's banged up, but there doesn't appear to be anything physically wrong with him," Perry replied, riding up front beside the driver.

"What about the guy in the trunk? Did he see anything?"

"He wasn't so lucky. He died on the way to the hospital."

Garrison blew out his cheeks. "When it rains, it pours. Where's Carr now?"

"The police have him in a holding cell at Penn Station. A pair of detectives questioned him, but everything Carr says is nonsense. They can't tell if it's an act, or if there's something seriously wrong with him."

"What's your gut telling you?"

"I think Carr's flipped his wig," Perry said. "We do know one thing for sure. The knapsack is loaded with enough Novichok to take down half the city. The recipe was in a hidden compartment in Carr's wallet. There are a hundred variants of Novichok, and he chose the most deadly strain. He manufactured several pounds of it."

Peter watched the passing scenery, the images from the séance still fresh in his mind. Wolfe wasn't the Grim Reaper, it was Carr. How could the spirits have gotten it so wrong?

"What's the NYPD doing to catch this guy?" Garrison asked.

"They're conducting a manhunt," Perry replied. "He got away on foot, so they think he's still near Twenty-sixth Street, where the crash took place. The mayor's been briefed on the crisis, and has decided not to shut down the city. He's afraid it would cause widespread panic."

"That's the stupidest thing I've ever heard," Garrison said. "They have to shut down the city, until this guy is caught."

"I've got his number if you'd like to call him," Perry suggested.

"I'll save my breath."

They had reached Penn Station. The front entrance was blocked by police cruisers and unmarked police cars. Next door, a long line of people was wrapped around Madison Square Garden, waiting to see the Knicks play basketball. It occurred to Peter that not a single one of them had any notion of the danger they were in. Their lives might end tonight while watching some highly paid athletes throw a round ball through a hoop. He'd seen this coming on Friday night, and it was his duty to stop it.

"Let me talk to Carr. Maybe I can get into his head, and find out who stole the knapsack. If I gain his confidence, I can read his mind."

"Can you read a crazy person's mind?" Garrison asked, sounding skeptical.

It was a question that Peter did not have an answer to.

"I can try," the young magician said.

"You're on, hotshot."

They sifted their way through the mob of police and entered Penn Station. The terminal was filled with news crews jostling with one another to get a story. Peter kept his head down, and tried to avoid being seen. Entering an elevator, they descended into the basement where the police station was housed. The car landed with a dull thud, and they got out.

Penn Station was a magnet for the city's homeless, and the plastic chairs inside the station lobby were occupied by dispirited bag people. Garrison approached the booking area, holding his ID in front of his face. "I need to see Dr. Carr," he announced.

"Carr's being interrogated," the desk sergeant replied.

"Don't make me repeat myself," Garrison told him.

The desk sergeant glared at them. Cops were fiercely territorial, and reacted unfavorably when their turf was encroached upon. Perry stepped between the two men, and batted her eyelashes.

"Please," she said sweetly.

"What's this about?" the desk sergeant asked.

"We think there's going to be an attack on the city."

"Why didn't you say so?"

The desk sergeant escorted them down a hall to a small room with a two-way mirror. On the other side of the glass, Carr was slumped in a chair with a deranged look on his face. The doctor was wrapped in a wool blanket and shaking uncontrollably. A pair of balding, overweight detectives were raking him over the coals. Their voices were harsh, and carried through the glass. "No more screwing around. Tell us who took the knapsack," the first detective said.

"He was the Devil," Carr replied, hugging himself fiercely.

"You ever see this devil before?"

"Never."

"How close did you get to him?"

"Close as I am to you," Carr replied.

"Think you could pick him out of a book of mug shots?"

Carr cast his eyes downward and laughed hoarsely.

"Look at me when I'm talking to you," the detective said.

Carr looked up. "He was the Devil. That was who took my knapsack. The Devil incarnate. That's all I have to say."

"He's been giving us this same line of crap since we hauled him in," the desk sergeant said, cracking a piece of gum in his mouth.

"Think you can get into his head?" Garrison asked Peter.

"I don't see why not," Peter replied.

"Go for it."

Peter moved for the door. He'd never plumbed the thoughts of a crazy person before, and supposed there was a first time for everything. The desk sergeant blocked his way.

"Hold on a second," the desk sergeant said. "What are you going to do? Put him under hypnosis?"

"Something like that," Peter replied.

"You don't look like a shrink," the desk sergeant said.

"I'm not. Tell your detectives to stop. I need to be in the room alone with Dr. Carr."

"No can do. It's against department rules," the desk sergeant said.

"Do it anyway," Garrison told him.

The desk sergeant didn't like it. He looked at Perry, thinking she might come to his aid. When Perry didn't respond, he left the room in a huff.

54

Fear had a smell. It tinged the air like rotting flesh, and so much desperation. The room in which Carr sat had such a smell. It was pouring off the doctor like bad cologne. Peter got up close to him anyway, and pulled up a chair. He sat so their knees were touching. Touching was important. It established intimacy, and created a physical bond. Carr stirred in his chair.

"Who are you?" Carr asked.

"My name's Peter. I need to talk to you."

Carr rocked forward in his chair. "You look like that young magician fellow. What's-his-name. My daughter dragged me to his show once. It was dreadful."

"You don't like magic?" Peter asked.

"Hate it."

"But your daughter does."

"Katie loved magic," Carr said. "She always made me hire a magician for her birthday party. Had to have a rabbit." His eyes glistened with tears. "I loved my daughter so much. When she and my wife were killed, it was a like a piece of my heart was torn out."

"I understand."

"No, you don't," he said furiously. "There's no way you could understand. You're too young to know that kind of pain."

"My parents were killed when I was a boy," Peter said quietly.

"You're not making that up?"

Peter shook his head. "No," he added for emphasis.

Carr hugged himself with the blanket. "I'm sorry to hear that. Were you angry after they died? I was so angry after I lost my wife and daughter. I lost control, and did a terrible thing. And now I'm going to pay for what I did. Both in this life, and the next."

Carr had let his guard down. Peter gazed into his eyes, and read the doctor's thoughts. It was like watching a disjointed movie, the scenes cutting into each other for reasons that only the doctor understood. In the first scene, Carr was taking his wife and daughter to a show in the city. In the next, a car was tumbling down a ditch on a darkened road. Badly shaken, Carr climbed out, but his wife and daughter did not. It was there that the movie ended. How ironic that Carr's last good memory with his family had occurred seeing a show in the city. *Just like me,* Peter thought.

"Tell me about the Devil you saw this afternoon," Peter said.

"Who told you about the Devil?" Carr asked.

"I heard you tell the detectives."

"You were listening in?"

"Tell me about him."

"God sent him to punish me."

"How did you know he was a devil?"

"Easy. He wasn't human."

Carr wasn't making sense, so Peter took another look inside his head. The doctor sat in the back of a cab with a child's knapsack resting on his lap. The door flung open, and a man reached in, and stole the knapsack. The man was only there for a brief moment; just long enough for Peter to get a fleeting glimpse at him. What he saw did not make sense. The man's clothes looked burned. His face was dark. Not black or brown, but a sickly purple color. There was no life in his eyes. Peter wondered if the man was real, or a figment of Carr's distorted imagination.

"How did you know this man wasn't human?" Peter asked.

"It was his skin," the doctor replied.

"What was wrong with it?"

Carr glanced suspiciously at the two-way mirror. He dropped his voice to a conspiratorial whisper. "It was the skin of a dead man. He wasn't alive."

"He was a corpse? You saw a corpse?"

"That's right," Carr whispered.

Peter felt his body slowly deflate. Carr was insane. Dead men did not hijack cabs and steal knapsacks loaded with deadly nerve agent. The images he'd seen inside Carr's head weren't real, but the product of a sick mind. He was wasting time. He needed to help the police find the man with the knapsack. Rising from his chair, he went to the door.

"Are you leaving?" Carr asked.

"Yes."

"You don't believe me, do you?"

Peter was not going to lie, and shook his head.

"Just wait," Carr said. "You will."

Peter entered the hallway outside the interrogation room to find the two overweight detectives waiting for him. Both were smoking cigarettes. It was against the law to smoke inside buildings, but these were not the kind of men you said something like that to. Peter started to tell them that Carr was crazy, but stopped the words from coming out. He'd been reading minds since childhood, and not once had a person been able to substitute an image. Why should it be different for a crazy person?

"Learn anything?" one of the detectives asked.

"He told me a dead man took the knapsack from him," Peter said.

"Hah," the detective said.

Peter returned to the viewing room where Garrison and Perry were waiting. Garrison stood in the corner with his cell phone pressed to his face. The veins were popping on his forehead, and he looked like a candidate for a stroke.

"What's going on now?" Peter asked.

"I'm not sure," Perry admitted. "Garrison is talking to some cops downtown, and keeps swearing under his breath. This case is going to kill him if he's not careful."

Him and me both, Peter almost said.

"Did you hear what Carr told me? He said the man who stole the knapsack was a corpse."

"Yeah, we heard him," Perry replied. "There's a hidden mike in the light fixture in the ceiling. It's sensitive enough to pick up a fly buzzing around."

"He was telling the truth."

"Excuse me?"

"Carr was telling the truth. I looked inside his head, and saw the dead guy. That's what caused Carr to flip out."

Perry's face betrayed her. She didn't believe him. Peter wasn't going to argue with her. When it came to the supernatural, nothing would change a nonbeliever. Perry didn't believe in the spirit world, or that the forces of evil regularly did battle with the forces of good, often in plain view of people just like herself.

"I'm just telling you what I saw, that's all," Peter said.

"Right," she said under her breath.

"I'm not making it up. Carr saw a dead person."

"Uh-huh," she said.

Garrison had finished his call. He said something to himself that sounded like "So help me, God." He jerked open the door, and looked back at them.

"You coming or not?" he asked.

"Where are we going?" Perry replied.

"To the morgue," he said. "There's a dead man on the loose."

55

The Office of the Chief Medical Examiner of the City of New York was located in Kip's Bay, in a steel-and-glass building overlooking the East River. Garrison remained silent during the drive. He looked shaken to the core. Something had happened inside the morgue that rocked him. Peter had tried to glimpse Garrison's thoughts to find out what it was. The wall of resistance he'd encountered was impenetrable.

They parked on the street in front of the building. Several uniformed cops stood on the sidewalk, blocking anyone from entering. Garrison identified himself and had a brief conversation with them. The cops looked equally rattled.

They went inside. The lobby looked like a cyclone had run through it. An employee stood on a ladder, righting a sign that hung on the wall. It read, LET CONVERSATION CEASE, LET LAUGHTER FLEE. THIS IS THE PLACE WHERE DEATH DELIGHTS IN HELPING THE LIVING. Looking around, Peter didn't think that death had delighted anyone recently.

They took an elevator to the basement. Peter felt the cold return to his bones as they entered the harshly lit autopsy room, an antiseptic chamber with eight steel examining tables where the city's dead revealed their secrets. The same cyclone had run through here as well, with broken equipment scattered about, the TV monitors used to film autopsies pulled off the walls and ripped apart. A maintenance man stood in the room's center, mopping chemical preservative off the floor. "Can I help you?" he inquired.

"Who's in charge here?" Garrison asked.

"That would be the chief medical examiner, Dr. Fiesler," the maintenance man said.

"Where can I find her?"

"She's down the hall, trying to calm everybody down."

"What do you mean? What exactly happened here?" Garrison asked.

"I'm not allowed to say."

"Why not?"

"Dr. Fiesler's orders. I'm sure you're somebody important, otherwise you wouldn't be down here. But I could lose my job, so I'm not saying anything."

Garrison turned to Perry. "See if you can charm this guy into telling you something."

"Will do," Perry replied.

Peter and Garrison went to a room at the end of the hall. Garrison entered without bothering to knock. Six physicians wearing lime-green scrubs stood in the center, talking in hushed tones. Behind them were the stainless-steel coolers where the newly dead were stored. Inside the coolers was a construction worker who'd had a heart attack, a homeless man who'd died peacefully in his sleep, and a house painter who'd fallen off a ladder. Their spirits whispered to Peter as he entered, telling him their darkest secrets. Normally, Peter would have talked to them, but today there was no time. He tuned out their voices.

"I'm looking for Dr. Fiesler," Garrison announced.

"That's me," replied a smallish woman with sun-bleached hair.

"Special Agent Garrison, FBI. I want to know what happened here."

"If I told you, you wouldn't believe me," Fiesler said gravely.

"Try me."

"We had a corpse come back to life while being cut open on an autopsy table."

"Name?"

"Wolfe. He was brought in yesterday. Fell from an apartment building."

"Dead people don't come back to life," Garrison said. "There has to be something else going on here. I'm sure you've considered that."

"We have," Fiesler replied. "There's no other explanation. Not one that we can think of, anyway."

"If you'll excuse me, I need to speak with my associate," Garrison said.

Garrison pulled Peter into the hallway and dropped his voice.

"Is this possible?" the FBI agent asked.

"The dead don't come back to life," Peter said. "It's one of the rules of the game. The only other explanation is that Wolfe's body is possessed."

"Is *that* possible?"

"It is if a group of psychics are involved. No one will admit to it, but that's what really started the witch trials in Salem. A group of witches were possessing dead people's bodies."

"How do we find out for certain? I need to know what we're dealing with."

"The TV monitors inside the autopsy room were pulled out of the walls. Maybe they were filming Wolfe when it happened, and he tried to destroy them."

"Would you know if you saw a film?"

"I think so."

Garrison went back into the room. The doctors were still in a huddle. Peter sensed they were having a hard time dealing with what had happened. *The things I could tell you,* he thought.

"Was Wolfe filmed during his autopsy?" Garrison asked.

"All our autopsies are filmed," Fiesler replied. "So was Wolfe's."

"I'd like to see it. It may explain what happened."

Fiesler took them to her office. It was a messy affair with stacks of papers hiding her desk. She got onto her computer and made magic on the keyboard. Soon they were watching a film of Wolfe's autopsy. The dead man lay naked on an autopsy table. Rigor mortis had set in, and his body had gone stiff, his mouth open like someone in a deep sleep. Looking at him, there was no doubt that his spirit had left this earth long ago. A doctor holding a scalpel began to slice open Wolfe's sternum. The tattoo on the dead man's neck began to glow.

"See that?" Peter asked.

"Yeah, and it's creeping me out," Garrison replied.

"Somebody give me a hint what's going on," Fiesler said.

"He's being possessed," Peter explained.

Wolfe's eyelids snapped open. Knocking the scalpel away, he sat bolt upright, and hopped off the table. In a mad fury he began destroying things, his movements stiff and awkward. The doctor performing the autopsy fled from the room.

Wolfe went to a closet in the autopsy room. He pulled out a cardboard box filled with clothes, and removed a tattered pair of pants and a shirt. He dressed himself, and staggered away.

"What's with the clothes?" Garrison asked.

"Good question," Fiesler replied. "He had a choice of clothes, including a brand-new pair of scrubs hanging inside the closet. For some reason, he took the clothes he was wearing when he was brought in. I guess he had some sort of attachment to them." She paused. "So let me ask you gentlemen a question. How do my staff and I explain this without looking like lunatics?"

"You don't," Garrison answered.

"Come again?"

"Keep a lid on it," the FBI agent said.

"But that's not ethical."

"No, it's not. But how's it going to look if you start telling people you saw a corpse come back to life?"

"Not good," she admitted.

"I'd call it career-threatening. People would question your ability to do your job. My advice would be for you and your staff to make up a story, and stick to it. That's what we do in the government."

"You're saying we should lie," Fiesler said.

"Through your teeth."

"Whatever you say. Anything else I can do for you gentlemen?"

"Can you e-mail me a copy of this video?" Peter asked.

"I don't see why not," the doctor replied.

Peter wrote his e-mail address on a slip of paper. Fiesler got onto her computer, and through the magic of the Internet, the e-mail appeared on Peter's cell phone seconds later.

"Much appreciated," he said.

"Last question," Fiesler said. "What should I do with this film?"

"Make it go away," Garrison answered.

Fiesler erased the autopsy of Wolfe, and walked out of the office.

Peter forwarded the autopsy film to Holly, with Garrison looking over his shoulder.

"I have a friend who's a witch," Peter explained. "She has the ability to track people down if she knows what they look like."

"Can all psychics do that?" Garrison asked.

"No, they can't."

"So you're not all the same, then."

"Hardly. Our gifts come from different places, and let us do different things. The thing we share in common is the ability to communicate with the spirit world."

"Can your witch tell me where Wolfe's hiding?"

"To a degree. She'll able to tell us if he's hiding inside a building, or on a rooftop, or in a bedroom. Hopefully, she'll spot some landmark that will tell us his location."

"How long will this take?"

"Hard to say. I have to talk to her first."

Garrison consulted his watch. The frown on his face grew more pronounced. The thoughts racing through his head were as easy to read as a ticker tape. He was going to call his superior in the FBI, and tell him to override the mayor, and shut down the city. If Wolfe did release the nerve agent, it would reduce the number of lives lost. It was the best Garrison could do, considering the circumstances.

Peter followed him upstairs. Perry was waiting outside the building for them. Garrison headed for his car, then stopped, and came back to where Peter stood.

"Explain something to me," Garrison said. "How did the Order of Astrum know to have Wolfe intercept Carr, and steal the knapsack? You said they didn't know what was going on."

"They didn't," Peter replied. "When Wolfe was killed last night, the Order realized their plan was in jeopardy. They figured out it was Carr the same way we did."

"So how did they find him?"

"Carr's incident at the lab was on the news. The Order must have seen it on CNN, and realized he was the one. They probably used astral projection to search for him, and saw all the police gathered around Penn Station. That was the clue they needed. They possessed Wolfe, and sent him to intercept Carr."

"So you're saying they got lucky."

"Afraid so."

Garrison was burning up inside. He'd never had an assignment break this bad.

Peter's cell phone vibrated. He pulled it out, and stared at the face.

"That's my witch. I'll call you when I know something."

Garrison hurried with Perry to his car.

Peter stepped under the building's awning to answer the call.

"That was fast," he said.

"I just watched the film you sent me," Holly said. "Is this a science fiction movie?"

"Wolfe's body has been possessed, and he's got his hands on a deadly nerve agent. You have to find him. Ask Max and Milly to help. The more eyes the better. He's hiding out somewhere south of Twenty-sixth Street, on the west side of town."

"Why's he hiding? Why not release the nerve agent now?"

"He's waiting until dark. It will make things easier."

"There are only so many places a dead man can hide. I'll call you when I know something."

"Thanks, Holly."

"No need to thank me. We're all in this together, you know."

Peter started to say good-bye, then stopped. Nemo had predicted that he would die at Wolfe's hands tonight. That had not seemed a reality, until now. There were some things that even a psychic couldn't change, and he realized he might never speak to Holly again.

"I'm sorry I've been such a shit lately," he said. "You deserve better. Please forgive me."

Holly's voice softened. "You've been under a lot of pressure lately. When this is over, we need to talk. I have a special gift for you."

He swallowed hard. Would he die not knowing what it was?

"What kind of gift?" he asked.

"It will change your life."

"Really? Tell me."

She laughed. "You hate being kept in the dark, don't you? You'll have to wait."

"Come on. Please."

"I'll give you a hint. It's three hundred years old, and came from Mary Glover."

"The witch? What is it, a magical talisman?"

"That would spoil the surprise. I'll call you once I've located Wolfe."

He smiled into the phone. Holly wasn't angry with him anymore. If he died tonight, he would know that at least he'd ended things right with her.

"Good-bye, Holly," he said.

56

H olly folded her phone with a smile on her face. Peter sounded like his old self again. More than anything else, she wanted Peter to be happy, and not to suffer. If that wasn't a definition of true love, she didn't know what was.

She glanced at her aunt. The sleeping pill had knocked her out cold. She decided that it would be a bad idea to awaken her. Better to ask Max to help her track down Wolfe. Max had a keen eye for that sort of thing.

She found the old magician snoring on the couch in the living room. Several vigorous shakes were required to rouse him from his dreams. Max awoke with a start.

"What's going on?" he asked excitedly.

"I just spoke with Peter. He wants us to find Wolfe."

"That should be easy enough," Max replied. "Wolfe's in the morgue."

"Afraid not. He's become possessed, and is about to release a nerve agent on the city. He's holed up somewhere below Twenty-sixth Street on the West Side. Peter wants us to locate him."

Max dragged himself off the couch. The sleep was slow to leave his face. Shaking it away, he said, "He's possessed? That makes him easier to find. Where do you want to do this?"

"How about right here? That way, if my aunt wakes up, we'll hear her."

"Fair enough. Get the potions, and I'll set up by the window where the light's good."

Holly retrieved the herbs and potions from her aunt's closet. Upon returning, she found a round vase filled with water sitting on the table. Max sat at the table, waiting.

"Isn't that vase a little big?" she asked.

"My eyes aren't what they used to be," Max said. "The bigger the better these days."

She prepared the potions, mixing them together with the tip of her little finger. "Unless Wolfe's hiding someplace obvious, we'll have no idea where he is. Will we?"

"The possessed are easy to find," Max explained.

"You've lost me, Max."

"Do what needs to be done. Then I'll explain."

Holly poured the potions into the vase, and the water turned a milky white.

> *"Spirits all so knowing,*
> *I'm looking for a man who's stopped growing.*
> *His name is Wolfe, and he's become possessed,*
> *and now hides somewhere in the city.*
> *Show me where, and I'll be forever thankful,*
> *that you chose to show me pity."*

"Not bad," Max said, nodding approvingly.

"I've been working on my rhyming." Holly pulled up a chair, and sat next to the old magician. "Now tell me why the possessed are easy to find."

"It's because of the baggage they inherit," Max explained. "When a person dies, their soul leaves their body, and leaves behind things which are no longer of use to them. I'll give you an example. Let's say Wolfe was a smoker. When he died, his craving for nicotine stays behind. When Wolfe's body became possessed, the possessor becomes a smoker."

"How does that make Wolfe easy to find?"

"The human instincts also stay behind. Wolfe is now in hiding, correct? Well, I can tell you that he's hiding in a place that is comfortable to him. A place that he knows."

"Like a child would do."

"Exactly. Just like a child. The possessor can't control this."

"What kind of places would Wolfe find comfortable?"

"Someplace he's already been to. Perhaps a bar, or a restaurant. We'll have to see."

The water inside the vase had gone from cloudy to crystal clear. An image of a man appeared. It was Wolfe, wearing the same clothes which had been burned after his fall. The skin on his face was hideous to behold, with rigor mortis setting in. At his feet lay a child's knapsack.

"That's him," she whispered. "It looks like he's in a basement."

Max leaned in. His bushy eyebrows came together as he stared. "I believe you're right. He's in the basement of a building. I can see the outline of a stairwell on the far wall."

"I see it, too," Holly said.

"Beneath the stairwell there's a large object beneath a sheet."

"You're right. It looks like a child's dollhouse."

"Yes, it does." Max brought his hand up to scratch his chin. "Damn it. Excuse me for swearing, but I've seen that shape before."

"But where, Max?"

"It will come to me. Just give me a little while."

They watched Wolfe pace back and forth. The dead man's movements were stiff, yet animated. Once darkness fell, he would venture outside, and wreak havoc upon the city.

"We're running out of time, Max."

"I can't rush this, Holly," the old magician replied. "My brain is filled with thousands of pieces of useless information. It's the curse of growing old. I need time to sort through it."

"I'm going to call Peter, and tell him what we've found. Maybe he can make sense of it."

"By all means. Peter is good at this sort of thing."

The haunting blast of an air raid siren filled the apartment. It was frighteningly loud, and drowned out all other sound. Her aunt called from the bedroom.

"What is that awful racket?" Milly asked.

Holly rose from her chair, and put her face to the window. A long line of police cruisers were snaking down Central Park West with their bubble lights flashing. The lead cruiser had a loudspeaker on its roof from which came a policeman's voice.

"Go inside! There is about to be an attack on the city," the policeman warned. "Seek shelter at once. Do not come outside until told to."

The street cleared out, with not a soul to be seen. Holly felt her body start to shake. The attack Peter had warned them of was about to happen. And only Peter could stop it. She dug out her cell phone while looking at Max.

"I'm trying," the old magician said.

"Try harder," she told him.

57

An air raid siren pierced the air. Peter had never heard one, except in old war movies on late-night TV. It was haunting enough to instill fear in a person, which he supposed was the point. People ran past. Before long, he was the only person remaining on the street.

A steel-gray sky blanketed the city. It was like a dreary canvas waiting to be completed. Would the picture be happy, or sad? Even he could not predict how it would look. There was another hour of sunlight left, maybe less. He tried to guess where Wolfe could be hiding. He'd read about trackers who could locate people in vast forests, but this was the city, with no footprints to be found. The expression "finding a needle in a haystack" came to mind.

His cell phone vibrated. He hoped it was Holly calling to tell him that she'd discovered Wolfe's hideout. Instead, he saw that it was Liza. They hadn't talked all day.

"Hi," he answered. "I hope you're not angry at me for not calling."

"How about livid?" his girlfriend said icily.

"I'm sorry. Really."

"I'm sick and tired of hearing you say that. I'm at the theater. Where are you?"

"What are you doing at the theater?" he asked, hearing the panic in his voice. "I told Snoop that you guys needed to stay at his place. The city's in danger."

"Don't you remember? A foreign tour group booked the theater this afternoon. You were supposed to give them a private show. I had to send them back to their hotel. They were heartbroken. I've never been more humiliated in my life."

"I'm sorry. I forgot all about it."

"Look Peter, I don't know what your deal is, but I've had enough of this. I don't want to be a puppet in your life anymore. You're manipulating me."

"I'm sorry."

"Say that one more time, and I'm hanging up."

"But I am. I should have come clean long ago. You had a right to know who I am."

"You can't undo what's done," Liza said.

"At least give me a chance to try."

A motorcycle cop rocketed down a deserted First Avenue. The cop spotted Peter standing outside, did a sharp U-turn in the street, and drove back to the building.

"Get inside," the motorcycle cop ordered him.

"Yes, sir," Peter replied.

Peter feigned going inside. The motorcycle cop sped away, and he returned to where he'd been standing. There were people inside the lobby, and he didn't want them overhearing his conversation with Liza. His life was already complicated enough.

"Who was that?" his girlfriend asked.

"A cop. The city's being shut down. There's about to be an attack. I've been trying to stop it with the FBI. They asked me to help, and I couldn't say no."

"Still playing superhero?"

He didn't feel like a superhero. Superheroes didn't fail.

"This isn't a conversation we should be having over the phone," he said. "I want to be with you. Please give me a chance to make things right."

"You want another chance?" she asked. He heard hesitation in her voice, and knew he was doomed.

"Yes. That's all I'm asking for."

Peter heard a loud beep. Someone was calling him. Caller ID on his phone said HOLLY. She wouldn't be calling unless she'd found where Wolfe was hiding.

"I need to take this call. Let me call you back," he said.

"Are you kidding?" Liza said in disbelief.

"This is life or death," he said.

"I'm sure it is. Call me when you have a spare minute to devote to our relationship." Liza hung up on him.

He brought his hand up to his face. The world was spinning out of control, and he was about to fall off. He took Holly's call, hoping she had good news to share with him. Anything would have lifted his spirts at this point.

"Tell me you found Wolfe," he said.

"Max and I are looking at him right now," Holly replied.

"That's fantastic."

"Don't get too excited. We haven't pinpointed where he is. Here's what we do know. Wolfe's hiding in the basement of a building. He keeps glancing at the ceiling, which makes us think there are other people in the building. Max says it's a building Wolfe's been to before."

"How does he know that?"

"Max said that the possessed revert back to old habits, and return to familiar haunts. Even though Wolfe's mind is possessed, his body is still functioning as if it's his."

"Are there any other clues?"

"There's something stored beneath a sheet in the basement. It looks like a large dollhouse. Max is convinced he's seen it before, but can't place where. I'm guessing it's a prop to a stage production, and that Wolfe is hiding in a theater."

"How many theaters are there below Twenty-sixth Street on the West Side?"

"I've found six on Google so far."

Holly started to recite the names when Peter heard a noise. The motorcycle cop had returned, and parked his bike at the curb. Seconds later the cop was standing beside him. "I told you to get inside," the motorcycle cop said angrily.

"I have a lead on the man you're looking for," Peter replied.

"You and every other joker in this city. Get inside the building. That's an order."

"Listen to me. He's hiding in the basement of a theater on the West Side. I'm getting the names of the theaters where he could be right now. He's in one of these buildings."

The motorcycle cop pinched his arm and began to drag him inside. He had a steel grip, and looked like he lifted weights when he wasn't running down bad guys. When Peter resisted, the motorcycle cop twisted his arm, causing a jolt of pain to shoot straight into his shoulder.

"Don't make me cuff you," the motorcycle cop warned.

"You're not listening."

"Just do as I tell you."

It was like talking to a wall. Peter felt defeated. Could anything in his day go right? He stopped resisting, and the motorcycle cop released his grip. His arm still hurt. If he'd learned anything in life, it was that nothing good came without a little pain and suffering. At that very moment the things Holly had just told him came together like a jigsaw puzzle inside his head. Wolfe had run to a theater he was familiar with. *His* theater. He was hiding beneath the stage, probably right below the trap door he'd fallen through during his previous visit. The object Max had seen draped beneath a sheet was the Dollhouse Illusion, which Peter had recently retired from his show. It would have looked familiar to Max, because he'd given it to Peter as a gift when he started performing over a decade ago.

The last clue was the worst of all. Wolfe was listening to the people directly above him. Snoop and Liza. Their lives were in imminent danger. He had internalized his anger long enough, and felt the rage boil to the surface.

"I'm sorry," Peter said.

"For what?" the motorcycle cop replied.

His actions were a blur. A quick blow to the helmet with the palm of his hand, and the motorcycle cop was lying on the ground. The next moment, he was straddling the cop's bike, and attempting to kick-start the engine. It roared to life, and he pulled onto the street.

He called Liza and Snoop as he drove, and got voice mail. Either they were ignoring him, or were still dealing with the mess he'd left them with.

He raced across town in the pouring rain. It had been a long time since he'd ridden a motorcycle. The good news was, the streets were deserted, and he wasn't going to hurt anyone if he spun out of control and crashed. Perhaps his streak of bad luck was finally over.

He could only hope.

58

Peter parked the stolen motorcycle in the alley behind the theater. Normally, the back door was kept closed. Now it was open, the lock jimmied. If he'd learned any lesson watching TV cop shows, rushing into an unknown situation was never a smart idea. He again called Liza and Snoop. When neither answered, he called Garrison, who picked up right away.

"I can't talk right now," Garrison said. "I'll call you back."

"Wolfe's hiding in the basement of my theater," Peter said.

"*What?* Are you sure?"

"I wouldn't call you if I wasn't."

"Did your witch find him?"

"It was a group effort." Peter gave him the theater's address, then said, "How quickly can you get here? I don't want him to slip away."

"I'll be there as fast as I can," Garrison said. "I'm on the rooftop of an apartment house on Twenty-first Street, running down some crazy guy we thought was Wolfe."

Peter was calculating how long the FBI agent might be when he heard Liza's screams from inside the theater. "That's not fast enough. I've got to go."

"Don't go in there yourself," Garrison said. "Let me get a team over there."

Peter heard another scream. It sounded like Snoop.

"Too late," Peter said. "Wish me luck."

He rushed inside. The back of the theater was dark and foreboding, and it took a moment for his eyes to adjust. Sound was magnified inside a theater, and Liza's cries for help could have been coming out of a loudspeaker. He charged across the area behind the stage.

Coming through the curtains, he found himself bathed in a soft yellow spotlight. Wolfe stood at the foot of the stage with his hands around Snoop's throat. The deadly knapsack lay at Wolfe's feet.

Liza lay on the floor, looking dazed. Peter had fallen in love with her the first time he'd laid eyes upon her. The effect was no different now, only painful, knowing that she was in peril. She saw him as well. Her smile melted his heart.

"Peter, help us," she shouted.

"Hold on. I'm coming."

Wolfe's head snapped at the sound of the young magician's voice. Wolfe's eyes were dead, and his frozen expression did not change. Hideous scratch marks ran down the side of his face where Liza had raked her fingernails across his rotting flesh.

"I've been waiting for you," the dead man said.

They met in the center of the stage and squared off. Peter struck his nemesis in the face with all his might. To his surprise, the blow had no effect. Wolfe threw his hands around Peter's throat, and began to choke him.

"Die, you little bastard," Wolfe said.

Peter struggled to break free. Wolfe hadn't been this powerful the last time they'd fought. Staring into the dead man's eyes, he was taken to another place and he saw three men in black robes and wearing masks sitting at a table covered in astrological symbols. Then he understood. He wasn't wrestling with Wolfe, he was wrestling with the elders of the Order of Astrum.

His knees buckled as the air was cut off to his brain. He gazed up at the posters of the great magicians of yesteryear hanging from the ceiling. Their faces mocked him. *Do better*, they said. *This is not the way you want to die.*

Wolfe tightened his grip. Pools of black appeared before Peter's eyes. He tried to summon the demon inside of him, but the demon refused to come out. Without the demon, he had no chance. His world turned utterly still, and he felt himself relax. *So this is what it's like*, he thought. *You black out, and end up somewhere else. No different than falling asleep on an airplane, and waking up in a different place when the plane touched down.*

His world changed. He was now floating on the bottom of the frozen lake in the town of Marble with his parents and their three little friends. His parents had bubbles pouring out of their mouths, and were drowning. So were their friends. So was he. He had gone from one end-of-life experience to another.

A large, circular light appeared before him. It was the Seal of Satan. One by one, the children were drawn into the seal, and disappeared. His mother was the last to go. She turned her head to look at him, and offered her hand. *Take it,* her eyes said. *Do not be afraid of what's on the other side.* He had nothing to lose, and clasped her hand. Together, they were pulled through the seal, the beginning of a terrifying fall through space.

The fall ended. He was standing inside a cave covered in human skeletons. The children of Marble were gone and he was alone. Tortured groans and the sounds of chains being dragged across the floor filled the air. He'd been transported straight to hell.

A purring black cat was rubbing against him. The cat crossed the cave, and jumped onto a throne of skulls. Before his eyes, it grew to human size, and became a man dressed in a long black robe. It was no ordinary man, but a towering figure with snakelike fingers that moved with a life of their own. One half of his face was handsome, the other half burned beyond recognition.

The wicked one.

"Are you ready?" his unearthly host asked.

"Do I have a choice?" Peter replied.

A demonic laugh that made Peter's hair stand on end came out of his mouth.

"Of course you have a choice," the wicked one replied. "Become one of us, and you will be sent back to earth with powers beyond any mortal's comprehension.

Refuse, and you will die a thousand deaths. Those are your choices."

Peter had never felt more afraid. Being a devil's disciple was not the life he wanted. But what other choice did he have? As he wrestled with his decision, Milly's words came back to him. No matter what evil spirit infested his body, he could always choose to be good. That option was always there, no matter what horrible transformation he underwent.

"I choose to be one of you," he said.

"Very good. Step forward, and give me your hand."

Peter approached the throne and stuck out his hand. His host clasped it. His flesh was cold and slimy, and felt like a reptile's.

"Repeat after me," his host said. "Darkness, take my hand and give me the power to destroy whoever stands in my way."

"Darkness, take my hand and give me the power to destroy whoever stands in my way."

"And rule the world as I see fit."

"And rule the world as I see fit."

"This is my destiny, forever and ever."

Peter choked on the words. This was *not* his destiny, and never had been. He'd been brought here against his will, just like his parents and their little friends.

"You tricked me. And my parents," he whispered.

"Yes, I did. Now, say it or die a thousand deaths!" his host thundered.

"This is my destiny, forever and ever."

"Very good. You are now one of us."

The wicked one's snakelike fingers ran up Peter's forearm, and sank their deadly fangs into his flesh. As their poison entered his body, Peter's head felt like it might explode.

He screamed.

His world changed again. He was back inside the theater wrestling with Wolfe. He had survived his encounter with the wicked one. But he had paid a terrible price.

Wolfe still had his hands around his throat. Peter pried back the dead man's fingers, breaking each of them with a sickening snap. Making a fist, he struck Wolfe squarely in the jaw. The blow resonated, and sent the dead man staggering backward.

"Way to go," Snoop called out.

"Yeah, Peter," his girlfriend exclaimed.

Peter nearly told his friends to shut up. They'd been nothing but trouble lately, and the thought of getting rid of them ran through his mind. He'd break their bodies like sticks and toss them in the river, and no one would suspect a thing. Just thinking about it filled him with euphoria. *Get rid of them,* a voice inside his head said.

What on earth was he thinking? He loved Liza, and Snoop was his closest friend. Yet the thought of killing them would not go away.

"Peter, he's getting away!" Liza exclaimed.

Wolfe had grabbed the knapsack and was walking stiff-legged across the stage. If he got outside and released the nerve agent, half the city would perish.

"Let him," he heard himself say.

"What did you say?" Liza asked.

"I said let him."

His girlfriend pulled herself off the floor and rushed toward him. "Why are you talking like that? What's come over you?"

"Do I sound different to you?" Peter asked.

"Yes. Your voice has changed. And your eyes look weird."

"How do I sound?"

"You sound evil, Peter, and it's scaring the crap out of me."

Milly's words again rang in his ears. Being good or evil was a choice. It sounded easy, only the evil had kidnapped his soul, and would not release it.

"Maybe I am evil," he replied.

He expected her to run away. Instead, his girlfriend wrapped her arms around his waist and gazed longingly into his eyes. "No, you're not. You're the most wonderful boy I've ever met. Now, please do this for me."

"Why should I," he heard himself say.

"Because I love you, that's why."

"You do?"

"Yes."

He read her thoughts. Despite the nightmare he'd put her through, Liza still loved him. It was the only thing he'd ever wanted, and he pushed the demon back into the farthest reaches of his soul. It was like pushing a boulder, and took all his strength.

"I'll do anything for you," he said.

"Good. Then stop him."

"Hey! He's going up to the roof," Snoop called out.

The wooden stairway that led to the roof was located beside the stage. Snoop was chasing Wolfe up the creaky steps by the time they reached him. Soon the three of them were standing on the theater's flat roof with its view of the gloomy Hudson.

"There he is," Snoop said.

Wolfe stood on the other side of the roof next to the building's ventilation system. He'd removed the bomblet from the knapsack, and held it above the system's powerful fans. If the nerve agent touched the fans, it would be distributed into the air, and spread across the city.

"Stay here," Peter said.

"Be careful," Liza said.

Peter sprinted across the roof. He needed a distraction, something to take Wolfe's mind off his deadly mission. Garrison had said that they'd found a girlfriend's snapshot in Wolfe's wallet. What was her name? Rona. No, it was Rita.

"Don't you want to see Rita?" Peter shouted.

Wolfe's head turned slightly, his face filled with pain. It was the first expression he'd shown. *Even the dead know love,* Peter thought.

Peter kept coming toward him. "Don't you?"

The pain in Wolfe's eyes grew more intense.

"I can take you to her," Peter said.

"She's here?" Wolfe asked.

"She's downstairs waiting for you."

"That's a lie."

"She's in a limo by the curb. Take a look if you don't believe me."

The temptation was too great. Wolfe moved away from the fans, and glanced over the side of the building. Peter seized the opportunity and ripped the bomblet from his grasp. He tossed the deadly device through the air to Snoop.

"Catch!" Peter said.

"You're not funny," Snoop said.

Wolfe spun around, and they began to fight. The images of Madame Marie and Reggie flashed through Peter's mind, and the demon inside of him reared its ugly head. He grabbed Wolfe by the throat, and lifted him clean off the ground. He shook the dead man, and broke every bone in Wolfe's body that wasn't already broken. The dead man's teeth flew out of his mouth, and his shoes fell off his feet. His head spun from side to side like a rag doll.

Peter gazed into the dead man's eyes. The elders of the Order had been jostled out of their chairs. Their masks had come off, exposing their faces. The elder in the middle had a twisted nose and crooked teeth. He'd finally found his parents' killers.

"I have a score to settle with you," Peter said.

He gave another violent shake, causing the walls around the elders to collapse. They screamed for mercy, something they'd never given to their victims. By the time the dust had settled, they were lying motionless in a heap.

It was over. Peter let Wolfe slip from his fingers. Then, he summoned all his strength, and forced the demon back into its hiding place. He could deal with this, he told himself. It was just going to take some getting used to.

He crossed the roof to where Liza and Snoop stood. His girlfriend had buried her face in her hands, unable to watch. Snoop shook his head in disbelief.

"I'm sorry you had to see that," Peter said.

Liza lowered her hands. "Are we safe? Is the city safe?"

"Yes, we're safe."

Tears ran down her face. She'd witnessed a side of him that no one was supposed to see. Without a word, she turned her back, and slipped into the stairwell.

"Liza, wait."

"No, Peter. No," he heard her say.

Snoop edged up beside him, clutching the bomblet to his chest.

"Remind me to never piss you off," his assistant said.

59

"**H**ey, superman. You okay?"
 Peter sat on the edge of the ventilator system, getting soaked by the rain. An hour had passed
since he'd shaken the evil spirit out of Wolfe, enough
time for the FBI to take away the nerve agent and the
dead man's body. The numbness had still not worn off.

Garrison sat down beside him, and handed him a
Coke. The tension was gone from the FBI agent's face,
and he looked like a new man. "You look like you could
use this."

Peter took a long swallow. "Thanks."

"You should come inside. It's cold and damp up here."

Peter did not reply. There were events in a person's
life that changed everything. This was one of them, and
he needed to be alone for a while to sort things out in
his head.

"You saved a lot of lives today. You need to go out
and celebrate. Life is good."

"I had nothing to do with this, remember? You
promised me that," Peter said.

"What am I going to tell my bosses?"

"Make up a story. That's what they do in the government."

Garrison laughed under his breath. "Whatever you
say."

Peter gazed out at the gloomy Hudson. A barge was
making its way up the river so slowly that it didn't appear to be moving. He felt Garrison's hand on his
shoulder.

"Listen. I know something bad happened up here,

and you're hurting inside, but life goes on. Tomorrow you'll feel a little better, and the next day, you'll feel even better. That's how it works. Eventually you'll heal, and whatever happened will be nothing more than a bad memory."

Peter drained his soda. Garrison meant well, but he was wrong. He'd lost Liza, and there was no getting her back. She'd seen the demon inside of him, and nothing could change that. Their relationship was already on shaky ground. Now, it was finished.

"Thanks for the pep talk," Peter said.

"Something tells me you don't believe me." Garrison slapped him on the back. "I'm sorry, man. You don't deserve this. Whatever it is."

The barge blew its horn. It was loud enough to raise the dead, and Peter laughed silently to himself. That was the last thing he needed right now.

"Time to head out," Garrison said. "Let me walk you down."

If this had been a movie, he and Garrison would have gotten drunk in a smokey bar right about now. Instead, he followed the FBI agent downstairs and walked outside the theater. The city was showing signs of life, with taxis racing past, honking their horns as they fought for fares. Across the street, his limo was parked at the curb. He'd called Herbie, and asked him to take Liza and Snoop home. He wondered why his driver was still here.

"It's been a pleasure, my friend," Garrison said.

"Glad to help," Peter replied.

A Lincoln Town Car came down the street and braked in front of them. Garrison hopped into the passenger seat. He started to close his door, then caught Peter's eye.

"Things will get better," the FBI agent said. "They always do."

"How can you be so sure?" Peter asked.

"You're not the only person who can see into the future. You take care of yourself."

Peter managed a smile. He'd always tried to find the bright side to every situation. Garrison was a good guy, and someone he could trust. He'd found a friend.

"You too," he said.

It was time to go home.

Peter crossed the street to where his limo was parked. The engine was running, and he saw Herbie slouched behind the wheel as if taking a nap. That wasn't like him, and Peter jerked open the passenger door.

"Herbie, are you okay?"

The breath caught in his throat. Herbie was out like a light. In the backseats, Liza and Snoop lay on their sides with their eyes firmly shut. He shook them, and got no response. Was this the Order of Astrum's payback for what he'd done? Hadn't he killed those bastards?

"They're not hurt, if that's what you're thinking," a voice said.

Peter pulled himself out of the limo. Holly stood beneath an umbrella on the sidewalk with a mischievous grin on her face. This was her doing.

"You didn't hurt them . . ."

"Your friends are fine. By the way, Max and I watched you dismantle Wolfe at the apartment. You were amazing."

Holly had a devious side to her; all witches did. He put his hands on her shoulders, and looked her squarely in the eye.

"Please tell me what you did to them," he said.

"I cast a spell on your friends. The potion once belonged to Mary Glover. It never fails."

"What kind of spell?"

"One that will make your life much easier."

Her eyes were twinkling, daring him to figure out the clever thing she'd done.

"You erased their memories," he said.

"Go the head of the class," Holly said. "When your friends wake up, they'll no longer remember any of the things you'd rather not have them know. I included your driver, too. You have a clean slate. Let no good deed go unrewarded."

"I think you got the expression wrong."

"I like mine better."

Holly had saved him. He didn't know how to thank her. Taking her hands, he gazed into her pretty face. She seemed embarrassed, and looked away.

"Why did you do it?" he asked.

"You didn't deserve what was happening to you," she replied.

"This gives me a second chance with Liza. You had to know that."

Her cheeks were wet, but not from the rain. Her voice wavered as she spoke. "I realized something years ago. You were babysitting me, doing your magic tricks. I was being difficult, and not playing along. It bothered you, and you left in a terrible mood. That night, I figured out why. You're easily the most unhappy person I've ever known. The tricks and clever one-liners are how you cope. You make other people happy to compensate for your unhappiness.

"But then you met Liza, and you changed. You were finally happy, and I was so happy for you. Don't get me wrong. I would have given anything to have made you that way. But I didn't. It was her. She was the one that stole your heart. That's why I did it."

"For me."

"Yes, Peter, for you. Oh, look. Your driver is starting to wake up. The others will soon follow. You should be there when they come out of the spell. It will make things easier for them."

"What should I say?"

Holly wiped away her tears. "I'm sure you'll think of something."

Holly had figured out his secret. And she'd protected him, as best she could.

"Thank you," he said.

She started to walk away. "See you Friday night at my aunt's."

"I'll be there," he replied.

Peter climbed into the backseat of the limo. Herbie had come to, and was wiping the cobwebs from his eyes. He looked slightly confused.

"Sorry about that," his driver said. "I must of dozed off."

"No more sleeping on the job. Put some opera on, will you?"

"Opera? Sure, whatever you say, boss."

Peter poured glasses of sparkling water for Liza and himself, an ice-cold Heineken for Snoop. He placed the drinks in holders for when they came out of Holly's spell. Placido Domingo's booming voice came over the limo's state-of-the-art speakers. Liza stirred.

"Hey, sleeping beauty, rise and shine," he said.

Liza slowly woke up. Gone from her face were the anger and distrust that had built up over the past few days. Life was good again.

"Boy, was that a weird dream," his girlfriend said. "Who put on the opera?"

"I asked Herbie to."

"That was sweet of you. Looks like it's finally stopped raining."

They looked out the window together. The storm had broken apart, leaving a vacant, slate blue sky. Like a curtain rising inside a theater, a new act was about to begin. He could start being a magician again, and forget about the evil that had consumed his life.

Snoop snapped awake, and grabbed the waiting glass of beer.

"Service around here is definitely improving," his assistant said.

They laughed. It was all back to normal. *The greatest trick of all,* he thought.

"Here's to the best friends in the world," he said.

"I'll drink to that," Snoop said.

"Me, too," Liza said.

They clinked glasses. Peter's drink burned going down. The searing ache in his heart was still there. He'd been living a lie, and it had nearly destroyed his relationship with Liza. He had to come clean with her before it happened again. The voice of his conscience told him to do it right now. He put his glass in the holder, and took her hand.

"I want to take you out to dinner. There's something I've been meaning to tell you."

"Sounds mysterious. I'm game," she said.

Peter breathed a sigh of relief. That hadn't been so hard, had it? He glanced across the seat at Snoop, and raised his eyebrow suggestively.

"Holy cow, look at the time," his assistant said. "You two have a nice night."

Snoop hopped out of the limo. He rapped his hand on the roof before walking away. Peter promised himself that someday, he would tell Snoop as well.

"Let's roll," he told his driver.

The limo glided down the street. Peter turned to Liza. "You hungry?"

"Starving."

"Me, too. Where do you want to eat?"

Liza snuggled up next to him, and rested her head on his shoulder. Her face was so close that he could feel her breath on his skin. Tomorrow morning they'd wake up together, and her face would be the first thing he'd see, her voice the first thing he heard. If he was honest with her, it would be that way for the rest of his life. If he'd learned anything during the past few days, it was that there could be no secrets between people in love. No secrets at all.

"Surprise me," she said.

TOR

Award-winning authors
Compelling stories

Please join us at the website
below for more information
about this author and other great
Tor selections, and to sign up for
our monthly newsletter!